# Queen

## of

# Diamonds

Scott Finley

ISBN: 979-8-9907909-1-9



Cover by Rossano Designs

# Acknowledgments

The great ocean liners from the golden age of trans-Atlantic travel are history now, save for the *Queen Mary* and *United States*. The *Queen Mary*, launched in 1936, has been since 1967 the property of the City of Long Beach, California where she serves as a floating hotel and convention center. The latest information on this historic ship, including shipboard events and event and hotel booking, can be found at www.queenmary.com/.

The *United States* was launched in 1951 and withdrawn from service in 1969. Various plans emerged over the years to return her to some sort of service, but at the time of this writing, she is destined to be sunk and turned into an artificial reef off the shore of Destin-Fort Walton Beach in Florida. Her two iconic funnels have been removed to act as part of a new visitor center at the location chronicling the fastest North Atlantic liner of all time.

The names of those other ships now gone forever evoke a grander and more elegant time when passengers dressed for dinner and socialites and social climbers aspired to sit at the Captain's table – the *Olympic*, sister ship to the ill-fated *Titanic* and *Britannic*, the *Mauretania*, the *Ile De France*, the *Normandie*, the *Queen Elizabeth*, the *Aquitania*, the *Leviathan*, the *Rex*.

With one notable exception – the *United States* – these grand liners were all of European construction. The United Kingdom, France, Germany, and Italy all had their ships on the North Atlantic passenger route, but no matter the nationality, they did have one fatal item in common: the rise of trans-Atlantic passenger jet service. The jets put an end to the ships as a means of routine transport back and forth across the Atlantic, though Cunard's *Queen Mary 2* continues to offer 7-day trans-Atlantic sailings along with her regular cruise ship schedule.

In doing research for this series to construct the fictional *Queen Victoria*, the flagship of the equally fictitious Stoddard Lines, a number of resources were consulted. Among them, *Queen Mary*, by James Steele, 1995; *Liners, the Golden Age*, by Robert Fox, 1999; *Record Breakers of the North Atlantic*, by Arnold Kludase, 2000; *The Fabulous Interiors of the Great Ocean Liners*, by William H. Miller, Jr., 1985; *Ocean Steamers*, by John Adams, 1993; *The Golden Age of Ocean Liners*, by Lee Server, 1996; *Pride of the North Atlantic*, by David F. Hutchings, 2003; *Images of America: RMS Queen Mary*, by Suzanne Tarbell Cooper, Frank Cooper, Athene Mihalakis Kovacic, Don Lynch, John Thomas and the *Queen Mary* archives, 2010; *Cunard White Star Quadruple Screw Liner Queen Mary*, reprint of souvenir issue of *The Shipbuilder and Marine Engine Builder*, 1936; *Queen Mary: Her Early Years Recalled*, by C.W.R. Winter, 1986; *The Cunard Liner Queen Mary*, by Ross Watton, 1989, and *Superliner SS United States*, by Henry Billings, 1954.

For a more in-depth look at life at sea and on a luxury liner, *The Sea My Surgery*, by Dr. Joseph B. Maguire, 1957; *A Million Ocean Miles,* by Sir Edgar T. Britten, R.D., R.N.R., Commodore of the Cunard White Star Line, 1936; *The Ile De France*, by Don Stafford, 1960; *The World's Greatest Ship: Leviathan* (six volumes), by Frank O. Braynard, 1974-1983; *Maiden Voyages*, by Siân Evans, 2020; and last but certainly not least, *The Only Way to Cross*, by John Maxtone-Graham, 1972.

Information about Harry Winston, "King of Diamonds" and arguably the best-known jeweler in the world came from *King of Diamonds: The Flawless World of Harry Winston*, by Ronald Winston and William Stadheim, 2023; *Harry Winston*, by André Leon Talley, 2012; and *Harry Winston, The Ultimate Jeweler*, by Laurence Krashes, 1986. Harry Winston can be found in major cities

STARBOARD FIRST-CLASS CORRIDOR
MAIN DECK 1ST CLASS CABIN ASSIGNMENTS

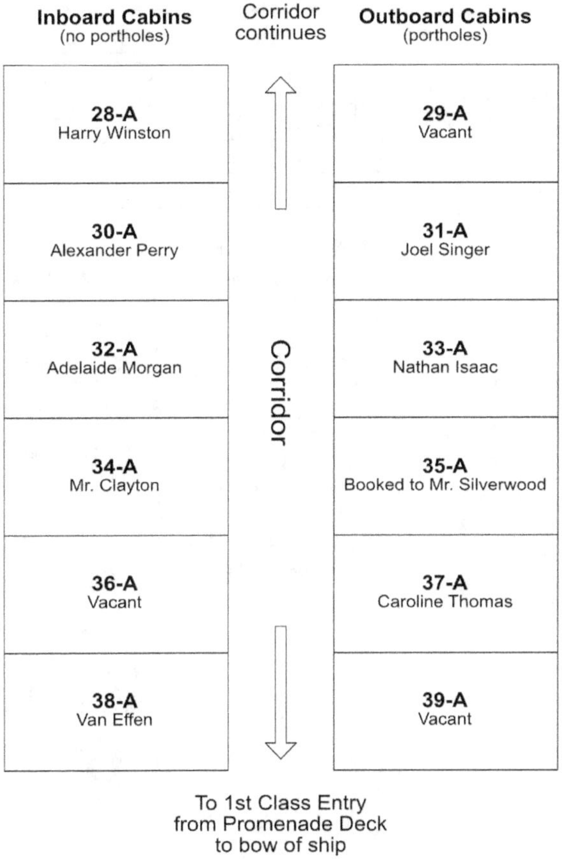

Inboard Cabins
(no portholes)

Corridor
continues

Outboard Cabins
(portholes)

Corridor

28-A
Harry Winston

29-A
Vacant

30-A
Alexander Perry

31-A
Joel Singer

32-A
Adelaide Morgan

33-A
Nathan Isaac

34-A
Mr. Clayton

35-A
Booked to Mr. Silverwood

36-A
Vacant

37-A
Caroline Thomas

38-A
Van Effen

39-A
Vacant

To 1st Class Entry
from Promenade Deck
to bow of ship

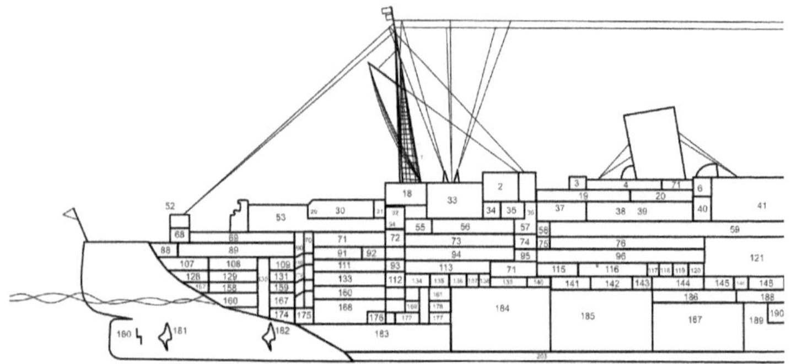



## KEY TO THE SECTIONAL PLAN OF THE QUEEN VICTORIA

### Sports Deck

1 Main Mast
2, 3, 4, 5, 6, 7 Ventilators
8 Staircase
9 Space for Deck Sports, Promenade, and Deck Tennis Courts
10, 11 Tank Room
12 Directional Aerials
13 Semaphores
14 Searchlights
15 Chart Room
16 Wheel-house and Bridge
17 Captain's and Officers' Quarters

### Sun Deck

18 Veranda Grill
19 Engineer Officers' Accommodation
20 Engineers' Ward Room
21 Cinema Projection Room
22 Engineers' Quarters
23 Gymnasium
24 Lift Gear
25 Wireless Receiving Room
26 Staterooms and Suites
27 Forward Staircase and Lifts
28 Staterooms and Suites

### Promenade Deck

29 Cinema Projection Room
30 Tourist Smoking Room
31 Pantry
32 Tourist Entrance
33 Smoking Room
34 Pantry
35 After-end of the Long Gallery (Port Side)
36 Staircase and Lifts
37 Ball Room
38, 39 Cinemas
40 Stage of Lounge
41 Lounge
42 Chair Stowage
43 Writing Rooms
44 Entrance
45 Main Hall and Shopping Centre
46 Drawing Room
47 Altar
48 Children's Playroom
49 Forward Staircase and Lifts
50 Cocktail Bar and Observation Lounge
51 Promenade

### Main Deck

52 Docking Bridge
53 Tourist Lounge
54 Tourist Staircase and Lifts
55 Tourist Writing Room and Library
56 Staterooms and Suites
57 Staircase and Lifts
58 Store Room
59 Staircase and Lifts
60 Main Staircase and Lifts
61 Furniture Store
62 Staterooms and Suites
63 Forward Staircase and Lifts
64 Third-Class Garden Lounge
65 Cargo Hatch
66 Fore Mast
67 Crow's Nest (Electrically Heated)

### 'A' Deck

68 Cinema Film Store
69 'A' Deck Tourist Lounge
70 Tourist Entrance, Staircase and Lifts
71 Suites and Bedroom Accommodations
72 Staircase and Lifts
73 Staterooms and Suites
74 Staircase and Lifts
75 Switch Room
76, 77 Staterooms and Suites
78 Staircase and Lifts
79 Purser's Office
80 Staterooms and Suites
81 Forward Staircase and Lifts
82 Third-class Hairdressers
83 Third-class Entrance
84 Third-class Smoking Room
85 Fore Hatch
86 Rope Store
87 Forecastle and Anchor Capstan

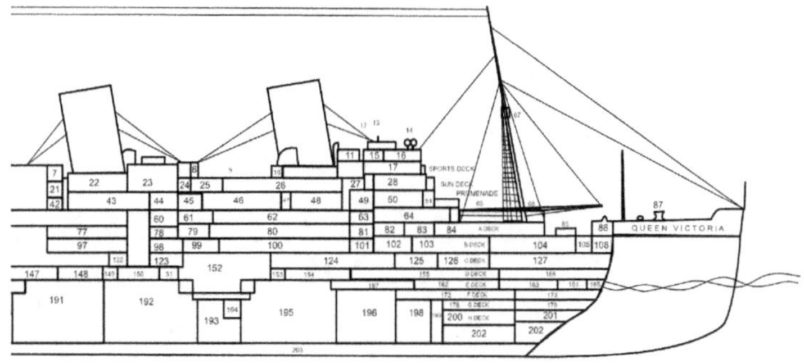


## KEY TO THE SECTIONAL PLAN OF THE QUEEN VICTORIA

### 'B' Deck

88  Crew
89  Suites and Bedroom Accommodations
90  Staircase and Lifts
91  Suites and Bedroom Accommodations
92  Hairdresser's
93  Staircase and Lifts
94  Suites and Bedrooms
95  Staircase and Lifts
96, 97  Staterooms and Suites
98  Staircase and Lifts
99  Hairdresser's and Beauty Parlor
100  Staterooms and Suites
101  Forward Staircase and Lifts
102  Third-class Children's Playroom
103  Third-class Lounge
104  Mail-handling Space
105  Capstan Gear
106  Crew

### 'C' Deck

107  Crew
108  Capstan Space
109  Bedroom Accommodation
110  Staircase and Lifts
111  Suites and Bedroom Accommodations
112  Staircase and Lifts
113  Tourist Dining Saloon
114  Baker's Shop
115  Vegetable-preparing Room
116  Kitchens
117  Grill
118  China Pantry
119  Bar
120  Private Dining Room
121  Restaurant
122  Private Dining Room
123  Foyer
124  Third-class Dining Saloon
125  Third-class Entrance
126  Third-class Accommodation
127  Capstan Gear and Crew Space

### 'C' Deck

128  Crew
129  Suites and Bedroom Accommodations
130  Baggage Lift Well
131  Suites and Bedroom Accommodations
132  Tourist Staircase and Lifts
133  Suites and Bedroom Accommodations
134  Ales and Stout
135  Stores Entrance
136  Ice Cream, Butter, and Milk
137  Fruit-ripening Room
138  Fruit Stores
139  Vegetable and Salad Room
140  Fresh and Frozen Fish
141  Butcher's Shop and Meat Store
142  Poultry and Game, etc.
143  Bacon and Eggs
144  Grocery Store
145  Hospital
146  Dispensary
147  Printer's Shop
148  Third-class Accommodation
149  Oil-filing station
150  Third-class Accommodation
151  Dressing-rooms of Swimming Pool
152  Swimming Pool
153  Kosher Kitchen
154  Third-class Kitchens
155  Third-class Accommodation
156  Crew

### 'D' Deck

157  Crew
158, 159, 160, 161  Suites and Bedroom Accommodations
162  Third-class Accommodation
163  Mail Discharge Room
164  Specie Room
165  Crew

### 'E' Deck

166  Tourist Baggage Room
167  Bedroom Accommodation
168  Tourist Swimming Pool
169  Beer Stores
170  Lift Well
171  Wines and Minerals
172  Garage
173  Registered Mail

### 'F' Deck

174  Baggage
175, 176  Mails
177  Linen Store
178  Baggage
179  Mail Space

### Machinery and Hold

180  Rudder
181, 182  Propeller Starboard Side
183  Shafts and Shaft Tunnels
184  After Engine Rooms
185  Forward Engine Rooms
186  Fan Rooms
187  No. 5 Boiler Room
188  Air-conditioning Plant
189  After Turbo-generator Room
190  Power Station
191  No. 4 Boiler Room
192  No. 3 Boiler Room
193  Forward Turbo-generator Room
194  Power Station
195  No. 2 Boiler Room
196  No. 1 Boiler Room
197  Fan Rooms
198  Water-softening Machinery
199  Tanks
200  Baggage
201  Mail Space
202  General Cargo
203  Double Bottom

# Prologue

When I was a young girl my older brother and I would play cards. We knew all the games any kids growing up in England would have known before the War – Snap, Brag, Rummy – even American poker with a couple of variants. (Where my Mum picked up the knowledge to play Texas Hold'em remains a mystery to this day.) Don't think I'm a big gambler, though, because I'm not. It's just that our parents provided a very eclectic education.

While my older brother was more inclined to go all in while holding a two, three, five, and seven of different suits with a Knave blithely serving as the face card, I was more inclined to discount the number cards and instead enjoyed the intricate drawings of the face cards. While all of them were pretty, to my eight-year-old eye the hearts, clubs, and spades couldn't hold a candle to the geometric precision of the diamonds. The others were all right, I supposed, in their own boring way, but the diamond – that just said something to me. It wasn't very many years later that it spoke in a more tangible fashion.

My Mum had received a pretty tear drop diamond necklace from my father on the occasion of their wedding anniversary. It sparkled with a fierce tenor from the hollow of her neck where it hung. By this time I had turned twelve, and to my young girl psyche it was something to be coveted. My brother, who had now reached the ripe old age of fourteen, saw it instead as something to be used in a scientific experiment. So naturally we threw in together and lifted it from Mum's jewelry box.

Our first stop with our hot rock was the garden shed, because my brother wanted to see if a diamond could indeed cut glass. One sacrificed pane later, we found that it could. His experiment being satisfactorily fulfilled, he handed it off to me and I retreated to my room, where I put it around my neck and preened in front of the mirror for hours as I gracefully met His Majesty and the Prince of Wales and anyone else I could think of worth meeting.

Finally, my fantasies satiated, I went to stealthily return it – only to find my brother frantically waving me off at the bottom of the stairs. He put a finger to his lips, and only then did I hear Mum on the telephone reporting that she had been robbed. Discretion being the better part of valor, as they say, I beat a hasty retreat back upstairs and stashed the gem in the drainpipe outside my window then sat down to wait.

It wasn't too long before the local rozzers showed up at the door to investigate. There were three of them responding to what was apparently the crime wave of the year, if not century, an indication of exactly how dull life in our small university town could be.

Long story short, as the Americans say, the law didn't find anything (they also being as dull as life in said university town) and left the house to pursue further investigation, where, I didn't know and didn't care – though I suspected from the way they talked it would be The Rum and Beagle, a popular town pub. The next day, as if by a miracle, the purloined piece reappeared in my mother's jewelry box. Nothing was ever said about it, and my Mum just "assumed" she had overlooked it in the first place.

My brother, who had covered his tracks by "accidentally" breaking the scratched shed window with a cricket ball, gave me a crooked look because he knew better. But I didn't care.

I had worn it, if only for a while, and was already looking forward to the day when I would be a grown woman and be able to wear as many jewels as I wanted.

But being a twelve-year-old girl, I just wasn't aware of what the cost would be.

# *Saturday, March 22, 1930*

**I**

**L**ord love a duck, I'll admit it – I truly enjoy going shopping in New York City. Unfortunately, there just isn't that much time for this expensive hobby when the *Queen Victoria* is doing her turnaround down at Pier 54 in Manhattan, across from West 13th and 14th Streets. Over the two days or less it takes for the *Victoria* to be provisioned, refueled, and cleaned up for the next round of passengers heading east, crew that can get shore leave take it, if only for a few hours. That's how my cabin mate Alice Johnson and I ended up on Fulton Street in the diamond district.

Like me, Alice is a nurse aboard the *Victoria*. Well, not entirely like me. I'm Maeve Chandler, head nurse, and I report to Doctors Harper and Bratton. Alice reports to me. And of course, we all report to the Captain, but neither he, Doctor Harper nor Doctor Bratton was with us now – Bratton in fact was in London attending his brother's wedding – so we just did as we pleased, at least until our shore leave was up.

"Look at all those lovely diamonds," said Alice, pointing through a particularly grimy shop window where the lovely diamonds in question were gamely doing their level best to glitter in the weak sunlight filtering down between the surrounding buildings. Even to my diamond-loving eye, they looked pretty sad.

In the diamond district on this Saturday in late March of 1930, barely five months after the stock market crash, few people were holding shopping bags, and even fewer had the cash to be interested in gems. While we were definitely interested, neither of us had the cash, so we stood with our faces close to the jewelry store glass like children at a confectioner's shop, intent on the gemstones laid out enticingly on the worn black velvet on the other side. After a moment I sighed and adjusted the shell-blue cloche on my head, a nice change from my regular nursing cap.

"Never in my lifetime," I said firmly. "Not even from a fly-blown store like this, not as long as I'm a sea-going nurse for the Stoddard Lines."

"You'll have to marry up a doctor, that's what you'll have to do," Alice replied, her South African accent lilting. I gave her a sidelong glance.

"Doctor Bratton's not really my type," I replied.

"Oh, 'coo, I was talking about Doctor Harper."

"Him, either. I have to work with them on board the *Victoria*, I can't imagine life with them on land." Well, I could with Harper, if he and I could ever properly cross paths without a corpse in the way.[*]

Alice took me by the arm. "Oh, pish, a doctor on land is the same as one at sea." She gestured at the window. "Haven't you always said you wanted to drip in diamonds, ever since you were a little girl? Let's go inside and have a closer look, shall we? Doesn't cost anything."

"Fine, all right, fine." I tried to check my make up in the window reflection but gave up as Alice pulled me to the door.

The silver bell over the entrance tinkled as we entered the dimly lit interior of the store. A gaunt, hollow-eyed man of indeterminate age, immaculately dressed in a neat

---

[*]  See Book One: *Shadow of the Queen*

if thread-worn black suit, came out from behind a dusty counter. He looked, I thought, like a cadaver.

"Good afternoon, ladies. How may I help you?" Yep. The melancholy voice matched the appearance.

"Good afternoon," said Alice. She put a delicate hand to her jet-black hair, coiffed in the vamp style made popular by Theda Bara, then gestured at the window. "The ring over there – might we see it, please?"

"Certainly, madam." The man walked with deliberate care to the display, produced a key from his vest pocket and opened the case. He gazed down at the assortment laid out on the velvet, then looked back at Alice. "I'm sorry, but could madam point out which ring in particular she was thinking of?"

"The marquis cut," said Alice. I rolled my eyes.

"Very good, madam. An excellent choice." The salesman bent for a moment, then straightened, the ring held delicately between his thin fingers. He walked slowly to Alice, holding the ring out for her inspection.

"It's beautiful," she said. "May I?"

"Of course, madam." The cadaver gingerly allowed Alice to take the ring from him. As she turned it in her fingers he spoke. "From one of the Kimberley mines in South Africa," he said. "A full five carats. It's pre-war; 1908, I believe. One of a few Mr Isaac has in stock, from his personal holdings. The setting is eighteen karat gold, of course."

"Of course," breathed Alice. The man gave us a considered look, appraising our dress from shoes up to hats with the finicky care of someone used to assessing a customer's ability to spend.

"You're English, aren't you?" he asked Alice.

"My sister is," lied Alice with a practised smoothness that always awed and scared me in equal parts. "I was born in South Africa. Our parents separated and we grew up apart from each other."

I fought hard to keep from rolling my eyes. Alice had always been unable to resist letting go a corker, and yes, she really was from South Africa, but the rest – "We're from the *Queen Victoria*," I added.

Alice nodded in assent. "And we're sailing home tonight, so we thought we might put in a bit of shopping before we leave New York."

"I see," said the man, a bit frostily. "Stewardesses?"

"Oh, no," I blurted, my professional feathers ruffled. "We're not stewardesses at all, we're - "

"First-Class passengers," said Alice smoothly. She handed the ring back into the man's willing hand. "And we've still more shopping to do today, don't we?" she pointedly said to me.

"Yes. More shopping," I said, giving her a look. "At Tiffany's," I directed at the cadaver as I took Alice by the arm and headed for the door.

"Tiffany's," said the man. He gave us a forced and icy smile. "I hope their luck is better than mine."

"I doubt it," Alice replied as the bell above the door jangled. A dour man leaning heavily on a cane entered the store, a man easily seventy plus years old, with a dried-up face and bushy black eyebrows shot through with gray. A battered bowler was jammed down onto his drawn skull head and a black scarf was wound around his neck. A jeweler's loupe hung from a delicate gold chain beneath the scarf. His stooped shoulders and outward thrust head gave him the appearance of a myopic and bad intentioned turtle, yet his build indicated that he had once been a powerful young man. A neatly suited man who looked to be in his early twenties was with him, courteously holding the door open. I felt Alice's hand close over mine. I

"Is there a chance I'll see you on board the *Victoria*, Miss Johnson?" Singer asked. "We can talk about the movies – or maybe see one."

"Yes, I understand the *Queen Victoria* has a very nice cinema on board," said Alice as I once again took her arm and began steering her toward the door.

"I'm sorry, but we've really got to go," I said, with no little irritation.

"I'll find you," Joel promised Alice as I opened the door. "I'll see you on board."

"Only if you hurt yourself," I said, keeping a firm grip on Alice and marching her out as the door closed behind us with a sharp tinkle of the bell.

## ||

Ask most anyone to name one of Shakespeare's plays, and almost without fail they'll tell you *Romeo and Juliet*. (Except for the neurotics, who always seem to go for *Hamlet*. You figure it out.) The star-crossed lovers are world-famous. Only the more realistic observers among us can look back at the story and remember that both handed in their dinner pails at the end. I seem to remember that Mercutio got it too, and maybe a couple more; as I said, most people prefer to remember the love story, not the body count rivaling the Chicago gangsters on half-price bullet day. Anyway, cast Alice as Juliet and Joel as Romeo, and all I could see was the downside to any shipboard romance between the crew Capulets and the passenger Montagues. But I could be wrong, and probably was.

"I tell you, Boss, I was never more embarrassed in my life. The cooing back and forth between them. Alice was everything but on that poor man, and him a passenger that's going to sail with us tonight, too." I stopped and looked at the Principal Medical Officer of the *Queen Victoria*. "Have you even heard a word of what I've been saying?"

"I'm sorry," said Doctor Harper. "I was trying to get an accurate count of our inventory, since someone came back late from her shore leave today." He pushed back his wire-rimmed spectacles, put his clipboard down and ran a hand through his sandy hair.

"Well, I just don't like this midnight sailing stuff," I said with a huff. "I like it better when we get into New York before noon on Friday and don't leave until Sunday afternoon."

"Nurse Chandler, what are you complaining about now?" said Harper. "You got to see a Broadway show last night, didn't you? And you got to get off the ship and go shopping this morning and early afternoon, didn't you?" He gestured around the small office in the ship's hospital. "I didn't get to take shore leave."

"That's only because Doctor Bratton is sitting this voyage out to attend his brother's wedding," I countered, taking the clipboard off the desk and running the pencil along the row of bandages he'd been counting. I made a quick note. "You even let Mister Reedy go."

"Our dispensing chemist doesn't sleep well," said Harper. "I thought some time ashore would do him good."

"He doesn't sleep at all," I replied. "And no amount of shore leave is going to take care of that." I finished the count, marked the total, and handed the clipboard back to Harper. "There. All done."

"Thank you." He set the board back down on his desk. "I don't know what I would ever do without you." He reflected a moment. "Except have a head nurse who addresses me as 'Doctor Harper' rather than 'boss.'"

"I only call you 'boss' in private. You know I'd never say it in public. Much."

"Yes, I can't imagine how a passenger or Captain Webster would respond to this informality." Harper smiled in spite of himself. "Can you just see Chief Engineer Duncan addressing Captain Webster as 'boss?' It boggles the imagination."

"They're not as progressive in their thinking as you are," I intoned. "You're willing to accept the fact that I'm a bit outspoken and have a mind that's good for something other than just counting bandages." I smiled. "They just don't work together as well, it's obvious."

"What's obvious, Emmeline Pankhurst, is that my discipline is becoming decidedly lax the older I get."

"You could always go back to His Majesty's navy, Doctor," I retorted.

Harper shook his head. "I'll take laxness on the *Queen Victoria* over discipline on a dreadnought any day." He pursed his lips. "Just try and behave with Doctor Bratton, will you?"

"Doctor Bratton's got a sense of humour you don't see. Remember, I worked with him before you joined the crew. He's very dry."

"Oh, I see it," said Harper. "He keeps me in – stitches. Yes, that's it. Stitches."

"Funny."

"Glad you liked it. Now, what were you saying about Alice? It sounded a bit like a love at first sight meeting. If so, good for her."

"She thinks it was. She just embarrassed me a little, that's all." I thought for a moment. "I don't know what she's going to do if he does ask for her during this voyage. He's under the impression she's a First-Class passenger."

"And who made that impression? Certainly not you two nurses, putting on airs and going jewelry shopping?" Harper said with a sly grin.

"Certainly not!" I said. "Maybe. I don't remember."

"Well, then, that's all right." Harper glanced at his watch. "We sail in six hours. I may go topside and see if Mister Harvey has anything going in the kitchens. Are you hungry?"

"No, thank you," I said. "I'll just stay here with my shattered dreams."

"Suit yourself," said Harper, then grinned. "But don't come crying to me at two in the morning when you haven't married into riches and you're hungry." He easily dodged the rolled bandage I hurled at his receding form.

"Impossible man," I muttered under my breath.

We made our way up to the First-Class dining salon where Chief Steward Harvey was directing the machinations of dozens of bus boys and stewards as the cavernous room was made ready for sailing. The stocky man looked over at us as we strolled inside.

"Good afternoon, Doctor Harper, Nurse Chandler," said Harvey. "What can I do for you?"

"I thought I'd rummage about for a bite to eat," said Harper.

"Help yourself. Maybe Bissell can find something for you."

"No, no need to disturb your assistant," I said. "I'm sure he is quite busy at the moment with a hundred details."

"Try a thousand," said Harvey. "That's kind of you not to want to disturb him, Nurse. I'd be lost without my right hand. Even with a midnight sailing, I've already got half the passengers on board, and then their visitors, and their visitors have visitors, and great heavens, you never saw so many requests for flower vases. I think Americans eat flowers." He took off his cap and scratched at his thick curly salt and pepper hair.

"I don't know about the flowers but they certainly carry a lot of baggage," Harper said.

Harvey nodded. "Did you see that lot out there at the top of the First-Class stairs? And more arriving every minute. I've been doing this for over twenty years with time off for the War and I still marvel that it all gets to the right cabins, and that the passengers even have enough room to move around all of it, though most of the stuff will just go into the holds. I don't know what they intend to do with it once they get to France and England. Start a shop, I suppose."

"I suppose."

Harvey wagged a finger. "I'll wager we have close to a thousand visitors today. Mister Collins will go insane."

I laughed. The thought of our prim and proper Chief Purser at the center of the sailing day maelstrom never failed to cheer me. "No wonder we don't see him until two days at sea. He's spending all his time recovering from sailing day." I nodded toward the massive fifteen-foot-tall open doors of the dining salon. "Here comes Mister Casey."

"Now what do you suppose he wants?" asked Harper.

"What he always wants – the big scoop." Harvey sighed as the diminutive ship's reporter and editor of the shipboard paper, *The Victory*, came up to us, cigarette dangling from his wizened face, ash falling to the floor. "Casey, do you bloody well mind? I'm trying to finish cleaning this place up."

"I know you don't vacuum until the last thing, Mister Harvey," said the newspaperman affably. "I've just come from the purser's office. No notables aboard on this trip. Got a few diamond merchants, though. Going to some big diamond trading show in Antwerp after they leave us in Cherbourg. None of them going through to our end in Southampton."

"Well, lucky for them," I said. "No one for you to irritate, eh?"

"Oh, I might be able to get a story about diamonds and what's popular this season from one of them," said

Casey. "Our passenger list is a bit down in the mouth right now. I suppose it's the stock market crash last year, heh heh."

"Anything else?" asked Harper. Casey took off his brown fedora and smoothed it between his gnarled hands, then put it back on.

"I think not. Just thought I'd pass along the word." He picked up a china coffee cup from a nearby table and flicked his cigarette ash into it. Harvey's eyes grew wide. "Well, it's not on your nice carpet, is it?" Casey asked.

"Is your hospital open?" Harvey asked Harper.

"Of course. Why?"

"Because," the Chief Steward said, turning to Casey, "I think our ship's reporter is about to have a grievous accident."

"I'm going, I'm going," Casey replied, shaking his head. "Come to do you a favor, and this is the thanks I get."

"Just a minute," said Harvey. He handed Casey the soiled coffee cup. "Stop by the steward's pantry and tell someone to bring another."

"What do I look like, a waiter?"

"You look like someone about to have a grievous accident," I said.

"Right-o," said Casey. He turned away, cup in hand, stopped long enough to light another cigarette and pointedly dropped the spent match into the cup, then paced off toward the pantry.

"Can you beat that?" Harvey said to Harper.

"It's just his style. He fancies himself a tough city reporter."

"Not in his lifetime," said Harvey. He looked after the diminishing form of Casey. "Which, if he keeps badgering me, is growing shorter all the time."

# *Saturday, March 22, 1930*

### ⦀

One of my favorite stories growing up was *Peter Pan*. Mum and Dad took us to see the play in London and I was in heaven, it was so magical. "Who would you want to be in the play?" my Mum asked afterward. I dutifully replied that I wanted to be Peter because he/she was the star of the show. To which my brother retorted that I'd be better served by playing Captain Hook. My older brother knew me quite well. Truth be told, from the moment he'd appeared on stage I had envisioned myself as Captain Hook and my brother as Mr Smee, but I said Peter for my parents (though I knew my Mum would have been secretly – or maybe not so secretly – thrilled with my choice of Hook). Looking back I find it faintly amusing that no one mentioned me as Wendy. Anyway, the point of this is that Peter, of course, never grew up. And that, I could see, was the situation I now found myself in with Alice.

"Do you think he'll ask about me?" Alice glanced over at me as she straightened her uniform for the tenth time in our cabin. I gave her my disapproving look, the one that could melt a hole in a steel bulkhead at fifteen paces.

"And if he does, what are you going to tell him, huh?" She frowned in response. "What are you going to tell him when he looks for your name at the purser's office and finds out you're not really a First-Class passenger?" I checked my makeup, then added for good measure and since I was thinking about Peter anyway, "Grow up."

My words went right past her. I saw them disappear through the cabin wall and the *Victoria's* thin hull and head for lower Manhattan. "I don't know," Alice said as she gazed approvingly at herself in the mirror. "Isn't he the most handsome thing?"

"I didn't notice." My tone was decidedly cold. Alice looked at me.

"What's the matter?"

"I just can't believe you're contemplating anything with that young man."

"Why shouldn't I? He compared me to a movie star." Alice preened in front of the glass. "He just walked right into my life. I had to grab your hand or just fall over. Anyway, you're the one always holding up those Walter Winchell columns in the *Mirror* and saying, 'look here, this could be me.'" She patted her hair into place. "Why should you have all the fun?"

I sighed. When she put it that way, I couldn't very well call her out. "Forget I said anything." I managed a smile. "You've got me on that Winchell point." I looked up at the clock. "23:30. I hate midnight sailings."

"So you've said." Alice gave me a look. "Repeatedly."

"But it does give a magnificent view of the city at night. I think I'll sneak topside and have a look before I turn in for the night. Want to go?"

Alice shook her head. "I'm thinking about Joel. I'll go to the hospital and look busy for a while before I come back here and hit the sack. Don't wake me when you come in or get up in the morning." She gave me a wicked smile. "I may be having really nice dreams."

"Don't be crass or I'll make you take the early shift in the morning." I adjusted my cap. "See you later." I opened the door and went out, then stood in the narrow corridor and listened with my entire body. I could feel the *Victoria* alive all around me; beneath my feet, in the slight vibration in the walls when I touched them, above my head in the ceiling as the vessel seemed to be gathering her strength for the five-thousand-mile journey ahead. The crew corridor I was in was nearly empty; with sailing time approaching everyone was busy with their own job to get the *Victoria* underway. Eschewing the lift, I stepped through a side door and immersed myself in the bustle of the passenger-only companionways and staircases and finally made my way up to the Chief Purser's office on A deck.

Mister Collins and his staff were, as always at this time, quite busy. Passengers were checking valuables into the ship's safe deposit vault, exchanging currency, setting up shipboard credit – the office functioned as a traditional sea-going Bank of England in almost every sense of the word, and I was almost certain that Mister Collins would bend heaven and earth to get a passenger a mortgage loan, too. He caught my eye as I stood next to a thicket of potted palms that dwarfed my small frame. The Stoddard Lines loved potted palms. They were all over the ship, something I never figured out.

"Someone ill, Nurse Chandler?" he asked. I shook my head.

"No. I just like watching rich people."

Mister Collins adjusted his green visor. "You need another hobby, Nurse."

"I need a lot of things. I just thought I'd stop by and see how you're doing. Mister Harvey and Doctor Harper were talking about you earlier."

"Oh?" He didn't look up as he counted out a stack of pound notes into the waiting palm of an obviously well-fed American not bothered by the recent Wall Street crash. "Nothing good, I suppose?"

"They said you were a very hard worker," I replied, paraphrasing the conversation as best I could. I took a nonchalant glance back at the crowd and froze. The old man from the jewelry store, Alice's heart throb's uncle, was approaching the curved counter of the bank. If he saw me in my nursing uniform that for sure would be the end of Alice's budding romance. I stepped back and squeezed myself in behind the now-welcome palms and their large planters, kneeling and making myself as small as possible. Mister Collins raised one eyebrow in my direction, then turned back to his work.

"Yes, sir?" he asked as Mr Isaac approached the counter, holding a shoe box sized metal case close to his chest with one hand. Isaac scowled at him.

"I want to put these goods into the ship's safe."

"What kind of goods would they be, sir?" Mister Collins pulled up a pad.

"Diamonds. I'm a diamond merchant."

"Yes, sir." Collins made a notation. "And your name?"

"Nathaniel Isaac. Cabin 33A. That's First-Class."

"Yes, sir, thank you, sir. Is this the box?"

"Yes, and it's locked. I have the key. Just put it somewhere safe."

"Yes, sir." Collins took the locked metal box from Isaac. "I'll put it into the vault myself. Here is your receipt." He pushed a piece of paper toward Isaac, who picked it up and scanned it with the practised eye of someone expecting to be cheated. "You know," continued Collins, "you're not the first person to be storing diamonds in the vault on this trip. There are several other diamond dealers aboard."

"Yes, I know." He gestured at the box. "Be sure that box doesn't get disturbed until I come for it when we reach Cherbourg."

"It won't move, sir."

"And make sure you give me back the right box." Isaac wagged a stern finger. "No substitutions."

Collins sounded pained. "Sir, I can assure you that the Stoddard Lines would never - "

"Yes, yes." Isaac turned away from the window, then stopped, coming up short against a gentleman about his own age, but that's where the similarity ended.

"Good evening, Mr Isaac," the man said. Isaac stared at him for a few moments.

"Mr Perry," he finally said. "The years have been kind to you." He gestured at himself. "Not so with me, I'm afraid. I'm glad you came."

"It's been thirty years, but I would recognize you anywhere, Nathaniel." Perry was tall and aristocratic, his silver hair combed back, his bearing regal. Both men gazed at each other with a tension that was palpable.

"You must know this is difficult for me after everything that happened in the past, but I had nowhere else to turn," said Isaac.

Perry gave a slight nod of his head. "Thirty years is a long time to be crossways with a man who was once like a brother to me. I'm happy to try and help your nephew, Nathaniel, but – "

"He's all I have, Alexander. My late sister's child. I've never been good as a father to him, and he's fallen in with the wrong sort of people." Nathaniel held up a cautionary palm. "No offense meant, of course."

Perry smiled. "None taken."

"Have you had any luck?"

Perry shook his head. "I'm afraid this is a hard row to hoe, Nathaniel. When I got your request I did go to Mr Schultz, but as you know he has a reputation for being very difficult to deal with. Where large sums of money are involved, he can be lethal to deal with."

"Joel didn't know what he was getting into," said Nathaniel.

"It doesn't matter to Dutch Schultz. He lent money, he expects to be repaid with interest. He told me as much and issued a thinly veiled threat that he would get his money, and more, back from Joel one way or another."

"He's nothing but a gangster. I don't know how you work for him."

"I turn diamonds into cash," said Perry. He gave Isaac a sad smile. "None of us are without darkness, I'm afraid. You of all people should know that."

Isaac lowered his chin and nodded. "I'll regret what I did at the camp until I die. I regret that and what it's cost me over the years."

"I'm just sorry you didn't come to me before Joel acted."

"If I had known he was going to act, believe me, I would have." Isaac shook his head. "Taking out a loan from the likes of Dutch Schultz to invest back into my jewelry store. I admit since the crash we've not been doing as well, but nothing to warrant what he did."

"He was only trying to help."

"I've been a pitiful excuse for a father," grumbled Isaac.

"I will keep trying to change Mr Schultz' mind," said Perry. "In the meantime I must warn you to take care. Dutch Schultz calls New York home but his tentacles are everywhere."

"Hopefully not in Antwerp." Isaac managed a sad smile. "It will be good to be at a show with you, Alexander."

"Yes," Perry nodded. "Mr Jenkins says you still have quite an inventory."

"I have an inventory, but none of it is moving." Isaac rapped the ferrule of his cane on the linoleum tiled floor and looked at the container in Perry's hands. "Checking in a box, are you?"

"Same as you," said Perry. "And just like you I am hoping to come away at least marginally in better shape than when I arrived. Will you and Joel have dinner with me tomorrow night? Say seven?"

"If you do not mind my company," said a voice. Isaac and Perry both turned. A tall man of muscular build, many years younger than either of them, was standing at Isaac's side. His face was sunburned to the shade of old walnut and his bright blue eyes darted from man to man. He wore an expensive and well-fitted suit, topped off with a broad-brimmed white woven straw hat on his head. Isaac again struck his cane on the floor.

"Ah, Van Effen. Of course you will be present." Isaac gestured toward Perry. "This is the gentleman I was telling you about who is trying to help Joel. Alexander Perry."

Van Effen doffed his hat with his left hand but didn't offer his right hand. "Mr Perry. A pleasure."

Perry nodded, warily. "The same, I'm sure."

Van Effen studied Perry. "You have known Mr Isaac long?"

Again, Perry nodded. "Yes, for many years, though we haven't kept in touch as much as we should have. Your accent, Mr Van Effen – are you Dutch?"

"I am."

"Boer, I believe."

Van Effen shrugged. "Does it make a difference?"

Perry pursed his lips. "Not anymore. I hope you will have a pleasant crossing, Mr Van Effen."

"I am sure I will." Van Effen looked at Nathaniel. "If you are ready to go, Mr Isaac," he said.

"If you could give us just a moment." Isaac looked at Perry. Van Effen nodded and moved away from the bank desk and out into the lobby area. Isaac turned back to Perry. "I should explain Van Effen. I thought it prudent to hire some protection. As you say, Dutch Schultz has a long arm."

"No need. After spending these years working for Mr Schultz I can recognize a torpedo when I see one. Tips his hat with his left hand, keeps his right hand close to his suit jacket shoulder holster. He looks very competent."

"He is," said Isaac. "He's costing me enough. We'll see you for dinner tomorrow night. Have a good evening." Isaac gave Perry a nod and stumped off, his cane thumping against the floor, Van Effen alongside. Perry watched them go, a curious expression on his face, then turned to Collins to do his transaction while I extricated my cramped body from the palms and made for the stairs.

When I got to the Sports Deck, I headed for the starboard flying bridge that jutted out over the ship's side far above the ocean. The flying bridges, one starboard and one port, were about three times the size of a soldier's sentry box on shore and fulfilled a similar purpose at sea. From inside, through its plate windows, officers could take in an unobstructed view of the bow of the *Victoria*, past the forward mast, the rigging and the steam cranes used for loading the forward holds, all the way up to the spare anchor mounted on the foredeck, as well as down to the ocean and aft to the ship's fantail, as far as the curvature of the hull would allow. While the box was closed on three sides from the wind and allowed viewing access through windows on those three sides, the fourth side, the entry, remained open to the elements. Depending on how the ship was berthed, one or the other flying bridges was usually vacant at departure. A green lamp indicating the starboard side of the vessel glowed beneath the sea-facing front window of the right side enclosure; a red lamp was housed on the left, or port enclosure. For those of you who spend most of your time on land, the red and green lamps serve as navigational aids for approaching ships to know which side to pass us on at sea.

I knew it was always Mister Harvey's favorite place to be as the ship embarked and by extension figured that's where I'd find Doctor Harper as well, and I was right. Both men looked over at me as I entered.

"Having a fabulous night," I said, "thanks for asking."

The men looked at each other. "Alice still being a problem?" asked Harper.

Harvey arched his eyebrows. "What's the trouble with Alice?"

"Nothing that time won't take care of," I said. Harvey gave me a look. "Oh, all right. She's fallen for a First-Class passenger, who also thinks she is a First-Class passenger."

"And how did he reach that conclusion?" Harvey mused. He looked at Harper. "As if I didn't know."

I shot him a sharp glance. "But there's more to the story," I said. I quickly recounted to Mister Harvey what I had earlier told Harper, then caught them both up on what had transpired at the purser's office. When I was done Harvey clapped a hand on Harper's shoulder.

"I'm glad she reports to you and not to me."

"Hush," I said to Harvey. I looked at Harper. "Don't you think there's something remotely suspicious about those two?"

"Three if you count the Dutchman." Harvey crossed his arms. "I was listening to you."

"Thank you, Mister Harvey." I turned back to Harper. "Three, then? What do you think of that?"

"I think you need to stay out of the potted palms and let our passengers go on with their business," said Harper.

"But Boss, the gangster. And Mr Isaac is worried enough to bring along his own security."

Harper shook his head. "It's not our problem, Maeve. Aren't you the one who told me to avoid passengers when I first came on board?"

"Fat lot of good that did," said Harvey.[*] He glanced down at his watch. "Last call," he said.

I knew that within the enormous public rooms of the ship, bellboys were walking through with their final announcement of "all ashore that's going ashore" and banging their brass gongs. Peering through one of the windows I could see the last of the visitors making their way down the gangplanks to the pier. The Stoddard Lines, like their competitors Cunard, White Star, and others, knew the value of having guests on board prior to sailing – today's guests may well be tomorrow's passengers. Looking through the open side of the flying bridge I could see directly into the *Victoria*'s well-lit bridge, where Captain Webster and First Officer Carter had turned over command of the ship to the Sandy Hook harbor pilot who would take the *Victoria* out of her berth, into the Hudson River, and from there to the *Ambrose* light ship – a small ship that serves as a floating light house, where we would stop to let the pilot off before entering the Atlantic ocean proper and beginning our voyage. Without warning, the

---

[*]    See Book One: *Shadow of the Queen*

*Victoria*'s horn gave a deafening three short blasts and then a long one.

Harper winced. "I still don't know how you put up with that."

"How did you put up with the sound of naval guns at Jutland?" Harvey said. "It's a matter of perspective. At least the *Victoria*'s horn isn't trying to kill you." He pointed down to the side of the ship where crews were detaching the last of the gangways. "Even money says there's still someone somewhere drinking in a First-Class cabin that isn't supposed to be there right now."

Harper nodded. "Probably. But as it's been pointed out to me, it's almost impossible to stowaway on board."

Harvey shook his head. "Oh, they're not stowing away, just overstaying their welcome. I'll just bet you that the pilot boat takes off someone else along with the pilot."

"I'll put a pound on it that we've gotten everyone off the ship that's not supposed to be here."

"Done." Harvey shook Harper's hand. I gave a sigh.

"Someday, Doctor, you'll learn not to bet against Mister Harvey." I watched as the final gangway retracted. "But I'm afraid you'll be learning the hard way."

"No doubt," he replied. "Just look at all the people showing up for a midnight sailing." The *Victoria*'s searchlights lit the pier far beneath us with a blaze of incandescence, showing a large throng of people yelling and waving up at the ship. I looked backwards through the enclosure and down. Passengers were lining the rails, waving back at those on the quay. Festive streamers of ribbon were launching from the ship, floating down in the chill breeze to hang down off the railings and lifeboat davits. "A man could get lost in all that lot," Harper commented.

"You should know," said Harvey. "You got lost coming up here, and I was guiding you."

"Don't you know your way around this ship yet, Doctor Harper?" I asked.

"I can find the hospital," Harper said. "And I can find my quarters."

"And the First-Class dining salon, as well," said Harvey with a grin. He winked at me. "Someone's put on some weight since he joined our merry crew."

"I may get lost, but I can always find something to eat." Harper smiled. "I'm not stupid, Mister Harvey."

"No, that you're not, Doctor," replied Harvey.

"Nor under-fed," I added.

Harper ignored my jab, pointing to a telephone pole on the dock that suddenly seemed to be slowly receding from the ship. "We're underway."

"Next stop, Cherbourg." Harvey pursed his lips. "I wish we were stopping long enough to allow shore leave, instead of just putting passengers off. I could take you all to the most fabulous restaurant."

"Sounds like a wonderful treat, Mister Harvey," I said. "Of course, you know Miss Kelly would also have to be invited." Kelly was the ship's Chief Stewardess. I gave him a speculative look. "And how is Miss Kelly, by the way?"

"Same as ever. Got all the stewardesses and housekeeping on the run. It's the Irish-Italian in her. What's a man to do?" Harvey spread his hands apart. "But I have to admit she does grow on me." He gestured toward the windows. "There's Brooklyn over there. And Staten Island there. I'll bet the Captain always sweats going through the Narrows before we get to the East Channel."

"From what I've seen of him since I've been aboard, I'll bet he never sweats," said Harper.

"Pound?" said Harvey.

"Pound," answered Harper.

"Big spenders," I said.

We stood silent for a time as the river pilot guided the *Victoria* along her delicate path. Soon enough the Statue of Liberty hove into view, alight in the darkness, with the city of New York glistening behind her. We gazed at the dignified behemoth, her glowing torch held aloft. "Say what you want about the French," remarked Harvey, apropos of nothing. "They know how to cook and how to build a statue."

"*Ambrose* lightship dead ahead," I said, pointing at a bobbing red light seeming to bear up directly in our path. The *Victoria*'s powerful lights illuminated the red-hulled craft, the word *Ambrose* painted in tall white letters along her 135-foot length. Warning lamps gleamed from the 67-foot lantern masts.

"Lonely job out there," said Harper.

"That's for certain," Harvey agreed. "I hear it's a six-man crew, and here they sit, stuck in the middle of the Hudson between Coney Island and Sandy Hook. Couldn't think of a better no-man's land."

"Oh, ask any of our War veterans that question. I'll bet they can." Harper nodded. "There's the pilot's boat coming up alongside."

We watched as the pilot left the bridge and made his way toward the ladder to go down the side of the ship. Sure enough, the *Victoria*'s massive Master-at-Arms Mister Armstrong appeared with two tuxedoed men in tow and set them on their way to follow the pilot. Harvey laughed. "You owe me a pound, Doctor." Harper withdrew his pocketbook, extracted the note and handed it to Harvey.

Harvey accepted gracefully. "I'll buy you a drink when we're off duty."

"And then you can buy Doctor Harper one," I said.

"What?" Harvey looked puzzled. I gestured over to the bridge windows where Captain Webster could be seen doing a very undignified stretch and covering a yawn with his hand.

"Doesn't look all sweaty to me," I said.

"Blast," said Harvey, handing the pound note back to Harper and adding one of his own.

"Boddingtons," said Harper. "Thank you for playing."

The harbor pilot quickly made his way to the waiting boat, then turned to help his two less agile guests aboard. When the all-clear was given, the ladder was pulled away and the harbor boat made her way into the clear. "Well," said Harvey, "show's over." He elbowed Harper. "Want to make another bet? I'll wager you anything you like that once we clear the limit and make it into international waters all of our thirsty Prohibition-suffering Americans aboard will be clamoring to have the bars stay open all night."

Harper grinned. "No bet there, Mister Harvey. You'd just be taking my hard-earned quid without a fight."

"Best way to do it," said Harvey. He grinned back. "I'm not stupid, either."

# IV

Have you ever been specifically trying to avoid someone, and then you run into them anyway? The thought pops into my mind about the line 'the best laid plans of mice and men,' etcetera. Actually, it's 'The best laid schemes o' mice an' men, Gang aft a-gley.' The Scottish poet Robert Burns wrote it in 1785, and I only know it because Chief Duncan likes to quote it, but if you want to say 'plans' instead of 'schemes,' it still gets the point across. The 'gang aft a-gley' portion can be loosely translated into several versions, not all of them suitable for print. It was into this latter category that I fell when I ducked into the First-Class Observation Lounge on the Promenade Deck to get out of the cold after leaving Harper and Harvey on the starboard flying bridge and ran smack into Joel Singer – and all I wanted to do was get to bed.

Mentally cursing myself for not wearing a coat over my nursing uniform, not only because it was cold outside but because it would have covered the uniform, I stood face to face with Joel in mute surprise. He blinked at me – twice, if you must know – and then opened his mouth. I cut him off.

"Yes. You saw me earlier today in your shop." I indicated my uniform. "And surprise confession. I'm not a First-Class passenger, I'm the head nurse aboard the *Victoria*."

"And the woman who was with you? Alice? Her too?"

Now we were at the proverbial fork in the road. As I saw it I had three choices. Either I could tell the truth and rat Alice out, completely deny knowledge of her (impossible to do now so really only two choices) or improvise. My brother, who had been one of Lord Baden-Powell's Boy Scouts and for a brief period of time could not tell a lie would have been proud that I took the first option. "She's a nurse, too," I confessed. "And we are not sisters." I felt this item had to be threshed out first. "Listen, can we just find a corner and talk?" I looked around anxiously. The bar was almost full. "I'm not even supposed to be in here."

"I'll tell people I had a medical question to ask you." The boy was good, I had to hand it to him. Unlike my brother in the Scouts, I had not gone in for the Girl Guides and could appreciate his speed in coming up with a suitable fib. He and Alice were made for each other.

"Fine." I navigated us to an empty table off the main floor and we sat. Almost immediately a waiter materialized to take our order. A pox on Mister Harvey and his efficient staff, I thought. The waiter looked at me carefully.

"Everything all right, Nurse?"

"Fine," I said again. "Why wouldn't it be?"

Joel interjected. "I had a medical question for the nurse. Too cold to stand outside, wouldn't you agree?"

"Oh, yes, sir," said the waiter. "What may I procure for you?"

"Gin and tonic," said Joel. He looked at me. "Nurse?"

If I could have gotten away with it, and more importantly if I could have reached him, I would have kicked him under the table. The last thing I needed was a drink and yet it was also the first thing I needed; funny how that worked. "We're not allowed to drink on duty," I said to Joel resignedly. I smiled at the waiter. "But I will have a cup of tea."

"Yes, Nurse." He shimmered away. I looked at Joel.

"Lord love a duck, I'm going to lose my job."

Joel leaned forward. "Is your name really Maeve Chandler?"

"Guilty as charged."

"Fine." He crossed his arms. "So," he said. "Tell me."

"Tell you what?"

"About her. Alice."

"Oh, Alice. Nice girl. In fact, I'm her boss. Look, aren't you at all upset that we were passing ourselves off as First-Class passengers today?"

He smiled. "Oh, I knew you weren't that at all."

"And just how, pray tell, did you know that?"

"When my uncle and I came into the shop, Jenkins said you were still going shopping at Tiffany's. Yet at that time it was about 45 minutes until First-Class boarding began and Tiffany's is on 37th Street and Fifth Avenue. It's over three and a half miles from my uncle's shop to Tiffany's, and neither of you showed any sign of being in a hurry. Plus, it's another mile and a half easy from Tiffany's to get down to where the *Queen Victoria* was docked. On the other hand, it's just over two and a half miles from my uncle's shop to go directly to the *Queen Victoria*, yet you two were going to traverse five miles in New York traffic and do some shopping at Tiffany's in the bargain – without being worried about what time you'd board the ship." He smiled. "I thought that two women who were in First-Class would be in more of a rush to get to the ship and board than you were, so if you really were from the

*Queen Victoria* you were most likely crewmembers who could come and go as you please." He sat back with a quiet air of triumph. "How did I do?"

I stared at him. "Other than saying we could come and go as we please, I think you did pretty well." Joel's drink and my tea arrived, the waiter giving me the fish eye, which I returned in kind. Joel lifted his glass.

"Cheers."

"*Slainte Mhath*." He gave me a questioning look. "It means to your good health," I said. "Traditional Gaelic."

"Ah." He took a sip. "Do you mind if I – "

"Not at all." I put my cup down. "Yes, she talked about you. Yes, she thinks you're handsome. Yes, she hopes to see you on board. Yes, she is single."

"All nice to know," said Joel. "Anything else?"

"Well, she was adopted, I can tell you that," I said. "No brothers or sisters. She really is from South Africa. Her adoptive father and mum moved to England to be closer to her and are not always in the best of health. Alice missed our new Principal Medical Officer's first voyage with us because she was home tending to her mum." I frowned. "If she lost her position here, she'd have a hard time taking care of them. That's one more reason why the two of you must be careful." I gave him a hard look.

"And yes, she and I share a cabin, so there will be no hanky-panky."

"Oh, none at all," he said, surprised. I believed him. "I'd like to see if she wants to have dinner with me Monday night, my uncle is occupying me tomorrow night."

The *Victoria*'s First-Class dining salon can seat 800 people at one time in comfort and yet, I thought, it wasn't going to be large enough for Joel and Alice and Isaac and Perry and Van Effen. "That's going to be a bit of a problem. I'm all for romance, but crew and passengers can't mix." His face assumed a downcast expression, like a freshly disciplined puppy. I sighed. "Fine. I'll ask her. There are a couple of smaller self-contained dining rooms at the aft end of the main salon that you might get into. They each seat 15 but perhaps Monday night they won't be booked. I'll have a note sent to your cabin with her reply." I took a sip. "Now I have a question for you." Joel nodded.

"I'm an apprentice diamond dealer. I'm single. I don't make much money. This is my first time on a ship like this. Actually, it's my first time on any ship."

"Well, thank you," I said. "But my question is what about your uncle?"

"What about him?" Joel took a swallow. "My parents were killed in an accident in 1910 when I was one year old and I've been living with him ever since. He's my mother's older brother. Never married or had children of his own. He and I are all that's left of the family."

"He seemed rather put out with you this afternoon."

Joel shrugged. "That's just his way. Right now he's worrying over something I did to help the store, but I think it will all work out at the end."

I hope so, I thought. "I'm just not sure of what he'll think of you and Alice."

"Ha. If he believes she's keeping my mind occupied – and she is – then that means I'm staying out of mischief according to his lights. He'll be fine with it. If not," Joel gestured with his glass, 'then he'll have Van Effen talk to me."

I turned and looked. Van Effen was sitting at a table with a very comely young lady, enjoying what appeared to be a bottle of champagne. "Who is Van Effen?" I asked, feigning ignorance. "That big man with the funny hat?"

Joel nodded. "My uncle hired him to protect us on this trip." He gave me a wan smile. "When I get into mischief I don't do it by halves."

"Now you've got my curiousity up. What did you do?"

"I took out a loan from a gangster to put money into the business. The loan's due with interest and right now I can't repay it."

Even knowing that this was the answer, his candor struck me. "So this Van Effen person – "

"I don't know what you'd call him in England, but in the States he's what's known as a hired gun." Again, the easy candor. "Looks like he's made a pretty friend. The last I saw him he was going off with my uncle to make sure my uncle's diamonds for the Antwerp show were properly deposited in the ship's vault." He leaned back in his chair. "Are we going as fast as the ship will go?"

I shook my head, both at his question and at the abrupt shift in conversation. "Not yet. Mister Duncan – he's the Chief Engineer – he really takes care of his turbines. He's slowly bringing them up to speed. If you're interested, we have a service speed of about 24 knots, which roughly translates to about 27 miles per hour." I finished my cup of tea. "And now, if you'll excuse me, I really need to get back to work."

I was just pushing my chair back when a dapper man came up to us. "Pardon the intrusion," he said. "Mr Singer, isn't it?"

"Yes," said Joel warily, eyeing the man and then glancing over to Van Effen across the room, who was still imbibing with the woman. "How do you know my name? I don't believe I know you."

"Oh! Sorry, my manners, you know!" The man smiled, holding out a well-manicured hand, replete with an expensive ring. He was, I guessed, somewhere in his early thirties. "I'm Harry Winston. I trade diamonds."

"I've heard of you," said Joel. He indicated me. "And this is – "

"Nurse Chandler." I indicated my uniform. "I work here."

"Charmed, Nurse. I hope to never meet you in your professional capacity."

"Actually, I'm in my professional capacity now. Mr Singer had a few questions, but I was just leaving."

"Nothing serious, I hope?" Harry pulled out a chair. "If the consultation is over, may I join you? Please stay, Nurse, you brighten the room considerably."

I sighed. This was certainly turning out to be a day for the books, if not a night. I sat back down and beckoned our waiter.

Winston's eyes flashed. "As to the how do I know your name, Mr Singer, I asked one of the pursers a few hours ago. I saw you and the older gentleman and something that looked like it stepped out of a horror movie come on board. In fact, the *golem* is across the room over there, isn't he? The older gentleman with you all was Nathan Isaac, the diamond dealer. Been in the business a long time, since the South Africa days."

"Nathaniel Isaac," corrected Joel. "Believe me, you'll only call him Nathan once. And yes, he's been in the business a very long time. The *golem* you referred to is his hired security, Van Effen."

"He looks rather intimidating," said Winston. "Not doing much in the way of security right now, is he?"

"My uncle is old and already asleep in his cabin," said Joel.

"Of course." Harry smiled. "You know, I've seen several of the old guard on board and I think you and I are the youngest dealers here."

Joel shook his head. "I'm only an apprentice to my uncle, Mr Winston, not yet a dealer." The waiter took a drink order from Joel and Winston passed. I ordered another spot of tea for myself and he departed, still giving me the eye. I just knew he was going to turn me in to Mister Harvey.

"Mr Isaac is your uncle?" asked Winston.

"Yes."

"I've heard old Nathan – rather, Nathaniel – is a real tough cookie."

"He can be, but he's always been fair to me when I deserved it, though right now I'm in some trouble with him."

"Nothing serious, I hope."

Joel took a sip of his drink. "If you don't think borrowing money from a gangster like Dutch Schultz to put into the business is serious, then no, nothing serious."

Harry stared at him. "You're kidding me."

"I wish I was. The interest on the loan is due and I don't have a cent to show for it." Joel inclined his head toward where Van Effen sat. "Believe me, he's not just along as window dressing. My uncle is asking his old business partner, Alexander Perry, to try and help. We're all supposed to have dinner tomorrow night. Perry works for Schultz. If that doesn't come through, my uncle has a box full of gems to sell at the show in Antwerp."

"I'm going to that show as well. Perhaps I can help you sell some of your stones. Don't be so hard on yourself. You made a mistake, learned a lesson, and you need to get out from under it and move on."

"That's what my uncle says."

"I'd listen to him. He's been around a long time. You always need to be careful of the people you do business with. I didn't, and it cost me everything. Everything."

"What happened?" I asked.

"I'll tell you," said Harry. "I had twenty thousand dollars' worth of diamonds in my store, and I came in one morning and they were gone along with my employee."

"Good Lord," Joel exclaimed.

"The Good Lord had nothing to do with it, Joel. That was back in 1922. I was twenty-five years old, and I was wiped out – not unlike a lot of the people from last October."

"What did you do?" I found myself fascinated by the story.

"Do?" Harry smiled. "I redoubled my efforts and went back to work. I did some very careful deals, got credit from a friendly banker, and rebuilt my business by getting into estate jewelry."

"Estate jewelry?" I asked. Harry nodded.

"Stuff that used to go for next to nothing when some rich old lady died. My first big purchase was from the widower of Rebecca Stoddard." He smiled at me. "No relation to your Commodore Stoddard, I'm afraid. Anyway, she was a very rich woman, and lived in New Haven, Connecticut. After she died, I got a pal of mine at a bank to write a letter of introduction for me to Mr Stoddard. With that in my hands, Mr Stoddard let me appraise his late wife's collection."

Joel nodded. "My uncle always says it's not what you know, it's who you know."

"I agree," said Harry. "Now, understand, I didn't have a penny to my name. I was operating on bank credit. But I looked at Stoddard's jewelry, and I offered him a million dollars for the entire collection."

"A million dollars? And he took it?" I asked.

Harry gave us a rueful smile. "Free advice number two. Don't shoot your bolt too soon. I thought that Stoddard wasn't going to do the deal, he was wavering, so I opened my big mouth and told him I'd sweeten the deal by two hundred thousand dollars more. Now, understand my commission would be one hundred and twenty thousand dollars, so Mr. Stoddard would be out in front by eighty thousand. Of course he took it. I hustled like never before, and within six months had disposed of the entire collection for a total of a million and two hundred fifty thousand dollars."

Joel's mouth dropped. "That's fifty thousand more than you promised him."

"Exactly. My final commission was one hundred twenty five thousand dollars."

"That's amazing," I said.

Joel glanced at his watch. "Do you have the time?"

"About 11:45, for you Americans," I said. "23:45 for us Brits."

"Thanks." He adjusted the stem on his watch. "I've really got to be heading to bed. The cabin is unbelievable. This is my first trip abroad and we're traveling in First Class. Uncle Nathaniel says we need to keep up appearances no matter what else. We can talk more in the morning? I mean if you're around?"

Harry leaned back and indicated the space around him. "We're crossing the Atlantic Ocean, Joel. Where else am I going to go? So, are you heading for the *Diamant Club van Antwerpen* or the *Antwerpsche Diamantkring*?"

"I'm not sure," admitted Joel.

"Well, no matter," Winston said easily. He crossed one sharply creased trouser leg over his knee, his foot swinging airily and smiled. "I'm trading at both. If you only do one, I can take you to the other."

"That's very generous of you," said Joel. Harry waved a dismissive hand.

"You'll do just fine in this business, Joel," said Harry. "I'll talk with Nathaniel in the morning."

"He'll be mortified," said Joel.

"Better him mortified than you in the morgue if you can't pay back Schultz." He settled back in his chair. "We just need business conditions pick back up again." He gave us a close look, his face becoming serious. "You know how bad it is?"

I nodded. "It's starting to be felt at home, back in the UK." I looked at the two men. "Not as bad as it is in America right now."

"My uncle has mentioned it," said Joel.

"Mentioned it!" Harry shook his head. "The price per carat of a rough diamond right now on the London market is about three pounds and some pence." He clicked his teeth. "Scarcely worth the effort. Of course, if the Diamond Corporation comes through, it may help somewhat."

"I don't know that much about them," Joel said.

"Well, the news isn't that old. The Diamond Corporation, that is. They just formed last month, in February. De Beers, CDM, Premier, all the other leading producers are in on it. We'll see what happens. I'm afraid if things don't improve, the big producers will have to curtail production. A glut of roughs on the market that no one can sell is just going to depress prices even further." He shrugged. "I do all right though. My business is the Premier Diamond Company, at 535 Fifth Avenue. You should come by some time."

"I've heard of it," said Joel.

"Well, I hope so," remarked Winston with a broad smile. "I've worked really hard at it."

Joel smiled. "I've got a lot of work to do before I reach your level, Mr Winston." He looked at me. "Walk you to the door, Nurse Chandler?"

"Thank you, Mr Singer." I stood. "I live here, remember? I can find my own way home."

Both men stood. "A pleasure to meet you, Nurse Chandler," said Harry. "If you're ever in the market for a diamond - "

"I'll look you up Mr Winston." In about forty years, I thought, at my current rate of pay. I hoped he'd still be around in 1970.

# Sunday, March 23, 1930

## I

You and I both know there are days when you shouldn't even bother with getting out of bed. I remember back in my university days when I stayed out rather late prior to an early morning class. No idea what possessed me to do it except I was with some of my girlfriends, and we didn't want the evening to end; I'm sure you've had the same experience. The upshot of it was that I got called down by the professor for sleeping in class (in my defense it was a deathly boring lecture on inorganic chemistry; any of you would have done the same) and was sentenced to extra reading, with a test just for me the following morning. The point is, if I'd stayed in bed and just skipped class with the excuse that I was sick, I probably wouldn't have been punished (at least as much) and the way this day was going to unfold, staying in bed would have been the best option. Hindsight, as they say...

"How was the rest of your evening, Nurse?" Harper asked as he walked into the hospital at seven Sunday morning. I stifled a yawn and rolled my eyes.

"Which do you want first? The medical report or my personal life?"

"Let's take it in priorities. Medical first."

"Thanks a lot." I enumerated the list. "Since I came on duty at five this morning, I have treated nausea due to a moving ship and too much alcohol, a sprained ankle and one broken finger."

"Broken finger?" Harper took off his cap and set it on the desk. I nodded.

"Passenger got his finger stuck in a lift gate as it closed." I shrugged. "Honestly, Boss, I don't know what they're thinking sometimes."

"They're not." As Principal Medical Officer of the *Queen Victoria*, Harper had the responsibility to sign off on all the final medical reports. He took the clipboard I handed him, gave it a professional check through, initialed the treatments and gave it back. "Now let's hear about your personal life."

"I barely know where to begin," I said. "Did you know that the price per carat of a rough diamond on the London market is about three pounds plus?"

"I must admit I did not. Nor does it make any difference to me. What has that to do with your personal life?"

"Plenty." I adjusted my nursing cap. "I'm running in high circles now, so you might treat me with the deference I'm due, Boss. Diamond dealers."

Harper raised an eyebrow. "There's more than the one Alice is infatuated with?"

"Lots more." I exhaled. "I sat in the First-Class lounge listening to Alice's man – Joel – talk with another man named Harry Winston. It really was a fascinating backstage peek at the diamond business."

"I beg your pardon?" Harper looked down his aquiline nose at me. "You were in the First-Class lounge? With two passengers? Talking? How did that happen?"

"After visiting you and Mister Harvey, I took a shortcut through the First-Class lounge and got caught by Joel. You remember at the jewelry store yesterday we told him we were First-Class passengers? Well, now he knows we're not. I confessed for both of us."

"I'm sure the uniform tipped him off," said Harper with a smile.

"Shush." I leaned against the desk and folded my arms. "After that, he wanted to know all about Alice." I sighed. "He's just as smitten as she is."

"The difference being he's a paying passenger and she's a paid nurse like you."

"If it's any comfort, Joel shanghaied me by saying he needed to discuss a medical issue." I pulled a chair over. "Do you mind if I sit down? This is a long story." To his credit, Doctor Harper said nothing while I relayed the events after I had left him and Mister Harvey the previous evening. When I finished his face was serious.

"This gangster money-lending issue sounds serious. The Captain will want no trouble on his ship from any underworld debt collector."

"I don't think anything will happen. Mr Schultz is in New York and we're at sea."

"Maybe you're right," said Harper. "Have you told Alice?"

"No, she went straight back to our cabin when I relieved her last night. She's still getting her beauty sleep, the poor lamb, which is something I desperately need." My eyes felt gritty. "But I'm going to go wake her up now, that is if you can do without me."

"I think I can manage," said Harper. "But this crew-passenger romance is a bad idea, in my opinion."

"I keep telling them that, Boss." I sat on the edge of the desk, yawned and swung my legs, hitting a chair in the process. "But I'm not going to worry about it," I grimaced. "She's a big girl and can take care of herself."

"Unlike you," said Harper as I rubbed my shin. The 'phone rang and he picked it up. "Hospital, Doctor Harper speaking." He listened for a moment, nodding.

"Right. Goodbye." He hung up the receiver and looked at me. "Mister Harvey has an elderly First-Class passenger who's not answering his door. In fact, he doesn't appear to be doing much of anything at all. His nephew is so worried he's called Mister Harvey to come and open the cabin."

"Nephew?" My sleepiness left me. "This elderly passenger wouldn't be named Nathaniel Isaac, would he?"

"He would." Harper picked up his bag. "I'm anxious to meet this man of mystery. Shall we go?"

"After you, Boss." I slid off the desk, lost my balance and caromed into that bloody chair again. Harper gave me a studied look.

"You really are the clumsiest thing," he said.

Mister Harvey was in consultation with Joel when we got to Nathaniel Isaac's cabin on the Main Deck, along the port side toward the bow.

"I'm sorry, Mr Singer," he was saying. "I can't just open another passenger's locked door without a good reason, even if you are a relative. It's a privacy issue." He looked over at us. "Doctor Harper, Nurse Chandler," began Harvey pleadingly, but Joel interrupted him.

"Nurse Chandler, my uncle never sleeps this late," he said to us. Harvey cocked an eyebrow at me and nodded at Joel.

"You know him?" he whispered.

"Alice's beau, for want of a better word," I said out of the side of my mouth.

Harvey nodded. "Of course, why wouldn't he be?"

Harper stepped up to Joel. "Mr Singer, I'm Principal Medical Officer Doctor Harper. Does your uncle have any underlying medical conditions?"

"Other than being old, nothing I know of."

Mister Harvey walked up to the door and gave a sharp rap. "Mr Isaac? It's Chief Steward Harvey. Are you there?" The cabin remained quiet.

"It was like this earlier this morning, too, said Joel. "I guess I came by here about an hour ago or so, after I first got up. There was no answer. I went back to my stateroom, got cleaned up and dressed, then came back again to see if he was awake yet. You can usually hear him stumping about with that cane, but I heard nothing. I was supposed to meet Mr Winston for breakfast but asked a steward to help me get into my uncle's room. He sent for Mister Harvey and here we are."

"Which room is yours, Mr Singer?" asked Harper.

"Right next door, 31-A. Please, he's always up at dawn. Goes to sleep before nine, usually, but always an early riser." Joel chewed his lip. "He might have had a stroke or a heart attack or something. Can we please just open the door?"

The door to cabin 37-A, three doors down from Joel, suddenly opened and a woman about my age stepped out into the corridor. I recognized her as the woman who had been with Van Effen in the bar last night. "What's going on out here? Can I not get some sleep?"

"I apologize, Madam." Harvey came as close as he ever could to giving an uncomfortable squirm. "We have an older gentleman in cabin 33-A who is not answering our calls."

"Could you call a bit quieter?" The woman, by her tone an American, drew her robe tighter around herself and put a hand to her forehead. "By the saints, what kind of champagne do you sell on this boat?" Mister Harvey began to open his mouth but I elbowed him in the ribs. The woman continued. "I thought it a bit of luck that I had an empty cabin on either side of me, but it seems my hopes for a quiet voyage were unfounded."

"Apologies, Madam," began Harper but she cut him off.

"Madam? I am not the proprietor of a house of ill repute. My last name is Thomas."

"Apologies, Miss Thomas. I'm the Principal Medical Officer of the ship and it's my belief this is a medical emergency."

"That so?" She appeared skeptical. "Well, keep it down, then." She gestured down the corridor. Another door had opened directly across the hall from Isaac's room and an older woman was peering out. "You're disturbing the paying passengers," said Miss Thomas. She withdrew and abruptly shut her door. I turned around and looked back at the other half-cracked door. It quickly shut.

"May we get on to my uncle, please?" asked Joel.

"Yes, of course." Harper looked at Harvey and nodded. "I'm declaring a medical emergency."

"As you say." Harvey pulled out a key ring and fitted one to the mortise lock. "Master key," he explained. He began to push it in then stopped, pulled the key out and knelt by the door to peer into the lock through the keyhole.

"What is it?" asked Harper.

"There's another key in this lock. And it's turned."

"It's locked from the inside, you mean?" asked Joel. Harvey nodded. "Can you get the key out?"

"Of course." Harvey pushed his master all the way in and we heard the key on the inside fall out and strike against the door on its way down to the carpet

"All these years working with you and I never knew you were so prepared," I teased. Harvey shrugged.

"You never know when you'll need a master key to get into a cabin. I had one passenger lock himself in and then accidentally drop his key down the tub drain." Harvey turned his master key. The door opened easily, revealing a gloomy interior with shades drawn on the portholes. Harvey stepped inside and switched on the light, illuminating the sitting room, then stopped short in the doorway.

"Uncle Nathaniel?" Joel called softly from behind Harvey. There was no reply. Joel pushed past Harvey, followed by the rest of us and we all stood still.

Nathaniel Isaac was upright in an armchair in the center of his sitting room, his arms resting on the chair, his head back and his mouth closed. His eyes were wide open, and his face had a bluish tinge. Harper and I quickly went to his side, Harper dropping his medical bag on the floor and touching Isaac's cheek and forehead.

"Stone cold," he said. I felt for a pulse.

"No pulse, Doctor."

"Is he dead?" Joel had come up behind us from the doorway.

Harper nodded. "I'm afraid so." I gently closed Isaac's eyes and looked up at Joel.

"I'm so sorry, Mr Singer." Joel made as if to speak but remained silent, staring at the dead man. We stood for a moment until Mister Harvey spoke.

"What killed him?" he asked, tactful as always. I again elbowed him in the ribs and jerked my head toward Joel. "Oh," said Harvey. "Well, I was just curious."

Harper rubbed his chin. "It looks like he suffocated, but his body position seems awfully calm for that to have happened. Rigor mortis hasn't set in, so he probably died between midnight and six this morning."

"I thought that happened right off," said Harvey.

"No," I said. "Anywhere from an hour to six hours after death."

"Suffocated?" said Joel. He looked wobbly. I guided him to a chair and had him

sit with his head down between his knees.

Harper took Isaac by the shoulders and looked at Harvey. "Help me get him into the bedroom."

"Right." Harvey took Isaac's slippered feet and they gently lifted him out of the armchair. "Doesn't weigh much, does he?" Harvey commented, then stopped, looking down at the chair. Harper and I followed his gaze.

"It's nothing," I said. "That's where he voided his bladder when he died. Be careful where you put your hands."

"Thanks," said Harvey. They deposited the body on top of the coverlet. His head lolled back and mouth drooped open. Harper's eyes narrowed. He took his glasses out of his uniform jacket and put them on.

"Maeve, open those curtains and turn on the overhead. Get a little more light in here."

"What is it?" I asked.

"Not sure. I thought I saw something." Harper knelt beside the bed and ever so gently touched Isaac's mouth. It remained slack. I heard sound from the bedroom doorway and looked back to see Joel standing there.

"You don't have to watch this."

"I want to."

"As you wish." Harper gently pulled Isaac's chin down and winced.

"What is it?" asked Harvey.

Harper looked at Harvey, then at me, and finally at Joel, a curious expression on his face. "I'm sorry, Joel," he said, standing up and stepping away from the body. Again we crowded in to see, and again, recoiled. I looked at Harper.

"What is all of that glittering at the back of his mouth?"

Joel's expression was grim. "Diamonds."

If you know me you'll find this hard to believe, but I actually won a scripture prize at Sunday lessons when I was young. The teacher was using common idioms and relating them to the Bible. When I was asked a question about reaping what you sow, I was able to answer Galatians 6:7. For those who don't know it, the verse reads, in part, 'a man reaps what he sows.' In faith, the only reason I knew this bit of religious trivia was because reaping what you sow was one of my father's favorite expressions. Looking down at the late Mr Isaac, I wondered exactly what he had sown to reap this ending.

For a few seconds, again, no one spoke. As usual, it was Mister Harvey who finally broke the silence.

"Bloody hell," he said quietly. Joel turned away, clenching and unclenching his fists.

"Who would do such a thing?" he said. "That looks like a fortune in diamonds in his throat."

"And how would they do it?" I said. "As Doctor Harper observed, he's very calm. I can't imagine anyone sitting still for that." I looked at Harper. "You know, as children my brother and I had marbles, and we were warned strongly by our parents not to put them in our mouth or we'd choke on them. Could someone consciously choke on diamonds?"

Harper shrugged. "I don't know. I would think one's mental state would have a great deal to do with it, but I'm not a psychiatrist." Harper gently closed Isaac's mouth.

"So he locks the door from the inside and commits suicide by diamond?" Mister Harvey sounded skeptical and I couldn't blame him.

Harper looked at Joel. "What was your uncle's mental state?"

"He was worried about the store. He was worried about me. I can't believe he's dead." He glanced around the room then looked at me. "Where the hell is Van Effen? He's my uncle's bodyguard. He's being paid to prevent this."

"I am here, Mr Singer." We all turned. Van Effen was standing in the bedroom doorway, immaculately dressed, holding his straw hat in one hand.

"My uncle's dead," spat Joel. "How did you let this happen?"

Van Effen looked at Harper and Harvey. "I heard one of these gentlemen say as I was coming in that Mr Isaac locked the door and committed suicide? I am sorry, and I am sorry for your loss, Mr Singer, but I can scarcely be faulted for not preventing a suicide behind a locked door. May I see the body, please?"

Harper and I stepped away from the bed. Van Effen approached and looked down. "What did I hear about diamonds? 'Suicide by diamond,' I think, was the wording."

"His throat is clogged with diamonds," said Harper. "He choked to death."

"And you are?"

"Principal Medical Officer Leslie Harper. This is Chief Steward Harvey and my nurse, Miss Chandler."

"Will you open his mouth, please, Dr Harper?"

Harper shook his head and skyrocketed in my already high estimation of him. "Out of respect for the deceased, I will respectfully decline, sir."

Van Effen nodded. "Respect for the dead. I understand. My apologies for making your acquaintance under such sad circumstances." Van Effen turned to Joel, his inspection of Isaac's body complete. "I will, of course, continue to look out for you, Mr Singer through the course of the agreement I made with Mr Isaac."

"I saw you last night in the bar," said Joel. "You were with a woman instead of guarding my uncle."

"I also saw you, Mr Singer, with this woman" – he indicated me – "and a man who sat with his back to me. As for myself, Mr Isaac had been safely deposited in his cabin and I heard him turn the lock from the inside before he dismissed me for the remainder of the evening."

"So you saw and heard nothing?" I asked. Van Effen shook his head.

"I stopped to listen at Mr Isaac's cabin door when I returned but heard nothing. It was my belief he had retired for the night. I did the same."

"And what time was this?" I asked.

"Shortly after the bar closed."

"The woman you were with, we saw her a little while ago. She looked like she was nursing a vicious hangover," I said with some satisfaction.

"Caroline Thomas," said Van Effen. "We met as strangers in the bar and began talking. Her company was a tonic. I offered to walk her back to her cabin and was pleased to see it along this corridor near mine."

"I'll just bet you were," said Joel.

Van Effen ignored the remark and turned to Harper. "Of course you will report this to the master of the ship. What will you do with the body?"

"That's up to Mr Singer here."

"I see." Van Effen thought for a moment. "Mr Singer, please keep me apprised of where you go on the ship and who you talk with. You may not always see me but please know I will always be close by. I regret Mr Isaac's passing, but again, I could not guard against a suicide."

"That makes me feel so much better," Joel said bitterly.

Van Effen tapped his hat against his thigh. "I have seen many things in my life, but this – odd. Very odd." Van Effen nodded to himself. "I will return soon, Mr Singer. Please do not open your cabin door to anyone you do not personally know until that time. I am pleased to have met you all." He took his leave, clicking the cabin door shut behind him.

"That was interesting," said Mister Harvey. "First time I've ever met someone in his line of work."

Joel ground his teeth. "Sorry. I guess you need to know why he's here, now that the cat's out of the bag."

I frowned. "I'm afraid I already told them about your remarks with myself and Mr Winston last night, Mr Singer. And we all know about a conversation I overheard between Mr Isaac and Alexander Perry last night at the purser's office, too."

"So you know it all, then?"

"I'm afraid we do. I'm sorry."

"God, what a mess," said Joel. He swallowed. "I suddenly feel very tired."

Harper rummaged in his medical bag, withdrawing a syringe and a bottle. "A bit of Luminal to help you sleep for a while." He looked at Joel. "Would you please roll up your sleeve? Nurse, alcohol swab, please."

"What's Luminal?" asked Joel as Harper filled the syringe.

"Phenobarbital," I said.

Harper finished the injection and snapped his bag shut while I stuck a Band-Aid on and rolled Joel's sleeve back down. "This will take effect rather quickly," said Harper. "Let's get you to your cabin."

"What about my uncle?"

"He's staying where he is," I said.

"But he can't stay alone," began Joel, then passed a hand across his forehead. "I don't feel – " He began to sway and Harvey caught him in his arms.

"I guess you're going to be wanting Mister Armstrong?" asked Mister Harvey.

Harper nodded. "And the Captain. I'll go topside with you after we get Mr Singer situated in his cabin."

"Bearers of bad news just like Rosencrantz and Guildenstern," muttered Harvey. "And you know what happened to them." He thought a moment. "Who's minding your shop while Bratton is on leave?"

"Nurse Johnson should be on duty now, so we're covered," I said. "And Mister Harvey, if you happen to run into her – she doesn't need to know that anything's happening right now."

Harvey looked at Harper and shrugged. "Like I said before, I'm glad she works for you and not me. Help me with the boyfriend, won't you?"

Harper took Joel under one arm and Mister Harvey shifted his load to the other. I lagged back and Harper gave me a questioning look.

"Joel was saying his uncle can't stay alone just before the drug took effect."

"So?" said Harvey. "It's not like he's going to know. Joel or his uncle."

"I'll stay until someone else comes," I said, remembering my first encounter with Mr Isaac at the jewelry store. "He's Jewish," I said by way of explanation.

"One of my husband's friends in the War was Jewish. When he passed his body couldn't be left alone. Someone had to stay with him, and my husband was honored to sit with another friend who was Jewish." I looked at Mr Isaac. "Until Joel is back on his feet I guess I can do the job." I looked at the body and frowned. "I don't guess Mr Isaac would mind too much if I stepped out every once in a while to check on his nephew."

Harper narrowed his eyes. "You wouldn't be thinking of poking around in here, would you?"

"Me? What makes you think that?"

"Five months ago is what makes me think that," he replied.*

"Ditto," said Harvey, shifting his load. "And I hate to complain, but the nephew is considerably heavier than the uncle. Could we please go?"

I sat down in a chair. "Look. I'm sitting. Mister Harvey, would you find out who's directly next door to Mr Singer in 29-A? And also who's in 35-A?"

"Yes, Nurse." Both men looked at each other and then walked a very unsteady Joel from the cabin without a backward glance. The door closed and I was alone with the mortal remains of Nathaniel Isaac. I looked at my watch. I probably had fifteen minutes, but to play it safe I banked on ten. I stood up, took a deep breath, and plunged in.

There were no immediately discernible marks of violence on Isaac; no bruises or cuts or abrasions that I could see. He was clad in silk red striped pyjamas and a tatty dressing gown, cinched at the waist. His bare feet were inside of a pair of worn black leather slippers; in overall aspect he reminded me of Ebenezer Scrooge, even down to his cane leaning against a wall near the bed. I pushed Isaac's now stiffening mouth closed then pulled a folded blanket up from the end of the bed, covered the body and walked to the sitting room.

The key that Mister Harvey had pushed out of the lock was still on the carpet. I stooped and picked it up, examining it closely. The steel key was of the skeleton type, issued to every cabin on the *Victoria*. It was just under three inches in length with a slender cylindrical shaft slightly less in diameter than one might find on a child's lollipop, and a single, flat rectangular tooth projecting out to one side at the bottom. Two tiny, raised notches protruded off the tooth. The top of the shaft was turned in a stylized open oval, with an inverted 'v' notch with the cabin number stamped into the top of the oval, and the lock maker's name stamped on the opposite side. The inside of the lockset below the doorknob offered little help either. To prevent peeping through keyholes, a brass escutcheon on a pin was supposed to swing down by gravity to cover the keyhole from the inside when the door was locked from the outside, and also perform the same function when the door was locked from the inside and the key removed from the lock, but the escutcheon was apparently jammed in the open position; at least I couldn't force it down to cover the keyhole. I set the key on the table and went back to the bedroom to turn my attention to the armchair where Isaac's body was found.

The chair offered no story at all, other than mute testimony to Isaac's wetting himself. I held my breath, got down on hands and knees and looked up underneath it, then for good measure turned it over, carefully avoiding the damp seat, but there was nothing to see. No marks that Isaac may have been bound to the chair. No marks of anything unusual on the chair. In fact, no marks at all. I righted it and went next door to check on Joel.

A gentle snore greeted me upon opening his door. I walked to the bedroom and glanced in. He was flat on his back. I took off his shoes and covered him with a blanket, then went back to Isaac's stateroom and sat down to wait. Who would have wanted to kill Isaac, and in such a fashion? My mind went back to the conversation between Perry and Isaac at the purser's office. Had Dutch Schulz reached out to send a not too subtle reminder that his payment was due in full? And where had Van Effen been? Of course, as he said, he couldn't very well prevent a suicide but still, the shade of Isaac must be railing to the heavens about the poor service provided by his hired protection. I got up and walked back over to the bed and pulled the blanket down.

The collar on Isaac's pajama top was askew. I reached out to straighten it then sharply drew my fingers back. Something was sticking up through the collar. I leaned in for a closer look and saw a very tiny glint of steel. If I hadn't happened to brush it with my finger tips I would have never seen it. Thanking my lucky stars that whatever it was hadn't punctured my skin, I went to Harper's bag, opened it and took out a pair of tweezers, then went back to the body.

Slowly dragging my fingers over the collar with a very light and delicate touch, I located the item again. With a careful hand I used the tweezers to grasp and pull it out, sliding it up through the thin silk, then held it close to my eyes.

Glittering in the light was the tiny broken beveled end of a thirty-gauge injection needle.

As you know by now, I'm clumsy and accident prone. I would bet that during my time on the *Victoria* there are very few pieces of furniture or railing that I haven't met up close and personal. Doctor Harper and Mister Harvey can tease me all they want, but the truth is that accidents are sometimes a blessing. Look at Alexander Graham Bell and the telephone. His words – 'Mr Watson, come here, I want you' – were the first words spoken over the telephone and uttered because Bell had spilled acid on his work apron. Or take Alexander Fleming, who discovered penicillin just two years ago quite by accident in a mouldy petri dish. And add me to the list – if I hadn't accidentally brushed across it when straightening Isaac's collar, the way he was made to ingest diamonds until he suffocated might never have been known.

I wrapped the needle fragment in some toilet paper and stuffed it in my pocket, then returned Harper's tweezers to his bag and sat back down, my mind racing. Despite what the men thought, I had felt it extremely unlikely that Isaac would have swallowed diamonds until he choked, no matter the condition of his mental health. Equally unlikely was the fact that he sat still while someone force fed him diamonds. Isaac had no visible bruises or marks on him from fighting back, which he would have done no matter how feeble he may have been. The broken needle point meant he had more than likely been injected with a paralyzing agent, probably something like pancuronium bromide or succinylcholine. He would have been rendered physically incapable of defending himself. I closed my eyes to the thought that he may have been paralyzed but alive as his killer placed the stones in his mouth; it was too horrible to contemplate.

My thoughts were interrupted by the stateroom door opening. The Captain, Doctor Harper and Mister Armstrong filed in and closed the door behind them. Harper gestured toward the bedroom.

"He's in there," he said quietly. I stood, smoothed out my uniform and came out to greet them.

"Nurse Chandler?" said the Captain.

"Yes, sir? I was sitting *shiva*," I replied. The Captain raised his eyebrows.

"I didn't know you were Jewish."

"I'm not. My husband had a close friend who was in the War." I gestured toward the bedroom. "The body isn't supposed to be alone."

"Well, take me to him."

"Yes, sir," said Harper. "This way." I stepped aside as Harper and the Captain went into the bedroom, leaving me behind with Mister Armstrong. The burly Master at Arms looked at me.

"Bad business, Nurse," he rumbled.

"And no doubt bad for business," I replied. "Sorry, that seemed callous of me."

"You've had a trying morning, Nurse," said Armstrong. "He was stuffed with diamonds?"

"Like some 50 carat Christmas goose. Doctor Harper will take them out."

"And then what? Run a notice in the paper that some diamonds have been found?"

"Mister Armstrong, I doubt anyone is going to come forth and claim them."

"No one in their right mind, anyway."

"No one in their right mind would have done this."

"Mister Armstrong," commanded the Captain from the bedroom. "Will you join us, please?"

"Straightaway, sir," said Armstrong. He gave me a brief smile. I was left alone in the sitting room. I did a quick walk around to see if there was anything I might have missed from the first pass, but the room remained quiet and gave up no secrets. I was glad when the bedroom door opened and they trooped back into the sitting room.

"Mister Armstrong," said Harper, "please get a stretcher team and take Mr Isaac down to the hospital. Try and avoid the passenger areas."

"No," I said. The Captain and Harper looked at me.

"No?" said the Captain.

"Yes, sir," I said. "I mean, no. My husband told me there are a lot of rules to be followed regarding a Jewish death. The body is considered sacred."

The Captain frowned at me. "I bow to no one, Nurse, in your medical skills, but are you certain you're qualified in the rabbinical world?"

"I'm just remembering what my husband told me of his experience. It was thirteen or fourteen years ago." I thought a moment. "I'm sure if we have any Jewish passengers on board they can fill us in. Or the dead man's nephew can guide us when he comes back around. We gave him a mild sedative."

"Yes, the Doctor and Mister Harvey told me."

"What shall I do, sir?" queried Armstrong. The Captain looked at me.

"All right. Have it your way, nurse. Leave him here for the moment."

"I can take the diamonds out of his mouth here," said Harper. "No need to move him."

"Fine," said the Captain. "Now to the more pressing point – who did this and why? Doctor Harper filled me in on what all you've overheard, Nurse. I find it disconcerting to say the least that an American gangster may be exacting his own justice on board my ship, not to mention the fact that we are also hosting a private security officer."

"'Officer' is not a word I would use in conjunction with Mr Van Effen," I said.

"Nor I," said Mister Armstrong.

"Whatever you want to call him, Nurse," said the Captain. "What about this man Schultz?"

"He's not on board, Captain. But maybe someone is who's working for him."

"Sir," said Harper, sparing me the Captain's look, "perhaps it really was a suicide. The door was locked from the inside, and while I've never heard of such a thing, I think someone in a diseased state of mind could choke themselves to death by swallowing items."

"That's a horrible way to go, Doctor Harper," said the Captain.

"No doubt, sir, but that's the only thing that fits our facts."

"Except for the fact that the body was at repose," I said. "Begging your pardon, Doctor Harper," I said, "the facts have slightly changed since you were here last."

The Captain cocked his head toward me. "So, what have you, Nurse?"

"Sir," I said, "I think we would all agree it's a fair assumption that no one would voluntarily sit still and be force fed diamonds until they choked, and no one would lock the door and then swallow diamonds until they suffocated, either."

The Captain thoughtfully stroked his trim beard. "What are you getting at?"

"Joel told us he was in and out of his stateroom and heard nothing," I said. "Van Effen also says he heard nothing and there are no signs on Isaac's body that anyone had a physical go at him. He looks like he went down without a fight." I looked at all three men. "So how was it done?"

"He was drugged," said Harper.

"Yes, sir." I looked at Harper and reached in my pocket for the little wad of toilet paper and placed it carefully on the table, then unfolded it to expose the broken needle tip.

"I'll be damned," said Harper. "A broken injection needle. Where did you find it?"

"I was straightening Mr Isaacs pajama collar and felt something sticking up out of the silk. I used a pair of your tweezers to pull it out. The puncture location is above the middle scalene muscle in the neck."

Harper nodded. "Some kind of paralyzing agent, then." He looked at the Captain. "I'll draw some blood and see what we can find out."

"This makes it premeditated murder," said the Captain. "Carefully planned out."

"Yes, sir."

"Why go to all the trouble with the locked room shenanigans, then?" said the Captain. "Why not just leave?"

"And how did they manage the door locked from the inside?" asked Harper. "They had to get out of the cabin somehow."

"To answer your question, sir, it's like Doctor Harper suggested. To make us believe it was suicide, and a very rugged suicide at that. As to the other," I shrugged. "I'm sure there's an explanation for it, it's just not presenting itself to my mind at the moment."

"The portholes are too small, and even if anyone could get through one there's nowhere to go but down into the ocean," said Armstrong. "And there aren't any air vents large enough for a man." He looked around. "And this is not one of the connecting cabins, either."

Harper shook his head. "As Nurse Chandler says, there's an explanation for it. In the meantime I think there's another big question begging an answer. Who had these diamonds and was willing to part with them in such a fashion? It seems a very expensive way to kill a man."

"Did you ever price the naval artillery shells we used in the War, Doctor?" asked the Captain. "That was a very expensive way to kill a man."

"Point taken."

"But why the diamonds?" asked Armstrong. "Once he's paralyzed, they could have stuffed a washcloth in his throat or held it over his mouth and nose and gotten the same result."

I gently cleared my throat. "I have one other thing."

"Yes, Nurse Chandler?" said the Captain.

"Isaac's cane. It's not in this room. It's still in the bedroom, propped at the night table."

"We saw it," said the Captain.

"Well, in the two short instances that I saw Mr Isaac alive, he was leaning on that cane. I personally don't think he could have gotten around well without it."

"So?" said Harper.

"So, why is he in here and his cane in there?"

"Mister Armstrong," said the Captain. "Bring that cane in here."

"Sir."

Harper looked at me. "Are you thinking he was drugged in the bed and then carried in here to the chair?"

"That would explain why the cane's not here," I said.

Mister Armstrong reappeared with the cane. "This is heavier than it looks."

"A man needing a cane to walk with doesn't want something flimsy, Mister Armstrong," I said.

Armstrong hefted it in his hands, giving it a critical eye. "This would have made one hell of a knobkerrie," he said.

"A what?" Harper asked. Armstrong smiled.

"You were in the Navy, Doctor, so you may not have come in contact with one. A knobkerrie is a type of club, popular among the Zulu and other tribes. We adopted the idea for our own use. I had a stout one with a big heavy head on it like this for clearing trenches in the War. Those coal scuttle helmets the Germans wore made a satisfying clang when you got off a good strike." He gave the cane a loving look. "Man would hit the ground like a sack of Mister Harvey's potatoes."

I shuddered to think of a man the size of Armstrong swinging Isaac's cane like a club and took it from him, leaning it against a wall. "Be that as it may, Mister Armstrong, Mr Isaac was not in prime physical condition for using this to bash heads. I did see him lift it to part a curtain with at his own store yesterday, but as I said I believe he needed it to walk any distance and he didn't use it to come in here from his bedroom. So, someone carried him in and plopped him in the chair."

The Captain took his cap off and ran a hand through his hair, then turned to me. "All right. Let me know when the nephew is back on his feet, I'll come and talk with him. Mister Armstrong, we'll do a separate meeting with Mr Van Effen."

"Sir." Armstrong opened the stateroom door to reveal Mister Harvey standing in the corridor.

"I was just about to knock," said Harvey. "Thank you, Mister Armstrong."

"Yes, Mister Harvey?" said the Captain.

"Sir, Mister Collins would be appreciative of you stepping around to the purser's office."

"He doesn't have a passenger who's been suffocated with diamonds, does he?"

"No, sir," said Mister Harvey. "Quite the opposite. He has a shortage of diamonds. A box of them has gone missing from his vault."

# IV

I'm sure you've heard the phrase "knocked me over with a feather." The actual phrasing is "You might have knocked me down with a feather." It comes from *Porcupine's Works*, a book by the English agitator and reformer William Cobbett somewhere around 1801. If I remember my father's teaching on this correctly, Cobbett didn't originate the phrase, he was just the first person to write it down, him having heard it from others. In any case, whether it was knock me down with a feather or knock me over with a feather, Mister Harvey's bit of knowledge sufficed to warrant use of the phrase, take your pick.

The Captain's reaction was simply one of another problem to deal with, which is why after a long career at sea he was in command of the Stoddard Lines' flagship vessel.

"Whose box?" he asked Harvey. The Chief Steward silently pointed a finger toward the bedroom. "Of course it is," said the Captain. "You didn't happen to tell Mister Collins that you found a cache of diamonds stored in something other than a safe deposit box?"

"No, sir. I thought it prudent to leave that to you."

"Thank you for giving me something to look forward to, Mister Harvey. Mister Armstrong, let's go pay a visit to Mister Collins. We'll chat up Mr Van Effen later on." The Captain's face remained imperturbable as he walked out.

Like most of the crew, I believed he had ice water in his veins.

"So," said Mister Harvey as the door closed. "Anything new on this end?"

"The box that Mr Isaac checked in is gone?" asked Harper.

"Are you saying Mr Isaac was killed with his own diamonds?" I added.

"I didn't say that," said Harvey. "I just said his box has gone missing, but at a first guess I can certainly see why you might think its contents ended up inside their owner. After I notified the Captain I stopped at the purser's office. You know what a fuss-budget Collins can be, and after what Maeve told us about Isaac and the other man checking in boxes of diamonds, I thought it might be prudent to make a wee check."

"You're starting to think like me," I said. "I'm so proud of you."

"Sad, isn't it? Anyway, I told Collins I knew he'd been under a bit of a crush last night, and just wanted to make sure everything was right-o. He said yes, but as his clerks were busy, would I witness him checking the vault, to which I replied certainly." Harvey looked at Harper. "You've only been with us a few months, Doctor. Mister Collins prides himself on the fact that no passenger has ever lost as much as an American penny or English pence on the *Victoria* under his watch and he's easily the most scrupulous man I've ever met. Imagine his reaction when he opened the vault and found that he was one deposit box short."

"He must have fainted," I said.

"Close to," agreed Harvey. "I rang up the hospital and waited with Collins until your mate Alice arrived to tend to him." Harvey sighed. "Collins says that box was lifted in only one of two ways. Someone either took the risk to tumble the lock, or someone already knew the combination."

"What does he think?" I asked.

"He refuses to believe it was anyone on his staff. That would be an inside job, I think the Americans call it." He looked around the room. "How did it go in my absence?"

I filled him in and then asked about the status of the cabin on the other side of Mr Singer. Harvey looked chagrined. "I forgot. I was going to tell you. 29-A is empty. I checked with Collins when I was in his office. Cabin 35-A on the other side of Mr Isaac is also empty but it was paid for by a person named Mr Silverwood. However, Mr Silverwood never took possession, so it's empty."

"That's a bloody expensive cabin for someone not to claim it after paying for it," said Harper.

"I thought so, too." Harvey crossed his arms. "It's even more expensive because it's a round trip booking for Mr Silverwood back to New York from Southampton. Odd that someone would make the trip to Southampton via Cherbourg and then have two days before the ship leaves for New York, but there it is. Maybe he took ill. Or someone in his family did. Who knows? So, you have Mr Singer on one side, Mr Isaac in the middle, and no one home to the other side. And of course the charming Miss Thomas in 37-A next to the empty cabin booked to Mr Silverwood, though from what you say she seems to spend a great deal of time in the company of Mr Van Effen, who's at the end of the hall in 38-A." He gave a polite cough. "And there's another question. Your deductive work is impressive, Maeve, but you didn't quite mention a disposition of the body. I know in the past you've preferred my 24-hour service."*

"Mr Isaac is staying put here for the time being," said Harper. "Our resident expert over there says he shouldn't be moved."

"Did you now?" Harvey said to me. "You know we've got about four days to go before Cherbourg. I don't suppose anyone brought up going back to New York to put him off. Maybe dropping him with another ship already headed in that direction?"

I pursed my lips. "You know as well as I do the Captain and the Stoddard Lines keeps a tight schedule. Heaven help us if we ever have to answer a distress call miles out of our way. I didn't even consider broaching the matter with the Captain."

Harvey nodded. "Perfectly understandable but judging from my experience and Doctor Harper's in the War, as well as any number of other men on this ship, I think we're going to have to deal with it well before four days are up." He took a sniff of air, glancing up at the round louvers set in the wall above the built-in shelving. "The ventilators are good here, but they're not that good."

"Mister Harvey, please."

"I'm just saying." He looked at Harper. "What's your medical opinion? Public health and sanitation and all of that?"

"Afraid I have to agree with you. But let's wait until his nephew wakes up. He's the next of kin, as far as we know."

"He's positively next of kin," I said. "He told me he was raised by his uncle since he was one. His parents —

---

*    See Book One: *Shadow of the Queen*

Isaac's sister and brother-in-law — were killed in an accident."

"Sad," said Harvey. "Well, if there's nothing else for me here, I'll be on my way. Quite the morning." He gave us a nod and took his leave.

Harper sighed. "I'll get a towel from the bathroom and take those diamonds out of Mister Isaac's mouth."

"And the blood sample," I reminded him.

"Yes, that too." He looked at me. "Don't worry, I'll be reverent about it all."

"I know." I glanced toward the bedroom. "I'm not sure if what you're doing in there counts as sitting *shiva*. "But we're kind of in a bind, I suppose."

"I suppose." Harper took off his jacket and began rolling up his sleeves. "Why don't you go check on Joel and then get some sleep?"

"That's the best advice I've had all day. See you later." Harper waved over his shoulder as he picked up his bag and walked into the bedroom. I heard the light snap on and the door closing as I went to the mirror in the sitting room to check my appearance — there was no need in me scaring Joel half to death with the way I felt I was looking right now — but the reflection wasn't too bad. At least I didn't feel the need to call on the ship's carpenter to do work.

# V

I remember when my family got the news that my older brother had been killed in action in the War. After he had enlisted his possible fate was not something we would let consume each passing hour, though certainly we knew and were aware of the fact that he would be in the line of fire, serving in the Royal Navy as he was; we just didn't expect him to die as the result of his hospital ship, the RMS *Britannic*, hitting a mine in the Aegean Sea in 1916. In retrospect I supposed we should have expected it, the unlucky *Britannic* being a sister ship to the *Titanic* that had gone down only four years earlier. I guess the point I'm trying to make is that we – my parents and myself – were, in a sense, prepared for the worst to happen though we tried not to dwell on it. However, Joel's uncle was a complete surprise. Not an inkling it would happen and not a moment of preparation. and it was with a sense of trepidation that I knocked gently on Joel's door. People take things so differently.

"Come in," Joel said to my tentative knock. I let myself in and walked to the bedroom. Joel was now sitting up, pillows behind him and the blanket to one side. His tie and suit jacket were on the floor next to the bed. "I got warm," he said to my questioning look. "Someone put a blanket over me."

"That was me," I confessed. "How are you feeling?"

"How should anyone be feeling whose uncle committed suicide?" Joel considered for a moment. "Honestly, I don't know how I feel."

I pulled a chair over to his bedside. "I think that's understandable. It was rather a shock."

"You can say that again." He gazed at the porthole for a moment, then shook his head. "I never thought I'd see anything like that. Never."

"I know," I said. "We've found one thing out, though."

"What?"

"Your uncle didn't commit suicide. He was murdered."

Joel's eyes flew wide. "Murdered?"

"Yes. It appears he was injected with something that paralyzed him, making it easier for the killer to do his work. I found a sliver of a hypodermic needle stuck in his neck. Doctor Harper is drawing a blood sample to test. And there's more."

"More than that?" He made a face. "Maeve, I don't know how there could possibly be more than that."

"It's possible the diamonds used to kill him were his own. The box he had checked in at the purser's office is missing."

Joel blinked at me. "Gone? The entire box?" He slumped back against the pillows. "I take it back. You topped yourself."

"I'm sorry. Mister Collins and Mister Harvey made that discovery a little while ago."

"Does Van Effen know any of that?"

"No. He hasn't been seen since he stopped at your Uncle's stateroom." A sudden thought occurred to me. "Did you know how many diamonds were in that box?"

"No idea. But I see where you're going. You want to know if all of them were used on my uncle, or did the murderer keep some back for himself."

I nodded. "Doctor Harper is removing them now. We'll soon know how many were used."

"But that doesn't tell us if any were pocketed," said Joel. "I'll have to send a wire back to the shop. I need to tell Jenkins – you remember Jenkins, he was the salesclerk you and Alice were toying with. I'll ask him if he knew how many were being carried. Clear all of it up."

"I remember," I said. "Joel, you told us you were back and forth from the corridor to your stateroom this morning. Did you hear anything at all unusual from your uncle's cabin?"

He shook his head. "Nothing."

"And Mister Harvey says the cabin on the other side of your uncle is vacant this voyage. So is the cabin next to yours."

Joel was quiet for a moment. "Does Alice know?" he asked with some concern. Obviously cabin assignments were of little interest to him.

"No."

He frowned. "I think you may have a more lucid grasp of all that's happened. Would you mind telling her?"

"Of course not." I smiled. "And I'll have her come up to see you." I held up a warning finger. "In a purely professional capacity, you understand."

"Of course. I don't want her to get in trouble."

"I don't either. This may be your first Atlantic passage but it's not the first time I've encountered a romantic assignation between passenger and crew member."

"No, it's much more than that," he said earnestly. There's something I want to ask her." He peered intently at me. "And I think you know what it is."

"I've got an idea," I said. "And I can't recommend it. Your uncle's been murdered, you're a potential target for a gangster, and you're thinking of love. Honestly, you Yanks. Don't either you or Alice think you're moving too fast? I mean, really. You've only known each other since yesterday afternoon." I stopped at the serious expression that had come over Joel's face. "I'm sorry. I don't mean to be a dark cloud, but don't you think you should perhaps wait a bit?"

"I've been waiting my entire life," he said. "My uncle always told me he would pass the shop down to me, so now I've got it, unless he changed his mind and left it to Jenkins. And I met the woman I want to marry. What's there to wait for, Nurse Chandler? Having someone kill me like they did my uncle?"

"Of course not. But we need to find out who killed your uncle and why."

"Yes, of course."

"And I'm sorry to bring this up, but we need to talk about what you want to do with your uncle's body."

Joel nodded. "In our faith, burial is usually required as soon as possible and in the ground. No embalming, no cremating."

"Well, there's not much ground around here," I said. "You just need to remember that we're about four days away from making port. And we really don't have facilities for embalming, much less cremating, so no worries on that issue. We can put him in cold storage, but once we reach Cherbourg you're still going to have to get him embalmed to ship him back to New York and as Mister

Harvey gently reminded me, dead bodies don't have much of a shelf life."

"What would you suggest?"

"I'm afraid that there's only one option open to you. Burial at sea."

"Sounds romantic," said Joel. "Nathaniel Isaac's last resting place will be the floor of the Atlantic Ocean." He pondered. "That's doable. I think we're allowed that if the person has died some ways off from landfall."

"I'm sure we could do that, Joel. I'll check with the Captain to make certain."

"Maybe there's a rabbi on board."

"I'll ask at the purser's office. If we don't have a passenger in that capacity, maybe one of the other liners out there does, or we can send a message to New York. We have a powerful wireless." There was a knock at the door. "Come in," I said.

Doctor Harper joined us, setting his bag on the dressing table. "How are you feeling?" he asked Joel.

"Better," said Joel. "Nurse Chandler and I have been talking."

"Yes," said Harper. He glanced at me. "Nurse Chandler is a great one for talking. She didn't bore you with anything about Walter Winchell, did she?"

"No." Joel smiled at me.

"Excellent. Then I suspect you'll live." Harper reached over to take Joel's pulse.

Joel looked at both of us, the smile suddenly gone from his face. "What's going to happen now? No one thinks I had something to do with what happened, do they?"

"Of course not," I said.

"Yes. Yes, of course," said Joel. "Nurse Chandler said you were drawing a blood sample to test?"

"Yes. I don't know if she told you or not. Your uncle was apparently injected with some sort of drug to induce paralysis."

"She told me. And the diamonds?"

"I removed them. They're wrapped up in a hand towel in my bag."

"How many were there?"

"Eighteen, in various sizes and shapes. Mostly small."

Joel shook his head. "Don't carry them around loose in a towel. You need to separate them. Get some stationary or other paper and wrap each one so it can't touch the other one."

"Why?" I asked.

"Diamonds can not only scratch glass, they can also scratch other diamonds," said Joel. "They always travel padded and physically separated from each other to prevent damage. Though my uncle's killer obviously didn't care that much about it."

"They all looked about the same to my eye," said Harper. "I kept two out to show you." He took what appeared to be a medium engagement ring-sized diamond out of a vest pocket. "This is what made up the bulk of them." He tried to hand it to Joel, who refused.

"May I?" I asked. Harper gave me the diamond and I examined it. "A little ostentatious for a ring setting, but I wouldn't turn it down." I handed it back to him.

"Then you'll love this one." Harper reached into his other vest pocket and withdrew a glittering gem about the size of the end of my thumb, its many facets sparkling.

"Fancy that," I said in awe.

Joel gazed at the diamond. "I may only be an apprentice but I know enough to tell you that's what we call an old mine cut. Probably from the *Chapada Diamantia* field in Brazil back in the middle of the last century. It was a popular cut up until about 1900 or so." He thought a moment. "If these are my uncle's diamonds, will I get them back?"

"Well, the obvious question to be asked is – can you prove that they belonged to your uncle?" I asked.

"You told me yourself his box had been stolen. And then these turn up in his mouth." Joel looked annoyed. "Who else would they belong to?"

"I'll have them put back in the ship's vault for the time being," said Harper, slipping the large stone back into his pocket.

"Fat lot of good that did before," replied Joel.

"Point well taken," I said. "Until we know how the vault was opened, best hide them somewhere else."

"I'll keep them in my bag," said Harper. "No one is going to look there."

Joel nodded. "What about his things? His cabin? My cabin? He had all the money."

"Don't worry about expenses, Mr Singer," said Harper. "And your uncle's cabin will be locked up and you'll get the key. Nothing will be disturbed."

"Thank you," said Joel. "Dr Harper, we were talking about what to do with the body. Jewish funerals are usually within 24 hours of death." He rubbed a weary hand across his forehead.

"I'm going to check with the Captain for a burial at sea," I said to Harper. He nodded.

"I don't see an issue with it. We certainly know the cause of death, and I don't mean to be insensitive, but keeping a dead body laying out until we reach port without any attempt to preserve it or slow down decomposition does raise some health issues."

"You both know best," said Joel, leaning back against the pillows. There was another knock at the door. I looked at him. "You're very popular today," I said getting up and walking out of the bedroom.

Harry Winston was standing on the other side of the door. He gave me a quizzical look. "Nurse Chandler? Joel isn't ill, is he?"

I shook my head. "No, but you had better come in all the same."

"Thank you. I got out of my cabin at six this morning and took a leisurely stroll around the ship, exploring, as it were. Not many people abroad at that hour, it was like I had the entire ship to myself. After that I went in for the most amazing breakfast I think I have ever enjoyed. Afraid I lingered over it too long." He stopped short as he caught sight of Harper with Joel. I made the introductions.

"This is our Principal Medical Officer, Doctor Leslie Harper. Doctor Harper, this is Harry Winston, the man I was telling you about."

The pair shook hands. "Happy to meet you, Mr Winston," said Harper.

"The same. Joel, what's going on? You're not ill are you?"

"My uncle's dead, Harry."

A genuine look of concern flooded Harry's face. He looked at the three of us. "What happened?"

"I think you should sit down, Mr Winston," I said, indicating the chair beside the bed.

"Not to put too fine a point on it, Mr Isaac was murdered," said Harper.

"Where? When?"

"In his own stateroom, next door," I said. "It probably happened between midnight and six this morning. You say you were out at six this morning – did you hear or see anything unusual outside in the corridor?"

"No, nothing. It was very quiet. I'm so sorry, Joel." Harry looked at me. "If it's not too much, how did it happen?"

"I'm afraid it was rather ruthless," I said. "We found him sitting in an armchair with his mouth and throat stuffed with diamonds."

"That's horrific."

"It gets worse," said Joel. "Doctor Harper and Nurse Chandler think he was injected with something to paralyze him, and then the diamonds suffocated him. On top of that, it looks like they were his own diamonds he had checked into the ship's vault last night."

"Unbelievable," said Harry.

"But there it is," Harper replied. "And the thing was made to look like a suicide."

"By swallowing diamonds?" Harry looked incredulous.

"Isaac's cabin was locked from the inside," I said. "If I hadn't found the broken tip of an injection needle in his neck we might have believed it."

"What kind of twisted state of mind would you have to be in to kill yourself that way?"

"That's a question for a psychiatrist," said Harper.

"Not in my uncle's case," said Joel. "He always thought people were stalking him, out to get him. He frightened at the slightest discrepancy in his daily routine or a shadow on the wall. He did it all his life. We lived above the store, and he had bars put on the windows both inside and out."

Harper nodded. "Paranoid schizophrenic," he said.

"I don't know the medical term for it, Doctor, but his behavior was always odd. And ever since I was old enough to pay attention, there were always rumors circulating about my uncle and how he lived in South Africa before my parents died and he adopted me. Some people said he had to flee Kimberley and the diamond fields because he killed someone. Others that it was a falling out with Mr Perry. Anyway, it appeared that bygones were bygones as far as Mr Perry was concerned and we were all to have dinner this evening and try and clean up my issue with Dutch Schultz."

"I've never met Mr Perry, but I've heard of him." said Harry. "Older fellow, very sharp, very elegant. People don't like him, but they don't dislike him either. He's one of the last of the old diggers, a direct living link back to the Kimberley fields at the end of the last century, just as your uncle was. Unfortunately, as you say, he's fallen in with Dutch Schultz."

"I apologize," said Harper. "People keep mentioning that name. I'm not up on my American culture as much as I should be. Who is this Mr Schultz besides a gangster?"

"A successful and murderous New York bootlegger," said Harry. "Like all of his kind he's looking to branch out into other criminal business. With Mr Alexander on his payroll it certainly sounds like he's going into the diamond trade."

I nodded. "And according to what I read in the *Mirror*, he's not someone you want to cross."

"Nothing we can do about any of that right now," said Harry. He withdrew a jeweler's loupe from his coat pocket. "Show me these diamonds you have, Doctor."

Harper opened his case and withdrew the folded hand towel. "I apologize for them being loose. Joel has let me know they should be stored in individual wrappers."

"That's right," said Harry. "Joel, you're absolutely correct." Winston gently took the towel from Harper and placed it on his lap, then opened it up and studied the contents. After a moment he gingerly took one of the stones in his hands, rubbed his fingertips across it then held it up to the light and examined it through the loupe. After a few moments Winston laid it back down on the cloth with a frown. "Beautiful work," he said, touching a finger to the stash.

"And then there's this." Harper took the Brazilian stone and the smaller stone from his pocket and handed them to Harry. Winston gave an appreciative nod and set the loupe back to his eye.

"What a lovely old pillow cut," he said, holding the larger stone. "You don't see a lot of these around anymore. I'm going to guess it's from the end of the last century." He glanced at Joel. His attention was totally focused on Winston. "What do you think?"

"I agree," said Joel. "I told them it was probably Brazilian."

"And this one?"

"I don't know."

Harry nodded and gave it a cursory examination, then placed it on the cloth with the others. "Since you were able to recognize the large stone as Brazilian, you can be forgiven on the other."

"What other?"

Winston held one of the smaller diamonds up to the light again. "I started my career buying and selling what we used to call costume jewelry," said Harry. "I'm talking about those overbearing gimcracks from the turn of the century. Huge, gaudy things. The corset decorations. Tiaras. Dog collars. You name them, I bought them - from estates, widows, whatever – and then I broke them down and either sold or remounted the diamonds." He leaned forward. "The thing you had to be careful of were the imitations. Many of those pieces were exactly copied using amethyst or quartz cut to simulate a diamond."

"Why?" I asked.

Harry shrugged. "Simple enough reason. No one wanted to lose anything that valuable, so an imitation was created to wear for more regular use, while the real thing was held in a safe at home to only come out on very special occasions. An untrained or inexperienced eye would never spot the subterfuge."

"Are you saying—" began Joel.

Winston gave a wan smile as he handed the cloth and diamonds back to Harper, then addressed Joel directly. "You can forget about separating these from each other with paper. These 'diamonds' that the doctor removed from Mr Isaac, with the exception of the Brazilian stone, are nothing more than very, very good fakes."

# VI

We've all encountered fakes and fakers from time to time. Seems like you just can't get away from them. For instance, there's the occasional expert malingerer that I'm particularly well acquainted with, the person who is faking illness or injury to get out of doing any work. Once they are exposed aboard ship, that's the end of their service career with us. They are put off, kit and all, at the next port of call and not let on again; I believe the Captain would prefer a desert island but those are few and far between on the North Atlantic passenger run. Then there are the really glamorous high-flying fakers – the art forgers. I seem to remember a case when I was still a girl about the *Mona Lisa* being stolen from the Louvre and forgeries made of it and sold to rich Americans. And then, of course, for sheer unmitigated effrontery in faking it, there are the out and out money counterfeiters, most of whom, at least in the United Kingdom, ended their days dancing at the end of a hangman's rope. But until Harry Winston made his pronouncement, I had no earthly idea that diamonds could be fake. I had just accepted them on face value, and I don't mind telling you it put a good-sized dent in my previously unshakeable belief that diamonds were a cure-all panacea for whatever might be ailing a girl.

"Fake?" Joel's voice was strained. "Impossible!"

Harry's voice was soothing. "Don't beat yourself up over it. You're not the first person to be taken in by something so well-made." He took one back from Harper. "I realize this is evidence, Doctor, but would you and Nurse Chandler mind if I kept one? Excellent craftsmanship. I'd like to study it if you don't mind. I'll get it back to you before Cherbourg." He slipped it into his coat pocket. "Joel, as for this Brazilian stone, it needs to go into a lock up. I can place it in my box for the time being if you like."

"I appreciate that," said Joel. "As for the rest of this *khazeray*," he began through gritted teeth.

"Sorry, what?" Harper asked.

"Junk," said Joel. "I don't care what happens to it. I want to know where my uncle's diamonds are."

"What do you mean?" asked Harry. He indicated the glittering horde in his lap. "Aren't these what killed Mr Isaac?"

"Yes, of course," I said. "But here's where the confusion over real and fake diamonds comes into play. The box belonging to Mr Isaac turned up missing this morning after we discovered his body. It was taken out of the ship's vault, we don't know when, and we naturally assumed that what we thought were real diamonds in his throat came from that box and were used to kill Isaac. But now you're telling us the diamonds that killed him are fakes, leading to Joel's question of where are the real ones?" I looked at Joel. "Your uncle wouldn't have checked fake diamonds in at the vault, would he?"

"Of course not," said Joel. "And why would he have fakes, anyway? Any legitimate dealer would spot them in a heartbeat."

"But no one would use a fortune in diamonds to accomplish murder," said Harry. "They'd just be leaving them there for someone else to profit off of." He watched Harper fold the towel up and place it in his bag. "These fakes accomplished the same end as using real ones, and much more cheaply, too." A sudden knock on the door caused me to jump.

"Who's there?" asked Joel apprehensively.

"Van Effen," came the reply. Harper took up a position near the door and glanced at Joel, who nodded. Harper opened the door wide.

"Doctor Harper," said Van Effen. "How good to see you again. And Nurse Chandler." He looked at Harry. "You are Harry Winston, the *diamantaire*."

"Yes."

Van Effen nodded and reached into his inside coat pocket, withdrew a pack of Pall Malls, selected one, tapped it against the door frame and lit it, then took a deep draw, exhaling the smoke through his nostrils. "I have heard of you. You are very successful."

"I've been fortunate enough to be in the right place at the right time," said Harry guardedly.

"It is better to be lucky than good, I have found. What is the saying? 'Fortune favors the bold.'"

"Something like that, yes."

Van Effen nodded and turned to Joel. "I hesitate to ask how you are, Mr Singer."

"My uncle has been murdered, Mr Van Effen. How should I be?"

"Murdered?" A quizzical look came over Van Effen's craggy features. "I was given to understand earlier that it was a suicide. Choking on diamonds was the cause."

"As Mr Singer said, Mr Isaac did not commit suicide. Mr Isaac was murdered." Van Effen turned his head to me as I went on. "What we know now that we didn't know earlier is that he was injected with something to immobilize him, before someone fed him diamonds."

"Interesting." Smoke issued from his flaring nostrils. "And speaking of interesting, I have found that Mr Isaac's box of diamonds, which I watched him check into your ship's vault on Saturday night, is now missing."

"That's old news, Mr Van Effen," I said. "Mister Harvey and Mister Collins discovered that a while ago."

"Did they? Your Captain Webster related it to me when I went by the vault to check." He inhaled a lungful of smoke and blew it out. "A no-nonsense sort, your Captain. We had a nice chat."

Good, I thought. Less for me to chat about with the Captain later. "I'm sure you did," I said. "Nothing like getting it out in the open and talking about it."

"Yes, nurse," said Van Effen. "Which reminds me. Mr Singer, do not forget we have a dining invitation for this evening with Mr Perry. Despite what has occurred I believe it would be wise of you to accept it."

"Go," said Harry. "We can catch up later."

Joel shook his head, swung his legs off the bed and located his shoes. "I need to sit with my uncle. He can't be left unattended until his service."

"I'll do it," I said.

Harry nodded. "We both will. You go on."

"No," said Joel. "But if you wouldn't mind, I'd like both of you there tonight." He glanced up at Van Effen. "If that meets with your approval."

"I see no reason why not," said Van Effen.

"All right," I said. "I'll impose on Alice to take over the watch."

"Can you ask her to relieve me about five this afternoon?"

"I think she will want to see you much sooner than that. In the meantime, I'll try and pull together the arrangements for Mr Isaac's burial at sea."

"Thank you," said Joel. Van Effen's face remained impassive. "Will you sit outside my uncle's cabin today while I'm inside?"

"Yes, Mr Singer."

Joel finished tying his shoes and stood. "Thank you all. Let's go, Mr Van Effen." They left the cabin and a moment later we could hear the door to Isaac's cabin open and close. Harper exhaled.

"I don't know about you two, but Mr Van Effen gives me the creeps."

"You handled him very well." I looked at Harry. "What are you thinking about, Mr Winston?"

"Symbolic gesture," he said, almost musingly.

"What?" I asked.

"Symbolic gesture." Winston looked at us. "The murderer or murderers could have used plenty of other means to finish Isaac after paralyzing him. Run the bathtub with an inch of water and lay him in it face down. Same result. And yet the method chosen is an obvious and very flamboyant gesture, using fake diamonds and one very real one. If that's not a symbolic way to kill a diamond dealer, I don't know what is." He pondered for a moment. "I wonder if they knew the smaller stones were false?"

"Would it have made a difference?" asked Harper. Winston shrugged.

"I think your question, Doctor, should be 'would someone have knowingly used a small fortune in real diamonds to accomplish this end?' As a *diamantaire* myself, I find that rather hard to believe. Still, people will go to extremes. Maybe the point was in making Isaac eat his sins."

I shivered. "That's ghoulish."

Harry looked at me. "We've no idea what he did back in the old mining days. I'm sure a lot of animosity still runs deep among the old timers; they were a pretty rough and tumble bunch from what I'm told." He thought for a moment. "You said Mr Isaac's cabin was locked from the inside. How did the killer get out?"

"I have no idea. I do have a couple of thoughts about how the murderer gained access, though. Perhaps Mr Isaac let his murderer in, which means he knew the person. The only other way into a room is with the room key, which was on the inside of the door, a master key such as we used to get in, or picking the lock from the outside, and it's kind of obvious to stand there in the open and try the lock pick route. Anyway, the cabin locks on the *Victoria* are mortise warded locks and very difficult to pick."

Harper looked at me. "How do you know all this?"

I shrugged. "You know me, naturally curious. I happened to see one of the engineering crew replacing a cabin lock once and I just asked."

Winston nodded. "Dr Harper, mortise refers to the way the lock mechanism is inserted into a kind of pocket cut into the side of the door."

"And warded means the inside of the lock box has built in obstacles, also called wards," I said. "They can only be opened by a pass key or a key that has cutouts exactly matching the wards inside the lock. Simple."

"You never cease to amaze me, Nurse Chandler."

I smiled. "I think it makes for an excellent working relationship, don't you? As to the getting out of the room and leaving the lock turned on the inside of the door, I don't know."

"You said you used a master key to get in?" asked Harry.

"Yes. Mister Harvey pushed his master through from the outside to reach the key already in the door from the inside, at which point it fell out of the lock and onto the floor in the cabin. After the lock was clear he just turned his pass key to let us in."

Harry rubbed his chin. "So we have a killer who may have been let in by his victim, who was prepared with a drug of some sort to sedate his victim, then killed him in a rather showy fashion, and left the room, somehow managing to lock the door after himself from the corridor side but leaving the key in the lock from the cabin side, apparently hoping Isaac's death would be seen as suicide?"

I looked at Harper, then back at Harry. "Yes. In our favor, our murderer doesn't know that we are aware of the broken needle and paralyzing injection, so maybe they're still hoping we'll take it that Isaac committed suicide behind a locked door, as improbable as that seems." I shrugged. "As far as the passengers and crew outside of our circle go, I'll have the ship's paper print that Mr Isaac simply died in his cabin overnight of natural causes. That's it in a nutshell."

"That's a pretty big nutshell, Nurse Chandler," said Harry. "More like a coconut." He smiled. "Do you read a lot?"

"That's a loaded question," said Harper.

I ignored the jibe. "Yes, Mr Winston. I read a lot of Agatha Christie."

"Have you ever read *The Mystery of the Yellow Room* by Gaston Leroux?

I shook my head. "I'm afraid not."

"It begs the question of how a killer got out of a room locked from the inside." Harry sighed. "Almost every diamond has a flaw, no matter how small. We've just got to find the flaw in this one."

# VII

Gobsmacked is a word we Brits use for when we are, as the Americans usually like to term it, completely blindsided. Broken down it roughly translates as 'gob' meaning mouth, and 'smacked' meaning, well, smacked. So, 'smacked in the mouth' is one way of looking at it. People react to being gobsmacked in different ways. Some find the situation humorous, some find it annoying, and some find it completely unacceptable. It was into this last category that Alice fell when I finished telling her of everything that had transpired last night and this morning.

"My poor lamb!" she finally said. "Do you think this Mr Perry and Mr Van Effen can be trusted?"

Inwardly cringing at Joel's poor lamb status, I nodded. "Van Effen is rather cold, but I think Mr Isaac's death wounded his professional pride. Mr Perry seemed glad to have renewed contact with Mr Isaac after years apart. I haven't seen him this morning and it's quite possible he doesn't know about Mr Isaac's murder." I thought for a moment. "And apropos of nothing, I've got to tell Mister Casey about this, but we'll just say Mr Isaac died in his cabin and leave it at that."

"I don't know how you can think of it all and be calm," said Alice.

"I had experience at it when you were out tending your mum."* I smiled at her. "Now, much as I'm trying to disapprove, I know you want to fly to Joel's side."

"I do," said Alice. I gave her a resigned nod.

"Then go – but you have a job to do. He's sitting up with his uncle's body in Cabin 33-A. He'll be leaving you around five this afternoon to get ready for dinner." Alice's face broke into a smile. I leaned forward and took her by the hand. "A dinner that you are not invited to, I'm afraid."

"What am I to do, then?"

I gave her hand a squeeze. "You will continue sitting next to the mortal remains of Mr Isaac until someone comes to relieve you. Try and avoid sitting on the armchair in the front room."

"Why?"

"Just don't sit on it. Van Effen is going to be parked outside the door in the corridor, but he knows you are coming."

"How will I recognize him?"

"Six plus feet tall with a broad brim white straw hat. You can't miss him." I gave her a close look. "Remember that your sitting with Joel is purely on a nursing basis. He's had a shock this morning."

"Of course," said Alice.

"There's also a passenger named Harry Winston who may be about. Don't worry about him. He's on our side."

She nodded. "What are we doing with Mr Isaac?"

"Looks like it may be a burial at sea," I replied. "I've still got to arrange it with the Captain and find someone to officiate."

---

* See Book One: *Shadow of the Queen*

Alice shook her head. "Paralyzed and then murdered with fake diamonds. I can't believe it."

"Yes but remember what I said I was telling Mister Casey. As far as anyone knows he simply died of natural causes in his cabin."

"But he didn't simply die in his cabin. He choked on diamonds."

I sighed. "Yes, dear, he did," I said as if explaining to a small child. "However, the entire ship doesn't need to know that."

I got up off the bunk I'd been sitting on in the women's quarantine ward – the *Victoria* has both a men's and women's quarantine ward located near the hospital, and while they are rarely if ever used, I found them handy places to take a private conversation – and opened the door. "Pop off, now."

Alice trickled out and I went around the corner to the hospital.

"Fancy meeting you here," said Harper as I walked in. "I dropped Isaac's blood sample off with Reedy in the dispensary." He moved his Gladstone medical bag out of the other desk chair so I could sit. "Where have you been?"

"Giving Alice the latest before sending her to sit with Joel." I sighed. "A lot's happened since they saw each other on Saturday afternoon."

"That's an understatement. Did you include Joel's history with Dutch Schultz?"

"Yes, I'm afraid I did."

"Of course you did." Harper indicated the paper on the desk in front of him. "I've got to write up a death certificate for Mr Isaac."

"Won't you need Mister Reedy's report?"

"Yes, but I can get the basic report underway now. I'll do an informal listing here then go up to my quarters and finish the rest of it. By the way, I went ahead and asked Mister Harvey to have the ship's carpenter round up what we need for a burial at sea."

"Thanks. If you don't mind, ring up Mister Casey and tell him Isaac died of natural causes. I don't feel I'm up to dealing with our ace press man right now."

"Certainly," said Harper. I rose, checked my sad reflection in the mirror then walked directly into the chair Harper had just vacated and uttered a muffled curse.

"Do you keep score of how many times a day you run into things?" asked Harper.

"It would just depress me, Boss. I'm going up and talk with Collins."

I took one of the crew lifts from C Deck up to the purser's office on A Deck. Normally I would have climbed the crew access stairs for the exercise, but I was about worn out and my knee hurt from the recent collision with the chair. Collins looked up when I rapped on his open door.

"Nurse Chandler? Really, I'm fine. It was a bit of a shocker for Mister Harvey and I to find that Mr Isaac's box had disappeared, but nothing compared to when the Captain and Mister Armstrong showed up and told me they'd found the stones." Collins involuntarily flinched. "And where they'd found them. I just can't imagine."

"There's a lot of that going around this morning, Mister Collins," I said. "Don't feel like you have to hold a monopoly on it." I sat down opposite his desk. "By the way, another diamond dealer named Harry Winston examined the stones we found in Mr Isaac's throat. With the exception of one, they were all fakes."

"Worthless?" Collins looked confused, then brightened. "So that means nothing of value was in the box taken from my vault? I'm glad to hear that."

I frowned at him. "Except the nothing of value, as you say, was used as a murder weapon."

"Yes, of course. Terribly sorry."

"However, as I said, one of them was real. Mr Winston will be putting it in his box for safe keeping." I sighed. "And another thing, if you please. We're officially saying Mr Isaac died in his cabin of natural causes."

Collins looked perplexed. "Just died?"

"Just died, Mister Collins. We're not going into how it was accomplished."

He nodded. "As you wish." Collins toyed with a pencil on his desk. "I'm curious, though, about one thing."

"Yes?"

"Why did you dive into the potted palms last night when Mr Isaac showed up at my desk?"

I sighed "It's a long story. Alice and I met him at his shop in New York yesterday morning and he thought we were First-Class passengers but of course we aren't and then we met his nephew and Alice began to swoon and – " Collins held up a hand.

"Stop. I'm sorry I asked. How may I assist you?"

"A couple of things. First, can you go through your passenger lists and see if there's a rabbi on board?"

"A rabbi?"

"Mister Isaac was Jewish," I explained. "His nephew has opted for a burial at sea if I can get the cooperation of the Captain."

"Ah." Collins made a note on the paper in front of him. "And the other?"

"Doctor Harper recovered eighteen items from Isaac's throat. Do you know how many were in the box to begin with?"

Collins frowned. "I'm afraid not, Nurse. The box wasn't opened in my presence. I just took it from him and put it in my vault."

"So you didn't know, and Joel says he didn't know."

"Joel?"

"Joel Singer. Mr Isaac's nephew. He's traveling with us in the cabin next to his uncle."

"You're right." He shook his head. "I believe I heard the name mentioned in another conversation earlier. You'll have to forgive me."

"Don't worry about it. This has been a rough morning." I leaned forward. "Do you think I might see the box checked in by Mr Perry last night?"

"That's highly irregular, Maeve."

"As previously noted, it's been a highly irregular kind of day, Mister Collins."

He nodded. "No disagreement there, Nurse." He stood up. "All right, come with me." We walked out of his office to an area just behind the front desk, where a clerk was busy exchanging money for a passenger. The stainless-steel vault door of the Specie Room glittered a few feet behind him. "Excuse me, Simpson," said Collins. "Right behind you." Simpson nodded and continued counting out paper currency. Collins rubbed his right hand on his trousers and began to deftly turn the combination dial. After a few clicks he took hold of the massive wheel in the center of the door and turned. The vault opened with ease. He pulled the door all the way open and latched it in place against the wall, then stepped inside. I followed at a respectful distance, eyeing the latched door and hoping that Simpson or another clerk had the vault combination in case that latch suddenly failed and we became trapped inside.

"Mister Harvey says you believe the vault was breached by someone who knew the combination or is a very good safe-breaker," I said.

"Yes," said Collins. "Explosives would have been a bit obvious, I think. The vault was closed and locked when I arrived this morning. Here we are." He lifted a box and handed it to me. "I can tell you that Mr Perry's box is identical to the box that went missing."

I took the box. It was very lightweight, made of steel and had a key lock at one end with a hinged top that ran the length of the box, very much like a bank safe deposit box. I gave it a tentative shake but heard nothing. Mister Collins closed his eyes. "Please don't do that, Maeve."

"They're diamonds," I said. "I have it on good authority that they are carefully packed and padded. It's not likely to disturb anything." I handed Mr Perry's box back to Collins. "Wait." I took the box back from Collins and shook it again. "What do you hear?"

"Nothing," he said, cringing.

I shook the box a second time. "And now?"

"Still nothing. What are you about?"

"What I'm about is that a box filled with diamonds and padded makes exactly the same noise when shaken as a box that's empty of diamonds and padded. That is to say, no noise at all."

"Are you suggesting that this box is empty?" Collins looked positively aggrieved.

"I don't know what I'm suggesting, Mister Collins," I said wearily.

"Why would someone check an empty box into the vault?"

I handed the box back to Mister Collins. "I don't know if they would or not. I'm just remarking on the sound similarity between a filled box and an empty box."

Collins pushed Perry's box back into its slot. "I wonder though, now that you mention it – did Mr Isaac's box actually hold real gems, or fakes or nothing at all? I guess we'll never know for sure."

At once I wanted to kiss Mister Collins, but looking at him I was able to restrain myself. I hadn't considered that point of view. Did someone take a box of real gems or a box of fake gems? If the former, where did the latter come from? Or were the fakes in the box with the real ones? Or maybe there were never real ones, only fakes? Or, was the box empty the entire time?

"Thank you, Mister Collins," I said, "you've been a tremendous help."

And I meant it.

Sort of.

# VIII

The county fair, or show, would pop up in our town once a year, bringing with it clowns, dog races, massive draft horses – the descendants of those horses bred to carry the full weight of an armored knight and his weapons – as well as cows, chickens, goats, sheep, and other examples of animal husbandry. My brother and I would gorge ourselves on all the sweets, pies, pastries, and puddings we could get our sticky hands on while our parents walked slowly up and down the tables of exhibits, pausing first in front of this one and next in front of that one. Examples of knitting, of iron work, of gardening, of vegetables, of flowers crowded into each other, with the occasional blue ribbon from the judges attached to one. There were also rides on ponies, and a small carousel to make you dizzy, and swings, and swaying rope ladders to climb and ring a bell at the top for a prize. The most interesting to me, though, were the pitch men, the barkers, and the gamesmen. There was one fellow I remember being mesmerized by. I spent an hour trying to guess which of the three cups the ball was hiding under as he whisked them around on his board faster than my eye could follow. I never did win but looking back on it now I must have been good for business because he let me stand there quite a while, saying "Blimey, mates, even a little girl can play this game!" even though I never guessed it out. (In fairness he did let me win one or two, even though I hadn't a tuppence to wager.)

And now I was a big girl and still playing the game, and apparently my skills hadn't improved much since the age of six. Was the box empty in the first place? Was it full? If the latter, was it carrying the false stones or was it carrying real stones? Again, if the latter, where did the false stones come from and where did the real stones go?

All of these thoughts were jostling for space and attention in my head when I left Collins and made my way to the bridge to try and plan a Jewish funeral at sea. The Captain's reaction to my request was really quite moving and no less in keeping with his character than I expected.

"You wish to do what, Nurse Chandler?" he said, one eyebrow raising millimetrically.

"Sir, Mr Isaac is Jewish. His nephew, who is also Jewish, states that in their religion the body must be buried as soon after death as possible. Landfall in Cherbourg is Friday morning, but of course the other option is that land is closer if we turn back to New York right now, but then there's the matter of preserving the body. Embalming is not encouraged in the Jewish faith and what we can offer in the way of cold storage would count as embalming. The body would have to be offloaded at Cherbourg or Southampton to be embalmed, which, as I said, is frowned upon and then reloaded to make the trip back to New York."

"Why this ship? Why not another one?"

"Sir, he purchased a round trip ticket on the *Victoria*. I'm no barrister but I think that's a contract. Anyway, Doctor Harper considers it a health hazard. A burial at sea seems to be our only option." The Captain stared down at me in that way he always did whenever we had a conversation, jaw muscles clenching beneath his beard. I managed a weak smile—usually one of my best defences – and was beginning to wonder what my Presbyterian funeral at sea would involve when there was a respective cough behind the Captain's back.

"Yes, Number One?" said the Captain, still looking at me.

"Sir," said First Officer Carter. "I think I might agree with Nurse Chandler and Doctor Harper about the burial at sea."

"You do, do you?" The Captain turned and scowled at him. "You've been my First Officer for five months and you're already taking someone else's side?"*

"Sir," said Carter, "I really think it's for the best." The Captain sighed and turned back to face me.

"Fine, then. Nurse, if you don't mind handling the preparations, all we need to know is when to bring the ship to a full stop. Mind you, I don't expect to be at a full stop much more than twenty minutes." He thoughtfully stroked his beard. "I will, of course, be happy to make any remarks as needed."

I mentally smacked myself. The Captain loved a stage. I should have led with that. "Thank you, sir," I said. "Mister Collins is looking to see if we are carrying a rabbi among the passengers." The Captain blinked at me. "But of course," I added hurriedly, "I'm sure his nephew would be proud to have you say a few words."

"No doubt," said the Captain. Was that a bit of preening I detected in him? "Have you informed Mister Casey of what's happened?"

"Yes, sir. As far as Mister Casey, passengers and crew know, Mr Isaac died of natural causes."

"Very well. Keep me informed, Nurse."

"Sir," I said and made my retreat from the bridge as inconspicuously as possible.

------

*    See Book One: *Shadow of the Queen*

Doctor Harper was waiting for me when I finally returned to the hospital after noon. I was contemplating the gentle kindness of my bunk until whenever I might wake up, but as usual, it was going to have to wait.

"Maeve," said Harper. "How are you doing?"

"I'm completely knackered, if you must know." I related my visits with Collins and the Captain. "Everyone seems to be very busy," I said, leaning against the desk. "But the Captain has given the go-ahead for the burial at sea."

"That's good. When we get the time set I'll ring Casey and he can add that to his story about Isaac dying in his cabin of natural causes."

"Thanks for doing that, Boss. You know I briefly toyed with keeping his death a complete secret, but with a burial at sea the entire ship will have to know about it." I frowned. "There's just not much disguising coming to a dead stop and disembarking a passenger into the ocean."

"Hard not to miss," Harper conceded. "But it will give the passengers something to write home about."

"Stop it. You're getting just as jaded as Mister Harvey."

"Not at all. Mister Harvey would have said something about giving the paying customers extra value for the money."

"Of course he would." I sighed. "Mister Collins is looking through the passenger list to see if we're carrying a rabbi who can officiate."

Harper nodded. "If not, we may be able to pull someone in from another ship via radio."

"That's what I told Joel." My eyes felt gritty. "I'm a little overwhelmed at the moment. Joel invited me to a dinner tonight with himself, Mr Winston, Mr Van Effen and Mr Perry."

"I'm sure it will be a feast of reason and flow of soul."

"Oh, and Alice is not just keeping Joel company. She's taking over to sit with Mr Isaac while Joel is at dinner."

"Fine," said Harper. "She can talk with him all she wants about the latest movies and he'll never get bored."

I frowned. "What's got you into this mood?"

"Hard not to be in a mood when I get lab reports like this." He held up a paper. "Blood sample results."

My tiredness temporarily left me. "And?"

"Take a seat for this one." I did as Harper directed and he held the paper out. "The first thing our dispenser noted was that the blood sample was cold; I had to tell him it was drawn off a dead man."

"To which Mister Reedy no doubt asked why."

Harper nodded. "I told him the whole story. After that experience last October, I didn't expect him to be nonplussed and he wasn't." *

"Of course not," I said.

"Here's his informal report. I'll just touch on the high points, shall I? 'Sample presented was heavy with alkaloids, placing it in category of muscle relaxant or some kind of neuro-muscular blocking agent. Note that onboard *Victoria* we use ether or succinylcholine for this purpose. Compound was apparently injected directly into the middle scalene muscle of the neck, with tip of injection needle breaking off at site.'"

______________

* See Book One: *Shadow of the Queen*

"Nothing we didn't know already," I said. I reached into my nursing smock and felt the wad of toilet paper. "I've still got the tip of the needle with me."

"Leave it on the desk, I'll put it in an envelope later." Harper resumed his story. "Now here's where it gets strange. Reedy asked me an odd question: when I was a boy, did I ever read any of H. Rider Haggard's works? *King Solomon's Mines* or anything like that?"

I nodded. "The African adventures? Spears and blowguns, hidden treasure? That sort of thing? My brother did. Couldn't get enough of the stuff. Why?"

"Let me go back to his report." Harper cleared his throat and began to read again. 'Consulting source book *British Pharmaceutical Codex, 1929*. I am copying the reference verbatim into this report.

*CURARA.*

*Curare.*

*Synonyms — Woorara; Worari; Woorali; Ourari; Urari.*

*Curare is an extract made from the bark of Strychnos toxifera, Schomb., and other species of Strychnos (N.O. Loganiaceae), probably mixed with other, possibly inert, substances. It is prepared as an arrow poison by tribes of Indians in British Guiana, French Guiana, Venezuala, Northern Brazil, and Colombia.*

I also consulted the 1918 edition of *The Dispensatory of the United States of America*. Again, I have copied the reference verbatim.

*This powerful South American arrow-poison was first brought to Europe by the celebrated traveler Waterton; it was in the form of a thick syrup, but as it now occurs in commerce it is a blackish extract, brittle, somewhat resinoid in appearance, encrusting the sides of gourds or little rude earthenware jars, into which it has been poured in a liquid state. The drug varies much in strength.'"

Harper stopped reading and looked at me. My eyes were

wide. "But this last bit is the most damning of all," he said. "This is from the *Codex.*"

"*The principle effect of curare is to paralyze the motor nerve-endings in striped muscle, death occurring from respiratory failure. In larger doses, it also paralyzes nerve cells.*'"

I started to speak but Harper held up a finger and resumed reading. "'Also from the *Codex*, I found this:

*INJECTIO CURARE HYPODERMICA, B.P.C.*

*Hypodermic Injection of Curare.*

*Curare, in powder 10.00/44 grains*

*Sterilised water to 100.00/ to 1 fl. ounce*

*Make the Curare into a paste with some of the sterilised water, transfer the paste to a small funnel plugged with cotton wool, and gradually pour more of the water upon it until the required volume of filtered liquid is obtained.*

<u>*Dose*</u>. – *6 to 36 centimils (0.06 to 0.36 milliliters) (1 to 6 minims).*'"

"Bloody hell," I said.

"Yes," said Harper. He turned the paper over. "Here's his concluding thoughts."

"'I am unable to determine the exact size of the dosage involved here, but I surmise it was greater than what was called for in the *Codex*. I'm also unable to surmise if the drug came from Brazil proper or another location in Central America, but I can tell you that it was mixed with sterilised water. The only sterilised water on board *Victoria* is in our dispensing area and the hospital, and access is very limited and controlled, leading me to believe that the syringe was ready for use before it ever came on board.'"

I shook my head. "If Reedy's conjecture is right, then someone came on board carrying that syringe with the express intent of using it in just the manner it was used. This wasn't any crime of the moment; the door locked from the inside and the diamonds used to choke him and the prepared syringe of curare mean it was absolutely thought out well in advance." The telephone rang and I picked it up. "Hospital, Nurse Chandler. Yes. And he's willing? All right, thank you, Mister Collins. I'll get a time set." I hung up the receiver.

"Well, at least that went right. We do have a rabbi on board and he's consented to do the service for Mr Isaac at ten tomorrow morning on the fantail. Rabbi Aaron Hoffman. Could you please get that to Mister Casey?" Harper jotted the information down as I hoisted myself up out of the chair, yawned and stretched. "Is it really only 12:30?" I asked.

"Afraid so. Of course, you were out late last night."

"Seems like a hundred years ago." I pulled out my compact and checked my face in the mirror. "Looks like a hundred years ago, too."

Harper crossed his arms. "I'm going to give you a prescription. Go get some sleep."

"And miss all of this fun?" I shook my head. "Not hardly."

# IX

Having dinner in the first-class restaurant aboard the *Queen Victoria* is one of those things for which you run out of superlatives. The room is massive, with smaller (relatively speaking) private dining rooms that can be closed off from the main floor. The mezzanine dining section is reached by a graceful curving wide stair built expressly for allowing the ladies to show off their finery ascending or descending. You'll note that I said it was massive. The restaurant can serve the entire First-Class of over 800 people at one sitting. Beautiful wood paneling glows along the walls. Crisp white linen tablecloths and napkins, cut crystal and silver service, and, I'm told by Mister Harvey, over 27,000 pieces of chinaware are available. The ambient lighting glows, the live band plays softly in the background and for all of you Americans happy to be away from prohibition, (and you know who you are) the alcohol flows freely. You would think it impossible for anyone to take all of this in and not feel good about their current situation.

And you would be wrong.

I may have been at less happy gatherings in my life, but I honestly couldn't remember when. Despite my earlier bravado with Doctor Harper, I was glad I'd at least gotten a few hours of sleep before arriving to join our oh-so-happy throng.

"Thanks for letting Alice come up early," Joel whispered to me as a waiter held the chair. I'd swapped my nursing uniform for a more sedate and conservative black dress. I wasn't supposed to be in here, but since Doctor Harper came on board it seemed that rule had gone by the wayside, but honestly, none of it had been my fault. *

"Of course," I replied. "I hope she didn't mind staying the distance tonight."

Joel gave me a half smile. "If she did she didn't show it. We talked the entire time I was with her, but I'm afraid the conversation tonight will be rather one sided. She brought along some magazines to read."

Van Effen leaned over to Joel's other side. "Mr Singer – here is Mr Perry." Joel stood as Perry approached our table.

"Mr Perry – I'm Joel Singer, Nathaniel Isaac's nephew." Perry smiled.

"I'm pleased to meet you," said Perry. He glanced around the table. "Mr Van Effen I've met. I recognize you, Harry Winston, though I don't understand why you are here. And you are?" he asked, looking at me.

"Ship's nurse Maeve Chandler," I said. "Mr Singer asked me to be here."

"Oh?" Perry gave me an appraising look. "Are you expecting someone to be ill?"

"Mr Perry, please have a seat," said Van Effen. Perry eased his slender frame into a chair and looked about.

"I don't see Nathaniel here," he said. "Nurse Chandler, is he under the weather? He seemed fine when I saw him last night."

"No," I said. I looked at Joel.

"I'm sorry to say my uncle died overnight," said Joel.

---

*   See Book One: *Shadow of the Queen*

Perry leaned forward in his chair, but otherwise showed no emotion. "Did you say died?"

"We found him this morning," I said.

Perry frowned. "I'm sorry to hear that. I am a very heavy sleeper and was very tired last night. I thought about knocking at his cabin door when I awoke around eleven this morning, but thought he may well be doing as I did and catching sleep. I took a late lunch and then an extended walking tour of the ship and came back to my cabin to rest and dress for dinner. What was the reason?"

"Natural causes," I said quickly with a knowing glance at the others. "We think he had a heart attack." Harry raised an eyebrow while Van Effen studied an invisible point on the ceiling. Joel pursed his lips.

Perry shook his head. "A heart attack. What an ignominious end for Nathaniel, after all he'd been through. All we'd been through."

The conversation was interrupted by a waiter taking drink orders. When he departed I looked at Perry. "There will be a service tomorrow for Mr Isaac. He's being buried at sea."

"You managed to arrange it with the Captain, then?" asked Joel.

"Yes. Ten in the morning. Rabbi Aaron Hoffman is a passenger and has agreed to conduct the service. It will be in the ship's paper tomorrow."

Perry bowed his head for a moment, as if in prayer, then looked at Joel. "This changes nothing of what I told Nathaniel I would try to do for you, Mr Singer. As a favor for an old friend that I regret losing many years with." He idly glanced at his menu, then looked around the table. "To change the subject, do Nurse Chandler and Mr Winston know why we're here at Mr Isaac's behest? I will assume that Mr Van Effen does." Van Effen gave a slight nod of his head.

"Yes, they have the picture," said Joel.

"Then perhaps you won't mind giving it to me so I can tally it with what your uncle previously told me." Perry steepled his fingers and leaned back in his chair. "What are you involved in that Nathaniel wanted me to talk to Schultz about?"

"I have some debt," said Joel. "But who doesn't these days?"

Perry nodded. "Debt, I think, is probably not the issue. Would I be correct in saying the issue may be to whom it's owed?"

Joel began to speak but was interrupted by the waiter taking orders. When he had gone Joel nodded. "This is very difficult for me. I hated working for my uncle and wanted to go out on my own. Unfortunately, banks are not lending on hopes and dreams. I had to go elsewhere for money."

"And you didn't get your loan from a legitimate bank, did you?" said Perry.

"No. I knew my uncle's shop was slipping. I help Mr Jenkins keep the books. The path we were heading down was unsustainable, so I took out a rather large loan to try and turn things around."

"From my boss. From Schultz," said Perry. Joel nodded.

"Yes. Nathaniel was furious with me when he found out where the cash infusion into the business had come from. I told him I would pay it all back, he wouldn't lose a dime."

Harry and I exchanged glances.

"But you haven't," Perry said. "And the interest and the loan are due."

"Yes."

Harry looked at Joel. "How much?"

"$28,000," said Joel. We must have appeared thunderstruck. My annual salary was about $1,100 in American dollars depending on the day's exchange rate. A sum like Joel mentioned may as well have been the moon. "Mr Perry," he continued, "I bet that the economy would go into an upturn, but it didn't. I was told that if at least some of the money wasn't repaid by this past Friday – the day before yesterday – there would be consequences. I'm terrified, just waiting for the shoe to drop. And yes, I'm ashamed." Joel's face reddened. "I've always lived in the shadow of my uncle and I wanted to make my own name. It just got out of hand."

"And your uncle wanted me to intercede on your behalf." Perry nodded to himself. "I didn't tell your uncle, but to do that would be putting myself at great personal risk."

"Mr Perry is correct on that count, Mr Singer," said Van Effen. "You are in deep and dangerous waters."

"Here is what I can do for you, Mr Singer," said Perry. "I'll send a message to my boss that I have talked with you. I'll tell him you've agreed to sell out your store to make up the debt and have transferred power of attorney to me. Since we're both going to Antwerp, I'll assist you in trading the diamonds that your uncle brought on board. I don't know what he has, but I'm sure it's worth a nice tidy amount. That will help you seed a new business that you can grow without the help of any future dubious loans." Perry stopped. "Why are you all looking at me?"

"There's an issue with that, Mr Perry," I said. "Joel doesn't have Nathaniel's diamonds."

"Of course he does. I saw Nathaniel check them in last night."

"And someone made off with it late Saturday or early Sunday," I said.

"Stole it?"

"It's gone," said Harry. "Contents and box."

"It is true, Mr Perry." Van Effen's face was devoid of emotion. "I had it straight from the Captain this morning."

Perry looked stunned. "Oh, Joel. I'm so sorry. First Nathaniel and now this?"

Joel nodded. "It's been a real red-letter day, Mr Perry. But thank you for your offer regarding the store. I will have to think on it."

"If you don't mind, Mr Perry," said Harry, "and if Mr Singer doesn't mind, when we return to New York I'll do an inventory of his store with him prior to any sale or transfer."

"Suit yourself. I will hold Mr Schultz off as long as I can."

"I can't ask you to do all of that work, Harry," said Joel. Winston shrugged.

"It's nothing. I don't want to see you taken advantage of."

"And I don't want to see him dead," said Perry. "Which he will be if this doesn't get cleared up. Ah, cocktails." He smiled appreciatively as the waiter returned and began doling out our drinks; not, I thought, the smile of someone who had just lost a thirty-year friend, no matter how little he had seen of him. I looked over at Joel.

"Are you all right to stay?" He nodded.

"I have to eat one way or another." He took a sip of wine. "Mr Perry, how did you know my uncle?"

"I knew Nathaniel from the time we were both in our mid-twenties. We were both from the lower East Side in New York, and both determined to get out of it as soon as possible and had decided that diamonds were the only way to go, and South Africa had the diamonds. "We took a work passage to Great Britain in the summer of 1879 on the *SS Arizona*, shoveling coal." Perry smiled at the far-away memory. "We were both quite fit in those days, you understand."

"And how did you come to be in South Africa?" asked Harry.

"We may have been young, but we weren't fools. At the time there was a war going on in South Africa, the first Boer war. We waited out the end of it in London, working as waiters and kitchen help. When the war ended in 1881 we made our way to Kimberley and got to work." He took a swallow of his whisky. "It didn't take long before we had amassed a tidy number of raw diamonds. Back then it was almost like they were laid out on the surface in the dirt, waiting to be picked up." He slowly shook his head. "Those were the days. We stayed and worked, it seemed almost every nation in the world had sons in Kimberley. The years passed quickly and we amassed quite a tidy fortune."

"What happened to it?" asked Harry.

"Happened? The big combines happened. Men like Cecil Rhodes happened. They bought up everything in sight and drove the independent diggers, like your uncle and me, out of business. We were wiped out. The work of 18 years gone." He looked at me. "And then what you Brits call the second Boer war erupted. We were caught up in it."

"Why? You were both Americans," said Harry. "That was a British affair."

Alexander gave Harry a weak smile. "Ah, Mr Winston, we were trapped in country. There was no getting out and we had to eat. So, we enlisted with the English."

"Why not the Boers?" Van Effen asked.

Perry shrugged. "I've often wondered about that. I guess the short answer would be because neither of us spoke Dutch or Afrikaans. I have to say that politically, I leaned toward the Boer cause. I saw their fight as one against a foreign usurper; the Boers, of course, being the original colonizers of South Africa, tracing their heritage back to the Dutch, and now fighting the British who wanted the land. No offense meant, Nurse, but I thought of it as that whole 1776 thing all over again."

"None taken, sir."

Perry nodded. "We were put to work with others building a detention compound. When it was finished the British herded their Boer prisoners into it – many more people than it was designed for – gave us rifles and put us on guard duty." He shook his head. "I began to rethink my position at that time. It was dehumanizing."

"I'm aware of the history, Mr Perry," I said. "It's a shameful episode in my nation's past."

Perry looked sad. "You should have been there. As a nurse you'd have been absolutely appalled. It was mainly women and children shoved into the camps, without proper hygiene or food or medical attention. Do you know nearly thirty thousand Boers died in those hellish places and over twenty thousand of them were children under sixteen years old?"

"Yes," said Van Effen. "It was, as the nurse says, shameful."

Perry nodded, a far away look in his eyes. "You know, it haunts me to this day. But it never bothered Nathaniel. I don't wonder that he never told you what happened. I think he was always afraid that I would someday meet you and say something to you, Mr Singer." He fell silent for a moment as if marshalling his thoughts. "Do you really want to hear this, Mr Singer?

"Yes."

Perry indicated Harry and me. "And your friends?"

"Yes."

"Mr Van Effen?"

"Yes, please."

"Very well." Perry sighed. "One cold night a woman who had just given birth wandered out of her prison barracks hut in a delirium, screaming and crying. I ordered her to go back into the hut, and she turned to face me. That's when Isaac came around the corner of the barracks, and all he saw was her from the back, with her arms raised in the twilight, screaming gibberish at me. He shot her right between the shoulder blades. The bullet broke her spine and deflected into her breastbone, otherwise it would have gone right through and probably hit me." Perry took a deep breath and screwed his eyes shut for a moment, then opened them. "Nathaniel was standing there, the rifle butt still up to his shoulder, and he gave me the most malevolent smile I never hope to see again. I'll never forget that. By that time soldiers and other guards had come running at the sound of the shot. I could see faces pressed against the windows in the nearby huts, including the one the woman had come from. From that moment I wanted nothing more to do with him. I managed to get transferred to another camp. I heard that he'd adopted you, Mr Singer, after your parents were killed – your mother was his sister, of course – and was raising you as his own. I've purposefully stayed away from him since, and I have to tell you it was a bit of a shock when he reached out to me regarding the missteps you had taken." He shook his head. "And now he's dead. If it was justice it was a long time coming."

"My uncle did that?" Joel was unbelieving.

"As God is my witness," said Perry. "Your uncle did many things you would not be proud of." Joel looked stunned. Perry gave him a weak smile. "If it's any solace, so did I. So did many others. It was the nature of the beast."

"Were there no repercussions to what happened in the camp?" Van Effen asked.

"From the British, Mr Van Effen?" Perry gently shook his head. "No, we were just a couple of hired hands – American hired hands at that. The Limeys – sorry, nurse, the Brits – just didn't care. It was one less Boer mouth to feed."

"My uncle said he had not talked to you for years," said Joel.

"That's true. It was thirty years. I would see him from time to time at a sale or show in New York, or in Antwerp, and I'm sure he saw me. But we never talked again. We met briefly on Saturday night here on the ship to set up this time to discuss your problem, and that was the physically closest I had been to him in decades." Our dinners began arriving and Perry began to exercise his knife and fork with a vengeance. "This is really quite delicious, Nurse Chandler. You must give my compliments to the chefs."

The rest of the meal passed in a gloomy silence.


Harry stayed behind to talk with Perry while Van Effen, after spotting the woman he'd been with the night before, issued strict instructions for Joel to return to Isaac's cabin and lock the door securely until such time as Van Effen would return. Joel and I stopped at his cabin long enough for Joel to pick up some toiletry articles, then we went to Isaac's cabin. Alice unlocked the door after we established our bonafides.

"How did it go?"

"Swimmingly," said Joel. "My uncle is a murderer. No wonder he put bars on all the windows at our shop."

"What?" asked Alice.

"He's telling the truth," I said. "Why don't you have a seat and I'll explain it all as best I can."

Joel took off his tie and suit jacket. "Thanks for sitting up with Nathaniel. I'll take over now." He headed for the bedroom. "Back in a minute, I just need to pay my respects. I hope he didn't give you too much trouble." We heard the door close.

"Well?" asked Alice, settling onto the sofa.

To her credit she said nothing as I recited the litany of what may have passed for The Last Supper, as filled with gaiety and spontaneity as it was. When I was done Alice slowly exhaled.

"That's incredible. The prison camps were never discussed in my home while I was growing up. My parents knew people who had perished in them."

"I'm sorry."

Alice waved a hand. "Scarcely your fault, Maeve. I'm just amazed by how quickly everyone caught on to your false explanation of Mr Isaac's death."

I nodded. "I didn't want to give away the real cause to Mr Perry, at least not yet."

"What is *The Victory* printing?"

"That Mr Isaac died of natural causes and as much of an obituary as Joel wishes to provide."

"I'll write something up," said Joel, emerging from the bedroom. "Thanks for all you've done, Maeve."

"Don't thank me yet. There's more."

"More?" Joel sat next to Alice, taking her hand in his.

"I'm afraid so. At least we know now what drug was used on your uncle," I said. "Curare."

"Curare?" said Alice. "Like some poison-tipped blow dart or something?"

I nodded. "Substitute the syringe for the blow dart, and Bob's your uncle."

"Where did it come from?" asked Joel.

"It was definitely brought on board. *Victoria* doesn't carry it in medical stores."

"Curare goes with South America," said Alice. "I know that much."

"Yes," said Joel. "I've heard how some of the Venezuelan and Amazon Indians use the drug to hunt and paralyze their prey. Diamond diggers in the area have told me stories you wouldn't believe." He was quiet for a moment. "At least we didn't find him with an arrow sticking out of his back," he said with a touch of gallows humour.

"No, the syringe was a bit more subtle," I said. "Joel, did your uncle have any dealings with anyone from South America?"

He shook his head. "South Africa, yes. South America, no."

I nodded. "I'll check with Mister Collins to be sure, but I'm reasonably certain we don't have any indigenous South American tribe members on board. Still, there's little doubt our killer has had some practical experience with the stuff." I thought a moment. "Had your uncle had any contact with anyone you didn't know in the past few days? Made any trips?"

"He went out alone on Friday. He was gone most of the day; I don't know where he went. I suspect that's when he engaged Van Effen. He was back in time to light candles for *Shabbat*. On Saturday morning he asked – or rather, ordered – me to go with him for a walk. We met no one he knew, we discussed nothing. We got back to the store and met you and Alice, and after you both left I finished my packing and when Van Effen arrived at the shop we caught a cab to the pier." Joel sighed. "If you wouldn't mind arranging for a meeting between Rabbi Hoffman and myself, we'll iron out tomorrow's arrangements."

"Certainly," I said.

"I've been doing nothing else but thinking about those fake diamonds. Why would he do that? And one of them real?" Joel frowned. "What am I supposed to do with that? And another thing. Unless I can get into his pocketbook, I have very little cash. It's embarrassing, but he had me on an allowance. I know Doctor Harper said not to worry about it, but still – "

"Well, the cabins are bought and paid for," I said. "Otherwise, Mister Collins would be hovering about."

"There's that," he nodded. "And at least I have a return ticket." Joel smiled ruefully. "Two, if you count Uncle Nathaniel, but he won't be using his."

"Oh, Joel," said Alice, taking his hand and giving it a squeeze while giving him a light kiss on the cheek.

"Hoy!" I said. "It's fine if you want to do that sort of thing, but only in front of me. Nowhere else."

"Yes, Mother." Alice stood, and Joel rose with her. "Since you're back to take watch, I suppose I should leave, Joel."

"I think that's a fine idea," I said. "Joel, what needs to be done to prepare your uncle for the service?"

"This rabbi you've found can assist me," he said. "Nathaniel's body must be washed and shrouded. Normally it would be placed in a simple wooden coffin, but since it's a burial at sea – " he broke off. "I'm not sure."

"I'll ask. Doctor Harper was getting with Mister Harvey to gather the necessaries. The Doctor was in the Royal Navy during the War. For that matter, so was the Captain and Mister Harvey. I'm sure they've seen their share of over-the-rail burials and will have some insight into the niceties of how exactly one does it. As far as the shrouding for Nathaniel, I'll get something from the linens storeroom."

"I can sew," said Alice. Joel shook his head.

"No, but thank you. Only men are allowed. It's something I'll have to do alone."

"And once the body is ready?" I asked.

"As you said, that's where we need the professional expertise in moving him over the side." He pursed his lips. "But I'll need some help to get him there. I'll ask Harry if he could serve as a pallbearer."

"I'm sure Doctor Harper and Mister Harvey would also help. Possibly Mister Collins and the Captain," I said.

"That's good. And because I'm a nephew and not a child, I can serve. That makes six. That's all we need." He glanced toward the bedroom. "I doubt he weighs that much."

"I know this is hard for you," I said. "No matter how you got on with him, I know this is hard." I put a hand on his shoulder. "We'll find out who did this and why. I promise."

Joel offered a half smile. "I believe you."

"And I believe you, too," added Alice.

I looked at their expectant faces. Now, if only I could believe it myself.

# I

My parents being educators we always subscribed to a fair number of newspapers when I was growing up. Among the ones I remember are *The Daily Telegraph* (that one is still going, I believe), *The Times* (also still in business), and *The Globe* (sadly, gone since 1921). I firmly believe that these newspapers – and there were more, believe me – were part of what turned my brother and I into such voracious readers, and by voracious reader I mean that most of my reading is confined to trashy novels as I drop off to sleep. (*Dracula* being the exception that kept me up all night.) While I do try to stay informed of world events, I'm afraid that, other than *The British Medical Journal* and *The Lancet*, about the only newspaper I read with any regularity anymore is the *New York Daily Mirror*, and that primarily for Walter Winchell's column. (Don't roll your eyes at me, I know you read it, too.) Having said all of that, I will admit that I also read our ship-board newspaper, *The Victory*. It's pretty much a one-man operation, run by Mister Casey and a couple of saintly office assistants for writing and operating the press and delivering the paper every morning. It carries announcements for the day's activities, how far we traveled overnight, which ships we encountered and exchanged greetings with in our travels, estimated time of arrival, what's playing in the ship cinema, weather, profiles of interesting and noteworthy passengers, and bits and pieces of international news gleaned from a friendly radio operator in the wireless room.

It also contains the occasional obituary, or rather, notice of ship-board death since Mister Casey rarely has enough material on the deceased to do an out-and-out *London Times* obituary.

This morning's edition noted the sad passing of one Nathaniel Isaac, New York City diamond merchant. If that wasn't enough, the real meat of this front-page story was that the *Victoria* would be stopping at ten this morning, ship's time, to consign the mortal remains of Mr Isaac to the tender mercies of the North Atlantic ocean, and the service would be held on the fantail of the ship. The story asked that proper decorum be observed by passengers and crew as the ceremony took place. I wasn't sure what that meant for the passengers but it meant crew in attendance had to wear dress uniforms.

"How do I look?" asked Harper as I folded the paper and laid it aside.

"Resplendent, Boss," I said, getting up from my chair in the foyer of the First-Class dining salon. "The Captain, you, Mister Harvey and Mister Collins are very nice to perform this with Joel and Mr Winston."

Harper shot his cuffs out from his uniform jacket and never disturbed the dress cap he kept between his body and upper left arm. "I can't speak for the others, but I'm honored to have been asked."

I smiled. "That's almost verbatim what the other three said, too." I adjusted my nursing cap. "And thank you for the help with the technicalities."

"Some things I wish I didn't know and could just forget." He placed his officer's cap on his head. "A polished board to serve as a bier, lead weights to sink the body and a shroud of thick sailcloth. Just the way we did it in the War." He gave me a gentle smile. "You were on the right track going to the linen stores, but the sailcloth from the ship's carpenter is much more durable."

I nodded and looked at the ornate clock on the wall. "09:15. We've got a few minutes. Do you want to hear about last night's dinner?"

"I've been on pins and needles."

"Pins and needles? Ha. Wait until you hear this." I launched into the story of The Last Supper, leaving nothing out. When I had finished Harper took a deep breath.

"Good Lord. Do you think it's all true?"

"I don't know. I'm not sure. It's a tale, though, isn't it?"

"I'll say." Harper rubbed his chin. "This is starting to remind me of when Mittens the cat would knock over my grandmother's knitting basket and pull the skeins of yarn everywhere."

"Well, Boss, I'll tell you – right now my money is on Mittens." I sighed. "You'd best be getting along to Mister Isaac's stateroom to meet the others. I'll see you on the fantail."

"Right." I watched him go then made my way to the nearest exit and mounted the stairs for the Sports Deck. The weather was pleasant, a clear blue sky, though somewhat chilly. I realized I should have brought a coat, but it was too late for that now – I could feel the *Victoria* beginning to slow. The Captain – or rather Mister Carter, since the Captain was also presumably on his way to join the others – was beginning what's termed a controlled speed reduction.

A ship like the *Queen Victoria*, as expensive and as grand as she is, lacks one component that, if you bought a new motor car and found it missing, would have you screaming. The *Queen Victoria*, like all other ships, has no brakes. You may be wondering, then, how something about a thousand feet long and weighing 78,000 tons give or take an ounce and moving at about 27 miles per hour (or about 24 knots) can, as the Americans say, "hit the brakes."

Chief Engineer Duncan explained it to me over a beer in the ship's crew pub, the Boar's Head. (Don't think this place is something fancy like the passengers have. It's a knocked together affair about as far aft on C Deck as you can go without getting wet, but it's a friendly place for us.) Anyway, there are apparently several ways to stop a ship in mid-ocean short of sinking it, but only one has the added advantage of not hurling passengers over the railings. According to the Chief, the bridge will ring down to the engine room on the telegraphs to cut our speed from full speed – since we would presumably be doing that in the open seas – down to half speed ahead, then after a short interval there would be another signal to slow ahead and another short interval later the telegraph would ring down dead slow ahead, then down to standby and finally full stop. This step-by-step reduction in speed keeps water flowing over the propellers and past the rudder to maintain control of the ship as she glides to a stop over the course of a mile or so. The process takes about fifteen to twenty minutes to complete. Of course, once we're no longer under power we can't just drop anchor in the ocean, it's too deep. Some length of anchor may be paid out to hold our position, but otherwise we just sit there quietly until the Captain gives the order to make way again. All of this is naturally dependent on fair weather; the Captain isn't going to endanger ship, crew, or the passengers.

As I made my way to the stern a quick glance up at the three funnels towering overhead told me that most of the *Victoria*'s boilers were in the process of losing pressure; the amount of black smoke from burning oil was decreasing and the valve off of boiler steam no longer going to the turbines was increasing. By the time I reached the aft end of the Sports Deck and went down the flight of open stairs to the fantail at the aft end of A Deck, the loss of ship's speed was perceptible.

A good-sized crowd was already gathered, lining the railings of the Sports Deck where they could get a look at the proceedings, and more were crowding the limited space on the fantail. It looked like about half of the ship's passengers were there (the other half no doubt sleeping last night's exertions off, or maybe they just didn't read the newspaper) and scattered among them were some crewmen and stewards standing quietly until the service was over and they could resume their duties. I cast an eye about to see if I could spot Perry or Van Effen, but neither man fell into my limited field of vision. I could see a knot of deck officers in dress uniform at the exact center of the rear of the fantail, as well as Mister Collins and Mister Armstrong and of course Alice. The crowd grew quieter as the *Victoria* finally came to rest. Without preamble the ship's horns blew three short blasts indicating she was stopping, and then went silent. I gently pushed my way forward through the passengers, my uniform providing a pass key they all observed.

Alice caught my eye as I neared and with a final shove I got free of the mass of people and joined her at the fantail railing. Directly behind us was a sheer drop into the ocean; the rudder was also below us but hidden from sight by the overhang of the ship where we were standing. I hadn't been to this area of the ship in about five months, the memory of what had happened here still very fresh on my mind.[*] Alice squeezed my hand as the people again became hushed. I stood on tiptoe and could just make out a man I took to be Rabbi Hoffman walking in front, with Joel and Mr Winston slowly stepping in unison behind him, a board about two feet wide between them at shoulder height. The shrouded body of Nathaniel Isaac was strapped to the board, and as the pall bearers advanced the people quietly stepped back to make way for it, the men removing their hats.

I wondered that they had carried the body all the way from the stateroom, then remembered what Harvey had said to Doctor Harper about Isaac not weighing much. The Captain and Harper were behind Joel and Harry, with Mister Harvey and Mister Collins bringing up the rear. They walked in a somber lock step to join the officers near the rail. The board carrying the body was set with what I presumed was the foot end on the railing, and the head end was placed upon what appeared to be a saw horse with a linen tablecloth draped over it for decorum. Their duty done, the six men stepped away and Rabbi Hoffman came to the microphone stand.

"Welcome, friends," he began. "I say friends because there are no strangers aboard this ship. We are our own community while at sea." There was a murmur of assent, and he continued. "I am Rabbi Aaron Hoffman. It is both my honor, and my sad duty, to perform the *hesped* – the eulogy – for Nathaniel Isaac, late of New York City, who passed from this life yesterday." I looked at Joel, but he was staring straight ahead. Rabbi Hoffman continued. "The Jewish faith prefers a burial in the ground within 24 hours of death, but we are at sea and far from land." He

---

[*]    See Book One: *Shadow of the Queen*

raised his arms heavenward. "So we ask forgiveness, and blessing, for this service." The people gathered responded as one with a spontaneous quiet 'amen.' Rabbi Hoffman smiled and nodded. "Thank you."

"He's good," Alice whispered to me. I nodded.

"Mr Isaac had only one living relative, a nephew, Mr Joel Singer," said the rabbi. "Mr Singer is with us now, and I'll ask him to come forward and say a few words." The rabbi stepped back as an obviously nervous Joel walked to the microphone.

"Thank you, Rabbi Hoffman." He looked out at the gathering. "Good morning," he said. "Thank you for coming, and – " he said, looking at the Captain, "I apologize for the interruption to everyone's schedule." The Captain gave him a nod. "My uncle Nathaniel could be a hard man," said Joel. "He was a diamond dealer, and he came up in the trade through the rough and tumble of the diamond fields in Kimberley, South Africa. He didn't speak of it much, but I know he was active in the Boer Wars. When my parents died in 1910 he took me in." Joel stopped, searching for words. "It was a difficult life at times. As far as I knew he had never married, never wanted children. And then he was suddenly raising the one-year-old son of his late sister." I glanced over at Alice, who was sniffling. "He was a difficult man to know," continued Joel. "But he did the best he could in the circumstances that had been dealt him. On his behalf, thank you for your attendance." Joel stepped back into the line of pall bearers and the rabbi resumed the microphone.

"Thank you, Joel. Well said." He turned to address the audience. "I will now perform the service of the *K'vurah*. This is the burial service, and will be said in Hebrew, so I beg your indulgence." He cleared his throat and began. His voice as he intoned the words was a rich baritone. I saw that Joel and Harry had closed their eyes. The other four pall bearers removed their caps and stood at attention until the rabbi finished. His head was bowed, and he was silent for a moment, then he looked across at all of us. "Lastly will be the *Mourners' Kaddish*. It is a traditional prayer, said in memory of the dead. It is in the form of a call and response. As I finish each line, I would ask you, in respect of Mr Isaac and no matter your religious beliefs, to respond by saying 'amen.' When we reach the end of the prayer, we will take a moment of silence, then the Captain has a few words, after which the burial will take place." A slight buzz of conversation greeted this information, but quieted down as the rabbi again raised his arms up. "Exalted and hallowed be His great Name." He stopped and looked expectantly at his audience. After a moment the crowd responded with an 'amen.' Hoffman nodded and continued. "Throughout the world which He has created according to His Will. May He establish His kingship, bring forth His redemption and hasten the coming of His *Moshiach*".

"Amen."

"In your lifetime and in your days and in the lifetime of the entire House of Israel, speedily and soon, and say, Amen."

"Amen."

"May His great Name be blessed forever and to all eternity. Blessed and praised, glorified, exalted and extolled, honored, adored and lauded be the Name of the Holy One, blessed be He."

"Amen."

"Beyond all the blessings, hymns, praises and consolations that are uttered in the world; and say, Amen."

"Amen."

"May there be abundant peace from heaven, and a good life for us and for all Israel; and say, Amen."

"Amen."

"He who makes peace in His heavens, may He make peace for us and for all Israel; and say, Amen."

"Amen."

After a moment of silence, Hoffman lowered his arms. "Thank you all," he said. "Captain Webster?"

The Captain took the microphone as Hoffman stepped back. "Thank you, Rabbi Hoffman." After a moment to stroke his trim beard, he quietly began. "A ship captain's duties are many," he said. "Most are of the everyday sort involved with running the vessel, but sadly, there is also what we are participating in today." He paused and looked about. "Burial at sea has taken place as long as we have been going down to the ocean. I, as did many of our crew and probably some of you, served in the Royal Navy in the War and participated in events like this more than I care to remember. I will tell you, whether it is a young man in the prime of life, or a man like Mr Isaac in the twilight of life, it does not get any easier." He took a paper out of his inside jacket pocket and put on his reading glasses. "With your permission, Rabbi Hoffman." He began to read. "And the Lord spoke unto Moses, saying, speak unto Aaron and unto his sons, saying, thus ye shall bless the children of Israel, saying unto them, the Lord bless thee, and keep thee: the Lord make His face shine upon thee, and be gracious unto thee: the Lord lift up His countenance upon thee, and give thee peace, and they shall put My name upon the children of Israel, and I will bless them." Rabbi Hoffman nodded, and the Captain resumed. "The last thing I will read is one that has always stayed with me, since I first heard it as a young man when I went to sea. It's by a Scotsman, George Bruce. 'The sea is the largest cemetery, and its slumbers sleep without a monument. All other graveyards show symbols of distinction between great and small, rich and poor: but in the ocean cemetery, the king, the clown, the prince and the peasant are alike, undistinguishable.'" There was silence; all we could hear was the wind singing around and over the *Victoria*. "Mister Harvey, if you will," said the Captain.

Harvey nodded and began to unbuckle the straps holding Mr Isaac's remains to the board. After a moment he straightened and nodded. "All clear, Captain."

"Mr Singer?" asked the Captain. Joel nodded. "Rabbi Hoffman?" The rabbi gave his silent approval. The Captain turned to the pall bearers. "Gentlemen, on my command," he said. There was a brief pause as the men got ready, then the Captain spoke. "Tilt." The board came up to a 45-degree slant and the body slid off, making the long feet first fall to the ocean. There was a discernible splash, and then it quickly sank out of sight, a trail of bubbles marking its wake. The Captain and officers saluted; Joel looked ashen.

The Captain gestured to Rabbi Hoffman who spoke into the microphone. "That concludes our service. Thank you all." A moment later the horns again sounded and seconds after that we could hear the water being thrashed by the propellers as Chief Duncan answered the bridge signal of dead slow ahead and the *Victoria* began the step-by-step process of coming back to speed.

**II**

At my age, I'm happy to say, I have attended more weddings than funerals – though a wise older friend once told me that the time would come when that cheerful ratio would be reversed. Until then, I could think of nothing worse than being the guest of honor at a funeral, unless it was just being a guest. Not that the service was bad; it was my first burial at sea so I didn't have any preconceived notions of how it should go. Tip, splash, done. Rather straightforward. Growing up in my small town, I do remember going to the occasional wake where the grownups tended to be very jolly, considering they had just laid a friend in the ground. All my brother and I cared for were the sweets, which were always in abundance. Unfortunately, the aftermath of Mr Isaac's funeral showed no such signs of an outbreak of jollity, much less sweets.

Joel, Harry, the officers, and the Captain all thanked Rabbi Hoffman for his work, as did Alice and I. He smiled, noted that it was his personal pleasure to be able to assist, and hoped the best for Joel, then was lost into the dispersing crowd.

"Fine man, that," said Mister Collins. "We should reimburse him something for his efforts."

"I'll take care of he and his wife's dinner tonight," said Harvey.

Collins nodded. "I'll throw in with you."

"And I've got your dinner tonight, Joel," said Harper.

Joel looked close to unleashing the tears that were absent at his uncle's funeral. "You are very kind," was all he could manage.

Harry glanced around at us. "If you all don't mind, I'm going to borrow Mr Singer for a few minutes. Captain, ladies, officers all, thank you."

"Before you go, Mr Singer," said Harvey. "I'm going to have the lock changed on your uncle's cabin door, just as a precaution. I'll have the new key sent to you."

"Thank you, Mister Harvey." Joel and Harry took their leave.

"That would be our cue," said the Captain. "Thank you, Nurse, for putting this together."

"My pleasure, sir," I said.

"Mister Collins, Mister Harvey, do you mind keeping me company back to the bridge?" The three men struck off. Harper looked at me.

"I suppose I should get back to the office." He nodded. "It was a good job, Maeve."

"Thanks, Boss."

Alice nudged me in the ribs. "Here comes Mister Casey."

"Bloody hell." I looked at Harper. "Save yourself. I'll answer his questions."

"Thanks." Harper did an about face and made his exit.

"Hey, Doctor Harper," called Casey, but Harper either couldn't or wouldn't hear him. A moment later and he passed from sight. Casey frowned, then turned to me with his notepad out. "That was quite the show. Interesting that the nephew serves as a pall bearer for his uncle. Who was the other chap?"

"Harry Winston," I said. "American diamond man." Casey jotted it down on his grubby notepad.

"Fine, thanks. And the medicine man was good, too."

"Rabbi," I corrected, my jaw tightening. "Make sure you spell his name correctly. Aaron Hoffman, Aaron with two 'a's.'"

"Will do." He put the pencil into the band of his fedora. "Nice turnout to see the old buster off."

"As much as I hate to admit it, Mister Casey, your article about it in the paper was good," said Alice. "It set the right tone."

"Glad to hear it, Nurse." He watched a pair of deck hands take down the microphone and stand, then pick up the board that had lately held Isaac's body. "Well, I'm away. Maybe get a reaction or two from these good people."

"But not from the bereaved, please," I said. Casey looked surprised.

"Nurse Chandler, I would never." He tipped his hat and made for the stairs leading up to the Sports Deck.

"Do you believe him?" asked Alice.

"Not for one minute," I replied. "Here comes your man back."

Joel and Harry, still in conversation, were crossing to us. Alice glanced at me. "How do I look?"

"Like someone who's just been to a funeral," I said. She appeared crestfallen. I sighed. "You look fine, stop with your worrying."

"Alice – Maeve," said Joel. "Thank you again for being here."

"Of course," said Alice.

"We're very sorry for your loss, Mr Singer." I glanced over at the railing. Everything had returned to normal. There was no longer any evidence of what had taken place earlier. "Were you happy with the rabbi's service?"

"Yes, he did a very good job. And the Captain's remarks were appreciated." Joel paused for a moment. "As far as other things go, I called the radio room this morning and sent a wire to Mr Jenkins to see if he knew how many diamonds were in my uncle's box."

"Good," I said. "Until you get a reply, nothing to do but sit tight."

"Oh, there's plenty more to do," said Harry. He looked at Joel. "Why don't you tell them?"

Joel smiled. "I'm going to go to work for Mr Winston."

Alice's jaw dropped. "Joel, that's wonderful!" She took a step toward him but I put out a restraining arm.

"Public," I said. "Time for that later."

Alice laughed. "So tell us about it."

"Well," said Harry, "I've been thinking about how best to expand my business. What I really want to do is open the doors under my own name, but I'm not quite ready to do that yet. As I told you I had an employee almost put me out of business when he ran out with my inventory, so I need someone I feel I can trust as I rebuild and focus on the future. I need someone who can mind the store while I hunt down the diamonds and gems. I need someone who's personable and knowledgeable and has the *chutzpah* to ask out a ship's nurse." He smiled. "In short, I need Joel Singer."

I held out a cautionary hand. "I don't want to have this come a cropper," I said, "but what about Mr Schultz?"

Joel looked at Harry and then at me. "I've been thinking about what Mr Perry said last night. I'll just liquidate what's left in my uncle's store. I don't want any part of it anymore. I want a fresh start. What I did was a stupid mistake, and I'm owning up to it."

"Oh, Joel," said Alice. There was entirely too much treacle flowing here for my liking and I decided to move before it became ankle-deep.

"That's all well and good," I said, casting a glance over to the railing where Nathaniel had recently bid farewell to this world. But let's not forget what happened to your uncle. If that was a warning, it was blown about as loudly as one of the *Victoria's* horns. I don't think you'll be safe until we find out who killed him."

"Mr Van Effen – " began Joel.

"Mr Van Effen has shown a tendency to wander off for a pretty face. Otherwise he seems quite reliable and dependable, when he's around. Except I don't see him now. Or Mr Perry." I looked at Harry. "Let's get Joel back to his cabin and safely put away."

Do you remember if you were disappointed or not when you found out that Father Christmas – Santa Claus to you Yanks – was being impersonated by your parents? I don't know about you, but I was a rather impressionable youngster, given to flights of fancy that usually included some kind of collusion with my older brother which inevitably ended poorly for both of us, me in particular. However, back to the story. Like most children, I was wildly impressed with Father Christmas. How could he do all he did in one night? My father told me it was Christmas magic. And I believed. I really, really believed – until that fateful Christmas when my brother woke me and had me come to the top of the stairs. Shaded in darkness, we peered around the corner and down to see Mum and Dad putting out presents beneath the tree. I will fair tell you that it absolutely leveled me. I had believed so hard in something that was magical and good, and now I was presented with something else entirely, forcing me at a young and innocent age to rethink my entire position not only on Father Christmas but also pixies, fairies, leprechauns and quite possibly unicorns.

That's the way I was feeling about diamonds right now. After depositing Joel in his cabin and dissuading Alice from joining him – after all, the girl had to do the work I wasn't doing in the hospital right now – Harry and I walked back up to the Sports Deck.

Winston put his hands on the railing and looked out at the sea. "I believe that we'll find Nathaniel's diamonds if they're on this ship. I found out early on that gems can turn up in the strangest of places. My father had a small jewelry store in New York, smaller than what Joel's uncle runs – or rather, ran. When I was twelve, I saw some jewelry in a pawn shop window. The sign said, 'take your pick, twenty-five cents.' I picked out a ring with a lovely green stone." He gave me a shrewd glance. "Do you know what it was? It was an emerald." I gasped involuntarily. "Not just any emerald, mind you, but a two-carat emerald. I sold it two days later for $800. The shop owner had no idea of what he had."

"Incredible," I said. He nodded.

"So if a twelve year old boy can find an emerald in a pawn shop window, the two of us should certainly be able to locate a box of diamonds on this ship."

"And find a murderer," I said. "But it is an awfully large ship."

"Yes." We walked along the Sports Deck in silence for a few minutes.

"That truly was a magnificent gesture you made to Joel about work," I said.

"Nothing magnificent about it. I need the help and he needs to be employed and put this deplorable episode well into his past. I've walked past Nathaniel's shop, but I was never impressed by what he had in the windows. And the inside was dark and dingy. I doubt Joel could make a go of it. I doubt anyone could make a go of it. Best to salvage what he can from the wreck and put in with me to learn the trade."

"You made Alice very happy."

Harry smiled. "It did seem so, didn't it? I suppose I should tell you there was one more part of the deal. I'm providing him with a ring so he can propose to her."

I ran my knee into an inconveniently placed bench. "Excuse me?"

"He's going to ask her to marry him."

"Bloody hell," I said, massaging my knee. "He alluded to that, but I didn't think he'd jump right in."

"Well, now, it's probably not all that bad," said Harry.

"Not that, I hurt my knee. I wish them all the luck in the world. They appear to have fallen in love at first sight on Saturday morning at his uncle's shop. I have to admit the romance is making me more than a little crazy." I stopped walking. "Look up there. Van Effen's at the rail, smoking." Harry followed my look. Van Effen appeared to be deep in thought, taking the occasional draw on a cigarette as he gazed at the ocean rolling past. "I wonder why he isn't looking after Joel?"

"No time like the present to ask."

Any thoughts I might have entertained about coming up behind him unnoticed were quickly dashed. Van Effen turned easily and sized us up in his professional manner as we approached. He took a last pull on his cigarette then flicked it over the railing and adjusted his tie.

"Nurse Chandler. Mr Winston."

"Mr Van Effen," I said.

"Shouldn't you be closer to Mr Singer?" asked Harry.

"He was safe in the crowd," said Van Effen. "Mr Perry and I watched him throughout the service."

"I didn't see either of you," I said. Van Effen shrugged.

"There were a lot of people." He steadied his hat in the breeze.

"Where did Mr Perry go?" asked Harry.

"Back to his cabin to rest. He seems to tire rather easily." Van Effen reached into his inside coat pocket, withdrew a pack of Pall Malls, selected one, tapped it against the rail and lit it, then took a deep draw, exhaling the smoke through his nostrils. "Thank you for seeing Mr Singer safely to his cabin."

"You saw us?" I said. Van Effen nodded.

"I followed you all at a discreet distance to see you lock him in his cabin. You are remarkably easy to trail." He blew smoke out. "Now, how may I help you?"

I didn't know if I should have been insulted by his remark or not, so I pressed forward. "I have a few questions that have crossed my mind since yesterday, Mr Van Effen."

"By all means, Nurse."

"You walked Mr Isaac to his cabin Saturday evening," I said.

"Yes, after he had checked his diamonds in at the purser's office."

"Then you were the last person to see him alive."

Van Effen shrugged. "I could not attest to that. My cabin is at the far end of the corridor by the stairs leading up to the First-Class entry. Mr Isaac's cabin is halfway down the corridor from me. Mr Isaac gave me Saturday evening off. As you know I went to the bar and did not return to my cabin until late."

"He brought you with him to watch himself and Mr Singer, then dismissed you the first night of the voyage?" Harry said. "Didn't you find that rather strange?"

Van Effen nodded. "I, too, felt the same way you do. But as his hired man, I did not call the tune. I merely danced to it."

"Did you have any other duties?" I asked.

Van Effen shrugged. "I understood from Mr Isaac that Mr Singer is still an apprentice," he said. "As I told you I have some knowledge of diamonds so I was to also help at the show."

Harry inclined his head. "Are you a dealer?"

"I have been, Mr Winston. I've also been an independent diamond hunter for many years. South Africa, Brazil, India."

"South Africa. You're Dutch?"

"Yes. Now." A thoughtful expression crossed his face. "I identified with the Boers in my younger days."

Harry nodded. "Boer. You're too young to have been involved in the unpleasantness."

"Not necessarily, Mr Winston. I was a boy in 1900." He gave Harry a careful appraisal. "We appear to be close to the same age."

"I was born in 1896."

"And I in 1895. I am only one year older than you, but that is where we diverge." Van Effen's face clouded over. "I was five years old in 1900 but I did my time as a guest of both Her and His Majesty's government during the Second Freedom War."

"An interesting life," said Harry. "You must have seen quite a bit."

"Oh, yes." Van Effen nodded. "Sometimes more than I cared to see." He put a hand up to again steady his hat in the wind.

"Unique hat," I commented.

"Yes, it is." Van Effen gave up on the wind and took off the hat with its broad black band running around the crown. His dark hair was brilliantined. "The Americans call it a Panama hat."

"It looks comfortable, but not warm."

"Nurse, you do not want a warm hat in South America." Van Effen turned the Panama in his hands. "This is meant to keep the harsh sun off your neck and face. I have been partial to these hats for years. I first wore them when I was a 16-year-old laborer on the Panama Canal, back in 1911." He put the hat back on and looked at Harry. "It is true, is it not, that we tend to keep the habits we develop as young men?"

"Yes." Winston nodded. "You actually worked on the canal?"

"It was my first real job. I left South Africa on a tramp steamer determined to make my fortune. I was on site for three years. Then the war broke out in 1914, and I returned to South Africa. I avoided the Maritz rebellion by the truly die-hard Boers and volunteered into the French Foreign Legion because while I dislike Germans more than I do the English, I couldn't bring myself to fight with the English. After the War ended and I was discharged, I went into diamond prospecting."

"Impressive curriculum vitae," I said.

"I am glad you think so, Nurse." He took another deep draw on his cigarette. "I put my life at risk more times than I can count to build it."

"Oh, if you'll pardon me, Mr Van Effen, I did mean to ask one more thing." Harry reached into his pocket and took out the small fake diamond he'd kept and unwrapped it. "Have you ever seen anything like this before?"

Van Effen put his hat back on then took the fake and examined it with interest for a few moments. After a close-up inspection including holding it to the morning sunlight, he handed it back to Harry. "This is not real," he finally said. "But it does certainly have the appearance, does it not, of a lovely diamond? It is beautifully made and would fool many people."

"I thought so to," agreed Harry.

"Where did you come by it?" asked Van Effen.

"A friend."

"Your friend was maybe intending to cheat someone?" Van Effen's face was calm. "Fine costume jewelry like this has been used before on the naïve, unknowledgeable, and unsuspecting. If there are no more questions, I will take my leave." He looked at me. "I believe your cinema is showing *Anna Christie* with Greta Garbo this afternoon. Something to look forward to. I may impose on you to keep a watch on Mr Singer, unless I can persuade him to attend with me." He gave a nod of the head and walked off. I watched him go then looked at Harry.

"I'm beginning to feel like Alice."

"Alice?" Harry wrinkled his brow. "Joel's Alice?"

"Alice from *Alice in Wonderland*. Do you recollect the title of chapter one?"

"Can't say that I do."

"Down the Rabbit-Hole." Van Effen disappeared from view around one of the large ventilators sprouting from the deck and I frowned. "I just wonder where we're going to come out."

# IV

You've heard the story of Pinocchio, haven't you? If you haven't, go out and buy a copy of *The Adventures of Pinocchio*, by Carlo Collodi. In this story a woodcarver makes a marionette out of a piece of magic wood, and the marionette, named Pinocchio, comes to life. He's not an upstanding citizen, though, and when he fibs his nose tends to grow. The book is charmingly illustrated and someday, mark my words, someone will use this new art of film animation and talking cartoons to make a movie and they'll make a fortune.

Unfortunately, that person would not be me because even though I felt one or both were fibbing, neither Mr Perry nor Mr Van Effen appeared to be experiencing any such uncontrolled rhinal growth in my presence. (That, and I can't draw a round circle to save my life.)

Following our interview with Van Effen, Harry had said he had a few things to attend to and slipped away. Left alone I realized that the wind had really picked up as the *Victoria* resumed her usual cruising speed after the funeral. Seeing that there was nothing to be gained by staying on the open Sports Deck and catching pneumonia, I made my way to the nearest stairs and descended to the warmth of A Deck to check on Joel in his stateroom. I hadn't gone much more along than the lobby when I was stopped by Miss Thomas.

"Nurse, I'm glad I ran into you," she began. "I was just going up to walk the decks for some exercise, but I wanted to apologize for my behavior yesterday morning, especially after I found that poor man died. I was at the service this morning, by the way. Beautifully done." She patted her perfectly coiffed hair, a stark contrast to my wind-swept hair curling out from under my nurse's cap.

"Well, thank you, Miss Thomas. I will pass on your condolences to Mr Isaac's nephew."

"You may call me Caroline. His eulogy was brief but seemed heartfelt."

"I think he did as well as anyone might under the circumstances." I looked over her clothing. "You're dressed rather thinly to be going out on deck."

Caroline gave a light laugh. "Like I said, exercise. I prefer to keep a brisk pace as I walk and a bulky sweater and coat just won't work."

"Exercise a lot, do you?" I eyed her trim body and tried not to think of my own curves.

"Oh, yes. Every day. Keeps me fit, don't you know." She smiled, showing beautiful white teeth that I hadn't noticed when she'd been reading us the riot act yesterday morning. I felt myself really beginning to be annoyed.

"Well, Miss Thomas, I mustn't keep you. I hope the rest of your voyage with us is less irritable and exciting."

"I'm sure it will be." She drew closer in a conspiratorial fashion. "I met a most interesting man, if you must know."

I thought to myself that I mustn't know, but knew she was going to fill me in on it, anyway. "Yes?" I asked, trying to put just the right amount of interest in the word.

Miss Thomas nodded and tilted her head to the other side of the corridor. "Man in cabin 38-A. Very sun-tanned and athletic. Wears a funny straw hat that somehow looks good on him, tailored suits, and has a fabulous accent. I'm surprised he can understand me with my New York accent, but he does."

With a start I realized she was describing Van Effen. I gave her a sweet smile. "He sounds lovely," I said. "But in my experience shipboard romances often end at the Customs Sheds."

She returned my smile with her perfect teeth. Again. "Oh, thank you for the advice, Nurse. I'm just looking to while away the empty days." She winked. "And nights. I'm sure you probably know what I mean."

"Yes, of course." The smile I gave her was brittle. "Have a pleasant voyage, Miss Thomas." I felt a momentary pang at not letting her know that the man she'd chosen as a paramour for the trip was a hired gun, but I managed to let it pass. Her impeccably coiffed hair, matching outfit, svelte and athletic body, and perfect white teeth deserved what they got. I watched as she athletically climbed the stairs, immediately wished I hadn't, and made my way down the corridor to Joel's cabin.

Not to my undying surprise, Alice opened the door to my knock. I frowned at her. "Don't you think you should at least ask who's in the corridor before you open the door?" I pulled a handkerchief out of my uniform pocket. "And you've made a perfect hash of your lipstick." I glanced over her shoulder at Joel. "And so have you. Can't leave you people alone for five minutes." I stepped in and closed the door.

"We were just – " began Joel, but I waved him off.

"I know what you were just, I wasn't born yesterday." I sat down. "I've got more information. Harry and I just had a talk with Mr Van Effen on the Sports Deck."

"What did he say?" asked Joel. I waved him off.

"Let me use the 'phone first." The operator put me through to the hospital and Doctor Harper picked up.

"Hello, it's Maeve," I said. "Yes, I'm fine. I just wanted to let you know that I'm in Joel's stateroom. Yes, she's here too." I rolled my eyes at Alice. "No, nothing is wrong. Just filling them in on a conversation Harry and I had with Mr Van Effen." I listened. "Yes, I'll be there directly and tell you. No, they're not in a clinch now. I can see light between them. Yes, right. Okay. Thanks, Boss." I rang off and looked at Alice. "Your love life is going to be the death of me."

"Sorry, Maeve." She gave me her sweetest smile, which, I had to admit, was rather fetching. No wonder Joel was putty in her hands. "But it will be worth it."

I started to say something, thought better of it, and motioned them to have a seat on the sofa. They both listened in silence, and when I had finished it was Alice who spoke up first.

"I think you should go to the movies this afternoon, Joel. Take your mind off things for a bit. Mr Van Effen would probably enjoy the company." I stared at her.

"I'm not that thrilled with the idea of sitting in the dark with Van Effen," said Joel. He looked at me. "My uncle never said anything about Van Effen having diamond knowledge."

"You mentioned that Van Effen rode to the pier with you and your uncle on Saturday. Did he say anything on the trip?"

"No. Nothing other than good evening. It was like being in a cab with a German Shepherd dog."

A sharp rap on the door interrupted our conversation.

"Mr Singer, sir. Message for you," a young voice said. I looked at Joel and shook my head, then went to the door myself.

"Slide it under the door," I said. After a moment an envelope appeared. I dug some coins out of my smock and passed them under, then stood and handed the envelope to Joel.

"What is it?" asked Alice.

"It's the reply to my message to Mr Jenkins, finally." He tore open the flimsy and pulled out the sheet. The color drained from his face.

"Joel?" Alice leaned forward. "Joel, you look like you've seen a ghost – what's wrong?"

Joel sucked in air. "It's from Mr Selber. He has a tailor's shop on the other side of my uncle's store. He says a messenger service tried to deliver my wireless to our store twice, but both times encountered a locked door and no one home so they finally came to him."

"And?" I asked.

"Mr Selber is old and stays in his shop. He rarely goes out. But when the messenger service told him they couldn't deliver next door, he went outside and looked in our store windows. And he saw nothing. No displays. No lights. No people. Nothing." Joel bit his lip. "The store is empty." He gave a mirthless laugh. "He does send condolences about Nathaniel."

"Bloody hell," I gasped.

"So much for my plan of paying off Schultz," said Joel.

"Oh, Joel," said Alice. She reached across and took his hand. "What are we going to do?"

"Do? Harry and Maeve and I are going to find the diamonds my uncle brought with him and go to those shows." He managed a smile. "I never did like that dark little store, anyway."

# V

One of Mister Harvey's delights is watching the American Western pictures. He's a big fan of the on-screen cowboys like Tom Mix, Warner Baxter (remember when he won the Academy Award a couple of years ago for his portrayal of the Cisco Kid?), and Ken Maynard. I remember sticking my head into the ship's cinema once to see what it was all about, and all I came away with was men on horseback shooting at and chasing after other men on horseback, or the town bank being robbed, or the train waylaid, or the stagecoach being held up, or – well, you get the idea.

What I'm driving at is that it was always something. No sooner had the good guy gotten the 'drop' on the bad fellow, than another 'bad 'un' popped right up. In our off-screen real world mystery which Mister Harvey might have named 'The Diamond Desperados at Victoria Gulch' it seemed we were facing much the same predicament, except that we had failed to get the 'drop' on anyone, and now another 'bad 'un' had popped up to bedevil us, and to make matters worse this one was now nearly two full days ahead of us. I took the paper from Joel's hand and read it myself, then handed it back to him.

"Not a word here about your Mr Jenkins," I said. "I wonder what became of him."

"Probably on his way to Rio with a suitcase full of gems," said Joel. "But why would he rob my uncle's store? The two of them had known each other for years."

"I don't know. What about insurance coverage?"

Joel shrugged. "I'm sure there must be some. At least I hope so."

"Was anything kept off site?"

He shook his head. "Nothing. Besides the store stock all he had was what he carried on board the *Victoria*, and now it looks like fakes have been substituted for those save for one." He put a hand to his head. "It's too much."

"Why don't you rest for a bit," said Alice. "There's nothing to be done right now."

"Alice is right. Go have a lay down. You've had a rough morning. We'll catch up later." I looked at Alice. "And you – "

"Yes, Mother. I'll behave."

"Right," I said, closing the door behind me.

Mister Harvey was visiting with Harper when I got to the hospital. He stood when I entered and slowly clapped his hands. "Welcome, Nurse Chandler. The only woman who ever had a poor dining experience in my restaurant. Was it the food or the conversation last night? Maybe the company? Doctor Harper wasn't quite clear on it when he told me the story."

"Bugger off," I said, leaning against the desk. "Now that you're caught up on that, do you want to hear everything that happened after you pushed Mr Isaac over the side this morning?"

Harper winced. "That's rather a macabre way of phrasing it," he said.

"Even flippant," added Harvey.

"You won't think this is flippant. Joel received an answer to his wireless to Mr Jenkins at the shop."

"How did Jenkins take it?" asked Harper.

I gave a hollow laugh. "Jenkins took it, all right. We think he took it lock, stock, and barrel. The shop is cleaned out. It was a merchant next door that ended up replying to Joel after the telegram service couldn't deliver a message to Nathaniel's shop."

Both men looked stunned. "You're kidding," said Harvey.

"I really wish I was, Mister Harvey. Coming on top of everything else this morning, it should have been a knock-out blow. I'll give it to Joel, he's got staying power."

"Does he need another sedative?" asked Harper.

"No. He's resting now. Alice is keeping an eye on him." Harvey raised an eyebrow. "In purely a professional sense, Mister Harvey." I hoped, anyway.

"What else?" said Harper. "I only ask because with you there's always another shoe to drop."

"More like a boot," I said. "Harry and I had a talk with Van Effen."

"When did you manage that?" asked Harvey.

"Sports Deck after the funeral." I recounted the conversation. When I finished Mister Harvey shook his head.

"That's something."

"It's all something if you ask me," I said. "But it gets us no closer to who murdered Isaac or why."

Harvey pondered a moment. "That woman who was killed in the camp. I wonder if Perry or Isaac knew her?"

"Sounds like she was just another prisoner," said Harper. "Don't you think that if he had known her he would have personally shepherded her back into the hut before Isaac could take action?"

"Maybe." Harvey shrugged.

"Mister Harvey," I said. "I just remembered. Did you ever check with housekeeping about any missing master keys?"

"I did, thank you. Nothing has been reported. Sorry." He headed for the door. "Thanks for the news from the front, Maeve." Harvey left, closing the door behind him.

"And that's where we stand now," I said to Harper. "It's irritating." I slapped my hand down on the examining table. "Bloody hell, I forget to tell you both something."

"Yes?"

"Remember the woman with the bad attitude in the cabin two doors down from Nathaniel?"

"How could I forget her," said Harper.

"I ran into her again today. She was going out for a stroll along the decks."

"It's getting cold out there. Hope she carried a coat."

"The weather doesn't seem to bother her and I hope she catches pneumonia. But this is interesting. She's really attracted to Van Effen."

"You saw them having drinks Saturday night," said Harper.

"And I'm pretty sure he was with her again last night after our dinner." I frowned. "And from what she said to me I'm reasonably certain that they are having a lot more than drinks."

"I guess it takes all kinds, right? As long as she isn't killed on the *Victoria*, it's none of our concern, I think."

"Boss," I began, then let it go. Sometimes the shot on the board wasn't worth the effort to make it.

# VI

You remember Napoleon? Short, stout chappie who came a cropper at Waterloo a while back, finally putting paid to his career as Emperor of the French and sending him into a forced retirement on St. Helena island in the South Atlantic Ocean. Up until that time he had a pretty good run (discounting all the dead people associated with his career) and he owed much of that pretty good run to being a peerless military tactician. But all it takes is one thing to slip up; the Prussians arrive in the nick of time, the British and other allies stand their ground even though they are taking a pounding, the weather delays Napoleon opening the battle by several hours, and the French cavalry is sub-par to the English. The end result is *soufflé* a la Napoleon.

When I was a young student, my father said that Napoleon could have dealt with any one of those things, but all four at once was too much. I agreed with him then, and I had to agree with him now. I was feeling much like Napoleon must have felt when he saw the Prussian reinforcements coming over the hill and realized that the jig was up, and, like Napoleon, my problems just kept riding over the top of the hill.

I spent the rest of the day in the hospital and surgery with Doctor Harper discussing what we'd learned so far. Every track we followed took us to a dead end, so our discussion was much like our day – nothing happened.

The seas were running calm, the cold was keeping most passengers indoors, and our medical services were fortunately not needed. Alice finally deigned to join us in the hospital about an hour before I was ready to leave because Joel was going to meet Harry for dinner and needed time to do his toilet and dress.

"Anything new happening?" I asked her. She shook her head.

"Van Effen stopped by a couple of hours after you left to check on things. He said he would be back to escort Joel to the restaurant and turn him over to Mr Winston. I think he was still intent on going to the movie."

"And I bet I know who he's going with," I said. Harper barely concealed a smirk; if Alice hadn't been there I would have punched him on the arm.

"Joel called Harry on the 'phone and told him what had happened to his shop," continued Alice. "Judging from Joel's reaction, Harry offered him plenty of sympathy."

"I shouldn't wonder," I said. "Harry told Joel and I on Saturday night that he had been the victim of just such a mishap several years ago."

Alice was surprised. "Really? How did he come back from it?"

"Hard work and perseverance. Those seem to be two qualities that Harry Winston possesses in more than ample supply. I'm sure he's always going to go from success to success. As for Joel, if this run of bad luck continues, we may be getting on to changing his name to Job." I sighed. "Alice, I know Joel hasn't been sitting still, no matter what you tell him. What's he done?"

"He sent a wireless to the New York police and reported the crime," said Alice. "The Yank Bobbies are going to take a statement from his neighbor Mr Selber, go into the shop to investigate, and begin looking for Mr Jenkins."

"Best of luck to them. He's got at least a two-day head start." I sighed. "What's your opinion, Boss?"

Harper shrugged. "I think you're probably right. He could be in Chicago or approaching Los Angeles by now. Or on a boat headed to who knows where."

I rubbed my forehead. "You're a lot of help. I guess I should go update the Captain on our progress, or rather, lack thereof." I looked at Alice. "And then I'm going to eat and get a decent night's rest. So mind the door when you come in."

"Yes, Mother."

"And stop calling me mother," I said, closing the door on their laughter behind me.

The Captain, predictably, showed little emotion as he listened to me relate everything that had happened starting with dinner the previous night. When all was said and done (and I have to admit I was getting pretty put out with having to constantly update people; I'm sure that never happened to Hercule Poirot) the story told by Perry evinced no more than a comment or two; he was more interested in the robbery of the store and how it might connect to Isaac's death. With an admonition to keep him up to date (again), I was dismissed from the Presence. I descended to the Promenade Deck to take a turn in hopes the brisk wind would push the little grey cells into action, but the brisk wind won out and I went inside and down the stairs to A Deck.

Whether by accident or design I found myself in the corridor that led to the staterooms of Joel and his uncle. I tried the handle on his uncle's stateroom and found it securely locked; Mister Harvey, true to his word this morning, had apparently had the old lock changed. A closer inspection of the lock revealed that to be the fact. There were no scratches around the keyhole as they always got from constant use, and presumably, Joel had the new key. I bent and peered through the keyhole. The escutcheon still seemed to be stuck in the upright position; through what little ambient light reached the cabin I could very faintly make out what I thought was the couch in the sitting room, but everything else was too dim. I straightened just as a door opened a few cabins away and Harry Winston stepped out.

"Nurse Chandler. How nice to see you again. Have you had any success yet?"

"If by success you mean answering any questions, no, I'm afraid not. There are so many little mysteries surrounding Mr Isaac's murder that I think they're obscuring any path toward a solution."

He nodded. "I have to agree with you. I spent the afternoon thinking over what Perry and Van Effen told us, and then those thoughts were pushed out when Joel told me about the store being robbed in New York." Harry frowned. "This case has more facets to it than a round brilliant cut diamond."

"Honestly, I'd rather have the diamond."

"So would I," he said and glanced down at his watch. "I've got to go meet Joel for dinner. We're dining in the Observation Lounge."

"What about the robbery at the store? Doctor Harper thinks Mr Jenkins may be halfway across the United States by now."

"Maybe," said Harry. "But I don't think he'll be carrying all those gems with him. If we are to believe he cleaned out the store, he already had someone who was going to take the loot off his hands."

"A fence, you mean. Someone who deals in stolen goods, buys and sells them."

"Yes, that's right. For a sea-going British nurse your knowledge of the American criminal underworld is astounding, and possibly troubling." He gave me a grin.

"I read the *New York Daily Mirror*, Mr Winston." I paused. "Well, not entirely true, I read the Winchell column in the *Mirror*, but it has plenty of gangland stuff in it. I know that once a jewel has gone through several hands in quick succession, it's almost impossible to find it again. Mr Jenkins may have been working with several fences to distribute the goods."

Harry nodded. "And I always thought Winchell was there for the entertainment value. Who knew?" He consulted his watch once again. "I really must go. Let's catch up in the morning, say around ten? I'll meet you in the writing room." He strode away, leaving me with another problem riding over the hill toward what I fervently hoped would not be my Waterloo, viz.:

Who was powerful enough to fence an entire store inventory of gems, even a store as small and shoddy as Nathaniel Isaac's? That's the thought I was pondering as I rapped on Joel's door, and the answer that was forming at the back of my mind gave every indication of being unpleasant.

A moment later I heard the key being turned and then the door opened. "Maeve," Joel said. "Come in."

"Don't you ever ask who's out there first? I could have been the last person your uncle saw."

He hung his head sheepishly. "You're right. I'm far too trusting."

"Well, don't worry. I'm sure your coming association with Mr Winston will cure you of that ailment. Speaking of, I was just talking with him in the corridor and he said the two of you are having dinner tonight. He was on his way up to the Observation Lounge. I don't want to keep you. Have you heard any more news from New York?"

He shook his head. "Nothing."

"Mr Winston thinks Jenkins may have already had someone lined up to take all the jewelry in your store off his hands."

"Does he know who that person might be?"

"No. But I have a suspicion. Dutch Schultz would have the power to take on a store like your uncle's and move the gems."

Joel frowned. "If he's fenced it, I'll never see it back."

I pursed my lips. "If Dutch Schultz fenced it, I think getting the diamonds back is way down on your priority list. Staying alive would be at the top."

Joel paled. "You think he had something to do with my uncle's death?"

"You tell me. You're the one who's been getting threatening phone calls."

"The caller just said there would be big changes in my life if the money wasn't repaid by the due date, but I never thought it would involve killing Isaac."

"You're not exactly dealing with the Bank of England here." I frowned. "What happened to the money? Twenty-eight thousand bucks is a lot of change. Surely there must be something left to return as a show of good faith."

Joel looked uneasy. "I made some bad business decisions to get more money for the store, then tried to recoup my losses gambling. I don't have to tell you how that went."

I frowned. "No, I don't suppose you do."

"What about Mr Jenkins?" I asked.

"What about him?"

"How long had he worked for your uncle?"

"I don't know. I'm twenty, going to be twenty-one in a few months. It seems to me Jenkins has always been there." Joel shrugged. "Maybe he was there from the beginning, when my uncle opened the store in 1903."

"After he got back from the war in South Africa."

Joel nodded. "Yes, that's right. I guess he made enough there while he was partners with Alexander Perry that he could come back and start right up in New York." He paused a moment. "And I still find that story Perry told about the shooting in the camp hard to believe."

"As far as we know Mr Perry has no reason to lie to you. He not only seems to be going out of his way to treat you in a friendly manner but it sounds like he's willing to work behind the scenes to afford you some relief."

Joel frowned. "That's good of you to think so, but I'm not holding out much hope. The diamonds my uncle carried on board are missing, and his store has been cleaned out. I've got nothing, Maeve, except some time in an Antwerp hotel without a cent to spend and a return trip ticket to New York on the *Queen Victoria* to what will probably be my own funeral if I can't pay that money back." He looked around the cabin. "Or maybe they won't even wait until I get off the ship."

The way he laid it out did make it seem pretty bleak, I thought, but I tried to put a light on the positive. "Not true, Joel. You have Alice and you have a dinner with Mr Winston that I'm making you late for. I'm sure he'll want to discuss his future business plans for you, so no, you do not have 'nothing' as you say. You've got plenty and I promise you we'll sort out the rest."

"Well, here's something to sort out that I haven't come up with an answer for yet. Have you figured out how my uncle's killer got out of a locked room?"

I inwardly winced as he touched on a sore spot. "No, sorry. That remains a mystery. And as far as suspects go, it seems the only person on board who had a real grudge with your uncle is Mr Perry. Given recent developments from my point of view the grudge seems to have ended before your uncle was murdered, and Mr Perry doesn't impress me as the phantom-through-the-door murdering type."

"Van Effen?"

I shrugged. "He was hired only Friday and was working for your uncle and now that Isaac is gone he's working for you." There was a polite knock at the door.

"Mr Singer?" asked a voice.

"Speak of the devil," said Joel. He unlocked the door and the imposing bulk of Van Effen entered the room.

"Has everything been quiet?" he asked.

"Yes. Nurse Chandler and I were just discussing some matters."

"As long as it does not pertain to your security."

"Only to my financial security, or rather insecurity. My uncle's shop has been robbed and his long-time clerk is missing."

Van Effen's countenance remained impassive. "I am sorry to hear that. I trust the police are looking into the matter?"

"Yes, but it's doubtful they will turn anything up." Joel shrugged into his coat. "I need to get going."

"Yes, of course." Van Effen and I followed him into the corridor and watched as he locked the door and pocketed the key. Joel gave me a wry smile.

"Not that locking the door does any good."

"I don't think you have anything to worry about," I said.

Joel smirked. "Go ahead and say it. What you really mean is I don't have anything worth stealing."

"Do you?"

"Of course not. I can't even afford dinner." He nodded at me. "Have a good evening, Maeve."

# *Tuesday, March 25, 1930*

I

The Americans have a saying: "Don't take any wooden nickels," and with good reason. A nickel, as you know, is not worth much. From what I've experienced in New York, it's good for a candy bar or cup of coffee, neither of which are very uplifting, unless you happen to be out with someone who carries a flask and offers to charge up your coffee for free. Why those items should be double the price of a copy of the *New York Daily Mirror* (two cents per copy, plus as Harry said, the entertainment value) is beyond me, but I'm no financial wizard. All I know is that a nickel will cover all expenses from one cent up to five cents, and of course, the Yanks, being the hard-headed business-minded folks they are, always expect a real, U.S. Treasury minted nickel in exchange for goods and/or services provided.

But I digress. As you know, a wooden nickel is worth far less than a real nickel which, as we discussed, can actually provide you with some purchasing choices. The wooden nickel, however, is worth nothing. In fact, it costs more for a merchant to have one made as a promotional item, though I suppose like most things they are cheaper when ordered in quantity. However, no matter the cleverness of the slogan or logogram imprinted on the wooden coin, the bearer is reminded by it to be careful in their financial or other endeavours so they don't get stuck with (presumably) wooden nickels. (And also, if the slogan or logogram is indeed clever enough, to grace that merchant with their business, but only by using real nickels.)

As I approached Harry in the Writing Room on the aft Main Deck this Tuesday morning, I couldn't shake the feeling that all I had to offer him was a nice big bag of wooden nickels.

"Maeve," he said, standing up and pulling out a chair from the small corner table where he was sitting. "The Writing Room doesn't appear very popular."

I nodded. "Honestly, I haven't been in here in a year." I looked around at the beautiful paneling and leather upholstered chairs. "Why anyone would write letters at sea has always been a puzzler for me."

"Status," said Harry. "And jealousy. Imagine how important your neighbor or relation will feel when they get a letter or postcard from you with a *Queen Victoria* cancellation on it." He smiled. "And, on the other hand, imagine how jealous they will be that you were on the ship and they were not."

I laughed. "Maybe, but Mister Harvey says more people take home the stationary than use it on board."

Harry smiled again. "I'm sure your housekeeping department also has a run on towels, too, like any upper-end hotel." He sat and beckoned to me to do the same. "Well, to business at hand." He gazed around the room. "I've been giving some thought to those *shloks*, those fake diamonds. They are exceptional craftsmanship; even Mr Van Effen thought so. I don't know of anyone making anything like them today."

"So they're old?"

He nodded. "I would hazard a guess at 1890's. Definitely the highest-end costume jewelry, meant to fool almost anyone. I've seen enough of it in my time."

"Where did it all come from?"

Harry shrugged. "Most likely European. The thing that interests me, though, is why an obviously valuable diamond was mixed in among all of the counterfeits."

"Maybe the killer thought it was a counterfeit, too."

Harry took a sip of water. "I thought of that. It would certainly explain why it was there. As I said before, I can't imagine anyone wasting a valuable stone in that fashion."

"So if the killer thought it was, what did you say, *shlok*?" Harry nodded. "Then they know little about diamonds."

"Or they know a lot and just aren't letting on."

"Not encouraging, Harry." I thought a moment. "You said something the other day about the Brazilian diamond being a symbol."

"Yes." Harry crossed his legs. "We know Isaac made his living with diamonds, and that diamonds – at least what looked like diamonds – ended his life. But with the one exception, this Brazilian stone, the diamonds that ended his life were all false. I believe it was to show that the killer was proving to Isaac and anyone else in the business that he, the killer, knows the difference between lies and truth, especially where Isaac was concerned."

"Harry, I hate to shoot holes in your balloon," I said. "But what if the killer believed all of those gems to be real?"

Harry shook his head. "Ah, there you have me. Then we just have someone with a grudge against Isaac who chose a symbolic way of killing him, though again I can't imagine any real *diamantaire* would waste precious stones that way knowing they would never get them back." He drummed fingers on the table top. "No, I keep going back to the fakes used knowingly by someone who knew they were *shlok*, but who also added the real diamond into the mix to tell the world they knew the truth about Isaac."

"And which truth would that be?" I asked. "From what we've learned about Mr Isaac the truth about him seems to be a commodity in short supply."

"How about the way he supposedly shot that woman at the internment camp? The story Mr Perry told us?"

"If it's a true story," I said.

"Why would Perry make up such a thing?"

"I don't know. He was my primary suspect but only briefly; as I pointed out to Joel he doesn't seem the sort. I believe he's truly trying to help Joel, through what misplaced sense of chivalry I don't know."

"What about Van Effen?"

"Now there's a question. He's hired as protection for Isaac, thoroughly mucks up that job, and now he's all over Joel." I frowned. "Except when he's at the bar or going to the movies, but then he makes sure Joel is locked in or in the immediate company of friendly faces."

"And did he make sure Isaac was locked in?"

"Good point. Much as I hate it, in his defence he did say that Isaac had given him the evening off. Maybe Isaac was expecting a visitor and wanted some privacy?"

"Something to consider," said Harry. "Is Isaac's cabin locked up?"

I nodded. "New lockset, new key, and Joel has it."

Harry paused a moment. "Did you ever locate Isaac's box that went missing from the vault?"

I shook my head. "No, and Joel doesn't have a good idea of what was inside of it. I wonder if anything was inside of it to begin with. But if it was holding the fakes, then we know where they are. If someone brought the fakes aboard to use on Isaac and Isaac's box was holding real diamonds, it's anyone's guess. I really haven't given it that much thought. I would imagine that the box itself has long ago been emptied of whatever was inside, fake or real, and it's sitting at the bottom of the North Atlantic by now, keeping its former owner company."

"What about this Jenkins fellow making off with the contents of Isaac's store. Have you or Joel heard anything new on that front?"

"Not a word. Jenkins is still missing."

"And no one has noticed any sudden flood in stones on the New York market."

Harry sighed. "I sent a wire to a friend in New York, asking him to keep an eye out for anything out of the ordinary. As you might expect, the diamond district is all a-flutter over the crime. I'm confident something will turn up."

"Even if something does turn up, even if those diamonds are recovered, they'll be held as evidence. It could be years before they are returned to Joel." I thought a moment. "Or they'll disappear out of the evidence room."

"Maeve, you're letting your imagination run away with you. Don't go begging trouble."

I nodded. "You're right. We've got enough to think about here on the *Victoria* without speculating on New York. Either they catch Jenkins or they don't. Nothing we can do about it from here. I just wonder, though – "

"What?"

"I wonder if the store robbery was something spur of the moment and convenient, or if it was part of some larger plan to even a score with Isaac or Joel."

Winston looked at me. "Have you always been so suspicious?

"Not hardly. I was once a carefree young girl, believe it or not."

Harry repressed a smile. "And what happened?"

"Life happened." I stood up from the table. "You know who would be big enough to handle all of those store diamonds? Dutch Schultz."

"Not someone you want to get tangled up with, Maeve. Even from this distance." Harry stood up and shook his head. "I'm sorry, this is a path I don't think you should follow."

"That's the thing about me, Harry. I don't choose the paths. The paths choose me."

**II**

Have you ever played the game Blind Man's Buff? No, that's not an error. Its actual name really is Blind Man's Buff, not Bluff. If you don't believe me, go look it up yourself. We called it Buff when I was a child. Anyway, whatever you call it, you remember how it's played. One person is blindfolded and spun around, and then they try to catch one of the other players. The other players, of course, try to avoid this by dancing away from the one in the blindfold, or by calling out false instructions, or by doing nothing more devious than hiding in plain sight. (In plain sight to everyone but the player in the blindfold, that is.)

I never liked wearing the blindfold as a child – given my propensity for tripping over and running into things when I could see, much less being blindfolded – and I liked it even less as an adult. Sure, I wasn't actually wearing a blindfold (and a good thing too, because I was still tripping and running into things) but there were still too many things that I couldn't see that were no doubt hiding in plain sight. The one thing I could see clearly, though, was the impressive sparkler Joel had gotten from Harry to give to Alice.

"It's beautiful, Joel. I'm sure Alice will love it." I handed the delicate ring back to him. "Harry did you well."

"I know." He examined the ring closely, holding it between his thumb and forefinger. "I don't think there was anything to match it in my uncle's shop." He slipped the ring into his inside tuxedo coat pocket. The evening wear, a rental, had been provided by Mister Harvey. "Not that I can remember, anyway. And not that I'm ever going to know."

We were seated in the lobby before the giant great doors to the First-Class dining salon. Van Effen, implacable as ever, was standing close by smoking a cigarette. The doors were closed; the evening seating wouldn't open for another fifteen minutes, though people were beginning to arrive and mingle. It hadn't taken much spadework on my part to have Mister Harvey secure one of the intimate smaller dining rooms in a corner off the main floor so that Joel and Alice could have some privacy for their big night; with the work Mister Harvey and I had put in on this I felt miserable that Joel had an air of gloom draped over his shoulders like a thread-bare blanket. I reached over and squeezed his hand. "Joel, don't give up. The jewelry from the shop may be recovered."

"Not a chance. Any trace of that merchandise has been erased by now."

"The police are looking for Mr Jenkins," I said. "They'll find him."

"Closing the barn door after the horses are gone." Joel stretched his legs out in front of him. "It's sad, isn't it? My uncle murdered in a horrible fashion and all I'm worried about is getting his jewelry back in my hands." He gave me a half smile. "Oh, and not getting myself and everyone around me killed because I owe money to some gangster." He shook his head. "You saw me yesterday. I couldn't even shed a tear for the old man. Sure, he put a roof over my head and tried to give me an education in the business, but beyond that I think he viewed me as a huge burden put on him."

"Well, put that out of your mind for tonight and think about this instead." I nodded my head toward an approaching vision in blue. "If that doesn't make you feel better nothing will."

Joel gaped. There is simply no other word for it. Alice was wearing a curve-hugging floor length bias-cut dress that flared out slightly at her slim ankles. The fabric clung to her form like the skin on a grape; her dark hair was freshly waved by one of the *Victoria's* female hair stylists. Alice and I had shared wardrobe items in the past, but neither of us had anything remotely resembling the slinky plunging firecracker she was wearing now. That dress had come out of one of the fancy shops on the Promenade Deck – a shopping area that rivalled anything Fifth Avenue or Regent Street could offer. Alice, being universally liked on the *Victoria*, had managed to obtain use of it for the evening. Finally, her neck was bare by design, not a single piece of jewelry adorned her; mere jewelry couldn't hope to compete with the image she was presenting. I glanced over at Joel. His mouth was still hanging open. I elbowed him in the ribs, none too gently, and he stumbled to his feet.

"A – A – A–," he stammered.

"Alice," I whispered.

"Alice," said Joel. "You look – "

"Beautiful," I said, *sotto voce*. Joel looked down at me.

"Thanks, Maeve, I think I can take it from here."

"Fine." I stood and sniffed. "I know when I'm not wanted." I reached out and took Alice's hands in mine. "You are gorgeous and I'm so happy for you." I leaned forward to whisper in her ear. "Make sure he gets down on one knee like all the movies."

Alice giggled. "Thank you, Maeve. For everything."

I nodded. The doors to the dining room were opening. "Go have a fabulous time. I'll leave the light on for you." I watched them walk forward, her arm through his, toward the maître' de station and Monsieur DuMont. DuMont, I have to tell you, can be a bit of a prig, but he wasn't going to be so tonight. I caught his eye and gave him a stare that meant he'd be washing dishes if he was lousy to the happy couple, then took my leave. Van Effen put out his cigarette and drifted inside the restaurant to take up station outside of the happy couple's private dining room.

On my way back down to the hospital I took a detour through the corridor where Joel and Harry's cabins were located, just to make sure things were still quiet.

The hallway was still. Without doubt, most of the guests staying in these opulent cabins had gone to the restaurant for their evening meal and then would be off to one of the bars until the wee hours. I knew Joel's cabin was empty, and I listened for a moment outside of Harry's door but heard nothing; ditto with Mr Perry's cabin next door. Undoubtedly both men were at dinner as well. A few more steps brought me to Isaac's former cabin. I tested the knob and the door was locked securely. Curiousity got the better of me and I stooped to peer through the keyhole.

The view was limited in scope, but nothing had changed. I could just glimpse Isaac's cane leaning up in a corner of his bedroom near the bed, and the death chair was still in the position we'd found Isaac's body in on Sunday morning. I stood and sighed, tried the locked door one more time, then made my way down to C Deck. Doctor Harper was still the only person in the hospital. I sat down in the chair behind the desk in the reception room.

"Yes?" he asked. "How goes the matchmaking?"

"Don't think of it as losing a nurse, Boss," I said. "Think of it as gaining a diamond salesman."

"Not much call for one of those around here." Harper leaned against the wall. "So, he's actually asking Alice to marry him?"

"Looks that way. Mister Harvey was lovely to give up one of the corner rooms. And I gave Monsieur DuMont the evil eye as I was leaving to keep him in line." I idly toyed with a pencil on the desk. "And of course, Van Effen is standing by just outside the door in case anything goes amiss." The thought of Van Effen bearing down on the prim DuMont cheered me up a bit. "The ring is beautiful, by the way. I don't know how much Joel is going to have to work to pay for it, but it's absolutely gorgeous."

"And Alice?"

I gave a deep sigh. "She was utterly entrancing. I can't thank everyone enough for pitching in for her."

Harper shrugged. "Remember what you told me when I first came to work here five months ago? That it's a big family?"*

"I remember." I rolled the pencil between my palms. "And now I'm going to have to break in a new nurse. I've barely gotten done with you."

"Thanks." Harper pulled up the chair on the opposite side of the desk and sat. "Anything new?"

I broke the pencil. "Does that tell you anything? There's nothing new. As I told Joel, I don't think Mr Perry is capable of sliding in and out of cabins unseen, much less killing someone, and this Van Effen character had just been employed by Isaac on Friday and had nothing to gain

---

* See Book One: *Shadow of the Queen*

that I can see – he's in the same situation Joel is in, a boat trip to Cherbourg, a train to Antwerp, a few days of vacation in Antwerp unless Isaac's diamonds can be found, a train to Cherbourg, then a boat trip back to New York. All expenses paid by the late Mr Isaac. And Van Effen has now transferred his security duty over to Joel, when he's not out with Miss Thomas."

Harper crossed his arms. "I'm sure she's a big girl and knows what she's doing."

"She's anything but big, if you remember. She's a trim little thing with perfect hair and teeth. I hate her. Let's talk about something more pleasant, like how Mister Harvey is fronting Joel and Alice's romantic dinner tonight."

Harper laughed. "Deep down Mister Harvey is a big teddy bear, for all his bluster." His face grew serious. "I've been thinking about that use of curare."

"And?"

"No one in the United Kingdom uses it. I did more reading in the medical library in the dispensary. The drug was discovered, at least by the English, in about 1595. The intrepid Sir Walter Raleigh trekked up the Amazon and encountered tribes using it on their blow gun darts and arrows. There were a couple of studies done in the last century that showed it effective in treatment of strychnine poisoning and tetanus. A man named Arthur Lawen tried to use it as an anesthetic around 1912 in Leipzig." He shrugged. "Other than that, nothing we didn't already know."

"I wonder if it's ever been used for hunting anything outside of birds and small animals in the Amazon? I'm sure someone in one of those tribes figured out it would be a perfect way to dispatch an enemy. Maybe we have a first for a murder using it outside of the Amazon basin. You could write it up in the medical journals, Boss."

"Not what I'd prefer to be remembered for, thanks." Harper stood and stretched. "I'm going to go get something to eat and retire early. Think you can hold down the fort until Alice gets back?"

"If she gets back, you mean?" I nodded. "Yes, I can do that. Go get your dinner. See you tomorrow."

"Well, if you go out, be sure to lock the door and turn off the light. Goodnight."

"Goodnight, Boss." The door closed gently behind him.

Lock the door and turn out the light indeed. Who did he think I was, a babe in swaddling? Of course I would lock the door and turn out the –

Light.

It suddenly blazed in on me that not a half hour before I had just looked through the keyhole into Isaac's cabin and seen it clear as day – which meant that someone had been inside that cabin and had left the light on.

Or worse, was inside Isaac's cabin right now.

'm sure you've all heard of those inventor types whose inspiration always seems to come to them in a flash. As a child I often wondered if that flash was accompanied by a boom or a puff of smoke, maybe with multi-coloured sparks in it. Maybe it set their hair on fire. I've seen pictures of Thomas Edison, and he looks pretty mild-mannered to me. I can't really imagine him running around his laboratory with his hair on fire, screaming "Eureka, I've got it!" or whatever it is that inventors scream when they figure out the electric light or anything else the man's come up with to date. All that my flash of inspiration gave me was a headache, and I went into the examining room to get a couple of aspirin.

Sadly, there was no way for me to investigate this new little mystery for a while. The only people I could get keys to Isaac's cabin from were both topside and both busy. I could either obtain the room key in Joel's pocket or the master in Harvey's; asking anyone else for a master was opening a can of worms I didn't care to get into. Joel had probably popped his question by now, and Mister Harvey had his hands full with overseeing dinner and the lovebirds in the First-Class salon; neither would be available for hours. I pulled out a chair and sat down to wait.

Why would someone turn a light on in Isaac's cabin? The answer, obviously, is because they needed to see – but see what? Isaac's body was consigned to the deep and there was nothing of value in the room. Why risk an entry when anyone could show up in the corridor, including Joel or Van Effen, to ask unsettling questions? I closed my eyes, leaned back in the chair, and immediately saw the flaw in my reasoning. While we thought there was nothing of interest in the room, someone else obviously thought otherwise. I glanced at the clock on the wall and gave a sigh; the wait to get a key and investigate was going to be interminable.

It seemed like I had just drifted off when a sudden jarring snapped me awake. My first thought was that we'd dropped a propeller blade. The *Victoria's* three propellers are huge, about 22 feet across with three blades each and weighing in at 30 tons per propeller; dropping a blade off one of them would certainly jolt the ship. I grabbed both sides of the chair with my hands and flashed my eyes open.

"Wake up, sleepy head," said Alice, standing in front of me in all her glory. She was holding a shoe after presumably taking it off to rap my chair and startle me awake.

"Seriously?" I said, waiting for my heart rate to drop. "You scared the bloody hell out of me."

"Can't help that." She waved her left hand under my nose. "Look."

The ring Joel had shown me earlier in the evening sparkled on her finger. I did an appreciative and expected 'ooh-ah.' "Beautiful," I said.

"Isn't it?" Alice admired it, moving her hand to let the examination room lights play across the diamond.

"So, spill it," I said. "How did it happen?"

"I feel just like a princess."

"That's the bee's knees, Cinderella. How did it happen?"

Alice clasped her hands and rolled her eyes. "I could relive this evening for the rest of my life." She dragged a chair over and sat next to me. "We had one of the little private dining rooms where no one could see or disturb us. Mister Harvey is such a dear to do that for us. Monsieur DuMont personally escorted us to our table – he's such a romantic, don't you think? All of the French are, I think."

I nodded. Personally, I felt it better to keep my feelings for Monsieur DuMont out of the conversation. "Yes, of course," I said.

"There was already a bucket of champagne at the table. Monsieur DuMont even poured our first glasses. I'm sure the waiter who took our order was personally selected by Mister Harvey; he was so nice."

"Yes, we've established that Mister Harvey is a saint."

"Oh, no, I meant the waiter."

I nodded. "Of course you did. Carry on."

Alice settled into the chair and leaned forward, at least as far as her dress would allow her without spillage. "It more than made up for the presence of Mr Van Effen standing outside the door." She reflected for a moment. "But he was all business and very quiet. Do you know he didn't even bring that silly hat with him?"

"Hard to imagine."

Alice nodded. "We had a lovely meal, and talked of this and that; Joel's future in the diamond business, and living in New York – "

"You're going to live in New York?"

Alice looked surprised. "Of course. That's where his business is, or will be, once all of this gets straightened out."

"You do remember that you are a British subject?"

She shrugged. "I was born in South Africa."

"Which makes you a British subject."

Alice looked perplexed. "Really?"

I shook my head in amazement. "Have you never looked at your passport?"

"A minor point to be overcome in the great scheme of things." Alice smoothed out her dress. "Anyway," she crooned, "no matter where we live will be perfect because we are so in love."

I managed a soothing smile for her fluffy pink clouds. "Of course you are."

She patted her hands on her lap. "So we got done with the dinner, another bottle of champagne came out, the waiter brought us our desserts, and then," she paused, milking the moment for all it was worth. "And then, he said the words I'll remember for all my life, just like something out of the movies. He said 'Mr Winston says he thinks I have a bright future ahead of me, and I'm going to learn a lot from him. All that's missing is you.'"

"Swoon," I said. Alice nodded enthusiastically.

"And then I said to him, 'I'm right here' and he said, 'And you're going to stay right there, if I have anything to do with it.'"

I had to admit to myself that it was getting exciting. I leaned forward. "And then?"

"And then he got up, came around the table, got down on one knee, and said 'I've only known you a few days, but I feel like you've always been a part of my life. And I want you to stay in my life.'"

If it wouldn't have completely compromised my devil-may-care exterior, I swear I would have squealed at this point. "And?"

"He presented the ring to me and said 'Alice, will you marry me?'"

I lost it anyway and squealed in delight for my best friend, reaching across to hug her. "I'm so happy for you, Alice."

"After I said yes, Joel said it was the happiest moment of his life. And I said the same." I reached up for a box of tissues on the counter behind me and offered them. Alice dabbed at her eyes, as did I. "And then he said the strangest thing."

"What?"

Alice sniffled. "He said that now his uncle would never take this prize away from him. He said that when he was only about six or seven years old, he wanted a bag of marbles. Other boys at his school had them, and when he asked his uncle for them he just griped at Joel. Told him they were nothing but glass baubles meant for fools."

"How horrible for a young child," I said.

"Yes," said Alice. "And then Joel said look at how he died. Glass baubles meant for fools." Alice shuddered. "And you know, Joel said he never got his bag of marbles, either."

I smiled. "But as he said, he has you and no one can take you away from him. As to the marbles, I think one of the shops on the promenade carries them."

"I've already picked a bag out. Call it an engagement gift." Alice laughed lightly. "It's about all I can afford, anyway."

"He'll love them," I said. "What are you going to do right now? Now that you're affianced, I mean."

"I'm resigning my position. As of our arrival in Cherbourg Friday morning." Alice gave me a weak smile. "I'm going with Joel to Antwerp to the diamond show. I'll find some part-time nursing work to do in the States when we get back, and I'll apply for citizenship." Alice frowned.

"I'll have to tell my mum, but she'll understand." She put out a hand to me. "Sorry to leave you short."

"Don't you worry about us. We'll get by. Not to change the subject, but where is Joel now?"

Alice smiled. "He was meeting Mr Winston in the Observation Lounge, I think." She smiled at me. "I just wanted to come down and tell you everything," she said, hugging me again. "And to also get out of this dress and these shoes, they're killing me."

"And it's a rental, kind of," I reminded her. "Wouldn't do to bring it back all tear-stained."

"Oh, no," said Alice. "I'll go get out of it and hang it up, then I'm going to bed. Do be a dear and try not to wake me when you come in?"

"I doubt a dropped propeller could wake you tonight," I said. "Again, very happy for you – for you both."

"Thanks, Maeve." Alice stood, albeit wobbly, and kicked her other shoe off as she put a hand on my shoulder. "I guess I had a bit more champagne than I thought I had."

I handed her the other shoe and rose and offered her an arm. "Need help getting back to the cabin?"

She shook her head. Barefoot, with pumps clasped in one hand, she meandered out of the examination room, if not on a straight course at least under her own power. A moment later I heard the main entry door open and close. I looked at the wall clock. It was 23 hundred hours. Hopefully no one would need medical care for the next hour or so. I left the hospital and headed topside for the Observation Lounge.

# IV

The *Queen Victoria*, like any fashionable hotel, has a couple of hot night spots that are always in demand – so in demand that the only way to rid them of clientele is to turn on the lights and regretfully ask people to leave. Mister Harvey says both places mint more money than the Crown, especially with the thirsty Americans taking a break from Prohibition.

All the way forward is the Observation Lounge, with its superb view over the bow of the ship. Almost all the way aft is the Atrium Lounge, with its skylights and glass-domed ceiling providing magnificent views of the stars overhead during clement weather, a rarity on the North Atlantic run, but spectacular on clear nights. Both spots are packed during daylight hours, and at night it's shoulder-to-shoulder.

There are several other smaller bars, of course, but they are much more intimate. There's the Rose Bar on the Main Deck, the First and Second Class Smoking Rooms on the Promenade Deck have their own bars as does the Third Class Smoking Room on A Deck (though people smoked all over the ship; I never knew why the ship's architects devoted very expensive and large rooms to it) and there's even a very tiny bar in the Writing Room on the Main Deck for those who couldn't channel their inner F. Scott Fitzgerald without a stiffish gin and tonic. And then of course I've told you about the crew pub, the Boar's Head, but I only knew of one passenger to ever make it down there and he was a music hall comic from America who just wanted to entertain the folks by trying out new material. (I think I remember he called himself Bob Hope, but I don't know if anything ever became of him.)

The good thing about the Observation Lounge is that it was crowded, and my nursing uniform stood out a little less. (Though not much.) The bad thing about the Observation Lounge is that it was crowded, which made finding people difficult, especially when you were my size. By standing up on my tiptoes I finally located Harry and Joel sitting together at a small table at one end of the bar, but not before painfully stumbling over two chairs and nearly knocking over a waiter with a full tray of drinks.

"Maeve," said Joel. "What a welcome surprise."

"I hear congratulations are in order."

He nodded. "Alice said she was going to tell you all about it."

"It sounds like a perfectly magical evening." I turned to Harry. "Mr Winston, how are you?"

"Ah, I'm just basking in the afterglow of providing the ring that made all of this possible and looking forward to putting my new employee to work when we reach Antwerp." He pointed at Joel. "Once we get checked in and set up I'll be examining the other wares while this young man minds the shop."

"I'll be meeting other dealers and taking names and enquiries," said Joel.

"And don't worry for your friend's financial health in this union, Maeve. I'll teach Joel how to have a good hand and find the *metsiya*."

"What?" I asked. Harry smiled at me.

"I'm sorry, Maeve. A 'good hand' simply means that someone has the skill, not to mention luck, that's needed to deal in diamonds and other gems. '*Metsiya*' means a bargain – like that emerald I found in the store window when I was just a boy."

I nodded. "Always happy for the chance to expand my vocabulary."

"I can't wait, Harry," said a beaming Joel. He glanced over at the bar and I could see Van Effen lounging against it, a drink in his hand. "Mainly I can't wait to be rid of my shadow."

"You're still alive, aren't you?" I asked. "I don't think you need to dispense with Mr Van Effen's services just yet."

"What do you mean?"

"Isaac's cabin has had a visitor."

Joel put down his drink. "What?"

Harry leaned forward. "Joel, don't you have the key?"

"Right here." He took it out of a pocket. "And that's a new lock that Mister Harvey had installed."

"Yes, it is," I said. "Which means our visitor used a pass key."

Harry frowned. "When did this happen? How did you find out?"

I shrugged. "I'm just naturally nosy. Last night I went by and peeped through the keyhole. There was faint light coming in from the outside deck, I suppose, through the bedroom porthole that we opened the drapes on Sunday morning. Tonight, at about the same time, I peeped through the keyhole again and saw the room. The faint light had been replaced by one or two electric lights that weren't on the night before."

"Was the door locked?" asked Harry.

"Both times, yes."

"I'll be damned," said Joel.

I looked around at the raucous crowd. "Do you think you two might be able to tear yourselves away from this bacchanalia and pay a visit to that cabin with me?"

"What about him?" Joel indicated Van Effen.

"I don't think you could stop him from coming," I said. "And God forbid we need him, but if we do, he's there." I shook my head. "I can't imagine any reputable Silver Ring bookie giving us good odds against a murderer," I said, "but then my faith in humanity has been sorely tested over the past few days." Joel collected Van Effen and we were off.

As we approached the end of the corridor Van Effen motioned us all to silence, indicating that we should take up positions on either side of the cabin door. He knelt and peered through the keyhole, then looked up at us.

"Very dim," he whispered.

"What if there's someone inside?" asked Joel. "Maybe they got here just ahead of us and went to turn off the light, and now they're listening to us out here?"

"Then there are four of us and one of them," said Harry. He looked at Van Effen. "Five if you count him twice." Van Effen gave Harry a crocodile smile and polite inclination of his head.

"Thank you, Mr Winston. Mr Singer, the key, please."

"Now?" Joel looked down the corridor. "What if someone comes by?"

"Then we are letting ourselves into your uncle's cabin," I said.

"No, no," said Joel. I meant, what if *someone* comes by?"

"Again, they'll see we are letting ourselves into your uncle's cabin." I glanced at my watch. "Look, it's late, I think everyone around is asleep. It's now or never."

"I agree with Maeve," said Harry. "Time is not our friend here. Let's do this."

Joel handed the key to Van Effen, who inserted it in the keyhole and turned. The bolt slid back smoothly. He twisted the knob and opened the door. No one jumped out at us, and within ten seconds by the faint glow of Van Effen's cigarette lighter we had ascertained that we were the sole occupants of the stateroom. Van Effen locked the door and put the key in his pocket.

"Great," said Joel. "Let's get some light in here."

"Don't turn on any light," I cautioned. "The keyhole escutcheon is jammed in the upright position."

"One moment," said Van Effen. We heard a faint grinding noise. "It is closed now."

"No light yet," I said. "Don't anybody move." I felt my way to the bathroom and picked up a towel, then came back and handed it to Van Effen. "Stuff it along the threshold," I said. "I'll go close the bedroom porthole curtains before I turn on the bathroom light and crack the door." Van Effen gave me an admiring look and did as he was told. In a moment I rejoined the group. "That will have to suffice. Do you see anything missing?" I whispered to Joel.

"No. And the last time I was in here was yesterday morning to help carry Isaac's body out for burial, and before that to prepare his body."

I nodded. "The last time I was here was the morning we discovered Isaac's body. As far as I can tell nothing's changed. The bed's still not been made, and the chair he died in is still in the same place, as is his cane."

"So why did someone come in?" asked Harry.

"Looking for something, of course. The question is, what was it and did they find it?"

"There's nothing out here," Joel said, indicating the sitting room. "Let's go to the bedroom." Joel led the way to the two-door mirrored armoire standard in almost all First-Class suites and pulled out a suitcase that he set on the bed. "This is Isaac's suitcase. I packed up his belongings inside when I prepared him for burial," he said. "My uncle traveled light, never with a trunk. I put his pajamas and robe in this case and hung his two suits in the armoire to pack later, since I dressed him in that burial shroud."

Van Effen ran his hands down both suits. "There is nothing inside of either of them," he said. Joel nodded, then moved his thumbs to the latches then paused, an expression of concern crossing his face.

"What is it?" I asked.

"These latches are unlocked. I'm sure I locked them when I was done the other day. The key is in my cabin."

"Let me see," said Harry. He knelt beside the bed to get a closer look at the latches, then pulled out his jeweler's loupe and brought it to his eye. "Can't see in this dim light. Close the bedroom door and turn on the light in here."

Van Effen did as instructed and Harry leaned in for a closer look. "There are some very faint scratches along the lock, along with larger scoring," he said. "I would ascribe the larger scoring to someone pushing a key in to open it and close it over and over."

"And the faint scratches?" I asked.

"I think those were done by someone very carefully picking a lock to leave as little clue behind as possible."

"Then why did they leave it unlocked? Seems sloppy to me," I said.

Harry shrugged. "Easier to use a lock pick to open it than a lock pick to lock it, I guess."

Joel popped open the latches and swung the top open. "Everything looks ok." He lifted out the pyjamas and robe, a shaving kit, a notepad and pen, two folded shirts, underlinens and the house slippers.

"Still a lot of room left," I said.

"The suitcase was also holding the box he checked in at the purser's office on Saturday, the one that's gone missing." said Joel. "That explains the apparent extra space." He dug around in the suitcase, then stopped and looked up at us. "Wait a minute. It's gone."

"What's gone?" asked Harry.

"When I was preparing him for burial I discovered he was wearing a delicate chain around his neck. I'd never seen it before. It was made of tiny gold links and suspended a large gold ring. Jews don't wear any ornaments when buried, so I removed it and put it in this side pocket of the suitcase to examine later."

"Why didn't you mention this before?" I asked.

Joel shrugged. "I thought it interesting, but not remarkable. My uncle, as you know, had a very – what's the word – mercurial temperament. I just chalked it up to his eccentricity and thought nothing more about it."

"Are you sure it's gone?" Harry asked.

"Hang on." Joel dug his fingers into a second pocket and after a moment let go with a sigh of relief. He pulled out a slender chain. "Here it is." He stared at it. "But there's a second ring on this chain now. I swear it wasn't there before." He held it out to show. In addition to the larger ring was a smaller ring. Harry took the chain from him.

"So, you're saying someone left this smaller gold ring behind?"

"Why would someone leave two gold rings behind?" I asked.

"I beg your pardon, Nurse Chandler," said Van Effen. "They did not leave two gold rings behind. They left an additional gold ring to the one that was already there."

"All right, fine, but why?" I asked.

Harry held the smaller ring up to the light and examined it closely. "No inscriptions, but I know what it is." He handed the chain and rings to me. "What do you think?"

I looked at the small ring, then on impulse opened the chain clasp, slipped the ring off and slid it onto my left ring finger. It fit perfectly. "This is a woman's wedding ring," I said. "Owner unknown. And the larger one belongs – or belonged – to a man."

"The question is," said Harry, "who?"

I turned to Joel. "Was your uncle married?

He shook his head. "No, at least not that I ever knew. He certainly never talked about having been married. There was never any evidence of it, no pictures, and no children around other than myself."

"Then what explains these rings?" I asked.

Joel shrugged. "Like I said, I saw the large one for the first time when I was dressing him for burial."

"Two wedding bands," said Harry. "Interesting."

The sound of someone unsteadily coming down the corridor who seemed to be caroming from wall to wall made my hair stand on end. Putting my finger to my lips to silence Joel and Harry I jerked open the door and flew out of the bedroom, crossed to the bathroom and hit the switch, choking down an oath as my hip connected with the bathroom sink in the dark. Behind me Van Effen had moved with surprising speed for such a big man, cutting off the bedroom light. By the faint light of the moon and stars shining through the portholes, I limped back to the bedroom and to my surprise saw no one.

"Maeve," hissed Joel. "Down here."

I looked. All three men were crouched behind the bed. "Shove over," I said and crawled in beside them, then glanced over at Van Effen. "Take off your bloody hat, you can see it over the bed." Van Effen removed it. We waited in breathless silence and I strained my ears, finally hearing a key fumbling at a door, a moment's drunken confusion and then the door solidly closing and the lock being turned. I exhaled slowly. Joel was starting to snap the suitcase closed but Van Effen cut him off.

"Put the rings back where you found them and do not lock the case," he said. Joel looked at me. I nodded.

"Van Effen's right. Leave it as you found it."

"I think," said Harry, "we've about pushed our luck as far as it will go."

"Agreed." We carefully made our way back into the sitting room. I put the towel back in the bathroom, opened the bedroom porthole drapes while Van Effen lifted the keyhole escutcheon and securely bent it in the open position and unlocked the door. The corridor was quiet. We slipped out and went our separate ways.

# *Wednesday, March 26, 1930*

I

I suppose you're familiar with the tale of Rip Van Winkle. It's a short story from 1819 by the American author Washington Irving. In it, a Dutch colonist in colonial America meets what turns out to be the ghost crew of Henry Hudson's ship the *Half Moon*, drinks their liquor, and falls into a twenty-year sleep. He awakens to find he's slept through the American Revolutionary War and almost everyone he ever knew is now gone.

I had no pretensions about sleeping twenty years and waking up in 1950, but I think Rip might have afforded me at least twenty minutes. Keyed up as I was over our visit to Nathaniel's cabin, I barely slept at all. In between all the questions racking my brain and the reverberations of Alice's champagne-fueled snoring, there was little left for me but to lie awake and think the remainder of the night away.

For starters, how could person "A" (Joel) live with and be raised by person "B" (Isaac) and never ask person "B" if he'd ever been married? Honestly, men can be such, well, men sometimes.

That the large ring had been Nathaniel's wedding band, I was almost positively certain of. And whatever had happened in that marriage, to whoever it was, he had felt remorse – or whatever he was capable of feeling – so much that he had kept the ring close to his heart all through the years. That someone should add a woman's wedding band to the chain after he died was the real puzzler. Why had it been done, and how had the person who added it known that Isaac wore the chain with the other band on it in the first place?

It was with some irritation that I finally heard Alice's alarm clock go off to signal the start of another day. It was with greater irritation that I watched her energetically throw back the covers and begin making ready for work, apparently with no damage from the champagne consumed the night before. All I wanted to do was pull the covers over my head, but Alice was in a chatty mood.

"I had such trouble falling asleep last night," she said, which I of course knew was patently false. "I wonder if Joel did, too?"

"I'm sure he did," I said, thinking of the rings.

"I'm sure he did, too," she said dreamily.

I sat up in my bunk. "Alice, has Joel ever mentioned if his uncle was married or not?"

"What a question to ask. No, I make it a point to steer conversations away from the subject of his uncle unless he specifically brings them up. Trying to give Joel some rest, you know." Alice finished gathering her toilet articles. "And I can't think of it now, I've got a wedding to plan."

"Are you really going to leave the ship when we get to Cherbourg?"

"Afraid so."

"So, you're going to be more useless than usual for the next few days."

"Probably so," Alice said cheerfully.

I wagged a finger at her. "Try to remember that we've still got other passengers besides Mr Singer."

"I'll do my best, Mother." She gave me a kiss on the cheek. "You'll be late if you don't get up soon." Alice blithely tripped out of our cabin.

"You're welcome," I said as the door closed. "And don't call me mother." I sat dejectedly on my bunk. Sometimes I could just scream.

Forty minutes later, following my morning wash-up and a quick breakfast in the crew mess I was assigned to I made my entry to the hospital. Only Doctor Harper was there to greet me.

"Where's Alice?"

Harper shrugged. "Breezed in and then breezed out to visit the boyfriend," he said. "I'm sorry, I meant fiancé. Did you see the ring?"

"I saw it."

"She's very happy."

"I know." Harper put down the file he'd been thumbing through. "You don't look all that happy."

"I'm not. Someone got into Mr Isaac's locked cabin."

"You're kidding."

"Cross my heart."

"How?" he asked.

"Used a pass key to let himself in, and then locked up behind him." I held up a hand. "Before you ask, Joel has possession of the new key that Mister Harvey sent to him yesterday after changing the lock on Isaac's door. The only way I found out was that I peeped through the keyhole the night before last and it was pretty dim in the stateroom. Last night I peered through the keyhole again and the room was lit up. Someone just forgot to turn out the lights after them."

"And you investigated."

"How could I not? Joel, Van Effen and Harry accompanied me."

"You took passengers on a break and enter? Getting a bit enthusiastic, aren't you?"

"Hardly that. Joel has the key to the cabin. And it was scarcely a break and enter." I reflected on all of us crouched behind the bed. "More like the Marx Brothers movie."*

"Was anything taken?"

I gave a bitter laugh. "No, but something was left."

"I don't follow you," Harper said, sitting behind the desk.

"Joel says Jews are not buried wearing jewelry. When he was preparing his uncle's body, he was surprised to discover his uncle was wearing a small chain around his neck with what appeared to be a man's wedding ring on it. He had never seen it before in his life, so he placed it for safekeeping in his uncle's suitcase, then locked it up and put it in the armoire."

"And the thief took that ring," said Harper.

"No. The thief left behind another gold ring."

Harper wrinkled his brow. "Left behind a gold ring?"

"Yes, a smaller gold ring, threaded onto the chain with the larger ring. Harry and I immediately identified it as a woman's wedding ring. Joel had never seen either of them before." I shook my head. "It kept me up all night, Boss."

"That' easy. It's a message, a forget-me-not," said Harper. "To quote Shakespeare, 'I'll note you in my book of memory.'"

"What?"

Harper leaned back in his chair. "'I'll note you in my book of memory' is a line from *Henry VI, part 2*. Richard Plantagenet was telling the Duke of Somerset that he

_______________

* Maeve is correct. In March of 1930 only one Marx Brothers film was in wide release, *The Cocoanuts*. Their second film *Animal Crackers* would not release until August, 1930.

won't forget the rude words and insults he endured from Somerset."

"So you're saying that in this case, by planting the second ring next to the first, someone was telling Isaac that even in death they'll reject him and won't forget insults from him?"

"Something like that," said Harper.

"I should have paid more attention in my English literature classes," I said. "You're a genius, Boss."

"I've been called worse. Where are you off to?"

"Need to talk with Harry. Be back later."

"Don't worry about me," called Harper as I left. "I can always draft someone from engineering to help set any broken bones."

Harry was engrossed in the day's copy of *The Victory* when I found him in the Observation Lounge. He looked up at me, folded the paper neatly and put it on the table. "To what do I owe this morning visit? Do you have another cabin that you want to investigate in the dead of night?"

I shook my head. "No, that was plenty for me." I sat down across from him. "I had an epiphany about those rings. Rather, Doctor Harper helped me realize something. They belong together."

"Surely that was obvious, Maeve."

"Yes, but not in the way you think. I know you, as a jeweler, will find this hard to believe, but sometimes a girl will return a ring to a hopeful suitor."

Harry smiled. "Not one of my rings, I hope."

"Of course not. But it does happen, you'll concede?"

"Yes, from time to time."

"Then I think that's what happened. Someone returned that ring to Mr Isaac, only they returned it thirty or so years late."

"Who? As far as we know, Isaac never married."

"That's right," I said. "As far as we know. But not as far as someone else may know. I think it's time that we talked to Mr Perry again."

"You didn't think he was telling the truth in that story about Isaac and himself in Kimberley?" asked Harry.

I shook my head. "I believe he was telling the truth. But I'm beginning to think he left some of the truth out. I wonder if he was ever married, for instance. He's a handsome older gentleman. Well spoken. As a woman, it's hard for me to believe he wasn't scooped up years ago."

"I'll take your word for it." Harry stood. "Where do you suppose we'll find him?"

"He impressed me as a rather gregarious person. I'm betting he's here on the Promenade Deck. Let's try the First-Class smoking room."

The First-Class smoking room was almost completely aft of the Observation Lounge, which was completely forward. On the hike to the rear of the ship I recounted last night's proposal scene as told by Alice. Harry laughed. "They're certainly starting out small, in rented dresses and such. Joel's a go-getter though. In a lot of ways, he reminds me of me."

"Well, he certainly thinks the world of you."

"And I of him. He's got a marvelous career out in front of him." Harry rubbed his forehead as we walked. "If we could only get our hands on all the diamonds he has coming to him."

"I know."

"His uncle's shop and the diamonds his uncle purportedly brought on the ship. All into thin air. It's dizzying."

"Agreed," I said. "And I believe there are common threads that run through it all. Revenge, deception, and an overall bitterness that would make quinine taste like sugar water."

"You have a way with words, Maeve." Harry nodded to the attendant who opened the door to the smoking room. The attendant gave me a look.

"Medical emergency," I said to him. He nodded.

"I've got it, Nurse. Mum's the word. Whatever you say, Nurse. Have a good day." He gave me a wink and closed the doors behind us, ignoring, as so many did, the look I gave him.

The First-Class smoking room loomed before us. Like the First-Class dining salon, the smoking room towered up two decks in height. From our vantage point, on the Promenade Deck, the ceiling of the smoking room pierced the Sun Deck above with a dome that let in light from outside and was at the same time lit from inside. Magnificent carpeting was throughout, the overstuffed chairs were all covered in a dusky maroon leather that looked like they had been stolen from one of the better clubs on Pall Mall, and rich wood veneers covered the walls. It was truly a temple to tobacco.

"Not too shabby," said Harry. "Makes you wish you had a pipe like Sherlock Holmes."

"Don't get carried away, Mr Winston. I should hate to have to begin calling you Watson." I pointed. "There's Mr Perry."

Alexander Perry was comfortably ensconced in one of the chairs, eyes closed, a tall glass of liquid refreshment on the light table at his side. He was puffing contentedly on a cigar.

"He looks so happy. Seems a shame to disturb him."

"I'll live with myself," I said. "Come on."

Perry opened one eye as we approached, closed it, then reopened it as if to hope we would have gone away.

With no such luck in the offing he set the cigar in the ashtray and waved a hand to greet us.

"Mr Winston, Nurse Chandler. How nice to see you both again," he said, but I don't think his heart was really in it. "May I offer you a libation or a smoke?"

"No, thank you," I said, though I would have enjoyed a cigar for later. (Don't look at me that way, I like an occasional cigar.)

We sat down. Perry took a sip of his drink. "How is your investigation going?"

"Which one?" I asked. Perry looked puzzled.

"I thought there was only the one. Isaac's death."

"Things have become complicated since we talked last," said Harry. "For one thing, Isaac's shop in New York was completely cleaned out and his clerk is missing."

Perry raised a white eyebrow and took a puff on his cigar. "When did that happen?"

"Joel got word on Monday evening. We really haven't seen much of you since our dinner on Sunday evening. Are you well?"

"I have a headache." He affixed me with what can only be described as a frigid patrician stare. "I can assure you that I had nothing to do with the store robbery, if that's what you're asking. And I'm still trying to make a deal on Joel's behalf." He swirled his drink and took a sip. "Hair of the dog," he said, "but I can't really tell if it's helping or not." He pursed his lips. "Damned difficult to do anything for Joel now if he's got nothing to offer."

"The New York police are on the case," said Harry. "I'm sure we'll hear something soon."

"I hope so, for Joel's sake. Mr Schultz is not a patient man at the best of times, and these can hardly be classified as the best of times."

"I appreciate your frankness." I leaned forward. "We came to ask another question."

"Or rather, get a clarification," said Harry.

"If I left anything out of my story, I'm happy to oblige."

I nodded. "Just one question then. Was Mr Isaac ever married?"

Perry's lips compressed into a thin line and he passed a hand over his forehead. "Why would you need to know that?"

"Because," said Harry, "someone let themselves into Isaac's cabin and made a deposit. A simple woman's wedding band. Gold. They placed it on a small chain carrying a large wedding band, also simple, also gold, that was already in Isaac's suitcase, and they went to the effort to pick the suitcase lock to get in and make this deposit."

"I'm not sure I follow you," said Perry, squeezing his eyelids shut and opening them again.

"Joel told us that in the Jewish faith, no adornments are carried into the grave," I said. "When he was preparing his uncle for burial at sea he was quite surprised to discover the slender chain carrying a large ring around his uncle's neck. He says he never saw it before." I crossed my arms. "So, was Mr Isaac ever married? You were close friends thirty plus years ago. Surely you would have known."

Perry took a drink. "I don't really see the bearing it has on the death of Nathaniel."

"It may help point us toward who killed him, and why," said Harry.

"I see." Perry closed his eyes and took a deep breath, then opened them. "It was all so long ago and I imagine everyone connected with it is dead now, except for me."

"It matters, Mr Perry," I said.

"As you wish." He rubbed his temple and took a reflective puff of his cigar, gathering his thoughts. "You may not have believed it to have seen him as you did, but in his younger days he was quite handsome, with a very talented turn of speech; had he been Irish it would have certainly been called blarney. Despite that, women did not figure into our equation; we were both intent on building our fortunes. Still, not even Nathaniel could dodge Cupid's arrow forever. At long last he met a South African woman a bit younger than himself named Annake Dirickson and fell head over heels in love, and she returned the sentiment."

I looked at Harry. "Sounds like Joel. It must run in the family. Please go on, Mr Perry."

"She was the widowed mother of a three-year-old boy. Fortunately for Nathaniel she was a very fluent English speaker, having learned it from missionaries when she was a child. As you'll remember me saying, neither Nathaniel nor myself was by any means fluent in Dutch or Afrikaans, despite the length of our stay. Picking up a foreign language just eluded us."

"Yes," I said. "Go on."

"Around that time the groundwork was being laid by both the Afrikaners and British for the second Boer war. It got started in earnest in 1899."

"And you said you and Nathaniel went in on the British side," said Harry.

Perry sipped his drink. "But not entirely for the reason I gave you Sunday night. Rather, we naively thought we might be in a better position to protect Annake. That was made difficult by her father, a tough old son of a goat named Ruben Dirickson who never approved of Isaac. I might also mention that Ruben was a chief in the Boer resistance movement. Anyway, you know how love is. Like Romeo and Juliet, Annake and Nathaniel paid no attention and got married anyway. For a few months everything was fine, and then the second war got started." Perry took a sip of his drink. "That's about the time Annake announced she was pregnant."

Harry and I looked at each other. "So Isaac has a child?" I asked.

Perry shook his head. "Not quite. As I told you, Nathaniel and I were dragooned into building internment camps for Boer prisoners of war. During the construction we managed to keep Annake and her father out of sight, but as I said, once the camps opened we were given rifles and the Brits began collecting prisoners. Annake's father was betrayed, and Annake was guilty by association, pregnant or not. In they went."

"That's horrible," said Harry.

"It gets worse, Mr Winston." Perry took another draw off his cigar. "I thought we might keep her out on humanitarian terms, but no luck. And it was about that same time I noticed a change in Nathaniel. His good spirits went away. Naturally I associated that with his wife being placed in internment, but there was more to it. When he saw her he spoke harshly to her. As her pregnancy advanced, he began to cut back on the food items he had been smuggling into the camp for her. When I noticed this I took up what slack I could, but it wasn't enough."

"What happened?" I asked.

"One night there was an escape attempt. Ruben Dirickson and several other men were shot and killed. I later found that the attempt had been orchestrated by Nathaniel, who then conveniently tipped off the officer of the watch to be prepared."

"His own father-in-law? Why?" Harry leaned forward.

"He was paying back Annake. And I finally discovered the reason why. I managed to get five minutes with her one afternoon. She told me that before she went into the camp she had discovered that Nathaniel had been cheating me on my share of our profits, by simply understating what we had. Annake was smart. In the beginning, she had volunteered to do our books for us, and what could have been better? Unfortunately for her, she was too smart for Isaac." Perry gave a heavy sigh. "I guess he blamed her for us losing it all, even though it had nothing to do with her. After her father's escape attempt, she was put under a strict watch. It became impossible for me to even try and smuggle any food to her. Malnourished and in ill health, she finally gave birth to a daughter." Perry looked at me. "As a nurse, I'm sure you can see the difficulties involved there."

"Yes, Mr Perry. I can."

He nodded. "Naturally, I became furious with Isaac. He all but dared me to make something of it. He would report me for fraternizing with a prisoner and he would deny any knowledge of Annake. My hands were tied." Perry's shook his head sadly. "Then that terrible night I told you about. Annake in a fever, stumbling out of her barracks when she saw me, rifle at the ready, standing in the yard. She slowly walked toward me, racked with fever. I can still hear the desperation in her voice as she asked for help for herself and her infant. And then the crack of the rifle, Annake falling face-forward in the dirt. And Nathaniel, proud of himself. I guess he thought he had silenced her from telling me how I'd been cheated by him." Perry took a long drink. "But I didn't care about it then, and I still don't care about it now. All I cared about was Annake. And she was lying dead at my feet." He picked up his cigar, tried a draw, then fumbled with his lighter to get it going again. Once he was able to expel a cloud of smoke, he gave me a sad smile. "That's the story, Nurse."

Harry was stunned. "Isaac killed his own wife?"

"And managed to have his father-in-law killed as well," said Perry.

"What about the infant girl and Annake's son?" I asked.

"What about them?" said Perry. "I was told by a prisoner that the infant perished. The boy, who knows. His father dead, his mother dead, him about five years old – I wouldn't hold out high hopes for him, either. At any rate, I never found out."

"Would you be able to recognize the two wedding bands?" asked Harry

Perry shrugged. "Maybe. I was Isaac's best man." He took a puff of his cigar. "But I doubt I could positively confirm it for you. It was a long time ago. Unless there's an inscription or a stone set in it, one gold ring looks very much like another to me, and I can tell you that neither ring had an inscription or a stone. They were just plain gold bands. Nothing to set them off from any other simple gold band." He picked up his drink. "Now, if you don't mind, I'd like to sit alone for a while. This has taken it out of me and I'm afraid I was up rather late last night."

"Oh?" I asked. He nodded, then put a hand to his head.

"Shouldn't do that. Yes. I was sitting up in the Atrium Lounge, watching all the young people and feeling sorry for myself. I'm afraid I had a bit too much to drink. A steward guided me almost all the way home and I stumbled the rest of the distance."

"I'm glad you made it safely," I said, realizing it had been Perry we had heard bumbling down the corridor the night before. The cloudbank the *Victoria* had been steaming beneath suddenly broke and a brilliant shaft of sunlight came down through the skylight dome of the smoking room, illuminating the gloom. I stared at his face. "Mr Perry, you appear a bit jaundiced to me."

"I am. Malaria. Got it in Brazil years and years ago, after I split with Isaac. It flares up from time to time."

"You spent time in South America?" asked Harry.

Perry nodded. "With the Tupiniquim Indians. I was working with a Dutch group of diggers who fortunately spoke enough English for me to get by." He rubbed the back of his neck. "I dose myself with quinine when it comes up."

"You should come to the ship's hospital, Mr Perry."

"No, thank you, Nurse." He took a swallow of his drink. "I've been fighting it for years. At this point in my life it's only a question of when, not if, my liver gives up." Perry raised his cigar to his lips. "So I try to enjoy myself. Each day is one day more."

"Well, thank you for adding to your story."

"You're welcome."

"Yes," said Harry. "I know reliving that was painful."

Perry took a sip. "I agree with you, Mr Winston. Whoever said time heals all wounds had no idea what they were talking about. If you'll excuse me, I think I'll go back to my cabin."

‖

We've all heard the expression about seeing someone in a different light. When I was about fourteen or so there was a boy that I had the most outrageous crush on. His name was Gerard, he was handsome (for a 15-year-old boy), he was articulate (for a 15-year-old boy), he was funny (again, for a 15-year-old boy), and most importantly he was geographically desirable (meaning I didn't have to hike through a meadow full of sheep and sheep dung to catch a glimpse of him after school).

The year was 1914, and the Great War would start in July, (my own marriage and subsequential widowhood was still five years away) but it was April and I was in love. Gerard asked me to go to the cinema and see *Mabel's Strange Predicament* with Mabel Normand and Charles Chaplin; as you know, Chaplin is still making movies, sadly, Normand died of tuberculosis just last month. I'm sure there was something else on the programme as well, those early films only lasted about 15 or 20 minutes. However, I didn't see it because about halfway through *Mabel's Strange Predicament* I found myself in my own strange predicament – Gerard was suddenly doing a very good imitation of an octopus. Ladies, hands up. How many of you went out with 15-year-old boys in your youth? Then you know what I'm talking about. I left the cinema alone and to this day have not found out how or if Mabel ever got out of her Strange Predicament; the scales had fallen from my eyes in a very biblical fashion and I never saw Gerard the same way again. I later found out that his middle name was Marmaduke, which, had I known, should have tipped me off more as to what to expect.

The point being, you think you know someone and then they drop a bomb on you proving that you really don't know about them at all, just like Alexander Perry did. Once the layers of what actually happened in that prison camp were peeled back, it was more than a little odd to me that after the epic falling out with Isaac, and despite his suave and genteel manner, Perry had never gone in for some good old-fashioned payback. The saying is that revenge is a dish best served (or eaten) cold, but someone waiting over 30 years to order a plateful seemed out of line. I didn't know how long Perry had been affiliated with Schultz, but surely if he had wanted to he could have put a bug in the gangster's ear and had Isaac delivered to the bottom of the East River in a pair of concrete overshoes.

On the other hand, maybe Perry was just one of those types who wear the transgressions committed against them like some sort of sacred hair shirt, carry a cross, and flagellate themselves once a day and twice on Sunday.

"What do you think?" I asked Harry as we walked forward to the Observation Lounge.

"I think he's nursing a vicious hangover."

I nodded. "No doubt. And he's paying for it today, and on top of a recurrence of malaria. I feel badly for him. At least it's calm right now. I've seen brutal hangovers coupled with rough seas. It's not pretty."

"I'll take your word for it."

We walked in silence for a moment. "Was it really that bad in the early days of the diamond trade in South Africa?" I asked.

Harry shrugged. "That's what I'm told. A lot of rough play in Kimberley between the early diggers back when the industry was being born. It was really cutthroat. Then layer on the animosity between the Brits and the Boers, and it became a vile and toxic stew. Still is, to a degree. I believe Perry's story. I only wish he had told it all to us on Sunday night."

"And we've got no way of proving or disproving it. Like he said, everyone involved is dead."

"Almost everyone," Harry reminded me. "Annake's infant daughter and son may still be alive."

"I don't think so," I said. "The girl was a newborn delivered of a sick and malnourished mother in an unspeakable prisoner of war camp. The boy was the son of a Boer resistance leader who was gunned down trying to escape. And the children's mother was shot dead in the camp yard. I have to agree with Mr Perry. It would be long odds on their survival."

"What's for certain is that Nathaniel Isaac was no angel. Frankly, with Nathaniel as a role model, I'm surprised that Joel has turned out so well."

"That thought has crossed my mind too." I glanced through the window of one of the shops as we entered the shopping arcade. Alice's dress from the previous night was already back on display. I wondered if the price had been lowered as one does a used automobile, or if someone would come in and say, 'I simply must have this dress, it's just like the one I saw a young woman wearing last night and she looked absolutely fabulous in it.' I saw that Harry was also glancing into the windows as we passed. "Amazing, isn't it?" I said. "Like Fifth Avenue or Bond

Street in the middle of the ocean. The dress Alice wore last night was borrowed from a shop we just passed."

Harry nodded. "Just another example that things are not always what they appear to be. Last night, Alice and Joel looked the part of the wealthy young couple, but without support from others, the evening would never have happened. Today they're back to penury."

"Maybe not that bad," I said. "Anyway, once you have Joel firmly beneath your wing, I expect the happy couple's finances to begin a steady move north."

"Has there been any news about the robbery at his store?"

I shook my head. "Nothing."

"If Dutch Schultz was involved, I'm afraid that's going to be a dead end." Harry paused outside the doors to the Observation Lounge. "If there's nothing more, I suppose I'll return to the ship's newspaper. It's entertaining in its own way, but it's not *The New York Times*."

"I'll be sure and let Mister Casey know. He's the writer and editor."

"Are you going to tell Joel the latest? That the woman his uncle shot was his wife and that he set up his own father-in-law to be killed?"

I frowned. "Bringing that information to Joel is not something I'm looking forward to, believe me. Would you care to assist?"

"Yes, of course. No need for you to shoulder that burden alone." The attendant opened the doors. "He and I have a lunch date at 12:30 today," said Harry. "Just come by my cabin then. We'll be waiting for you." He disappeared and I was left standing outside the doors. I turned around to go, took ten steps and almost ran into Van Effen.

"Good morning, Nurse. I see you and Mr Winston have been chatting with Mr Perry."

"Were you spying on us?"

Van Effen raised his hands, palms outward. "No. I just happened to be passing the Smoking Room and saw you all huddled inside. It seemed to be a very intimate conversation."

"Why aren't you with Mr Singer?"

Van Effen smiled. "Mr Singer is in his cabin with his fiancée."

"Of course he is."

"I believe they are quite safe."

"I'm sure they are." My lips compressed into a thin line.

Van Effen shrugged. "If you wish, I can evict her."

I shook my head. "That would only earn you enmity. Besides, Joel has a lunch date with Mr Winston at 12:30."

"I will make sure he is there." Van Effen took off his hat and ran a hand back over his smoothly pomaded hair. "Thank you for the adventure last night."

"I'm glad you enjoyed it. What did you think of those two rings?"

Van Effen replaced his hat. "If I were to hazard a guess, I would say – how do the Americans say it? – that the chickens have come home to roost."

"I would agree with you. Whoever killed Mr Isaac had a lot of unfinished business." I gave him a steady gaze. "Were you aware that Mr Isaac's store has been robbed?"

"Has it?"

"The manager, Mr Jenkins, has also disappeared."

Van Effen knit his brows. "When did this happen?"

"Joel received word yesterday. The New York police are looking into it."

"That is distressing, Nurse Chandler. Have they suspects?"

"Only the disappeared Mr Jenkins."

Van Effen nodded. "If you wish, I will send a wire to an associate in New York to see if he can find more information." He gave me a crooked smile. "Sometimes I can reach where the police can't."

I didn't doubt him and didn't want to know, so I didn't ask. "Thank you for your offer," I said.

"Of course," said Van Effen. "Mr Perry looked very – distraught, I think is the word – while you and Mr Winston were talking to him. Was he speaking of the old days in Kimberley?"

"What do you know of the old days in Kimberley? You said you're Harry's age, close enough."

"That is true. However, I have always had an interest in history." He took a cigarette from the rumpled pack in his coat and lit it. "Speaking of history, did you ever find out anything about the beautiful glass imitation that Mr Winston showed me on Monday?"

"No," I said cautiously.

"Too bad." Van Effen blew out smoke through his nostrils. "I think I could sell a lot of those at a good price to the right buyer."

"You mean defraud a buyer."

"As I am sure you have surmised, Nurse, I am not completely lily-white. I have to make a living too, and if it involves playing greedy people for fools, then *caveat emptor*, Nurse Chandler. Let the buyer beware."

"I know what it means."

"I am sure you do." He tipped his Panama hat to me. "I will see you at 12:30." He took another drag and walked off in a cloud of smoke.

"How is Miss Thomas doing?" I called after him. He paused and turned.

"Are you referring to the lovely woman who occupies a cabin across the corridor from myself?"

"She and I chanced to talk. Girl talk, you know. She is quite interested in you."

Van Effen gave a slight nod of his head. "She seems nice. But shipboard romances, you know."

"That's what I told her."

He took another deep drag. "Thank you for your concern."

"Not at all." Van Effen turned and walked away. I watched him go, then climbed the nearest flight of stairs to the Sun Deck to stare at the ocean and think.


Alice was sitting in one of the reception room chairs thumbing through the February issue of *My Home* magazine when I finally came through the hospital door an hour later. "You look a bit bedraggled."

"Thanks." I sat down next to her. "You look pretty good considering all the time you've been spending in Joel's cabin with him."

"We're just talking," she said defensively.

"Yes, I'm sure." I picked up the magazine she'd been looking at. "Colour Schemes You Will Love To Try," I read from the cover. "Full of Furnishing Secrets and Pretty Ideas." I handed it back to her. "Is this supposed to be you and Joel on the cover?"

"It could be. Did you have a busy morning? Joel said you all had a busy night."

"Joel needs to learn to keep his mouth closed about certain things," I said.

Alice giggled. "I'm just imagining the four of you hiding behind the bed. Did you find out who that was out in the corridor?"

"Mr Perry, coming back to his cabin after a night of heavy drinking. However, he was recovered enough this morning to talk with Harry and myself."

Alice listened attentively to the morning's activities. When I finished she nodded her head. "I feel sorry for Mr Perry."

"I'm not sure how I feel," I said. "I do think, as they say, he's more to be pitied than censured."

"What do you think about that wedding band joining its mate after thirty years? Do you think Mr Perry did that?"

"Honestly, I have no idea."

"Have you told Joel yet?"

"Told him what? That the woman his uncle shot was married to his uncle?" I frowned. "I'm meeting him at Harry's cabin at 12:30."

"I should come."

"Thanks, but no, Alice. Someone needs to stay and watch the fort. Where is Doctor Harper?"

Alice shrugged. "Meeting with a First-Class passenger in his private consulting room. The passenger apparently hears things that aren't there."

Harper's consulting room on A Deck was part of his quarters there, for those well-heeled, or in this case, slightly off-kilter passengers who didn't want to make the trek all the way down to the ship's hospital on C Deck. "Better Harper than me for that one. I'd give them some candy pills and sling them out on their ear." Alice laughed and I gave her a smile. "Forgot to tell you, Cinderella – I saw your dress back in the store window this morning."

"I'll remember every detail of that dress for the rest of my life," said Alice. "At least the *Queen Victoria* didn't turn into a pumpkin at midnight." She admired the ring on her finger. "I can hardly wait to start our new life."

"Sounds romantic. Don't forget your new life will also include Mr Van Effen, at least for a couple of weeks more."

"I don't think he's so bad."

"I ran into him this morning. He seemed curious about whatever conversation Harry and I had been having with Mr Perry."

Alice stood up. "Probably nothing more than professional curiousity. If you don't mind, I'll run out and grab something to eat before you head back topside. Shall I bring you anything?"

"Some toast and tea, thanks."

"Right-o." She turned to go, then looked back. "I haven't said it, but thanks ever so much for last night."

"Glad to have been of service. I wish all my problems were as easy to solve."

# III

My mother always used to say there was no such thing as a problem – only a solution that had yet to be found. I have yet to ask her if she meant 'a solution' as in one singular solution, or was it instead many solutions that would each solve the same problem but in different ways? For instance, suppose your assignment is to come up with a way to arithmetically arrive at the number two. To reach that number, you can add one and one. Or you can subtract one from three. Or you can divide four by two. Or subtract four from six. It goes on and on. All are different solutions to the same problem – reaching the number two – and all of them work equally well. There's not a one size fits all solution. There are many solutions.

Maybe, I thought, I was going about the Isaac problem in the wrong way. Maybe there were multiple solutions that, sewn together, would provide a complete blanket explanation for who killed him and why, instead of a one size fits all solution. So far it was all piecemeal items, like how does someone leave a room with the key locked from the inside, where did enough cut glass 'diamonds' come from to choke a man, who had access to curare and knew how to use it, why did a jewelry store in New York get robbed and the manager disappear and how did someone get into the *Victoria's* vault and make off with a box of diamonds? Not to mention the latest puzzler of who went into Isaac's room and left behind a woman's wedding band on a chain that already carried a man's ring? The one fact I was reasonably sure of after Perry's amended story is that the victim deserved his fate for what had happened in that prison camp thirty years earlier, but again, why in the world would someone wait thirty years to exact that kind of justice?

All of these thoughts were swirling around in my head as I made my way up the stairs to Harry's stateroom on the Main Deck following my oh-so-nutritious buttered toast and tea. (While you want to gain your 'sea legs' as they are called, the diet aboard does nothing to help your sea thighs, which is why I took stairs as often as possible.) I made a detour on A Deck to check on Doctor Harper and saw that his next door consulting room was closed. I toyed with the idea of opening the door wildly and sticking my head in and shouting 'booga booga' or some such nonsense but figured it would end with me being cashiered. I passed on the option and resumed the stairs up to Harry's.

Joel was already inside and seated on the couch with Van Effen standing near the door when Harry let me in. I took a seat at the table covered with a variety of jeweler's tools and paraphernalia, including an odd small mahogany box with a slot cut through it and a light bulb screwed into the top. A thin electric cord snaked out of the box and reached to the ceiling, plugged into the socket apparently recently vacated by the light bulb now on the box. Harry caught my bewildered expression.

"It's a demagnetizer."

"For what?"

"Demagnetizing," said Harry. "I have some small tools that work better when magnetized, but sometimes they accidentally magnetize other things. This device removes the magnetic field." He patted the mahogany box. "The model 840 Improved Electric Automatic Demagnetizer for Alternating and Direct Current." He looked at Van Effen. "As Mr Van Effen knows, it's also good for watches. I demagnetized his pocket watch Monday afternoon."

"How did you know your watch was magnetized?" I asked.

"It began gaining time for no apparent reason, a little over a minute a day," said Van Effen. "It is an expensive pocket watch, a Waltham. I took the opportunity of consulting with Mr Winston about it."

"You didn't say anything about that," I said to Harry.

"Nothing to say. As far as I'm concerned it's just a routine jewelry repair. Just took a few minutes." He stood on a chair to reach the overhead light fixture, disconnected the device, then unscrewed the hot light bulb with a handkerchief and replaced it in the ceiling socket. When he resumed his seat at the table Joel spoke again.

"Well, now that we're all here, Harry says the two of you want to talk with me?" asked Joel.

"We had a conversation with Mr Perry this morning, Joel," I said. "He was very forthcoming on some additional detail relating to the relationship between himself and your uncle in Kimberley during the second Boer War. It's not pleasant, but here it is."

Harry and I took turns telling the tale. When we had finished Joel was appreciably pale. Van Effen spoke first. "Forgive me, Mr Singer, but perhaps now I do not feel as bad for what happened to Mr Isaac."

Joel shook his head. "I can't believe I'm related to him. His own wife? It's impossible to think he was my mother's brother." He passed a hand in front of his eyes. "What's Alice going to think of me now?"

"The same thing she's thought since you met. I told her a couple of hours ago. She's picking out wallpaper for your little love cottage together."

"And it doesn't change anything with me, either," added Harry.

I stood up. "I know you two gentlemen have dinner plans, so I'll be going."

"Lunch plans," said Joel dully.

"Lunch, dinner, same thing to us Brits." I left the cabin and closed the door behind me. The corridor was empty. I walked down to Isaac's cabin and again put an eye to the keyhole. The same dim light from the drawn drapes over the portholes greeted me, so either no one had visited after we had departed last night, or if they had, they'd remembered to turn off the light this time. I jiggled the knob. It was locked. I turned away and went back up the corridor and around the corner, past the First-Class entrance from outside and the purser's offices, then down the stairs to A Deck and Doctor Harper's consulting room and quarters. The consulting room door was now open. I rapped on the door jamb. "Doctor Harper?" I queried.

"In here, Maeve." I walked through the small waiting area and into his consulting room. "How was your visit with Mr Winston?"

"Intriguing. Your vast Shakespearian knowledge opened a new line of thought." I offered a smile. "I hope you didn't have to tap Chief Duncan for any help. He's also a Shakespearian."

"Is he? We'll have to have a chat."

"Remind me not to be there. Before I really get started, Mr Perry is suffering from a malarial relapse."

"How advanced?"

"He's obviously jaundiced." I sat down, Harper following and closing the door. "He says he got it when he was working with Dutch diamond diggers in Brazil years ago, after he left Isaac. He's self-treating it with quinine, a lot of alcohol and cigars."

"Cure or kill approach, I see."

I nodded. "I told him to come see us at the hospital but he turned it down."

"His choice."

"Yes, but he's in his 70's."

Harper shrugged. "If he doesn't want treatment, there's nothing you can do."

"Probably not." I sat on the couch, drew my legs underneath me and smoothed my skirt. "But the fact that he contracted the disease in Brazil tells me we now have two people on board who probably have a good working knowledge of the effects of curare. And there's more. You remember that woman I told you about that Isaac shot at the camp?"

"Yes."

"Here's the news flash, as Mister Casey would say. That woman was Isaac's wife."

Harper's eyes widened. "Good Lord – that's – " He was speechless.

"Yes, I couldn't find the word for it, either. Harry and I had a nice chin wag with Mr Perry and he told us the entire story, including that there were two children involved. The woman had a son before meeting Isaac, and the child she gave birth to shortly before she was killed was a girl." I held up a cautionary hand. "And before you ask, Mr Perry believes the infant certainly died in the camp and the young boy perished as well. Given the conditions in the camps I've no reason to doubt him."

"I think you need to start at the beginning." Harper sat down in his chair behind the desk, listening in rapt attention while I went through the meeting with Perry, then the run-in with Van Effen and finally the most recent meeting with Harry and Joel. When I finished he gave a low whistle. "So Van Effen wants to cash in on the fake diamonds? You didn't tell him that they'd come out of Isaac?"

"No. As far as I know, he believes that the diamonds in Isaac were real, but he's not made any enquiry about them. He would just like to get his hands on some fakes to sell, like the one out of Isaac that Harry showed him. You still have them, don't you?"

Harper tapped his medical bag. "Still right here in the bag."

"Well, at least we know where those are. The real ones, if there ever were any, are still whereabouts unknown."

"You've had quite the morning. What are you planning for an afternoon encore?"

"Getting something to eat and telling Alice she's under house arrest until we reach Cherbourg."

"Good luck with that."

"Speaking of Alice, she says you had an interesting patient this morning."

Harper rolled his eyes. "An amiable old buffer but he says he can hear mice in the ceiling of his stateroom. He swears he heard them chewing wood a couple of nights ago."

"The cabin ceilings aren't made of wood," I said. "It's a veneer on steel."

"That's what I told him. Nothing for mice to chew on; still, he was adamant and the customer is always right. And it might interest you to know where this customer is – his cabin is 34-A, right across from the mysterious Mr Silverwood."

"That is interesting. What did you do with him?"

Harper shrugged. "I sent him away with instructions to have the steward bring a mug of warm milk with Ovaltine when he was ready to retire to help him sleep more soundly. He asked if he could add a tot of brandy to it and I said I couldn't see the harm of it." Harper leaned back and crossed his arms. "I'm hoping the power of suggestion will be enough to do the trick. Can't hurt, anyway."

I laughed. "I wish the doctor I had as a child would have prescribed Ovaltine for my brother and me. Think how much easier our parent's lives would have been." I turned to go. "You know, this affair with Mister Isaac is cutting into my sleep as well. Do you think Ovaltine would work on someone younger?" I gave him the eye. "I am younger, aren't I?"

"Of course, Maeve." Harper gave me a wicked smile. "Whatever you want." He reached for the prescription pad on his desk and jotted a couple of lines, then tore off the sheet and handed it to me. I looked at his scrawl.

"What is this? I only rate two mugs of Ovaltine before bedtime? After all I've been through lately?"

"Always thinking of yourself," said Harper. He grinned. "The other mug is for Alice."

# IV

I had an aunt – my father's older sister, if you must know – who had literally about seen it all. She was born in 1850 in Surrey, the same year Nathaniel Hawthorne published *The Scarlet Letter* and Millard Fillmore became President of the United States. In the 51 years leading up to my birth in 1901, she saw the American Civil War, the publication of Tolstoy's *War and Peace*, the arrival of the telephone, the phonograph, the electric light, the Eiffel Tower and Sherlock Holmes. I'm sure there were probably some other things, too, but that's all I can think of at the moment. I may have put some things at the wrong place on this list (I can't remember if the light or the telephone came first) but you can consult any historic timeline and set it straight. Having seen all of this, my aunt had a saying: what's past is prologue.

My father explained it to my young mind as meaning that what happens in the past merely sets the stage for what will happen in the present. Much later I found out that it's a line from Shakespeare's *The Tempest* by which two characters basically rationalize that the murder they're about to commit has been set up by what happened to them in the past. And no, I don't feel bad about not knowing the quote from *Henry VI* that Harper dropped on me earlier in the day; everyone knows that *The Tempest* is a much more popular play.

As far as the past being prologue, if what Mr Perry told Harry and myself about Isaac arranging the death of his father-in-law, killing his own wife, and abandoning his infant daughter and adopted son wasn't reason enough for someone to kill him, I don't know what was.

After leaving Harper I walked back up to the First-Class corridors and rapped on Perry's door. After a moment it opened.

"Nurse Chandler." Perry's face was impassive. "Again?"

"I'm sorry, Mr Perry. May I come in?"

"Certainly." He stood aside, closing the door behind me.

"I hope your headache is better."

"It's passing. Maybe the quinine I took helped, I don't know."

"You should really let us look at you."

"No, but thank you." He indicated the open deposit box on the table. "Since Joel appears to be bereft of diamonds, I thought I would see if there is anything I can part with to help his case."

"That's very generous of you."

Perry sat at the table. "Oh, I'm not just giving it away. There's a small price."

"And what would that be?"

"We both know that Nathaniel Isaac didn't die of natural causes, no matter what your shipboard newspaper says."

His words startled me. "Where did you come up with such a suggestion?" I said, frantically playing for time.

"His missing box of diamonds coupled with the interest you and Harry Winston have been showing in me. While I've been questioned by the police before, I've never been questioned by a nurse, let alone one as tenacious as you. You've been showing far too much interest in Isaac's history than there should be for an old man who died of supposed natural causes and was mourned by no one save his nephew, and it seems not much there, either. The more information I gave you, the more you wanted. You are quite adept."

"I don't know if that's a compliment or not."

"Take it as you like." He smiled. "Perhaps it's also a sign of my advancing age and knowledge of the reaper heading in my direction. I'm glad Isaac got justice." He leaned forward. "And I will keep trying to help his nephew."

"Why?"

"Because had things worked out, Annake would have been his stepmother. I'm doing it for her."

Realization dawned on me. "You were in love with her."

Perry nodded. "Yes. May I ask how Isaac passed?"

I bit my lip. That knowledge was an ace card, perhaps our only ace card. I reasoned that if Perry was the one who did it, I wouldn't be telling him anything he didn't already know, and if it was the opposite, perhaps he could offer some insight into the event. I delicately cleared my throat. "Mr Isaac was found in the sitting room in his cabin, with the door locked from the inside and the key in the door. He was seated in a chair in the middle of the room. No sign of a struggle. Someone had injected him with a dose of curare that paralyzed him, and then his throat was filled with imitation glass jewels. He choked to death."

Perry processed all of this while lighting a cigar. He puffed appreciably for a moment. "Harsh justice," he said, "but justice." He blew out smoke. "So apart from you, and of course Joel and Mr Winston, and presumably Van Effen, who else knows how Isaac died?"

"The Captain, the Master at Arms, the ship's Principal Medical Officer, the Chief Steward, the Purser, my assistant nurse, our chemist."

"Quite the cast."

"I'm trusting you to keep this to yourself, Mr Perry."

"Of course." He toyed with a pen on the desk. "What do you think of Van Effen?" he asked, then charged ahead without waiting for an answer. "I will tell you what I think. No, I will tell you what I know. Van Effen is a very capable hired gun. He's being very protective of Joel. I, for one, don't understand how someone slipped past him to get Isaac."

"That is a big question, yes." I nodded. "You impress me as a well-educated and sophisticated man, Mr Perry. If I may ask, what are you doing with a gangster like Dutch Schultz?"

"An operation like Mr Schultz runs employs different types. There are the Van Effen types, but there are also accountants and lawyers, and then there are those like me."

"I get the accountants and lawyers. What do those like you do?"

"You could say that I'm in sales. What else do you know of Van Effen?"

"He says Isaac also hired him to help at the Antwerp show. I will say that Mr Van Effen does appear to have a basic, and probably better than expected, working knowledge of the diamond industry."

Perry laughed. "Good for him. Joel, I'm not so sure. He strikes me as rather ineffectual."

I felt defensive. "Joel is completely alone in the world. If it wasn't for Harry taking him in, I don't know what he'd be doing. He's got nothing."

"Oh, he's not completely alone. I know about his relationship with the other nurse. Don't look so surprised. It's become rather an open secret among most of your crew."

I made up my mind. Alice would no longer be confined to quarters. She'd be sent to the isolation ward and strapped to a bed. "Yes, that's true," I said. "And they are engaged to be married." I pursed my lips. "As you seem to be in the know, perhaps you can tell me who killed Isaac and why."

"If you're asking if it was me, the answer is no." Perry spread his hands. "Like Nathaniel, I'm also an old man. As you've no doubt noted I spend most of my time in my stateroom or in the smoking room or lounge, and of course your magnificent First-Class dining salon. I'm just a businessman on what may well be my last overseas trip."

"You would have a reason for revenge."

"But I don't need more diamonds. Heaven help me if Schultz thought I was skimming."

"I suppose so." I stood up. "Thank you for the conversation, Mr Perry." He escorted me to the cabin door and opened it.

"My pleasure, Nurse Chandler," said Perry, but I didn't think he meant it. The door closed behind me and I was left alone.

# V

When I was a child I was often referred to as precocious. Not in the child-prodigy-Mozart-composing-music-at-the-age-of-five way, but rather in the pushy-or-cheeky-endearing-to-no-one-but-my-parents way. As I aged this tendency grew until now I had to remind myself to check it from time to time. Case in point: while Mr Perry seemed pleasant enough in our last interview, I got the feeling that he was beginning to think that what the world needed to be a better place was fewer and less inquisitive Maeve Chandlers, and for a man who had the ear of Dutch Schultz that was a distinctly disturbing thought.

However, I didn't have much time to dwell on it because I hadn't made more than a couple of steps before I was abruptly stopped by a gray-haired older man coming out of his cabin.

"Oh, good," he said in a cultured British accent. "Doctor Harper sent a nurse around to check on me. Thank you, dear."

I gave him a blank look. "I'm sorry?"

He took me by the arm. "I know I heard mice in the ceiling and all he told me to do was have the steward bring some Ovaltine before I retired. Fortunately I put brandy in it."

The light went off in my head. This was Doctor Harpers 'amiable old buffer.' While I was curious I didn't really have the time at the moment. "Oh, yes. The doctor told me about that, and it's sound medical advice. I'm actually on another call right now, so – "

His grip intensified; for an old codger he felt like an all-in wrestler. "Come in, dear, come in. I'll show you where I heard them." He ushered me into his stateroom and trapped me by closing the door. "Your Doctor Harper is very nice, but maybe I should have called housekeeping or your engineering department?"

I bit my lip at the thought of Miss Kelly or Chief Engineer Duncan dealing with a call about mice. "Sir, I'm sorry, I didn't get your name?"

"Clayton," he said. "Roger Clayton."

"Thank you, Mr Clayton," I said, glancing about the cabin. "Is Mrs Clayton not here?"

"I'm afraid not. I'm widowed. Mrs Clayton passed away back in 1927."

"My apologies. Mr Clayton, it's physically impossible to have mice in the ceilings of the cabins on the *Victoria*. The ceilings are made of steel frames with a veneer overlay of paneling."

"Well, young lady, I know I heard something. It was right back here." We were now standing in the entrance to his bathroom. "Maybe it was in the door. The doors are made of wood, are they not?"

"Yes, of course," I said. "But they're solid. There aren't any hollow spaces within a door for a mice – that is to say, a mouse – to crawl around inside of, Mr Clayton." I craned my neck. "The Chief Engineer tells me that some of the stale air discharge ventilation ducts do intersect, however. Perhaps you were hearing something coming from somewhere else.'

He considered this fact. "I hadn't thought of that," he said. "I heard them on Saturday night and last night. I'll be listening for them again tonight, and if I hear them I'll call you, Nurse."

"That's fine, Mr Clayton. Just dial for the hospital. If I'm not there someone will know where to find me."

"Thank you, dear." His face became concerned. "I was saddened to hear of the death of that elderly gentleman the other day. He looked to be about my age. You know, his cabin is just one up across the hall from me. I believe his young nephew is next door to him." He leaned in confidentially. "I do hope that young man is fine. I've seen a nurse coming and going from his cabin at all hours."

Making another mental note to smack Alice when I saw her next, I nodded. "Yes, he's fine," I said of Joel. "Just a bit of a shock for him when his uncle died. We've just been checking on him to make sure he's all right."

"That's so nice of you." He walked me back to her stateroom door. "You have certainly allayed my concerns. Perhaps I can finally get a good night's rest."

"The sound was that bad?"

Mr Clayton nodded and put a hand on my arm with, mercifully, less of a grip this time. "I'm a deep sleeper, but sometimes I even thought the mice were talking. Isn't that silly?" He gave a light laugh. "Mice can't talk, except for that Mickey Mouse of Mr Disney."

"Yes," I agreed, opening the door. "I hope the rest of your voyage goes smoothly, Mr Clayton." His stateroom door clicked behind me and I heard the key turning in the lock. I took one step and stopped short. Chief Duncan's words came back to me again. 'Some of the discharge ventilation ducts do intersect.' The cabin directly across the corridor from Mr Clayton's was booked to Mr Silverwood, who had never taken possession. Or had he?

I went across to 35-A and, taking the risk that a passenger or crew member might come by, stooped and peered through the keyhole.

Unlike Isaacs's cabin door, the escutcheon on the inside of this door was working and effectively blocked my view of the room. I stood and tried the door only to find it locked. I sighed. Nothing to be gained here until the door could be opened. I went on down the corridor to Harry's room and knocked but there was no answer. I tried Joel's cabin with the same results. Both men were obviously still at lunch. I turned back and headed for the forward stairs and lift station.

Mister Harvey was standing near the lifts, ever attentive to any passenger need, when I arrived. Honestly, I was surprised to see him. "Shouldn't you be in the restaurant now?" I asked.

"Giving Mister Bissell a chance to spread his wings," replied Harvey. "He was asking for more responsibility, so I asked him to take the midday service, and then I came forward so I wouldn't be tempted to stick my head in and see if he's making a mess of it or not. What's been happening in your world? Harper has filled me in on some of it and of course I know about Alice's engagement, but I'd like to hear it from you."

"What hasn't been happening is more to the point, and as far as hearing it, how much time do you have?"

He glanced at his wristwatch. "Until 14 hundred. Feel free to proceed." I did, and when I got to the end of the latest conversation with Perry it had taken 20 minutes. Harvey shook his head. "Sorry I asked. You've been quite busy, Maeve."

"And that doesn't count the old fellow I just talked with who is hearing mice in his cabin."

"Mice? Not a chance." Harvey looked positively affronted.

"I thought that would get your attention. The way he describes it, the sound may be coming through the discharge ventilation system shared with the empty cabin across the corridor."

"The one that was booked and never occupied?"

"The very same."

Harvey frowned. "Well, I can't check now, but – " He reached into a pocket. "Here's my master key. Go look in that empty stateroom. I know you won't rest until you do." He handed it to me. "I can't believe you haven't asked for it before this anyway. Sometimes I think you're slipping."

I took the key. "Thanks for the compliment. I'll bring it back."

"Off you go, then. I'm going to see if I've still got a restaurant left." He turned and headed down the stairs while I walked as quickly as I could back to the staterooms. The corridor was still quiet and empty. I slipped the key into the lock and noiselessly let myself into the stateroom.

A silent walk-through of the unoccupied cabin assured me there were no mice. I went to the bathroom and switched on the light. No mice in the bathroom either. I pulled back the curtain and looked into the tub, opened the lid on the loo and checked the sink, but there were no signs of anything at all that could have made any of the sounds that Mr Clayton described. I was just turning to go back into the bedroom and sitting room when I caught sight of what looked like tiny breadcrumbs on the tile floor near the bathroom door. I knelt and moistened the tip of a finger with my tongue and then pressed my finger to the crumbs and brought them up for closer examination, then gently touched my finger to my tongue and wrinkled my nose. They definitely weren't breadcrumbs, but there was something familiar about them I couldn't quite pinpoint. I brushed my finger off on my nursing apron and stood back up, thinking.

Mr Clayton had heard scratching in his bathroom from about where I was standing under this cabin's bathroom vent, but another look around told me there was absolutely nothing here that could have made any noise. On the off chance that the door – which had been open when I came in – had swung on its own in the night and made some slight noise, I closed the bathroom door from the inside.

When it hit the jamb, I started. There had been a definite noise from the door. I opened it and heard it again, then closed it and heard it a third time. The non-existent mice were exonerated, but there was definitely something inside the door. I opened it to the midway point and moved it back and forth briskly. The same soft, barely discernible rustle greeted my ears.

I went back into the sitting room and dragged a chair to the bathroom, then carefully climbed up on the seat and put a hand on top of the bathroom door and slowly felt along the top. After a moment my fingers encountered an area that wasn't solid; in fact, it felt like a soft depression. I withdrew my hand and fished in my smock for a small hand mirror, then held it up so I could see the top of the door.

A perfectly round circle greeted my eyes, dimpled into the top of the door and most assuredly a different color from the rest of the door. I stared at it for a moment, then remembered my father pursuing his wood craft hobbies in his little workroom. My brother had dared me and I had accepted, putting one of the very thin curled wood shavings into my mouth that had fallen as my father used his plane on a plank of wood. I could remember the odd taste to this day.

Those weren't breadcrumbs on the floor. They were the detritus of someone using a drill to put a hole in the top of the bathroom door, secreting something away, and then filling it in. Mr Clayton had been right about hearing something, but it wasn't a mouse. It was a big rat.

# VI

You may have participated in Easter egg hunts as a child; my brother and I did. We'd help decorate the eggs and then our parents would place them around the yard, or, if it was raining, around the inside of the house. When we were very young the eggs were seen in some very obvious places, like on the dining room table, or at the top of the stairs, or on a window sill. As we grew older, the hiding places for the eggs became a bit more complex: inside a shoe, behind a book on the shelf, in the branch of a tree. The point was that sleuthing for eggs was graduated to our ages. Nowadays, I imagine, if my mother was up to it (my father passed several years ago) the eggs would go on top of the chimney, or in the glovebox of the car, or perhaps under one of the more surly hens in the coop.

But in the top of a First-Class stateroom bathroom door on the *Queen Victoria*? Not even my brother could have conceived of that one.

Holding the mirror steady with one hand I reached toward the indentation, then quickly drew my hand back as if I had touched a hot iron. What was I thinking? Whoever made this hole and deposited whatever was inside of it was, sooner or later (and probably sooner) going to come back and get what had been secreted away. I didn't want to think about what would happen if they found it tampered with; I had little doubt that the items making noise when the door moved were diamonds, and probably the real diamonds that had belonged to Isaac.

Another thought suddenly intruded on my mind: what if the person who made this hiding place was on their way to check on it right now? That galvanized me into action. I stepped off the chair, dragged it back to its location in the sitting room, and returned the bathroom door to the position it had been in when I arrived. Ever so quietly I crept to the cabin door and opened it just a crack to peer out.

The corridor was empty. I slipped out, locked the door, and knocked on Harry's stateroom.

"Come in." Thank God he was back. With a last furtive look around the still empty corridor I went into his stateroom and closed the door behind me. He looked up at me from the table where he was working with his jeweler's implements. "Nice to see you, but I didn't know we had a scheduled meeting this afternoon. If you're looking for Joel he said he was going to walk the Promenade Deck and get some fresh air after lunch. Van Effen is with him." Harry set his tools down. "What's the matter? You look like you've seen a ghost."

"I think someone is using that empty cabin next to Isaac's as a hiding place for diamonds."

"What?"

I recounted Mr Clayton's story and my own reconnaissance. Harry listened intently.

"I think you were correct in not disturbing it," said Harry. "I've heard of a lot of ways to smuggle diamonds, but inside of a bathroom door on an ocean liner is a new one." He toyed with a tiny screwdriver for a moment, then looked up at me. "How exactly did you get into that room in the first place?"

"I ran into Mister Harvey and he let me have his master key to investigate. Which reminds me, I need to get it back to him."

"May I see it? I've been turning one of our puzzles around in my mind."

"Certainly." I withdrew the key from my smock and handed it to him. Harry weighed it in his hand.

"Almost identical to the room keys, isn't it?"

"Do you think someone used a room key as a pattern to make their own master?"

"It's possible. See here?" he pointed to the end of the master where the teeth were, then picked up his own room key off the table for comparison. "The skeleton key – the master key that you got from Mister Harvey – is missing some of the teeth you can see on my own room key. Those missing teeth help it slip past the wards that my regular key has to engage to turn the lock."

"So all someone would have to do is file or cut off the teeth somehow," I said.

Harry nodded. "But that's rather labor intensive and you have to keep trying it in the lock as you file. The easier way is to get a couple of small blocks of clay. Dust some talc on the two sides and blow away the powder that doesn't adhere, then press a master key between them and put some weight on the mold – something like a heavy book or two – and then you melt some alloy slug in a ladle by holding it over a medium flame. One of those Lenk blow torches I have with my tools would do the job. Take the master out of the mold, pour the molten metal in, wait thirty minutes, then separate the halves and gently tease the key out. I'm leaving out a few steps, but it's not a hard job and could be done in 45 minutes if necessary. It might need a bit of filing to fit it correctly, but that would be simple enough. Just want to mind that you don't burn yourself with the torch or the molten metal. As to how and when it was done, I have a theory."

"Yes?"

"We're told that no master keys are missing, so here's what I think happened. The last time the *Victoria* was in New York – not a few days ago, but maybe two weeks – someone came on board prior to departure when the ship is jammed with visitors and an extra body won't be noticed. They managed to get their hands on a master, made their wax impression, replaced the master and left the ship, no one the wiser. The intervening time until the *Victoria* was back in New York was more than sufficient to have a key cast. So, this past Saturday this person came on board, tried the key, made any adjustments with a file, and was instantly granted access to any room he wanted to enter."

"That's smart," I said. Harry shrugged and handed the key back.

"Just approaching it logically."

"Any logical theories for how the key got left on the inside of a locked door?"

He shook his head. "I'm afraid not. The door key from Isaac's room had no scratch marks on its barrel, so no one used a small pointed pliers to try and turn it from the outside through the keyhole while it was still in the lock on the inside. That part of the routine still has me baffled."

"Well, if your theory is true about the master key it means this was all planned out in advance and that the vacant stateroom booked next door to Isaac wasn't just a coincidence."

"That's what I think," said Harry. He put the master key down on the table and it was instantly drawn to a little black block about an inch away.

"What's that?" I asked.

"A magnet. I use it to hold very small parts that might otherwise fall to the floor and disappear forever. Of course if it's too strong I have to use the demagnetizer here to remove the magnetic field from whatever it was touching. It's a vicious cycle." He laughed and pulled the key away from the block and handed it back to me. "Don't forget to give this back to Mr Harvey. The brief exposure to magnetism it just had will wear off in a while."

"Thanks." I gingerly dropped it into a pocket then jumped as someone knocked on the door.

"Harry?" Joel asked. "Are you there? It's important."

I opened the door. "You scared the life out of me banging on the door like that."

"Sorry," said Joel. "I have news."

I looked past him into the corridor. "Where is Van Effen?"

"He went to buy cigarettes. I told him I'd be safe here until he got back." Joel sat on the couch. "I've heard from the New York police regarding the robbery at my uncle's store."

"They found Mr Jenkins?" asked Harry.

"In a way. He was located floating face down in the Hudson River. It took a while to get a positive identification on him. Apparently he'd been worked over pretty badly."

"Good Lord," I said.

"Any idea who did it?" asked Harry.

Joel gave a sardonic laugh. "Three guesses."

"Dutch Schultz?" I asked. Joel nodded. "Why?"

"No answer to that question. Police say it was a signature Dutch Schultz murder, but that's all they know."

"And the contents of your uncle's store?" asked Harry.

"Still unaccounted for." He shook his head sadly. "Completely vanished."

"Well, we may have a lead on the diamonds your uncle brought on board," I said. "I found a hole drilled in the top of the bathroom door in the empty cabin next to Isaac's. It's sealed with some sort of filler. When you move the door quickly, you can definitely hear something inside. The man on the other side of the corridor thought he had been hearing mice in his cabin, but it turns out he'd heard noise through the connecting discharge ventilation system, more than likely the drilling of the hole and sealing up afterward."

"When?"

"Saturday night and again last night, but I suspect that last night he was hearing us flailing around in Isaac's cabin."

"Did you open it and look?"

"No. I thought better of disturbing it and Harry concurred, though I'm of the opinion it's a stash of diamonds – hopefully real ones. For now, I don't think the person who created that hiding place has any idea we have any knowledge of it."

"Who could have done it?" asked Joel.

"Perry is tall enough to stand on a chair and reach the top of the bathroom door," said Harry.

"But he's not in the best of health. I noticed he appeared a bit jaundiced this morning when you and I were talking to him. Turns out he's having a recurrence of malaria that he acquired in Brazil as a young man after he and Isaac parted brass rags."

"Van Effen was in Brazil too," said Harry. "And he's plenty tall to monkey with the top of a door."

I nodded. "And no doubt both of them learned about curare in their time in South America."

"Do you think one of them did it?" Joel looked

"That thought crossed my mind," I said. "But I think Mr Perry is out."

"Why?"

I related my earlier conversation with Perry and when I was done, Joel shook his head. "So he's been willing to help me not for the sake of Isaac, but because Annake would have raised me had Isaac not killed her."

"Interesting that he came up with the revenge motif too," said Harry. "And what happened to Annake would certainly drive him in that direction. As for his rationale for not taking the diamonds, that makes perfect sense, especially in light of what Joel just told us about Mr Jenkins. No one in their right mind would cross Dutch Schultz."

"Never mind about the shop. I think we need to get a look inside that door," said Joel. "How did you get inside the cabin, Maeve?"

I fished out the master key and brushed an errant paper clip off it. "Borrowed a master from Mister Harvey this morning."

"Do you think he'd notice if you kept it a bit longer?" asked Harry.

"No. He's busy with post luncheon and getting the place prepped up for dinner." I glanced down at my watch. "If we're going to do it, we need to do it now."

Harry shook his head. "Broad daylight is different from late at night. It's running a big risk."

"We'll park Van Effen outside in the corridor. He can turn away any unwanted guests. And as far as the daylight goes, we don't have to worry about any light from the cabin reaching the corridor."

"You'll have to find something to open that hole with," said Harry. "And seal it up when we're done."

I gave Harry my sweetest smile. "Just leave that to me. I'll get what we need from the ship's carpenter and meet you back here in twenty minutes."

# VII

Did you play pirates as children? Yo ho ho and all of that? My brother and I would wrap one of my mother's scarves or father's ties around our heads, and my father made us little wooden swords in his shop. An eye patch was easily cut out of black felt with a string to tie it in place, and a fearsome moustache or goatee could be drawn using one of Mum's eyebrow pencils. Captain Kidd or Blackbeard had nothing on us. (Well, ok, they had ships and cannon, but that's where our parents drew a firm line.)

As you know, the most important thing about playing pirate is having buried treasure hidden somewhere. Otherwise, what's the point? We would bury a few shillings (generously provided by Mum) in a cloth draw string pouch. It went into the garden, or maybe at the base of a large tree. Then we'd sketch out a map with lots of dashed lines and paces marked off, prettied up with maybe stylistic compass points (though neither of us had a clue what was north, south, east, or west). The best part of the map, though, was always the big 'X' marking the location of the treasure.

And so now, here we were, gathered outside the door to cabin 35-A, ready to search for the treasure. Only Van Effen appeared dubious.

"I do not believe you should disturb it," he said. "Anything you do will certainly tip off the person who placed it there. My advice is to wait."

"No." Joel was firm. "I'm certain these are my uncle's diamonds. Since the store was robbed I have nothing, and I'm depending on the good will of Mr Perry to smooth my path." He looked at me "And as Nurse Chandler says, he's an old man dealing with a recurrence of malaria, plus he drinks a lot. What if he dies before he works anything out with Schultz?" Joel shook his head. "No, I'm going to get whatever is in there. Just keep an eye out for us."

Van Effen nodded. "As you wish, Mr Singer."

I glanced up and down the corridor. All was quiet. I slipped the master into the lock and turned, and in a moment the three of us were inside with the door closed. I turned and looked at them. "Be absolutely quiet," I whispered. "Remember the old gentleman across the corridor can hear through the ventilation system. With any luck he's taking a nap or something." I led them to the bathroom, stopping in the doorway. "Look down there. See that stuff?"

"Yes," said Harry. Joel nodded.

"Don't touch it. It's what led me to the door. Those are particles of wood shavings that someone missed cleaning up when they drilled into the top of the door."

"Why didn't they clean it up?" asked Joel.

"It was night, according to the man across the hall. They probably just didn't see it."

"Big mistake," said Harry.

"But good for us." I looked at our relative heights. "Joel, you're the tallest, but you're still going to need a chair. Hang on." I went back into the sitting room and took up the desk chair and returned. "Ok, up you go."

Joel clambered up onto the chair and nodded. "I see where the hole was made."

"Terrific, here." I handed him up the tool I'd brought. "Gently dig it out and give me what you remove." I unrolled a few sheets of toilet paper and placed them in the sink.

Joel bent to his task, carefully teasing out the filler material and handing it down to me. I took a look at the coloring and cursed. "Bloody hell," I said. "The patching material I brought isn't an exact match for this stuff."

"What do we do, then?" asked Joel.

"We'll have to reuse the original material and hope for the best."

"If no one tries it again until it's dark, it ought to be ok," said Harry.

"Keep going, Joel," I said.

After about a minute he stopped. "I hear something."

Harry and I listened. To my intense dismay I could hear Miss Thomas outside the door.

"Hello, Casper," said Miss Thomas.

In the bathroom we looked at each other. 'Casper?' mouthed Harry.

"Caroline," said Van Effen.

"What are you doing out here?"

"I just came out to get some air."

"Me, too. I was just up on the Sun Deck and thought about you. What do you say we take a spin around the Promenade Deck and then go to the Observation Lounge for a late lunch, honey bunch?"

"That sounds nice, thank you."

"Okie dokie. I'll just be a moment. Want to change my wrap and then we'll ankle on up."

"No," said Van Effen. "You look fine. Let us go now."

She laughed. "That's what I like, a man who makes up his mind. Race you to the top!" I heard her pounding steps, followed by Van Effen's slow, measured tread. After a moment I felt I could exhale, but barely.

"We've about shot our bolt," I said. "Get back to it."

"Who was that woman?" asked Harry.

"Casper's," I paused. "Rather, Van Effen's shipboard romance, for want of a better description." Joel resumed his careful scooping, handing material down to me. After a few moments he whispered.

"I see it."

"Take it out slowly. Be mindful it doesn't spill," I instructed him. He nodded and slowly withdrew a cylindrical oil cloth drawstring bag about five inches long.

"Clever," said Harry. "It just fits into the door. Someone thought this out carefully."

Joel handed me the bag and climbed down, and I handed it to Harry. He carried it to the bed and gently untied it with Joel and I anxiously watching. The first thing he pulled out was a bent piece of cardboard. He handed it to Joel.

"One of my uncle's business cards," he said. "I wonder why they scooped that up with everything else?"

"Probably in a hurry to empty the box," said Harry.

"And maybe to prove that they actually did steal from Isaac," I added.

"Possibly," said Harry. "Here we go." He began to remove glittering diamonds, each one nestled in a thin paper wrapper. "Your uncle used a nice grade of diamond paper," said Harry. "And they are loosely packed. I'm sure it contributed to the sound you heard when you opened and closed the door, Maeve."

Joel carefully opened one of the wraps. "Remember how it goes, you'll have to put it back," I said.

"I know. I just have to see one or two."

Harry had taken his loupe out and picked up one of the stones Joel unwrapped. He took it to the porthole to examine, then went back to trade it for another, and another, as Joel unwrapped and rewrapped them. Finally, Harry put his loupe back in his pocket and came over to us.

"Is there enough here to get me out of my jam and started on my own?" asked Joel.

"I'm still holding the Brazilian pillow cut for you," said Harry.

"And I'm glad it's safe," said Joel. "What about these?"

Harry shook his head. "If the other stones in that bag follow the lead of what I've looked at…I'm sorry, Joel."

Joel turned pale. "You don't mean," he began.

Harry slowly nodded his head. "This looks like your uncle had nothing to sell but *khazeray*."

# VIII

I'm sure you've heard the adage 'Fool me once, shame on you, fool me twice, shame on me.' The proverb has its beginning in a book written in 1651 by a man named Anthony Weldon. He writes that 'The Italians having a Proverb, He that deceives me once, it's his fault; but if twice, it's my fault.' Where the Italians came up with it I haven't the foggiest but I'm willing to bet that it originally had nothing to do with diamonds, and yet for us, had everything to do with diamonds.

Joel stared at Harry, and I have to admit I must have been goggle-eyed too. "Junk?" Joel squeaked out. Harry nodded.

"I can keep looking at the rest of them, but I'm going to say it will have the same result."

"Try one from deeper in the bag," I said. Joel dug down and removed a stone, handing it to Harry. In less than a minute he returned the verdict.

"The same. Well-made, could fool your average person, just like the ones that killed your uncle."

Joel sat on the bed. "Oh my God, what am I going to do?"

"The first thing we're going to do is put these back," I said, carefully loading the rewrapped gems back in the sack, finishing with the folded business card. I pulled the drawstring closed and handed it to Joel, then followed him into the bathroom. "Back it goes. I'll hand you up the filling and you can repack it."

Joel sighed and stood back up in the chair and began his work. "Kind of reminds me of filling in a grave. Mine."

Harry and I looked at each other. "Maybe this wasn't what was in Isaac's box," said Harry.

"Of course it was. You saw the card." Joel began to smooth out the packing material. "He brought a box of junk to sell. Maybe he meant to go out on the street with Van Effen and make people think they were getting a bargain." He clambered down from the chair. "After everything I've learned about him in the past few days I wouldn't not credit him with doing something along those lines."

"Me either," I said as I gathered up the tool and unused filler. A final glance at the floor and overall room told me everything was as it had been. "You two go on to the door," I said. "I'll put the chair back where I found it." Another quick stop to smooth out the bed covers where Joel had been sitting, then I joined them at the door.

"I wish Casper was still out there," said Harry.

"Can you imagine?" I said as I unlocked the door. "Hulking man like that and he's named Casper." I opened the door a crack and peered out. The corridor was deserted. "Ok, Joel, to your cabin and lock the door. Harry, you come with me." He nodded. I swung open the door and we bolted, me locking up after us. Harry followed me up the stairs to the Main Deck where we emerged into a sunny but chilly early afternoon.

"Never in my life," said Harry. I nodded.

"We Brits say 'never in my puff' but it means the same thing. And I have to agree with you. Who would have thought?"

Harry shook his head. "Not me. I refuse to believe that anyone, even Nathaniel Isaac, would stoop so low as to try and pass off fakes."

"So now it all depends on Mr Perry," I said. "Selling enough to give Joel a start on paying off Schultz, if he doesn't die first."

Harry gave me a sidelong glance. "Really, you need to curb this tendency toward pessimism."

"Hard not to be. We arrive in Cherbourg Friday at eight a.m. and we're no closer to solving Isaac's death than we were on Sunday afternoon." We climbed the stairs to the Promenade Deck. "Meanwhile I'm losing Alice who's leaving the ship at Cherbourg to marry Joel, who may or may not be alive a week from now if he doesn't repay some of his debt, which appears impossible since his New York store was robbed and out here we're apparently awash in fake diamonds." I looked at Harry. "I know Mr Perry has volunteered to help Joel out of a requiem for a lost love. But what if he can't do a deal for it?"

"I've been thinking on that," said Harry. "We still have the Brazilian stone, and I believe it would fetch a nice price, but that would leave Joel with nothing to begin his career on – unless any of the items Mr Perry is willing to part with are on a substantial scale. I obviously don't know what Mr Perry has in his trading stock, but I'm willing to help sweeten the deal for Joel with one or two items from my own."

I stopped in my tracks with a sharp exclamation. Harry's offer was amazing, but to be fair I had also run into a deck chair impolitely left in the promenade traffic pattern. "Would you really?" He nodded. "Harry Winston, you are a prince among – what is the word you use?"

"*Diamantaire*," said Harry, "and thank you for the compliment." He smiled. "Prince is good, but I'm aiming a bit higher."

"I've no doubt," I said, inclining my head to indicate the side door of the Observation Lounge. "Look who's coming out – Van Effen and his paramour."

Harry gave her a once over. "She matches her voice, doesn't she?"

"I'm afraid so. Let me introduce you." I hastened forward, mindful of the deck chair bump on my knee. "Mr Van Effen," I called. He turned around.

"Nurse Chandler," he said. "And Mr Winston." He gave me a brittle smile. "I hope your last endeavor worked out well for you?"

"Yes and no," said Harry.

Van Effen gave him a brief curious look, then indicated the woman on his arm. "Oh, I beg your pardon, Mr Winston. This is Miss Caroline Thomas."

"Mr Winston, a pleasure." She turned to me. "And of course Nurse Chandler and I have already met once or twice."

"Twice," I said.

"Yes." She sized me up before turning back to Harry and I felt more frumpy than ever. "Casper tells me you're a jeweler as well."

"Casper is correct," said Harry as I tried hard not to smirk. "And I believe Mr Van Effen also has some expertise in the field."

Caroline hugged Van Effen's arm. "Yes. I love a man who knows his diamonds. Surely you must feel the same way about all your men, Nurse?"

"Oh, yes," I replied, wondering if the Captain would put me in irons or just order me placed under cabin arrest after I tossed this woman over the railings.

"Where is Mr Singer?" interjected Van Effen.

"In his cabin," I said.

"And the other nurse, Miss Alice? Is she with him?"

"I wouldn't doubt it."

Van Effen nodded. "Well, I am sure he is fine." He turned to Caroline. "Shall we go?"

"So nice to meet you, Mr Wilson," Caroline cooed. "And Nurse Chandler, it's always a pleasure. We shall have to get together, just us girls, and talk about men and diamonds." She gave me an up and down look. "And of course, fashion."

"There's nothing I would like more," I said, wishing for my wooden sword of childhood days and grinding my back molars into dust.

# I

When I woke up Thursday morning the birds were chirping merrily, the sky was the most beautiful cloudless blue, and the grass was soft and newly mown, still damp from the dew and heavy with a scent that came straight from heaven. An absolutely glorious day, all in all.

Somewhere it was like that, I was certain. Just not here.

As I was coming to life the *Queen Victoria* was passing into a series of squall lines. The resulting whipping winds and driving rain made it impossible to be out on the open decks. If you're reading this and are not a sailor, here's what was happening. A squall line is an organized line of thunderstorms. They are accompanied by roll clouds and shelf clouds and can lead to severe weather events. Normally we have our share of rough seas from November through February, but somewhere in those months is when we usually put in to drydock for inspection and service, so we miss at least part of it. (But the North Atlantic lanes we travel are notoriously fickle, so you never really know.)

The rapidly changing wind direction means the ship is buffeted from all sides, and waves crash against the hull. Again, if you're not a seasoned sailor, it's not a pleasant place to be; honestly it's not that pleasant for those of us who already have our sea legs. For the medical staff, mornings like this mean plenty of quick seasick cabin calls.

For Mister Harvey's staff, it means plenty of uneaten breakfasts. And for housekeeping – well, you can imagine what it means for housekeeping.

In order to more quickly bring aid and succor to our passengers, Alice started at the bottom on E Deck and worked her way up, Doctor Harper started in the middle at C Deck, and I began on the Main Deck and worked my way down, bag in hand. Even in our modern age there's not a lot to be done about seasickness. Some of the more knowledgeable passengers had come on board with their favorite patent medicines for treating seasickness; Mothersill's Seasick Remedy, (a notion I was frankly skeptical of) while others carried Seajoy Anti-Seasickness Plasters (of which I was also a skeptic but they did contain a bit of morphine, so maybe people felt better afterward). The other non-prescribed cure is Roach's Sea-Sickness Draughts, so if you are so inclined, you can take your pick.

In my experience, however, treating *mal-de-mer* involves a light, very bland diet, plenty of water, and bed rest. Scopolamine is also a treatment alternative, but we only use that for really severe cases.

Like the one being inflicted on Alexander Perry.

Seasickness affects different people in different ways. Some brush it off as nothing more than minor indigestion and go about their day. Others feel absolutely nothing at all and acclimate almost immediately. Still others may need a day of bed rest and the bland diet I indicated. And then you have those who feel like they would have to die in order to get better. That's the category Mr Perry fell into. His cabin door was unlocked and he was wedged into his bed with pillows, looking like he was already at death's door – which, for a man in his 70's already suffering a bout of malaria, was alarming.

"I'm sorry to see you're not feeling well, Mr Perry," I said, placing my bag at the foot of his bed. I picked up his wrist to take his pulse. "You do look ashen." I frowned at him. "And still jaundiced."

"Ashen? The way I feel I should think jaundice and forest green would be more appropriate."

"Have you taken any sort of store-bought remedy?"

"No, just quinine for the malaria. He screwed his eyes shut and opened them. "How much longer is the ship going to heave about like this?"

I shrugged. "I'm told it's a line of thunderstorms cutting across our path. We should be out of it by one, in time for lunch."

"Lunch!" Perry clenched his jaws. "If I'm any indication you're going to have a lot of empty seats."

"The morning meal was also not well attended."

"I can believe that." Perry suddenly sat up and I quickly put the rubbish basket by the bed out for him. After a moment he leaned back weakly.

"Given the way it's affecting you, Mr Perry, I'm going to recommend that you let me give you an injection. It will help calm the ill motion effects you're feeling."

"Anything that will help, Nurse Chandler. What is it?"

"Scopolamine." I took a syringe out of my bag and began to fill it from a small vial.

"Never heard of it."

"Have you ever had any surgery?"

"No"

"Then you wouldn't have. It's primarily used to control any post-operative nausea and vomiting that can be side effects from anesthesia, but it's also been found to be beneficial at helping control heavy motion sickness like you're experiencing. Roll up your sleeve." I swabbed the injection site with alcohol, then gave him the shot. "Not too bad, was it?"

"No." He let his sleeve down. "When will it start working?"

"About twenty minutes or so. Just lay still and close your eyes. Avoid smoking for the next eight hours. And with your malarial reoccurrence I highly recommend you stop drinking. The less stress you put on your liver the better. I've got some more rounds to do, but I'll come back and check on you."

"Fine, thank you." He closed his eyes. "If I'm asleep, please don't wake me. Unless, of course, you think I might be dead, in which case feel free to prod away."

"I will." I snapped the bag shut and left the cabin, turning the light off behind me. Feeling it best to get my older passengers out of the way first, I knocked on Mr Clayton's door and was rewarded with a sprightly "come in".

"Ah, Nurse Chandler," he said. "What a pleasant surprise. I should have thought you would be very busy with the rough seas."

"Actually, I am. I'm just checking in on you. No ill effects, I hope?"

"None at all. And those mice that I was hearing seem to have gone away."

"Yes? You haven't heard them?"

"No, and it's the strangest thing, too. They seemed to go away not very long after I talked with you yesterday. I thought I heard one last rustle of them after you left me, then I heard some scratching early this morning, then quiet again. Isn't that odd?" He smiled. "Maybe they knew you were looking for them."

"Maybe." I took his wrist to check his pulse, but my mind was racing. "Well, as you seem to be in perfect health, I'll continue my rounds."

"You should get some help," he said, indicating my bag. "That looks awfully large for a little thing like you to be lugging about."

"It's not too bad." I smiled at him. "And it gives me something to use on recalcitrant passengers."

"Then I'm very glad I'm one of the obliging ones."

"You have no idea, Mr Clayton. Thank you." I closed the door and stood in thought. The first reference to the mice was obviously the visit with Harry, Joel, and me on yesterday. But then the second reference early this morning? I rapped impatiently on Harry's cabin door. "Mr Winston? It's Nurse Chandler. I need to talk with you."

"He and Mr Singer have gone to breakfast. The seas apparently do not bother either of them."

I turned. Van Effen was standing in the corridor, hat in hand, seemingly materialized from nowhere. "Mr Van Effen," I said. "The weather doesn't appear to bother you, either."

"No," he nodded. "But one thing does."

"And that would be?"

Van Effen took a step toward me. "What was in the door?"

"I'm surprised you didn't ask yesterday."

"The opportunity did not present itself after I guided Miss Thomas away from your investigation."

I set my bag on the floor. "For which we were intensely grateful. And how is Miss Thomas today?"

"She is quite ill."

"I'm sorry to hear that." I couldn't care less. "As to what was in the door, I'm afraid it wasn't what we were hoping for."

"Counterfeits?"

"Yes, and very well-made ones too."

"Were they?" Van Effen pursed his lips. "All of them?"

"All of the ones that we examined. We didn't go through the entire package, but there's no reason not to believe they all wouldn't be counterfeit."

"What did you do with them?"

"Put them back where we found them."

"I see," said Van Effen.

"In point of fact, they were quite like the ones we found in Mr Isaac's mouth."

Van Effen's eyebrows arched. "I was under the impression that those were real diamonds."

I shook my head. "Only one of them was real. The rest were fakes."

"And where is the real one?"

"In safekeeping."

"So what you are telling me is that unless the police recover what was taken from his shop, Mr Singer has nothing but one stone?"

"Does it make a difference?"

"No." Van Effen put on his hat. "I am contracted and paid to protect him until we return to New York. However, once he steps off the boat in New York, he is on his own." He adjusted his tie knot. "The City can be a large and violent place."

I ignored his jibe. "Have you heard back from your 'associate' in New York about the robbery?"

Van Effen shook his head. "Only that Mr Jenkins is no longer among the living, but I'm sure you already knew that. As to the store's contents – " He shrugged. "If you will excuse me, I will take my leave to check on Mr Singer and get something to eat before bringing him back to his cabin. Would you be good enough to look in on Miss Thomas?"

"Of course," I said with a smile on my face. Maybe I could give her something to increase her seasickness.

"Thank you." Van Effen steadied himself as the *Victoria* began encountering heavier swells.

"Are you certain you will be all right?" I asked him.

Van Effen nodded. "I went to sea many years ago." He turned and headed for the stairs.

I went to Miss Thomas' cabin and knocked. "Miss Thomas," I said. "Nurse Chandler. We're having some rough seas, I just thought I'd check on you."

"Just a minute." I heard stumbling feet and then the key turned in the lock and the door swung inward. With some smug self-satisfaction I noted her disheveled appearance and the way she staggered back and fell into the bed.

"Not feeling well?" I asked solicitously.

"Too much giggle juice last night," she replied. I nodded my head in sympathy.

"The bartenders on the *Victoria* are known for being generous," I said.

"Too damn generous by half." She clamped her hands to her head. "Can you make the damn room stop spinning?"

"You'll live."

"I doubt that."

"Bed rest, water, and water biscuits. It will go away, I promise."

Miss Thomas laid back on her pillows, a hand across her eyes. "What the hell are water biscuits?"

"Yanks call them crackers."

"Jesus, then why didn't you say so?" She rolled over and pulled a pillow over her head and I left, fighting the urge not to sit on said pillow. I let myself out into the corridor. Van Effen had apparently made a stop on his way out to check on Joel. I could hear his muffled voice through his cabin door, though not well enough to make anything of it; it sounded as if he was carrying on an argument with himself.

Maybe the strain of spending so much time with Miss Thomas was getting to him.

One could only hope.

**‖**

While I'm good at math and chemistry, I was never cut out to be an accountant. Adding never-ending columns of numbers all day long sounds like a special ring of Dante's *Inferno* that I really wouldn't wish upon anyone. And when you're done, Column A has to tot up perfectly with Column B. Close enough by a ha'penny or two won't cut it.

So, in the ledger devoted to the mystery of Nathaniel Isaac, Column A now held, thanks to Harry, the probable secret of the master key, as well as a hiding place drilled in the top of a bathroom door for more jewels that turned out to be fake. Column A also held the wedding bands that told the sad story of Nathaniel Isaac and Annake Dirickson.

Column B held a dead Isaac and a dead Mr Jenkins and a robbed jewelry store, as well as a former business partner of Isaac who seemed truly sorry for everything that had happened in the past, in addition to someone who was knowledgeable about curare and knew how to deliver a dose to cause paralysis but not death and also was capable of locking a door behind them and leaving the key turned in the lock on the inside without a trace of how it was done.

Finally, just because I'm unlucky, I had a bonus Column C. Contents: one nephew who was going to marry my nurse if he could keep from being killed for owing money to a New York gangster, one bodyguard for said nephew who was enjoying a shipboard romance, and finally a missing box of jewels, if indeed there were jewels in it in the first place. It was enough to give a girl a headache.

Alice was idly flipping through an old newspaper when I returned to the hospital around noon. "Did you get everyone taken care of?"

"Pretty much. Gave a few injections, but for the most part just prescribed bed rest, you know, the usual drill."

She frowned. "Did you check on Joel?"

"I didn't see him but I've no doubt he's fine. He and Mr Winston went to eat."

Alice laughed. "Sounds like they're both born sailors."

"Van Effen as well. Mr Perry, I'm sorry to say, was not doing well."

"I think he's nice to try and help. I hope he gets better." She nodded. "I've written out my resignation letter. It's on the desk."

"You're really going to do this?"

"Absolutely."

I passed a hand over my forehead. "I know you're in love, but I still think you should wait."

Alice shook her head. "If not now, then never." She smiled. "I don't think you'll have any trouble finding a replacement."

"That's scarcely the point, and you know it." I sat down next to her. "I just feel like things are too murky right now."

"What do you mean?"

"The body of Mr Jenkins was found in the Hudson River. As of now no jewels have been recovered from the store."

Alice blinked at me with that wide-eyed bunny rabbit stare. "That's horrible."

"There are people out there playing for keeps," I said. "And if Joel isn't able to make a payment on his loan, he could be hurt, or worse."

"You really are worried, aren't you?"

"Yes. And you should be, too."

Alice thought for a moment. "We're what, about a day, day and a half out?"

"Something like that. Arriving Cherbourg around 8 a.m. local time tomorrow."

"I'm glad you can keep all of that time calculation straight in your head. I never can."

"It's about the only math I'm capable of," I said.

Alice laughed, then frowned. "What will happen if we arrive in Cherbourg and don't know who killed Mr Isaac?"

"Then someone will have gotten away with murder."

"Is there anything else?"

I nodded and told her about the bathroom door with the hole drilled in it.

She frowned. "That's bonkers. I don't understand why anyone would want to hide fake jewels in the bathroom door. Beyond their value as costume jewelry, they're worthless, aren't they? Unless – "

"Unless what?"

"Unless the person that put them in the door thought they were actually real."

I stared at her. "Where did you come up with that?"

Alice shrugged. "Just trying to be helpful. Am I being helpful? It isn't right you and Mr Winston having to carry this out on your own."

In my mind's eye I could see my neatly ordered ledger columns, all three of the bloody things, A, B, and C, trying to rearrange themselves into new patterns. None too stable to begin with, they were now quivering on their foundations. I patted her hand.

"You're always helpful," I assured her. The telephone rang and I picked it up, glad for the distraction. "Hospital, Nurse Chandler."

"Good morning, Maeve," said Harry. "I hope I'm not disturbing you? I thought you might be on the job."

"Which one? Nursing or sleuthing?"

"I'm afraid the latter. Can you come up? I think I may be on to something for one of our riddles."

"Be right there." I rang off and took Alice's hands in mine. "One other thing you might bear in mind, your romance with Joel isn't the well-kept secret you may imagine it is. If someone is going to go after Joel while he's on board, they may go through you to get to him."

"What should I do?"

"For now, stay here in the hospital with Doctor Harper. Where is he, anyway?"

"Still making his rounds. He said he would return to the hospital afterward."

I nodded. "All right. Wait for him. Tell him what I told you. I need to go up to see Mr Winston."

When I returned to First Class Van Effen was sitting in a chair outside of Joel's cabin door. He nodded at me. "Mr Singer is fine. He and Mr Winston returned from breakfast a few minutes ago. He is laying down. I do not think it is the sea sickness, he is just tired."

"And with good reason," I replied. "I know I am." The corridor was empty save for the two of us. "By the way, I did go and check on Miss Thomas."

"How is she doing?"

I refrained from saying catty as ever, choosing to let my conscience be my guide. "I don't believe she's suffering from the sea, but from a galloping hangover."

Van Effen gave a thoughtful nod of his head. "We did drink last night."

"You seem to have made a full afternoon and evening of it then, Casper."

He flinched. "Please do not call me that name."

"Have it your way. I'm sure she'd enjoy a visit from you."

"Perhaps once Mr Singer is up and about, maybe in the company of Mr Winston, then I will call on her."

"Well, good luck. It's been a couple of hours since I've seen her. Maybe she's slept it off by now. Is everything all right with you?"

"Yes. Why would it not be?"

"Just making sure. I thought I heard you arguing with someone in your cabin a while ago."

"It was a minor disagreement with a steward," he said easily.

"All right, then." I gently knocked on Harry's door and after a moment was admitted.

"I think I've figured out how the locked door trick was worked," he said, guiding me to the table on which sat his jewelry repair paraphernalia. "It's blindingly simple, yet ingenious."

I sat across from him at the table. "Maybe to you. Me, not so much."

"Oh, Maeve, it was right in front of us – well, at least me – all the time." He picked his room key off the table. "Steel key. Issued for all the cabin locks on the *Victoria*, am I correct?"

"Yes."

"And we know this individual cabin key can be dispensed with if you have a master key, whether legitimately obtained or not."

I nodded. "Which I've still got to return to Mister Harvey."

"Yes, yes, of course," said Winston. "But what if there's a third way to open and then lock a door?"

"Without a key?"

He shook his head. "No, the key would still need to be placed in the lock. Turning the key is where the trick comes in."

"I'm not sure I follow you," I said.

Harry nodded. "Do you remember yesterday when I told you I'd de-magnetized Van Effen's pocket watch?"

"Yes, on Monday afternoon is what you said." I pointed to the demagnetizer sitting on the table. "Using that box there."

"Correct. Van Effen's pocket watch is very expensive," said Harry. "As he pointed out, a Waltham. An extremely accurate time piece costing about $300, so you don't want to monkey with it too much."* Winston frowned. "It's been bothering me the past few days, how someone as obviously fastidious and immaculate as Van Effen would let a valuable watch come into contact with a powerful magnetic field, much less how he himself would come into contact with one."

I thought a moment. "The *Victoria*'s magnetic compass is out in the open on the roof top of the bridge," I said. "But it's obviously not strong enough to affect a watch or the officers would have been complaining a long time ago. I'm sure Chief Duncan could point out plenty of things in engineering that could magnetize, but that area is strictly off limits to passengers."

"Good thought," said Harry, "but the watch would need to stay in close proximity to the generated magnetic field to become magnetized itself. So, that lets out your idea of dynamos or generators or whatever in the

_______________

* $300 in 1930 is roughly the equivalent of over $5,000 in 2023.

engineering rooms. Anyway, I don't picture Van Effen loitering about in the engine rooms, do you? So it would have to be something smaller." He took out his own watch. "Where does a man keep his pocket watch?"

"In his pocket, of course."

Harry nodded and slid it back in his pocket. "What else would a man keep in his pockets?"

"Coins, cigarette lighter, keys," I said. "None of which are magnetized."

"Right. So what would magnetize a pocket watch? It would have to be small to fit in a pocket."

I shrugged. "Obviously a magnet, of course."

"Yes, but not a cube magnet like I use to hold small parts. This would be a very special kind of magnet." He held up his cabin key. "A magnet that would slip over this steel key and hold it tight."

"I'm not sure I understand what you're saying."

Harry held his key up by the oval at the top. "This part of the key is called the bow," he said. He drew his finger down the shaft. "This is the shank, or stem." He touched the protruding tab at the bottom. "This is the bit, with the key wards cut into it."

Finally, he tapped the very end of the key's cylindrical body. "This is the pin. Now, what if you had a way to slip a magnetized sheath or cylinder of some kind over the pin at the end of the key? If the magnet is powerful enough and fits perfectly onto the pin, it would grip the key and, I think, allow someone to turn the key in the lock from the outside."

I have to admit I stared at him. "Do you think that's how it was done?"

Harry nodded. "As good an explanation as any, and it fits the magnetism issue Van Effen had with his watch." He toyed with the key in his hand. "The keyholes on the cabin doors are awfully small to put the jaws of a pair of needle nose pliers in, even the smallest pair of jeweler's pliers, and even if you could you wouldn't have a hope of gripping anything and turning it. On the other hand, if you had a thin tube of highly magnetized metal that would fit snugly over the pin, it would give you some leverage to turn the key in the lock from the outside."

"Cor blimey," I said. "How did you come up with that?"

"When you were in here earlier and that key was attracted to my block magnet," said Harry. "It got me to thinking."

I shook my head. "That's a better explanation than any I've tried to work out. I thought maybe someone might have used a piece of string looped over the door and through the bow of the key to turn it."

"Bit fussy, don't you think? Not to mention time consuming to stand out in the corridor and fiddle with," said Harry. "The magnet is more certain."

"And a powerful magnet carried next to a watch would cause problems?" I asked. He nodded.

"If the watch's hairspring gets magnetized, then part of the hairspring gets stuck together, making it shorter, which in turn makes the watch run faster. Van Effen said his watch had been gaining nearly ninety seconds per day. A fine pocket watch like that doesn't just start gaining time without good reason, so I began thinking about the magnetism route. One thought led to another, and there you have it."

"But Van Effen," I said. "I wasn't sure about him at first, but he's been nothing but helpful."

"Maybe too helpful," said Harry. "He's been in on what you've been doing about every step of the way."

"And he knows that if Isaac actually did bring real diamonds on board that they are still missing."

"Powerful incentive to be helpful."

I looked at Harry. "How do you feel about us talking with him?"

"Now? Just the two of us without anyone else?"

"He's in the corridor outside of Joel's cabin right now. He won't do anything."

Harry nodded "He won't do anything there," he corrected me. "But remember someone has a master key and they aren't afraid to use it. We'll have to spend the rest of the voyage in the Observation Lounge."

"Or locked up in the Isolation Wards." I waited until Harry had put his jacket on, then opened the door and looked. The chair was still outside of Joel's cabin, and while Van Effen wasn't in it his hat was. I picked it up. "Guess we can take it back to him. Maybe help ease into our conversation. I haven't seen him without it the entire voyage."

"I don't think there's going to be anything easy about this conversation," said Harry. We walked down the corridor to Van Effen's cabin and I knocked gently on the door but got no immediate reply. Harry looked at me. "Maybe he's taking a nap."

"Can you imagine Van Effen ever letting his guard down to take a nap?" I rapped on the door, with the same result. Harry tried the door knob.

"Locked."

I knelt on the carpet and peered through the keyhole. "And from the inside," I said. I dug out Mister Harvey's master key and inserted it through the keyhole and gave a twist. The key on the inside fell out and the master turned the wards. A gentle twist on the knob opened the door.

Van Effen's cabin was inboard with no portholes, and the suite was in darkness. I located the light switch and turned on the overhead. The sitting room was devoid of Van Effens, as was the bedroom. His shoulder holster and handgun were laying on the bed and his shoes were on the floor. His jacket was carelessly tossed over a chair.

"Like I said earlier, Van Effen always struck me as more neat and precise than this," said Harry. The bathroom door was closed. "What do you think?"

I shrugged. "The worst that can happen is we'll catch him in an embarrassing moment." I reached for the knob and twisted it, then turned on the light. Harry and I stood in silence for a few seconds. "I take it back," I said. "That wasn't the worst that could happen."

At the very bottom of a very full bathtub lay a very dead Van Effen.

# *Thursday, March 27, 1930*

Everyone knows that ships can, and do, sink. There was the *Titanic* nose-dive just 18 years ago, and of course my brother perishing on the *Britannic*, just one of the many ships making an unscheduled trip to the bottom in the recent War. And an irrevocable fact is that when ships sink, people drown. (Unless aboard a war ship, and then as Doctor Harper could tell you, they can also get despatched in other ways.) On the other hand, in my experience, I've found that people drowning at sea without having their ship slide out from under them is rare – so rare that this was the first time I'd seen it happen. (Of course, there was that incident on the *Victoria* last October, but I think that falls under a technicality.)*

Harry and I stood side by side and gazed down at Van Effen's water-logged corpse in silence. I pursed my lips.

"I don't think we're going to get any answers out of him, do you?"

"Nope."

"Help me get him to a sitting position." We each took a shoulder and dragged Van Effen upright, heedless of the water splashing out of the tub onto our shoes and the floor.

"Another door locked from the inside. Suicide?" ventured Harry.

"I wouldn't bet on it."

---

*    See Book One: *Shadow of the Queen*

"Me, either." He watched me begin to examine Van Effen's neck. "I hate to ask, but what are you looking for?"

"I'll know it when I see it," I said. Van Effen was wearing a white dress shirt, collar buttoned, and a knotted blue tie. He was still in his blue suit trousers with suspenders and socks. "Look at this, Harry." I pinched my thumbs and forefingers on either side of a small section of Van Effen's shirt collar at the side of his neck.

"What am I looking at?"

"Right here." I moved an index finger over it. "See it?"

Harry squinted. "There's a little hole."

I flipped the collar over. "And a tiny spot of blood. Unless I'm very much mistaken, that's where Mr Van Effen received a none too gentle injection."

"Curare?" said Harry "Again?"

"Probably." I stood and reached for a towel to cover Van Effen's face.

"And the killer pushed him under to finish him off." Harry shook his head. "I wasn't overly fond of Mr Van Effen, but that was a terrible way to go."

"Almost as bad as being stuffed with fake diamonds." I glanced at my wristwatch. "You know, not more than 15 minutes elapsed between the time I saw Van Effen in the hall outside Joel's door until you and I left your cabin and he wasn't out there any longer."

"So?"

"So, this bathtub is very full, Van Effen's water displacement notwithstanding. It takes about fifteen minutes for one of these tubs to fill."

"Are you saying someone had already filled this tub and was waiting for Van Effen?"

I shrugged. "All I know is when I was through this corridor earlier ministering to Mr Perry and Miss Thomas' bouts of seasickness, Van Effen told me he was going up to check on you and Joel having breakfast. Shortly after that I heard what sounded like him arguing with someone in his cabin. Just before I saw you he told me it had been a disagreement with a steward."

Harry shrugged. "Maybe his shoes didn't get shined to his satisfaction. All I can tell you is that he did a checkup on us and got his own breakfast while he waited for Joel and I to finish ours. After that he walked Joel back to his cabin."

"So it's possible someone could have let themselves in, filled the tub, and let themselves out again in that interim."

Harry nodded. "Or filled the tub and stayed inside the cabin to wait for Van Effen to return. Maybe this mystery steward."

I looked down at Van Effen's body. "Our stewards usually don't come in at nearly the same size as Van Effen; none of them in their right mind would pick a fight with him because they'd be squashed like a bug. And remember Van Effen's coat and shoulder holster and gun in there on the bed, like he'd taken them off in a hurry." I pursed my lips. "Maybe in a hurry to join someone in the bathroom?"

"Exactly," said Harry. "Which would indicate that when he entered his cabin he knew his killer was already here and let his guard down."

"You do have a multi-faceted mind, Harry. But who would want him dead and why?"

We were interrupted by a sharp knock on the door. "Casper?" said a woman's voice. I bit my lip.

"Miss Thomas again," I whispered. "She seems to have made a recovery from earlier this morning when I saw her."

"Maybe she'll go away," said Harry. The doorknob rattled and she knocked again. He looked at me. "Persistent, isn't she?"

"Casper, I'll be in the observation lounge. See you there." For a moment we could hear her heels clattering on the steps leading topside, then she was gone.

"What now?" asked Harry. "Can't just leave him here."

"Of course not. I'll call Doctor Harper. He and Mister Harvey will take charge of the body until we reach Cherbourg."

"It sounds as if you've done this before."

"Once or twice," I said.* "Just leave him sitting here." We walked back into the bedroom and I picked up the 'phone. After a brief explanation to an incredulous Harper, I rang off. "They'll be here soon," I told Harry. "In the meantime, let's have a look around."

"Do you think we should?"

"Van Effen is beyond caring." I began opening drawers, encountering plenty of empty space. "For an ocean voyage roundtrip and a stay in Antwerp, he sure traveled light."

"I don't know," said Harry, opening the wardrobe. "Several suits in here."

"That's nothing, Harry. You should see the trunks some of the women in First Class travel with. A different outfit two or three times a day."

"Well, Van Effen was nothing if not consistent. All of these suits are pretty much identical dark blue and smell of

---

*    See Book One: *Shadow of the Queen*

cigarettes. And more white shirts folded here. His hat seems to be the only thing that he wore to set himself off. Judging by these he certainly didn't seem to go in for high fashion." Harry thumbed through the suits. "Wait a minute. Look here." He pulled a suit out of the wardrobe and laid it on the bed.

"What?"

"Right here." Harry pointed out a small, white-colored crusted streak on the suit jacket, near the right-hand pocket. "What does that look like to you?"

I shrugged. "I don't know. Dried oatmeal?"

"How about the filler that was used on the door in that vacant cabin?" Harry gently put his hand in the suit pocket and withdrew a similarly stained and crusted handkerchief. "And, as the French are fond of saying, *et voilà!*"

"Oh, my sainted aunt!" I said. "And he asked me just this morning what we had found in the door. He knew all along – he was having a go at me." A sudden thought crossed my mind. "Turn out his trouser cuffs on that suit, would you?" Harry did as he was instructed. A miniscule collection of wood shavings surfaced. "Bloody hell."

Harry nodded. "Looks like we've found your man."

"Then the missing diamonds should be in here." I turned my attention back to the drawers and furniture, got on my knees to look under the bed, and even lifted the mattress. No diamonds. I walked into the front room where Harry was just closing a drawer on the writing desk. "Any luck?"

"Nothing."

I pointed at the air vents. "When Harper and Harvey get here we'll have one of them get on a chair and take a look in there. After that, we'll have looked everywhere there is to look in here."

"Not the top of his bathroom door."

"Good point." I dragged a chair over and climbed up, running my fingers along the door. "Nothing."

"Maeve?" Harper's voice came through the cabin door. Harry opened it and Harper and Harvey came inside.

"Van Effen's in the bathtub," I said, climbing down from the chair. "Could one of you please take a look in the air vents?"

"What are we looking for?" asked Harvey.

"A bag. Any sort of container that might hold diamonds." I left Harvey with Winston and ushered Harper into the bathroom. "There he is."

Harper knelt beside the tub. "And you found him under the water?"

"Yes." I pointed out the hole and blood on his collar. "With this to help him on his way."

"Curare again," said Harper.

"Undoubtedly, Boss. But who's large enough to manage sticking Van Effen? Isaac was an old man who walked with a cane. Van Effen's a professional torpedo."

"I hate to ask, but the door?"

"Locked from the inside again. I used Mister Harvey's master to open it. Which reminds me. Mister Harvey?" I called.

"There's nothing in the vents," said Harvey, sticking his head in. I handed him the master.

"Sorry to be so late getting it back to you."

"Keep it," he said. "I think you're going to need it more than I am for the time being." Harvey looked into the bathtub. "And now this. Landfall tomorrow morning and I'm thinking the Captain isn't going to want to stop for another service."

"Yes," said Harper. "I think we're close enough that we can safely leave him here until we port. Just get him out of the tub and on the bed."

"And drape a blanket or sheet over him," said Harry as he joined us.

"Right," said Harper. "For now, should anyone feel the need to know, let's just say he slipped in the bath, hit his head, and drowned."

"Mr Winston," said Harvey. "On behalf of the Stoddard Lines, I apologize for your crossing being so eventful."

"Not at all. I've actually learned one or two things." He gave me a wry smile. "Not that I'll ever have occasion to use them."

"Mr Winston knows how the doors were locked from the inside," I said.

"I think I do," corrected Harry. He explained his magnetized sleeve theory.

"Was that device here?" asked Harvey.

"The person who locked Van Effen's door from the outside took it with them," I said. "Just like they did with Mr Isaac."

Harper glanced down at the body. "Why was Van Effen killed?"

"I don't know. We found – Harry found – proof on him that he had drilled the hole in the top of the bathroom door and sealed it. It follows then that he was the person who put the fakes inside the door. But we also know he could recognize fakes. So why would he bother to hide them if he knew they were fakes?"

"Because he thought they were real," ventured Harry. "I think someone else was in there with him and handed him the closed bag for deposit. There was no time for him to look in the bag to check their authenticity and I'm guessing he had little reason to believe that the bag contained anything other than genuine diamonds."

"Well, he knew before he died. I saw him earlier today and he asked me what was in the door. I told him counterfeits, like the ones in Isaac's mouth."

"What was his reaction?" asked Harry.

"You know how he was," I said. "Hard to read, but I think that news got to him. It wasn't what he was expecting."

Harvey shook his head. "We're going to have to get the print shop to put out a programme to keep it all straight." He looked at Harper. "You have the counterfeits that we found in Isaac, correct?"

"Yes. Except for the one real stone. Mr Winston has that one."

"And what about the stuff you found in the door, Maeve?"

"Still there as of last night. I've been too busy to check."

"And Mr Isaac's original box with whatever he had in it?"

"Gone," I said. "And we never established if there was anything in it to begin with."

Harvey screwed his eyes tight shut then looked at Harper. "I've said it before and I'll say it again, I'm glad she's your responsibility, not mine."

# IV

Have you ever juggled, or watched a juggler? The really good ones are tossing and catching multiple items with blazing fire or something equally dangerous on one end, but of course they didn't start out that way. My brother and I saw a juggler at a friend's childhood party and were entranced. For whatever reason our father said no to us wanting to learn with knives, and instead got us Slazenger tennis balls with the proviso that we learn outside the house, away from breakables (as if).

I'd like to tell you that we were soon performing for our friends, but of course we weren't. We'd get one ball up in the air, maybe two, then lose one on its return. Every once in a while, for a couple of seconds, we'd get three balls moving at once, but then the entire enterprise would come crashing (or bouncing) down to earth.

Kind of the way I felt about my life right about now.

I asked Doctor Harper to take care of the formalities of informing the Captain that we were short another passenger, then Harry and I took our leave.

"Do you want to tell Joel the news?" asked Harry as we walked back up the corridor. I nodded.

"He might as well get it from me as anyone else."

"What about her?" Harry glanced down the corridor. Miss Thomas was approaching us.

"Oh, terrific," I said.

"Nurse Chandler and Mr Winston," said Miss Thomas as she drew near. "How nice to see you both again. And thank you for your advice earlier this morning, Nurse. I'm feeling much better." She tapped the corridor wall. "And of course, the ship's also stopped rocking so much. We must have passed through the storm. Have either of you seen Mr Van Effen? We were supposed to have an early lunch but I haven't seen or heard from him today."

I must admit that much as I disliked Miss Thomas, I wasn't going to enjoy what I was about to say to her. "I'm afraid I have some bad news for you, Miss Thomas. Mr Van Effen is no longer with us."

"No longer with us? What do you mean?"

"I mean he's dead. We discovered him in his cabin earlier this morning not too long after I had visited with you."

Miss Thomas clutched at the corridor handrail. "Oh, my God," she said. "What happened?"

"I think he was also suffering from the weather effects and ran a bath to see if it would help. It looks like he slipped and fell in, hit his head and drowned. Our Principle Medical Officer and Chief Steward are in the cabin now." I held up a restraining hand "I'm sorry, but you can't go in. The cabin will be sealed until we make port tomorrow morning."

"Poor Casper," she said. "What about his belongings?"

"They'll be handed over to the authorities when we dock, as well as his body. If no one claims it I would imagine he'll go into a pauper's grave or whatever passes for it in France."

"Poor Casper," she repeated, then gave a bright smile. "Well, I must be starting in on my packing for arrival. So sorry we never had time for our girl's chat, Nurse Chandler."

"The disappointment is all mine," I lied. She smiled again then brushed past us and up the corridor to her cabin where she disappeared. Harry looked at me.

"She's really a piece of work, isn't she?"

"I'll miss Van Effen much more than I will her."

Harry frowned. "Odd question, asking about his belongings. She certainly didn't mean his gun, at least I hope not, and the only other item of value I ever saw him with was his pocket watch."

"She's a gold digger, and they come in all shapes and sizes. Believe me, I've seen them before on this ship. They get their claws into a man they think is wealthy or exotic and before you can say Jack Robinson they've cleaned him out."

"You don't think," began Harry, then stopped. "No, of course not."

"Of course not what?"

"Van Effen wouldn't have told her about Mr Isaac's missing diamonds?"

"If he did I can certainly see how that may have piqued her interest." I gently knocked on Joel's cabin door.

"Who's there?" came Joel's voice.

"Nurse Chandler and Mr Winston," I replied. The key turned in the lock and the door swung inward.

"Ah, Harry," said Joel. "Good to see you again. I actually laid down and took a nap after we got back from breakfast."

"Did you sleep well?" I asked.

"Yes, with Van Effen parked outside the door."

Harry glanced at me. "About that," I said, coming inside with Van Effen's empty chair and closing the door. "Van Effen is dead. Murdered like your uncle, an injection of curare and then dumped in a full bathtub in his cabin."

Joel blinked at us. "Why?"

"He knew or found out something that he shouldn't have, and it cost him his life," said Harry.

"Did he say anything to you that might possibly be construed as out of the ordinary?" I asked Joel, putting the chair into a corner out of the way.

"No. Our conversations were always just civil, small talk. How was I doing, did I need anything, things like that." He frowned. "He did talk about how much he was enjoying that woman – Thomas is her last name?" Joel shook his head. "Hard to imagine a man like Van Effen being smitten that way."

"It takes all kinds," said Harry. "Best remember that when you start selling engagement rings."

"Joel, I'll have our Master at Arms detail a man to provide protection for you during the remainder of the voyage."

"Do you think I still need it?"

"Maybe the person who killed Van Effen thinks you know something, too," I said. "Yes, you need protection. I'll take care of that immediately. Until then, don't open your door unless it's someone you know and don't leave the cabin."

He nodded. "You two, Doctor Harper, Alice, Mister Harvey. What about Mr Perry?"

I uttered a brief expletive. With everything else going on, I'd completely forgotten about him. "I've got to go back and check on him. Harry, can you stay here with Joel until Mister Armstrong sends a man?"

"Yes, of course."

"Remember what I told you about opening the door," I said and stepped back into the corridor. It was quiet and empty; Harper and Mister Harvey were still inside of Van Effen's cabin. I walked across the hall and tapped on

Perry's door. There was no immediate reply so I knelt and put my ear to the keyhole. A gentle, rhythmic snoring could be heard. I stood and tried the handle, found it still unlocked from my earlier visit in the day, so I quietly opened the door and went inside.

The lights were still off and, like Van Effen's, Perry's was an inboard cabin with no portholes. I switched on the small desk lamp and placed a quick phone call to Mister Armstrong to let him know Mr Van Effen was a bit under the weather and could he send a substitute, then made my way to the bedroom.

The bedside light was on and Perry was asleep, propped up in the pillows. "How is the poor man doing?" a voice spoke quietly behind me. I whirled around, my heart jumping. A trim, nicely dressed and attractive woman in what I guessed to be her mid to late forties was standing in the bedroom door. She smiled down at me, something most people did since I'm barely five feet tall, but this woman was a good ten inches taller than me. "I was just coming back from a turn on the Promenade Deck and saw the cabin door ajar. I thought I'd look in on the man in case he needed aid after our rough weather this morning. I checked on the other gentleman earlier. In fact, Mr Clayton and I went up to the Observation Lounge for a drink. He was still there when I left." She smiled. "So fortunate for a widow like myself to be housed between two such handsome men as Mr Perry and Mr Clayton."

"Who are you?"

"Adelaide Morgan. Cabin 32-A, though I don't spend much time there. How do you do?" she proffered a hand.

"Miss Morgan," I began.

"Mrs."

"Mrs Morgan. While I'm sorry we have not had cause to meet socially and glad we have not met professionally, I must strongly complain that you can't just walk into another passenger's cabin."

"Oh, it's all right," she said. "I'm a nurse, like you. Well, I was a nurse. I retired after Dr Morgan passed away." She looked down at Perry. "And how else is a widow supposed to meet attractive men?"

"Socially is usually the accepted way," I said, thinking about my earlier admonishment to Harry about gold diggers.

"Mr Clayton and I have already had dinner three times and taken some nice walks about the Promenade in the afternoon and evening. Mr Perry not so much. He seems to have been rather preoccupied with personal matters. I believe he was a friend of that man who passed away earlier this week."

"Yes," I said, purposefully leaving it ambiguous. "And Mr Perry is also suffering a reoccurrence of malaria."

"I did notice that when I would see him outside his cabin. Poor man," said Mrs Morgan. "I talked with him a couple of times but could never get him to let me give him a closer look."

"Yes, well, if you don't mind, I'd like to tend to my patient now."

I turned back to the sleeping Perry. Or was he sleeping? It took a few moments of listening to realize he was carrying on a one-sided conversation. Mrs Morgan opened her mouth to speak but I held up a hand. "Shush. Listen."

"You know I love you. I've always loved you," said Perry. "Not Nathaniel, no, I promise we'll always be together." I cringed at the mention of Nathaniel. Mrs Morgan looked interested.

"That's very strange," she whispered. "What's happening?"

"I don't know. I gave him an injection of scopolamine to help control his sea- sickness."

"Scopolamine?"

I nodded. "We use it on board as a way to prevent nausea and vomiting after anesthesia. It's also a specific for treating some difficult cases of motion sickness, which is what Mr Perry is, or was, suffering from."

"Yes, I'm familiar with it. I was an obstetric nurse in the United States before I retired."

"United States? But your accent?"

Mrs Morgan smiled. "I have dual citizenship. My late husband was an American doctor. I came home with him after the War ended. Believe me, the post-war boom wasn't just in finance. Lots and lots of babies for returning soldiers. Dr Morgan and I were very busy." She looked down at Perry then at me. "You said you've used this drug on the ship, so you know the general effects of it. I'll tell you, I thought I did, too."

"What do you mean?" I asked, taking Perry's pulse.

"He shouldn't have done it," said Perry. "The Dutchman always gets what's his."

"I'm afraid it can also have side effects and I think we're witnessing one now." She crossed her arms. "He's being chatty, don't you think?"

I nodded. "He is, at that. I've never really noted this kind of reaction. How did you come across it?"

"In 1920 Dr Morgan and I attended a clinical gathering where one of the presenters was an obstetrician from Texas. He had noticed that beyond scopolamine's primary use of twilight sedation for women giving birth, it also seemed to help them more easily bring forward any hidden information, things they otherwise would have kept to themselves. In other words, it acted as a serum to make people tell the truth."

"You're having a go at me. There's no such thing."

"I'm so sorry," said Perry. "I should have done more."

"Poor man," said Adelaide softly, brushing his hair back off his forehead. "With the scopolamine, once my husband and I knew what to look for, it became almost like a game, listening to what they would say under its effects." She shook her head. "Not in the least ethical, I know, but interesting."

I looked at her. "What do you think this is all about, then?"

"He can have it," muttered Perry.

Mrs Morgan shrugged. "I think he just has things to talk about. When did you give him the injection?" I told her and she nodded. "He'll be coming around soon, then. Best that you're here when he wakes up, he may be a bit disoriented." She gently brushed his cheek with the back of her hand. "Poor sweet man," she said. "So much on your mind." Adelaide gave me a gentle smile and took her leave. I looked down at Perry.

A bit disoriented? I didn't see how Perry could possibly be more disoriented than I was right now.

# V

ave you ever had your fortune read? It's fun, but you really can't put much store into it. The prognostications you're given are almost inevitably murky and cloaked in shadow, and for good reason. What you get handed could mean something, or it could not mean something, depending on your immediate situation at the time. For instance, 'you will meet a tall handsome stranger' is all well and good if you are in the market for a tall handsome stranger. On the other hand, meeting said tall handsome stranger in a dimly lit alley generally bodes no good, even if he is handsome. The whole hit-and-miss of it is much like people talking under the influence of a drug, like scolopamine. You read into it what you read into it.

So it was with Mr Perry and his twilight sleep pearls of wisdom. I wasn't exactly sure yet what to make of what he'd said, though four items stood out in my mind:

'You know I've always loved you' 'The Dutchman always gets what's his' 'I should have done more' and 'he can have it.'

After greeting him on waking up (as Mrs Morgan had surmised, it was not too long after she had departed) and making sure he was suffering no ill effects from the sea, I pronounced him fit and ready to return to active service. He was a bit put back by the news of Van Effen's demise.

"Big strong fellow like that drowned in the bathtub?"

"I'm sure he was suffering seasickness as you were and got into the tub in the mistaken belief it would provide him with some relief from the weather. Our ship's doctor believes nausea overcame him, he hit his head against the side of the tub, slipped under the water, and that finished him."

"Well, thank you for watching after me, Nurse Chandler. If you don't mind, I'll get cleaned up and dressed then check on Joel. I assume he knows about Mr Van Effen?"

"He does, thank you."

Perry nodded. "Sad. If you wouldn't mind closing the bedroom and cabin doors on your way out. You can tell Joel I'll be by later."

"Of course." I turned to go, then turned back. "Mr Perry, may I ask you a question?"

"Of course."

"Have you met a woman named Adelaide Morgan?"

Perry nodded. "I'll say. She's next door. I've spent a lot of time avoiding her. If it wasn't for poor Mr Clayton down the hall I'm afraid she'd have caught me." I laughed and Perry smiled. "She had me out for cocktails a couple of nights ago. Very talkative."

"What did you talk about, if you don't mind my asking?"

"Oh, this and that. She attended Nathaniel's funeral. Of course, I didn't tell her any of the things I've told you and Mr Winston." He shook his head. "She's very charming. A nurse, of all things. If I wasn't a confirmed old son-of-a-bachelor, well, who knows. She reminds me of someone, but I can't place it. The malaria clouds my brain."

"She came by to minister to you while you were under the weather this morning."

"Did she?" He looked pleased with himself. "I trust I was appropriate."

I smiled at him. "Ever the gentleman. I'll go so you can get dressed." I closed the bedroom door behind me and let myself out of the cabin.

A burly seaman was positioned outside of Joel's door. He gave me a silent nod as I knocked and was admitted. "How is Mr Perry?" asked Joel.

"He's fine. He said he would be by to visit you later." I sat on the couch. "I had a visitor while I was with him. A retired nurse named Adelaide Morgan. She's in 32-A, right across the hall from your uncle's cabin."

Joel nodded. "I've seen her come in and out a few times. We exchanged pleasantries and she offered condolences on Nathaniel's death. Other than that, not much."

"You're too young for her, so be grateful," I said. "By her own admission, she's busy manhunting, and not in the bounty hunter sense. Mrs Morgan is apparently a wealthy doctor's widow – wealthy enough to be traveling in First-Class, anyway – and she's on the prowl. Count yourself lucky, she's been trying to have a go at Perry but seems to have clicked with Mr Clayton in 34-A who's been hearing the mice in the ceilings."

"Sounds like Mr Clayton is having more than his share of annoyance," said Joel.

"Doesn't it, though? Poor man. Anyway, Mrs Morgan stuck her head in to check on Mr Perry, who was under the influence of an injection of scopolamine that I'd given him this morning to help fight his seasickness."

"Did it work?" asked Harry.

"Yes, but not entirely in the way I was using it for. I found out from Mrs Morgan that she and her late husband had used scopolamine in his obstetrics practice to help calm women in childbirth, and when they were under its influence they could be very loose with their words."

"How so?"

"Well, for one thing, they are liable to speak out on things they'd normally keep hidden. Mrs Morgan referred to it as a truth serum."

"Good Lord," said Joel. "What did he say in front of her?"

"A bit of babbling that I trust she took as babbling and nothing else."

Harry crossed his arms. "What kind of babbling?"

"'You know I've always loved you' 'The Dutchman always gets what's his' 'I should have done more' and 'he can have it.'" I looked at them. "'I'll always love you' is surely about Annake. The Dutchman is obviously a reference to Dutch Schultz," I said. "The 'should have done more' probably refers to trying to help Annake, and 'he can have it' is anyone's guess."

"Nathaniel," said Harry. "Nathaniel's the only 'he' in this equation."

"Unless Perry's again talking about Schultz." I shook my head. "I don't know. How have you been occupying your time since I went to check on Mr Perry?"

"We've been discussing Mr Van Effen," said Harry. "I told Joel our theory that Van Effen may have known his killer, just as Nathaniel did."

"It makes sense," said Joel. "I can't imagine Van Effen going down without a fight, and it sounds like there was no struggle."

"There was absolutely no struggle," I confirmed. "And there's no doubt Van Effen knew his killer."

"Then who?" asked Harry. "Not Mr Perry, he was ill at the time."

"And," said Joel, "Harry said that Miss Thomas knocked on the door asking after Van Effen while you two were in Van Effen's cabin."

"Which, unless she's also a better actress than she is a person, leaves the list of people who already knew something was rotten in Denmark –and correct me if I'm wrong – to these." Harry began to call off names, ticking them off on his fingers. "The Captain. Doctor Harper. Mister Harvey. Mister Collins. Mister Armstrong. Mr Perry, whom you've already noted was ill at the time, Joel. Alice. Myself. You. That makes ten."

"Plus our First Officer and our chemist who isolated the curare in Nathaniel," I added.

Harry sat at the desk and pulled a sheet of paper toward himself, writing down names. When he finished he looked up at us. "So that group is around for Van Effen's death. Now let's go through those who knew Mr Isaac."

"Perry," I said. "Van Effen."

Joel shrugged. "Me, I suppose."

"Yes, I'm afraid so, Joel," said Harry. He looked at me. "Is there anyone else that had a direct connection to Mr Isaac?"

I shook my head. "No one."

"Unless you count Mr Jenkins," said Joel. Harry smiled.

"I'm sorry, I should have stated anyone on board who had a direct connection to Mr Isaac. There were three of you, and now there's only two."

Joel's jaw tightened. "I would say only one."

I nodded. "Mr Perry certainly had motive. And he and Mr Van Effen were familiar with curare from their time spent in South America." A polite knock on the door stopped me.

"Who's there?" said Joel.

"Alexander Perry. May I come in, Mr Singer?"

"Just a moment." Joel unlocked the door. "Apologies for the *golem* at the door," said Joel. "But since Mr Van Effen – "

"Yes, I heard," said Perry. "Shame about him having that accident in his tub. I do think he was truly trying to protect you." Joel and Harry gave me a look and I returned it with a millimetric shake of my head. Perry sat on the couch next to me and took a small package out of his coat pocket. "To other business. I went through what I have and I can afford to give you these." Joel began to protest but Perry held up a hand. "I'm thinking that I've had quite enough and am going to retire. I have funds put away that I can use to pay off your debt to Schultz. As for me, I'm an old man. I'll keep a few diamonds to hold body and soul together for whatever time I've got left." He handed the package over. "If your uncle's gems are recovered you can give these back if that's what you want to do, but I want you to have a start."

"You're sure Mr Schultz won't have something to say?"

Perry shook his head. "I'm old enough and I've seen enough that I don't really care anymore. Anyway, these are mine, not his. Take them."

"And you still have the Brazilian stone," said Harry. "It's a nice old pillow cut, Mr Perry," he explained. "And I'll add something to what Mr Perry's doing, Joel. Like he says, if we never locate Isaac's diamonds, you'll be set to start out, anyway." He gave Joel a smile. "Of course, you'll be starting your business on the side while you work for me and learn the ropes."

Joel was dumbfounded. "I can't thank you gentlemen enough," he managed.

"I'm sure you'll make us proud," said Perry. He crossed his legs. "I had a visitor this morning after you left, Nurse. Someone from the Purser's office."

"Mister Collins? He's the officer in charge."

"No, this was a junior ranking. Simpson, I think?" He shrugged. "Anyway, he had a curious question for me concerning two pretty little gems he had in his possession."

"Let me guess," said Harry. "He wanted to know if they were the real thing."

Perry looked surprised. "Yes, that's right. How did you – "

"Besides the ones we found in Mr Isaac, there seem to be a great many fake diamonds moving about the ship, Mr Perry," I said. "But please continue."

"Yes," said Perry. "As I said, this young man had a small envelope with a pair of diamonds inside. He said they had belonged to his late mother and he was carrying them back from New York to give to his sister in Southampton."

"Go on," I said.

"Well, he came to me because he said I looked trustworthy – " Harry raised an eyebrow and Perry held up a hand in response. "I know what you're thinking. Anyway, I took the diamonds and examined them. Cut glass. And very well done, too."

"More fakes," said Joel. "I don't believe it."

"What did you do?" I asked.

"Do?" Perry shrugged. "What else was there to do? I told the young man that what he held in his hand were very good imitations, and while they might command a moderate price for a fake they were not diamonds worthy to give to his sister."

"What did he say?" asked Joel.

"He thanked me and left, taking them with him." Perry was thoughtful. "He did appear rather annoyed."

"I guess so," said Harry. He looked at me. "Where do you think these new fakes came from?"

"I don't know." I got up off the couch. "But I have a feeling Mister Simpson is going to tell us whether he wants to or not. Coming?"

Harry grinned. "I wouldn't miss this for the world."

# VI

You know what a biscuit jar is. You Yanks call them cookie jars. No matter how it's referenced, on either side of the Atlantic, getting one's hand caught in the biscuit/cookie jar is generally not something seen as positive. While my brother and I did plenty of snaffling of biscuits in our time, we never got our hands actually caught in the jar; possibly because our hands were too small (or maybe the jars were too wide). In either case, while the supply of biscuits in the jar shrank visibly, as long as we closed ranks it could have been anyone thieving them. (Anyone but us, that is.) The nanny, the man who trimmed the hedges, even our little friends were all fodder for blame. However, in the case of this shipboard biscuit jar, there was only one person to blame for having his hand caught inside.

Mister Collins leaned back in his office chair and steepled his fingers. "So these were your mum's, and you were taking them back to your sister?"

Simpson nodded. "That's right, sir."

"Is that chair uncomfortable?" asked the Captain.

"No, sir."

"Then stop fidgeting."

"Yes, sir."

Collins held up the two fakes, one in each hand. "Mr Winston, you can corroborate Mr Perry's assessment that these are nothing more than cut glass?"

"Yes, Mr Collins."

"Not much of a gift for your sister, Simpson," said the Captain.

"No, sir," replied Simpson, his voice quiet.

Collins flipped open Simpson's employee file folder and glanced over at the Captain. "Especially when you have no sister and your mum lives in Canterbury." He shut the folder. "Come, Mister Simpson. These trinkets are worthless but your career is not."

The Captain leaned forward in his chair. "And may I remind you that a Mr Isaac was murdered on this vessel through the use of trinkets like this, and," he looked up at me, then back to Simpson, "I'm now informed that a second man has met a not dissimilar fate."

Simpson looked up at Harry and I, then back to Collins and the Captain. "Sirs, I had nothing to do with either of those. I didn't even know about them until you told me."

"Then where did these come from?" asked the Captain.

"I don't know, sir."

"Mister Simpson," began Collins.

Simpson shook his head. "No, sir, it's true. I found an envelope addressed to me at my station out front the night of sailing. Well, you know how busy it is. Anyone could have dropped that envelope there. I didn't open it until about the time we were closing up shop. One of these things was in it, with the promise of a second one by Sunday morning if I would leave the vault unlocked Saturday night. The writer said they would close and lock up after themselves, and nothing would be attached to me."

"Where is this note?" asked the Captain.

Simpson hung his head. "Gone. I tore it up and scattered it off the Sports Deck."

"So we've nobody's word but your own?" asked Collins.

"Sir, it's true. I didn't want to do it, but the way the world is now, I thought a little nest egg would come in handy, I didn't know there'd be any murder involved."

"Obviously not," I said. "So you did as the writer asked?"

Simpson looked at the Captain, who nodded. "Yes, Nurse," he said. "Like I just said, I thought I'd be making a nice profit."

"And you didn't stop to think that it was highly improper?"

"Only for a moment, Mister Collins."

The Captain crossed his arms. "And you left the vault open, and it was closed when you returned on Sunday?"

"Everything in place, just like the letter writer said it would be," said Simpson. "Except one box was missing that belonged to the late Mr Isaac and there was a second envelope with no note, just the other diamond."

"Glass trinket," corrected Harry.

"Yes, sir," said Simpson, looking up at him. "But I don't know diamonds, now, do I? And what with Mr Isaac dying – of natural causes, so I read in *The Victory* – I just sit on these two for a few days, pondering what to do with them, then finally decide to get them checked. I should have done it earlier."

"Yes," said the Captain. He stood. "Mr Simpson, the Stoddard Lines is on the hook for a passenger's box of diamonds that were taken from a secure vault as the direct result of your collusion with a person unknown. For all I know, you may have colluded in his murder as well." The Captain paused for a moment and then pronounced sentence. "Mister Simpson, you are relieved of duty and will be confined to quarters. You will be turned over to port authorities in Cherbourg and they will remand you to the police and the Stoddard Lines, whom I am sure will press charges."

Simpson stared at the floor. "Yes, sir."

"Very well, then." The Captain turned to Collins. "Mister Collins, if you'll take care of the details and have Mister Armstrong perform his service."

"Yes, sir."

The Captain nodded. "Nurse Chandler and Mr Winston, thank you for your assistance. You may go."

Once outside Collins' office we took the stairs up from A Deck to the Main Deck. The seas were calm and a freshening breeze blew across the ship in marked contrast to the weather earlier in the day. "That was interesting," Harry finally said as we walked. "What do you think will happen to that man?"

"I don't know. I do know he'll never set foot again on a ship belonging to the Stoddard Lines or any other ocean-going company."

"I thought the Captain was going to make him walk the plank."

"A little outdated for this century, but don't give him any ideas."

"Far from it." We walked in silence for a minute. "Maeve, I've been thinking."

"Yes?"

"Wasn't this person taking an awful chance by giving Mister Simpson counterfeits?"

"What do you mean?"

"I mean, how would you react if someone made a proposition to you like the one made to Simpson, and then pawned off a fake diamond as partial payment? Why take the chance that Simpson would have the diamond looked at as quickly as possible to ascertain its veracity?

And if you found it was a counterfeit, would you do what they requested or go straight to Mister Collins?"

"It does seem a chance not worth taking," I replied.

"Exactly. Which makes me think that the person who bribed Simpson didn't know they were using counterfeits. They must have thought that they were using real diamonds instead."

"Are you suggesting our diamond thief and possibly murderer can't tell the difference between a real diamond and a glass imitation?"

"Yes and no," said Harry. "If you remember I said the counterfeits in Isaac were probably placed there on purpose."

"So the killer knew in advance that those were counterfeits."

"Yes."

I thought for a moment. "Which means they brought on their own counterfeits for the express purpose of killing Isaac, and also had two they thought were real to bribe the vault open with."

"Correct. Unless someone tells them the difference between fake and real, they have no idea."

Harry nodded. "Yes."

"And Isaac's real diamonds, if he indeed brought any with him, are still out there?"

"That's what I surmise."

A woman's voice calling broke in on us. Caroline Thomas was coming up from behind.

"Well, hello you two!" she said in her chirpy manner. "Didn't it turn out to be a lovely day!"

"That's often the way of it, Miss Thomas," I said, with some annoyance, thinking it was a lovely day if you didn't mind having your boy-friend murdered – which she obviously didn't.

"Yes, isn't it?" Done with me she focused her attention on Harry. "Mr Winston, you know Casper spoke highly of you."

"You mean the late Mr Van Effen?"

"Yes, that's him. He spoke highly of you," she repeated. "I wonder if you could help me?" She dug into her purse and came up with a soft cloth which she unwrapped to reveal a small sparkling gem. "I found it on the floor in the First-Class corridor where my cabin is. Finders-keepers, you know. Is it worth anything?"

# VII

My parents instilled a love of words in me that's stayed with me all my life. Of particular interest to me has been the etymology of words – where they come from, how they've been used, how their meaning may change over centuries. One such word is 'brazen', which I fear is not used too much these days in the context it assumed in the early 17th century. While it descends from meaning something made of brass, and still does, the other definition I prefer has to do with sheer effrontery. For instance – and cover your ears if you need to – a man who is able to bluff and bluster his way out of trouble by blissfully ignoring the facts is said to have brass balls. You may have also heard of a woman in the same situation being described as a brazen hussy.

And right now if Miss Thomas didn't take the prize for 'brass (n.) from the Old English bræsen 'of brass,' I didn't know who did.

"I'm sure Mr Winston would have no problem with taking your find back to his cabin to examine it more closely," I said.

"Would you?" oozed Miss Thomas. "That would really be the cat's pajamas." She handed the cloth with the gem in it to Harry.

"Well, I suppose I – "

"What Mr Winston means is he'd be delighted," I said. "You found it outside your door? How famously lucky for you."

She smiled and scrunched up her shoulders. "I know," she said. "But remember, finders-keepers."

"Oh, yes, certainly," said Harry, giving me a hard look. "But don't you know, I'm certain it belongs to somebody. There are several diamond dealers, including myself, on that corridor."

She pressed her Clara Bow lips into a pert moue. "I just don't know who could have been so careless. Certainly not someone like you. It might not even be real, might it?"

"False gemstones made of glass or other material have been known to appear from time to time," I said. I'd certainly received an education on them the past few days. "Perhaps you'll be fortunate." I turned to Harry. "I have to go back to the hospital for a bit. I'll check in with Mr Singer on the way. Why don't you call me when you have something?" I smiled at Miss Thompson. "Then we can present you the good news together and possibly go to the lounge for a celebration."

"All right," she said. "Mr Winston, would you walk and take the air with me? I'd just love to hear about all you do."

Harry gave me an imploring look. I smiled back at him. "Well, that's settled, then," I said. "I'll hear from you later, Mr Winston. Best of luck, Miss Thomas." And with that, I headed for the stairs down.

Joel and Mr Perry were still in Joel's cabin when I knocked on the door. "How did you your chat with Mister Simpson go?" asked Perry.

"Not well for Mister Simpson," I said. "He's been cashiered. It seems he came into possession of those stones you examined from someone unknown who paid him to look the other way while they looted Nathaniel's box out of the vault. One diamond before the theft, the second after successful completion."

"All that glitters is not gold," said Perry with a tinge of sadness. "Poor man."

"Kind of risky for the thief, using fakes to get the clerk to turn the other way," said Joel.

"That's what Harry and I thought. So it's apparent the thief also thought the stones they were using to bribe Simpson were real."

Perry rubbed a hand against his forehead. "Are Mr Winston and myself the only ones on board with the genuine article?"

"It seems that way, doesn't it?" I sat down on the couch. "And according to our latest theory, our thief can't tell the difference between real and fake diamonds. On another topic, Harry and I were approached by Van Effen's girlfriend a few minutes ago."

"Van Effen's girlfriend?" asked Perry.

"The pretty woman he was squiring about the ship," said Joel. "Caroline Thomas is her name. Her cabin is at the end of this corridor by the stairs."

I nodded. "She's a real piece of work. When I told her that Van Effen was dead, she put on a very brief and melodramatic emotional display that could well have concluded with the words *c'est la vie,* and then blithely tripped off to her stateroom to begin packing for disembarkation tomorrow."

"How Van Effen was taken with her I don't know," said Joel. "What little he told me about her, I thought she was very shallow."

"But as I was about to say, she has an eye out for riches," I said, recounting our recent meeting with her on the Main Deck.

"Found it on the floor, did she?" said Perry. "I'll just bet she did."

"That's what she says. I can't wait to hear what Harry has to say about it." I stood up. "Mr Perry, you look well recovered from this morning. Why don't you and Joel go and get some lunch? I'll catch up with you later."

"Would you mind if I ring down to Alice to see if she'll join us?" asked Joel.

"Not at all. Since she's leaving the ship with you tomorrow, I'm sure you've got plenty to talk about."

"I'll leave you young people to it, then," said Perry. "I'll go to the smoking room, have a drink and a cigar, and try to avoid Mrs Morgan. If you don't mind, Joel, I'll take those stones and put them back in my safe box. We can settle up once we're off the ship tomorrow morning." He placed the parcel in his inside coat pocket and let himself out, closing the door behind him.

"Well, Joel," I began, then stopped. Voices could be heard from the corridor.

"Why Mr Perry," said a woman's voice I recognized as Mrs Morgan. "So good to see you up and about again. Have you had anything to eat this afternoon? I was just going up to see what I could find in the Observation Lounge. Would you care to accompany me?"

"Mrs Morgan," said Perry with what I thought was a touch of resignation in his voice. "I can think of nothing I would like more." Their voices receded up the corridor as they headed for the stairs.

I looked at Joel. "I think Mr Perry is a good man."

"Don't forget that the person he works for is a cold-blooded gangster who isn't happy with me right now."

"I'm not," I said, but truthfully Dutch Schultz was the farthest thing from my mind. So was the robbery of Mr Isaac's store in New York and the demise of his sales clerk. What was on my mind was a killer walking the decks of the *Victoria*, and if I couldn't come up with a case to present to the *gendarmes* in Cherbourg they were going to get clean away with murder.

# VIII

When it comes to literary sleuths, I'm a big Agatha Christie fan; I even got to meet her once.[*] Before her, though, was Sherlock Holmes. In fact, I believe his creator, Sir Arthur Conan Doyle, is still alive, though he must be getting on toward seventy or so. My father was a huge fan of his work, and Holmes remains immensely popular to this day – like Christie, I imagine people will still be reading him twenty years from now.

My father was fond of using Holmes' quotes: 'the game is afoot' and 'elementary, my dear Watson' (with my or my brother's name usually inserted instead of Watson). However, being an educator and preferring to teach using the Socratic method, I think his absolute favorite came out of the Holmes novel *The Sign of the Four*, published forty years ago. 'When you have eliminated the impossible, whatever remains, *however improbable*, must be the truth.'

Well, there were certainly things that were as good as impossible for me to figure out. The store robbery, Jenkins' death, even the presence of the shadowy but all-too-real Dutch Schultz.

So, taking those items away left me with what, by Sherlock's reasoning, should have been the truth no matter how improbable, except that the math didn't work.

Take the curare injections, for example. Only two people had knowledge of the use of curare; Van Effen was

---

[*]  See Book One: *Shadow of the Queen*

dead, and when he was murdered Perry had been down for the count because I had put him there.

Then there are the fake diamonds. Harry, Van Effen, and Perry could all tell a fake from a true diamond. Again, Van Effen was dead and Mr Winston and Mr Perry could scarcely be called serious suspects.

It was like looking into one of Harry's multi-faceted gems; so many shiny faces that I could easily get lost and had; it was no wonder I was in a downcast mood when I walked through the hospital door.

Harper and Harvey were seated at the desk; I waved them back down as they began to rise. "Ah, Maeve," said Harvey. "We were just talking about you."

"Nothing good, I hope." I slouched on the couch.

"Has there ever been?" Harvey said with a wink. "No, just wondering how long you'll be able to get along without Alice."

"What do you mean? She'll be gone tomorrow and we'll hire someone new."

Harper sighed. "He means that given the current economic situation, her position may not be replaced."

"I'm losing easily a dozen people," said Mister Harvey. "All the departments are taking cuts. The Captain announced it in this morning's department head meeting."

"Jolly terrific," I said. "Did he have anything to say about our worries?" Harper and Harvey glanced at each other. "Fine, lads, out with it."

"He's giving it until we dock tomorrow. After that he's turning the whole thing over to the British Consulate in Cherbourg," said Harper. "Sorry, Maeve."

Harvey nodded. "We haven't been much help to you." He frowned. "Of course, you haven't really asked, either." He seemed wistful. "Last time was ever so much fun."*

"I'm the one who should apologize," I said. "I've been trying to bull this through and all I've got to show for it is another dead man. At least we can get Van Effen off the ship quietly tomorrow without a big send off like Nathaniel. Oh, and Mister Simpson has been let go, by the way." I explained what had happened in Collins' office. Harper shook his head.

"Sold his career for some cut glass."

"I'm sure if he'd known they were cut glass he wouldn't have acquiesced so easily. Still, he should have reported the first one or at least made an attempt to have it checked out by someone like Mr Winston or Mr Perry."

"Well, that solved the issue of how Mr Isaac's box got out of the vault, anyway," Harvey stood.

"Don't go," I said. There's more. The woman Van Effen was squiring around – Miss Thomas – she shows up today with a diamond she says she found on the floor in the First-Class corridor. She gave it to Harry to check over and see if it was worth anything."

"How did she find a diamond on the corridor floor?" asked Harper.

I shrugged. "Fakes have apparently been going and coming through there like it's Picadilly Circus," I said.

"Was it worth anything?"

I shrugged. "Don't know yet. I let him be shanghaied into a walk on the Main Deck with her. And then there's that irritating wedding band."

"What irritating wedding band?" asked Harvey.

I shook my head. "I'm sorry, maybe I forgot to tell you that story." When I finished filling him in, including

---

*   See Book One: *Shadow of the Queen*

for good measure the cache of fakes in the bathroom door, Mister Harvey took a deep breath.

"That's a lot to think about, Maeve. Even for you." He stretched. "Off I go. Plenty to do before tonight's big farewell dinner. I'm sure Mister Bissell has it well in hand, but you never know. You two will be there to hold down tables and chat with passengers, will you not?"

"I can't guarantee what my appetite will be, but I'll be there," I said.

"That's all I can ask. Dress uniform. You know the drill. *Au revoir.*" He left Harper and myself alone. Harper unlocked a bottom drawer of the desk and drew out a bottle and two glasses.

"Purely medicinal," he said to me as he poured off the amber liquid. "Your health."

"Or lack thereof." I took a swallow of the whisky.

"Maeve, I think you've got too much you're trying to do," said Harper.

"I was having that same thought on my way down here."

"Well, then. Let me give you some advice from my days in the Navy. One, everything always has an answer. Two, if you can't find the answer, see number one. Three, what seems to be an insurmountable problem looks a lot better when you eliminate pieces of it that have nothing to do with the immediate issue at hand."

I took a moody sip. "Thank you, Sherlock Holmes. I've been doing that."

Harper topped me up. "Apparently not well enough." He swirled his glass. "You've been going almost non-stop since Sunday morning."

"With little if anything to show for it. No, Boss, someone's walking down the gangway tomorrow with a parcel of diamonds that aren't theirs and Joel's going to pay a probably fatal price for failure from Dutch Schultz when he returns to New York. I just hope Alice can stay clear of what's coming."

The door opened and Harry came inside. "Sorry," he said. "I got lost coming down here, or I'd have been here earlier. Joel thought this is where you'd gone to ground." He looked at me. "Actually, I'd have been here even earlier if someone hadn't tossed me to the wolves."

"Sorry," I said. "I can't stand that woman."

"I can see why," said Harry.

"Mr Winston," said Harper. He indicated our glasses. "Join us?"

"No, thank you Doctor."

I tilted my glass. "It's purely medicinal, or so I'm told."

Harry smiled, pulled out a chair and sat. "Did Maeve tell you about Mister Simpson and Miss Thomas and her lucky find?"

Harper nodded. "And that you've also been enjoying a walk with Miss Thomas."

"'Enjoy' is not the word I would use. 'Endure' comes to mind," said Harry, then grimaced. "How that woman can prattle on," he said. "But I wasn't the only one being coerced into a stroll. I saw Mr Perry and an older lady making the walk too."

"That would be the Mrs Morgan I told you about." Harper gave me a questioning look. "She's a gold digger in the cabin next door to Perry."

"She'd have to go the distance to compete with Miss Thomas," said Harry. "I don't see how Van Effen stood it."

"Stoic, I think, was our Mr Van Effen." I swallowed a bit of whisky. "I was just recounting to Doctor Harper my abject failure in figuring any of this out."

"Nonsense," said Harry. "There are a lot of moving parts. We just have to isolate the main spring." He took a handkerchief from his pocket. "And I think I figured out how we'll do it." He unwrapped the cloth to show the diamond that Caroline had given him to study. "It's a fake, too, but again it's extremely high quality, like the ones Mister Simpson had foisted on him or the ones used on poor Mr Isaac."

"So? How does that help us?" I asked.

Harry put the faux diamond on the desk. "Remember how adamant Miss Thomas was about finders-keepers? She obviously can't tell a real diamond from a fake one. If we're having trouble going to the source, let the source come to us."

"What are you saying?" Harper leaned forward.

"I'm saying we arrive in Cherbourg tomorrow, and – correct me if I'm wrong, Maeve – as far as I can see we've run out of time for subtleties. Let's give the suspect or suspects a reason to tip their hand."

"How?"

"Your ship's newspaper comes to mind. Have your editor put out a special edition. He can wrap it up in the usual end of voyage trivialities, but there needs to be a little item insert." Harry tapped the diamond with his fingertip. "A maintenance man doing work in a vacant First-Class cabin discovered a packet of small valuables. Please call at the cabin in question and identify the items to reclaim them."

"You're right. If she thinks this one is real, she'll think the others are, too. She'll come to get them."

Harper sat back. "Do you really think that will work?"

"I don't see any other options and as Harry points out, we're running out of time." I glanced at my watch. "I'll go see Mister Casey at his office and see what we can do while you go give Miss Thomas the good news that she's suddenly got a small fortune in her hot little hand."

"I'm sure Casey will love being the center of attention distributing a special issue at tonight's farewell gala," said Harper. He shook his head. "Mister Harvey won't be happy about it."

"Mister Harvey will have to get over himself," I said to Harper, then looked at Harry. "But I still don't see this brings us closer to finding who killed Isaac and Van Effen."

"Rome wasn't built in a day, Maeve," said Harry.

"I know. But a little less than a day is all we've got."

# IX

I think there's something to be said for ego. I'm not quite certain what it is, but there's certainly something to be said for it. To wit: the little university town I grew up in had its own small community theatre. The university itself, alas, focused primarily on hard materials like math and science curriculums. I don't believe there was even a dramatic club on campus, but no worries, our home-grown troupe of actors and actresses faced down many a sticky wicket to provide stout-hearted entertainment to the culture-starved locals.

I remember one woman in particular who, when not treading the boards, worked behind the counter at the local bookstore. Quiet there, even meek, she became Lady Macbeth with a vengeance on stage, no matter what the role was. As I recalled, it took quite the entirety of a fortnight after the production closed before her super ego got choked back down again. While hers actually would recede, that of Mister Casey would not, and that's what I was counting on when I visited his lair and the home of *The Victory* newspaper.

"Nurse Chandler," he said, rising from behind his buried desk. He stubbed out the ever-present cigarette into an ashtray that miraculously avoided igniting the mass of paper on his desk. "And what brings you here to the seat of shipboard democracy?"

I refrained from pointing out that the *Victoria* was an autocracy and the Captain was the chief autocrat. Better to put out honey than vinegar, I thought. "Mister Casey, since you and *The Victory* are so well read, I have a favor to ask of you."

"Anything you like. Have a seat, heh heh. What can I do for you?"

I sat and demurely folded my hands in my lap and plunged forward. "I want you to insert a false item and put out a special of *The Victory* in time for tonight's farewell gala in the First-Class restaurant. Make sure everyone gets a copy."

Casey slipped back down into his chair and lit a cigarette. "You don't want much, do you?" He took a deep drag. He and the late Van Effen could have paced each other smoke for smoke. "What is this false item?"

I steeled myself. If I confessed that Isaac's cause of death had been anything other than it was, I'd never hear the end of it from Casey. Anyway, I wasn't even sure if this charade of Harry's would turn up a diamond thief, much less a murderer. "The Captain ordered it kept quiet, so don't feel like you missed it," I prevaricated. "We had a theft from the ship's vault. A box of diamonds."

Casey leaned back in his wooden swivel chair and pushed his fedora up on his forehead. "Okie-dokie," he said. I knew he was picturing himself sitting in a big press newsroom somewhere. "Tell me more."

I gingerly dusted the detritus off the chair armrests, conscious that my nursing whites were probably never going to be the same. "Well," I said, leaning forward, "it seems that the stolen jewels belonged to the man who died, Nathaniel Isaac. His box was lifted out of the vault."

Casey pulled a pad toward him and produced a grubby pencil. "When?"

I shook my head. "That doesn't matter, and the Captain would rather not let it get out that we can't secure things in our own vault. You can see that, I'm sure."

Casey nodded. "Smart move."

"Right. So just by happenstance, a member of the engineering crew was doing some maintenance in an empty cabin in First Class when he discovered a packet of what turned out to be diamonds hidden in, of all places, the bathroom door."

"What?" His pencil jerked to a stop. "Hidden inside the bathroom door?"

"Yes. They'd used a drill to put a hole in the top of the door, dropped their packet in, and resealed it. Unfortunately for them, the door made a rattle when it was opened and got the repairman's interest."

Casey took another hit off his cigarette. "Well, that's a heck of a story, Nurse."

"Isn't it? Unfortunately, we don't want you printing that part of it." Casey looked crestfallen. "But here's what we want you to say that might help us catch the thief. I recited Harry's words. 'A maintenance man doing work in a vacant First-Class cabin discovered a packet of small valuables. Please call at the cabin in question and identify the items to reclaim them.'"

He jotted it down and read through it again, then looked at me. "Pardon me for saying, Nurse, but what kind of thicko would be dumb enough to answer this message?"

I stood. "Can you do it?"

"Sure, sure." He glanced at his watch. "Do you want me to just hand out papers to people going into the restaurant tonight?"

"That would be perfect. And yes, have the paper available only to those going into that restaurant. Make sure everyone gets a copy. Thank you, Mister Casey."

"Sure, sure," he repeated. As I closed the door I could hear him yelling "Stop the presses, we've got a special!" I smiled to myself. Mister Casey would live on that moment for a year.

The First-Class corridor was empty when I arrived. Harry answered my knock and ushered me in. I nodded toward the hall.

"All quiet on the Western Front, as they say. Except Joel's guard is gone."

"No, he's on duty. He went with Joel and Mr Perry to lunch. He was hovering nearby looking menacing while the two of them were having a deep discussion. I saw them for a moment after I met with Miss Thomas."

"And how did she react to your good news about her diamond?"

Harry smiled. "As one would expect."

"I'll just bet the love light of avarice was shining in her eyes."

"Something along those lines, yes. I think she repeated her trope about finders- keepers a couple of times. I'm sure she's mentally counting her money right now. Did you get the press squared away?"

"Yes. I feel kind of bad using Mister Casey like this, but he's the one always talking of the rough-and-tumble of the news business." I sighed. "As to tonight, I imagine that Doctor Harper and I will be holding down a table. Would you mind joining us?"

"Not at all. I assume you'll also be wanting Joel and Mr Perry. I'll leave my door open so I see them when they come back from lunch."

"Thank you." I thought for a moment. "You don't think, since she believes those are real diamonds, that she'll try and get them out now, do you?"

"In broad daylight?" Harry shook his head. "As far as we know she doesn't know we're on to her and she's no doubt the one with the pass key. She'll wait until late tonight, after everyone has retired. The note in your newspaper should only serve to whet her appetite and make her hungry for more."

"Fine by me," I said. "As long as we're not the ones getting indigestion."

_Thursday, March 27, 1930_

# X

ave you ever been to a movie or other show and someone in your immediate vicinity is making you crazy by rattling their sweets wrappers? It may not have been that much of a nuisance a couple of years or so ago before the sound movies came out; you could always read the title cards on screen and at any rate the theatre's organ was invariably playing too loudly for you to concentrate on any other noise, but with the talkies, ambient sound outside of the dialogue is a distraction.

It was the same way with the constant rattling of newspapers in the First-Class restaurant. The restaurant, normally a cathedral to fine dining, always had an undercurrent of quiet conversation buzz with the background of a live musical accompaniment. Tonight, it sounded more like the late afternoon rush on the Tube with everyone reading their evening papers. Mister Casey was out in the lobby hawking like a newsboy and had even enlisted the aid of two of Mister Harvey's staff to help him distribute _The Victory_ to passengers going into the restaurant. Patrons, surprised by the novelty of getting an evening paper with their formal gala last night dinner, snapped them up while Mister Harvey stood off to one side glowering. When he could stand it no longer he motioned me to him from the table that Doctor Harper and I were holding down with Harry, Joel and Mr Perry.

"You are ruining the dining experience, you know that." He gave me an accusatory stare and gestured at the crewman assigned as Joel's guard standing off to one side. "Not just the paper, but him, too. Even dressed up he still looks like a gargoyle that escaped Notre-Dame. Maeve, the *Victoria* is renowned for sea-going cuisine and atmosphere, and this stunt with Casey is ruining it. No one is looking at the surroundings, they're all reading that bloody newspaper." He glanced over at the guard again. "Except him, I don't know if he can read or not."

"I think everyone sees it as a novel experience, Mister Harvey," I said. "And much less stressful than what happened in here last October." *

"That was none of our doing and you know it." Mister Harvey huffed.

"Don't worry. *The Victory* isn't *The Times*. It won't take people more than a few minutes to go through it." I looked at the glittering array of women in evening wear and men in formal attire and had to admit to myself that the sight of open newspapers accompanying them was rather incongruous, but I put my best face on. "See, some are already done, their papers are on the table or the floor next to their chairs."

"Creating a trip hazard and throwing my place settings completely off kilter," groused Harvey.

"Cheer up, Mister Harvey. In a year you'll be seen as a pioneer, everyone will be setting out a newspaper, at least for breakfast. You'll single-handedly give the French Line something to think about." I gave him my best smile and went back to my table. A passing waiter politely pulled my chair out for me and got me settled at my place. Harper raised an eyebrow. I shrugged. "You know how Mister Harvey can be," I said. "He's worried I'm disturbing the atmosphere of this palace." I glanced up to the mezzanine

---

* See Book One: *Shadow of the Queen*

seating and caught the Captain looking down at me from his table. He disliked sitting with the passengers and apparently disliked it more when they were reading newspapers instead of paying attention to him.

"Look at all of these people reading. I think you're getting the word out," said Harry. Mr Perry nodded.

"Quite an interesting plan," he said. "I must admit I had my misgivings when you told Joel and I about it. Do you really think it will work?"

I took a sip of water. "I hope so. It's like baiting a mousetrap – it's up to the mouse to take the bait." Two waiters appeared and began serving our soup course. Everyone began to eat but Joel, who sat quietly looking at the one empty chair at our table. I rested my spoon. "Van Effen?" I asked him.

"Yes. I was never quite sure what to make of him, but he did grow on me."

"I understand. That's why I requested Mister Harvey provide us with a six-seat table. Maybe it's like having him here." The empty chair was tilted in on two legs to the table. "Plus I didn't think any of us were up to entertaining the strangers who'd have been seated at one of the eight or ten person tables with us."

"Your sensitivity and attention to detail is remarkable," said Harry.

"You don't know the half of it, Mr Winston." Harper smiled at me. "Though I will say, in all kindness, that Nurse Chandler can also make me a bit bonkers from time to time."

"Thanks for the compliment, Doctor. I do my best." I looked over toward the tall bronze entrance doors of the dining salon, open and swung back against the walls. "Look who's here."

Perry glanced backwards and then turned away quickly. We were a good 45 feet away from the entrance, but it apparently wasn't far enough for him. "It's that woman, Mrs Morgan," he said.

"And Miss Thomas," added Harry. Both men busied themselves with studiously looking down at their newspapers.

"Ah, Mr Clayton has resurfaced," said Harper. "He looks happier than the last time I saw him. A woman on each arm. I guess the Ovaltine did the trick."

"If you want a senior gold digger on one arm and a junior one on the other, then yes, it did the trick," I said acidly. Harper raised his eyebrows again and returned to his soup.

"Why is Mrs Morgan with Miss Thomas?" asked Joel. "I can understand the older man, but Miss Thomas?"

"Having only my shipboard acquaintance to judge by, I'd guess that Mrs Morgan saw Miss Thomas in the hall and dragooned her," said Perry. "Meanwhile, all I can say is God bless Mr Clayton. Once this is over I'm going to buy him a drink and a good cigar." He took a deep swallow of his whisky and soda. "Wish I could think who Mrs Morgan reminds me of, though." He gave us a gentle smile. "My advice to you all is not to grow old. You forget more than you remember."

A waiter arrived to seat the trio at their table, with, in a stroke of serendipity, their backs to us.

"No one's opened a paper yet," said Harper.

"Give them a moment. They're ordering cocktails." A pair of bus boys began clearing our soup course.

"Maybe they'll at least give us time to eat first," said Joel. "Look, they're getting company." A waiter had begun seating four more people at the table.

"That's what happens when you arrive late for dinner and end up on one of the eight toppers." I scrutinized the new arrivals. "No one I recognize."

Harry laughed. "But they've all got a newspaper, don't they?"

"Not that it's doing much good," I replied. By now most everyone in the salon had dropped their paper to the floor next to their chair; very few were in evidence out on tables. Whether anyone was talking about our little story was impossible to tell. I sighed inwardly and took a sip of wine and did my best to avoid looking at Mister Harvey or the Captain.

A half hour later I put down my fork and tilted my head. "Movement," I said to Harry. We all watched Miss Thomas rise from her table and make her graceful, head-turning way in the direction of the foyer. I pushed my chair back. "If you gentlemen will excuse me," I said as I picked up my clutch.

"Are you going to follow her alone?" asked Harper. "What if she's up to something?"

"If she goes past the restrooms in the foyer, I'll motion back for help. How's that?"

Harper shook his head and looked at Harry. "Like I said, makes me bonkers. All right, Maeve, play it your way. We'll wait."

Perry drained his glass. "Best of luck."

"Thanks. If I need you, make sure you bring Joel's muscular friend over there along. Mister Harvey will no doubt be happy to see him go." I sauntered off, being sure to keep Mrs Morgan's back to me as I walked. Mister Harvey was still on station at the doors, along with Monsieur DuMont. Fifteen paces in front of me I saw Miss Thomas enter the women's restroom.

"Anything?" said Harvey as I passed. I shook my head and kept going.

"Most irregular," sniffed DuMont, his Gallic nose in the air.

I promised myself that someday I'd put something in his coffee and show DuMont what irregular really felt like, then opened the door to the lady's and went inside.

# XI

This is probably not the conversation you expected to be having on this page, but I must tell you that using the First-Class women's public facilities outside of the Great Hall on the *Queen Victoria* is a religious experience. The intricate black and white hexagonal tiled floor is the foundation to a blindingly white forest of heavy porcelain wash stands overlooked by a pristinely polished mirror fully twenty five feet long enclosed in an intricate gilt frame. Individual stalls are wood panelled and seats are made of mahogany. A couple of small couches and a table with chairs is also provided, the whole lot seen over by a sweet and matronly attendant who can dispense perfumes, hand lotions, and any other necessity m'lady needs to do repairs or enhancements. The attendant even has a small sewing kit for wardrobe issues, and she's been known to offer a shoulder to cry on for those evenings that just aren't turning out the way one hoped. While I wasn't yet at that point, just the knowledge she would be there if needed bucked me up considerably.

"Oh, my, Nurse Chandler, don't you look fine tonight," said Mrs Tucker. She reached a hand out to straighten the shoulder of my dress. "I always love the last night events when you people get all dressed up."

"Thank you, Mrs Tucker." I cast a quick glance across the stalls. One door was closed. "Just came in to touch up the war paint, you know," I said, taking a lipstick from my clutch and leaning toward the mirror. "Mrs Tucker, would you mind absenting yourself for a few minutes? I need to speak privately with the young woman in that stall."

"Oh, dear. Medical issue, is it? Of course, of course. Let me get my bag. I'll be outside the door if you need me. Shall I tell people it's closed, then?"

"Would you? That would be very nice. It shouldn't take very long, but you never know how people will take things."

"Poor dear. Of course." Mrs Tucker left me to myself. I finished my lipstick and put it back in the clutch, adjusted my mid-calf length black dress and waited. After a few moments I heard a rush of water, and then the door opened. Miss Thomas stopped when she saw me.

"Well, if it isn't Nurse Chandler. And all dressed up. I thought I heard your voice, but then I thought, surely not."

"You heard it, Miss Thomas. I was just thinking that we never had that chance for a girl's chat you mentioned."

Caroline laughed. "Now? In the lady's room?" She eyed my dress. "And you're out of uniform."

"Doctor Harper and myself always attend the final night gala. He wears his dress uniform, I put on something less antiseptic than my whites."

"Do you now? Maybe you should do it more often." She smiled. "Now I really must get back to my table. If you'll excuse me?"

I smiled. "May I offer my congratulations on the diamond?"

She stopped and brightened perceptibly. "Yes, Mr Winston brought it to my cabin before dinner. He says it's quite a fortunate find for me."

"Finders-keepers, I know."

"Yes, and I'm not turning it in to lost and found if that's what you're going to ask. I'll probably sell it when I get back to New York. Maybe buy a new automobile."

"It's very lucky for you. You know, someone else on board came into possession of not one, but two stray diamonds."

Caroline gave me an intent look. "Two? Does that have anything to do with the little story in the paper tonight about a valuable packet being discovered?" She laughed lightly. "If I knew which room they were referring to I'd have a go at retrieving it myself."

"I've no doubt," I said. "Sadly, the two diamonds I'm talking about brought nothing but bad luck to their new owner. A man who worked in our Purser's office. I say 'worked' because he's been fired now."

"What happened?"

"Someone gave him a diamond with the promise of a second one if he would leave the vault unlocked on Saturday night. So he did, received his second diamond, and someone made off with a box of jewels out of the vault in return. The only problem is, besides obviously the illegal transaction and theft, the two diamonds he received for his services were fakes."

"But mine wasn't and the diamonds in the vault weren't."

I crossed my arms. "No one's seen the diamonds that came out of the vault. How do you know they weren't fakes?"

She gave an easy shrug. "Why would someone put fake diamonds into a vault?" Caroline opened her sequined handbag and took out a lipstick. "I've really enjoyed talking with you, Nurse, but I must get back to the table. Mrs Morgan was regaling us with tales of her life as a nurse. Maybe someday that will be you, except for the married part, of course. By the way, the shoulder of your dress is slipping a bit." She gave me her dazzling smile and pushed a paper note into Mrs Tucker's tip collection, then flounced out the door.

For about a half second I contemplated joining Mister Simpson in his ignominy, but realized poor Mrs Tucker would have to clean up the mess I would make with Miss Thomas. I sighed, ran some cold water out of the tap onto a hand towel and patted my forehead with it. Mrs Tucker came in just as I finished.

"Well, your news must not have been too bad, Nurse Chandler," she said. "That young thing looked as if she owned the world."

"She certainly thinks she does," I replied. "Thanks for helping me out, Mrs Tucker." I gave her a hug and headed back to the restaurant.

The dinner service had been cleared at our table and desserts were coming out. A waiter held my chair and I rejoined the group. "Discover anything?" asked Harry.

"She slipped up – or maybe she didn't." I told them what Caroline had said regarding the diamonds out of the vault.

"What are you thinking?" asked Joel.

"I'm thinking I'm working really hard at trying to keep my personal animosity for her out of what I'm thinking." I watched Mr Perry flag down a waiter and order another drink. If he was intending to kill his malaria with alcohol he was doing a great job. I took a sip of wine. "Between her and Mrs Morgan I'll be very surprised if someone – hopefully not either of you – doesn't walk off this ship tomorrow morning affianced."

Joel sighed. "This is not helping me any."

"I know. I'm sorry." I rubbed my forehead and picked up the newspaper at my place setting. "Looks like this was a bust, Harry."

Winston shrugged. "The evening is just getting started for most of these people." He looked about the vast salon. "Though it does seem most of them have finished their meals. Maybe they'll take another look before the band kicks in full blast."

"Maybe." I looked up at Mister Harvey. "Yes? Come to complain to me again?"

Harvey shook his head. "No, sorry to disappoint. I'm here for the good doctor."

"What can I help you with?" asked Harper.

"Not me. Passenger in second class. Slipped down some steps and from the description his wife gave it seems to be a compound fracture of the leg. I called Mister Armstrong to get a couple of his men down there and take him to the hospital."

"All right." Harper dropped his napkin to his plate and pushed away from the table. "Good luck to you all. I'll catch up when I can."

"I'll go with you." Harper shook his head and waved me away.

"Alice is there. Might as well get some work out of her before she takes leave of us tomorrow." He put on his cap. "*Au revoir.*"

"Tell her hello for me," said Joel despondently.

"I will. Have a good evening." Harper and Harvey took their leave of us, Harvey carrying a copy of *The Victory.*

"Mister Harvey will never let me forget this," I said.

"Maeve, as I said earlier, the evening is just getting started. Don't be in such a hurry to make a deal. The deal will make itself." Harry motioned to the dance floor. "It's filling up. I see that Miss Thomas has already snagged a partner."

"Of course she has." I looked in the direction he indicated. Sure enough, Miss Thomas was bubbling over with gaiety as she and a young man I hadn't seen before twirled away to the music.

Frowning, I turned my head back toward her table. One of the late arriving couples was missing, and presumably on the dance floor. Mrs Morgan was engrossed in what seemed to be a deep conversation with Mr Clayton.

Perry noticed where I was looking. "Looks like Mr Clayton is getting the hard sell," he said as he took his drink from the waiter.

"Really? I smiled at Perry. "Better him than you, eh?"

"I'm far too old to be domesticated now." He took a deep swallow. "But she is rather a charming woman."

"Yes, she is."

Perry nodded. "The joy of youth." He raised his glass. "I'm very happy for you and your girl, Joel. The world, such as it is today, is wide open for the both of you."

"It is, isn't it?" I said. "Even if I'm losing my only nursing staff member."

"Cheers to you, Joel," said Harry. "We'll get through this, don't worry."

"Try and think of happier thoughts." Perry settled back in his chair, sipping his whisky. "All of this really does bring back memories to me. The gaiety and joy of just being young and alive. Why, I remember when your uncle and I – " He stopped short, frozen, apparently deep in thought.

"Mr Perry?" said Harry, a concerned look on his face.

Joel grasped my arm. "Oh my God, is he having a stroke?"

"Mr Perry?" I asked. Perry's eyes fluttered and he looked at me.

"Jesus, Joseph, and Mary," he said. "I know who Mrs Morgan reminds me of."

# XII

Memories are funny things. I've talked with people who swear they remember things that happened when they were only a year or two old, and others whose earliest memory dates from the age of five or six. Now, I know you're going to ask, so I'll tell you. My earliest memory concerns a cow and a milk pail, and my mother tells me I was five years old. She had taken my brother, who was then six, and me to a local farm so she could purchase eggs. The nanny, I'm told, had been ill that day which is why mum had child duty and wasn't at her job teaching.

My brother and I watched in fascination as a cow was milked and the full pail set to one side of the cow. The milkmaid excused herself for a moment, but an unsupervised moment was all it took; my brother said I probably couldn't tip that heavy pail over if I tried. Well, I could, and I did. It cost me my first spanking and set up what would be an adventurous career in misadventure with my brother. That memory has always stayed fresh because neither my mother nor brother ever missed a chance to retell it.

Mr Perry's sudden memory epiphany, however, was quite different. Sigmund Freud, the Austrian neurologist, says repressed memories are usually of a traumatic nature. While I've not had the pleasure of conferring with the *Herr Doktor*, (he's in his early seventies now) I do know it's believed that repressed thought is a defense against painful past experiences and some sort of trigger opens the memory back up. Whether it was the whisky, the music, the food at dinner, his happiness for Joel and Alice or just general reminiscing about being young – or maybe a combination of some or all – something had clicked in Mr Perry's brain.

All three of us looked at Mr Perry. "Who?" I asked. "Who does Mrs Morgan remind you of?"

He took another swallow of his drink. At this rate he'd be on his fifth round in a few minutes. Perry took a deep breath. "I can scarcely credit it myself, but she looks just like Annake's mother."

"Impossible," said Harry. "She'd have to be in her late seventies or eighties."

Perry shook his head. "No, you misunderstand. I'm not saying she's Annake's mother. I'm saying she looks like her mother."

"How did you know her mother?" asked Harry. "You've never mentioned her in what you've told us."

"There was never anything to mention. There was a photograph of an older woman with Annake at the home she shared with her father before the troubles started. I asked Annake and she confirmed it was her mother in the photo, who had passed away since it was taken. It was just a tintype sitting on the mantel above the fireplace. That's what's been bothering me." Perry drained his glass, and, true to form, ordered another. "It was a happier time," he said.

I turned my head back toward her table. She was still talking with Mr Clayton. I looked back at Perry. "Did Annake have a sister?"

"Not that I ever knew of," said Perry.

"If Mrs Morgan looks like Annake's mother, then she must have," said Harry. "Unless Mrs Morgan is just some kind of doppelgänger."

"Or Annake's mother had a much younger sister." I looked at Perry. He shook his head.

"Bloody hell, why don't you just go ask her?" said an exasperated Harvey. I started and gazed up at him.

"I thought you left with Doctor Harper."

"I did. He asked me to come back and try and keep an eye on you." He held up a rolled newspaper. "And I'm armed."

"Well, I'd hate for you to have made the trip back for nothing," I said, rising. My eyes met an empty chair. "Hells bells, she's not there anymore. Wait a moment, I'll be back." I threaded my way through a phalanx of dancers until I reached the table. Mr Clayton was sitting back, watching the merry makers. He looked up at me.

"Nurse Chandler, what a nice surprise. I want you to know I never heard those mice again."

"That's terrific, Mr Clayton. "I'll let housekeeping know the good news. Didn't I see you sitting with Mrs Morgan a few minutes ago?

"Yes, lovely woman. We're both staying aboard at Cherbourg and going on to Southampton."

"How lucky for you." I smiled. "I need to speak with her for just a moment, do you know where she's gone?"

"The lady's room is what she told me."

"Thanks, Mr Clayton. Enjoy the rest of your evening." I rejoined my table.

"Well? asked Harvey.

"Gone to the loo," I said. "If I'm not back soon come after me." I paced out of the salon back to the ladies' and was back in a couple of minutes. "No one matching her description has been in," I said.

"She took the bait," said Harry. He stood up. Mister Harvey looked at both of us.

"Where do you think you're off to?"

"To see if there's anything in our rat trap," I said. "Joel, you stay here and keep an eye on Mr Perry. He looks like he could keel over any minute."

"Just the two of you?" said Mister Harvey. "Not bloody likely." He glanced over at the guard provided by Mister Armstrong. "I'm coming with you and I'm bringing Goliath over there with me."

I shrugged. "Fine, but remember, the bigger they are, the harder they fall." I nodded toward the empty chair. "Just ask the shade of Mr Van Effen."

Leaving Joel with a quietly musing Perry we four filed out of the salon, heading for the lift station to go up to the Main Deck and First-Class accommodations. Harry shook his head. "This woman was hiding in plain sight."

"Kind of like that twenty-five cent emerald ring you bought as a boy," I said.

"I thought it was going to be Miss Thomas."

"Ha. For purely personal reasons I had hoped it would be, too," I said. "But first I thought about Van Effen. He was in Panama and Brazil and knew diamonds and had knowledge of curare."

"You could say the same about Mr Perry."

"I could. But in my professional opinion he's lacking the physical stamina to do all that's been done. And then Van Effen was killed." We walked into the lift. "Main Deck, please," I said to the lift operator. He nodded, slid the gate and door closed and turned the handle.

"So you think Mrs Morgan killed Van Effen?" Harry looked at me askance. "Do you think she killed Isaac, too?"

"If she is indeed Annake's sister, don't you think she'd have a good reason?"

"But what did Van Effen do to deserve dying?"

"I'm betting he found out something and had to be gotten rid of."

"Kind of a physical overmatch, wouldn't you say? Mrs Morgan versus Van Effen?"

"Don't forget that curare is the great leveler." I tapped Mister Harvey on the shoulder. "I think we need a plan before we get there."

Harvey looked at me like I had cucumbers growing out of my ear. "Really? I was under the impression you were just going to wing it."

"Mister Harvey, I've had a very long week. If you've got a plan, speak up."

"You think this woman is heading for the unoccupied cabin of Mr Silverwood?"

"Yes. The cabin number was not mentioned in the newspaper item for the very reason that it keeps any false claimants to the throne out of the area. Only our thief would know which cabin we were referring to."

"Well, what I'm thinking is this. You and Harry go check the room. I'll block one end of the corridor and – what is your name, anyway?" he asked the large seaman.

"Hogan, sir."

"Great. I'll block one end of the corridor and Hogan will block the other. Keep people from coming in, keep people from leaving." He thought for a moment. "You don't think she's armed, do you?"

"I don't think so. Harry and I saw that Van Effen's gun was still in his room."

Harvey nodded. "You don't think so. You hear that, Mister Hogan, she doesn't think so."

"Yes, sir."

"I wish Harper was here. Why do people have to fall in bathtubs, Mister Hogan?"

"I couldn't say, sir."

"No, of course not." Harvey's face was grim. "You're not saying much, Mr Winston."

"I was just thinking how I had been looking forward to a relaxing ocean voyage. Fresh salt air, good food, pleasant surroundings."

"The Stoddard Lines prides itself on giving value for the money," I said.

"Maybe next time more money, less value," Harry commented wryly.

"I'll bear that in mind," I said.

The elevator boy stopped the lift. "Main Deck," he intoned. "Have a nice evening." Then, as an afterthought: "Whatever it is you're doing."

"Right," Mister Harvey muttered under his breath. We walked quietly to the cabins. The hallway was empty. "Hogan, go to the end of the corridor. I'll stay here by the stairs up."

"Sir." Hogan strode forcefully away. Harvey turned to us.

"Well, Maeve?"

"Mr Winston?" I asked.

Harry nodded. We started quietly down the corridor. To our left was 38-A, Van Effen's cabin. The door was now sealed shut, a padlock in place. Another couple of steps and Miss Thomas' cabin was on our right, then Mr Clayton on our left. I stopped and we both looked at the door to Mr Silverwood's cabin, directly opposite Clayton's.

Dim light filtered through the keyhole. I very gently tried the knob. "Locked," I whispered.

"Then unlock it," said Harry. I withdrew the master key I'd never returned to Mister Harvey, took a last furtive look up and down the corridor at Mister Harvey and Mister Hogan, then set it to the lock.

# XIII

There's an English proverb that runs something like 'give him enough rope and he'll hang himself.' The meaning is clear: allow or give someone the opportunity to overreach themselves, and sooner or later they'll crash into a wall. My older brother had a God-given talent for doing just that, and he never seemed to learn.

For instance, there was the curious case of the missing marzipan that had been made specifically to frost the Christmas cake one holiday season. He successfully made off with the pan, and emboldened by the ease of his crime, he tried again. My mum made it easy for him by leaving the second pan out in full view in an apparently empty kitchen. We watched from behind a slightly cracked cupboard door as he committed petty larceny, and then the long arm of parental (and sibling) justice reached out for him. Of course, outside of one's own kitchen and pantry, life is usually not so accommodating for catching a thief.

Or a murderer.

There was an almost imperceptible click as I slowly turned Mister Harvey's master key. It slipped past the wards and moved the bolt. I looked at Harry.

"*Alice in Wonderland*," I whispered.

"What, again?"

"The key Alice found after she went down the rabbit hole let her into Wonderland's garden." I silently withdrew the master and put it back in my clutch, then looked over to Mister Harvey standing only two cabins away. I nodded at him, then turned my head back to Winston. "I don't think we're going to enter Wonderland. Ready?" He nodded and I turned the knob, slowly and silently pushing the door inward.

A single light in the sitting room was on, and light streamed from behind the partially opened bathroom door. Now that we were inside we could also hear the sound of an instrument of some sort digging into wood. I leaned back into the corridor and, putting a forefinger to my lips, motioned for Harvey and Mister Hogan, then Harry and I stepped inside. Harry gestured to a purse on the sitting room sofa; I nodded and angled my head back toward Mister Harvey, who had just stepped inside. Harry quietly picked up the purse and handed it to Mister Harvey, then I crept toward the bathroom door.

Looking down I could see a chair leg and an empty pair of women's shoes. I was now well and truly at the proverbial crossroads. Should I retreat to the safety of the sitting room with Misters Harvey and Hogan and Mr Winston, or should I press my advantage and remove the chair and let the chips fall where they may, no pun intended? She could strike her head or break an arm or worse in a fall around the toilet, lavatory, and tub. On the other hand, as far as I knew she'd already killed twice and I was pretty certain I'd be giving up a wedding invitation to Alice and Joel if I checked out right now. I split the difference and jostled the chair. A wood chisel and small hammer fell past me and cracked the floor tile as she grabbed for the top of the door with both hands and I put in a distress call to the reserves.

"Lift her down and keep her arms pinned, Mister Hogan!" Hogan complied; Mrs Morgan struggled for a moment but then gave up, she'd have had an easier time breaking free from a python. "Bring her in the sitting room and put her in the desk chair and keep a firm hand on her shoulders," I told Mister Hogan. "If she moves you have permission to take whatever steps you think are practicable to immobilize her."

"Yes, Nurse Chandler." Hogan walked her in and seated her none-too-gently.

"Mister Harvey, if you wouldn't mind emptying the contents of her purse on the table." Harvey did as he was asked and looked through the pile. After a moment he held up a capped syringe.

"Three guesses as to what's in here," he said.

"Put it back in the purse. You can leave the rest of it on the table," I said.

"Gladly." Mister Harvey carefully dropped the syringe into the purse and clicked it closed. He looked at Mrs. Morgan. "I'll just hang on to this, if you don't mind."

She gave him a thin smile. "It does nothing for your outfit."

"Don't push it, madam." Harvey looked at me. "I'll telephone Mister Armstrong, he can round up the necessaries and meet us here."

"Don't forget Doctor Harper."

"I won't." Harvey lifted the receiver..

"No need for Joel, Perry or Alice," I said. "Tell Harper for her to stay put."

"Yes, your ladyship." I ignored the jab and turned my attention elsewhere.

"Mrs Morgan. I'm curious as to what you were doing up on a chair in the bathroom of an empty cabin with a hammer and wood chisel."

"Possibly looking for something?" said Harry.

"Vandalizing Stoddard Lines property?" added Mister Harvey, looking up from the telephone.

She gave us a shrewd look. "I think you know what I was looking for," she said. "Nice job, putting that little notice in the newspaper. I wonder how many others read it?"

"It only matters that you did," I said.

Harvey rang off. "Mister Armstrong's on his way. He's calling Harper. There's another possibility of some weather so the Captain is staying on the bridge."

"Do you mind waiting, Mrs Morgan?" I asked.

"I don't appear to have a choice."

"No, you don't." I looked her over. "Maybe we can clear up one item before we have visitors. Mr Perry had been wondering who it was you reminded him of, and it finally came to him. He says you are the image of your mother."

"I was always told so."

"Annake's younger sister."

"Yes. Her only sibling."

"How did you not end up in the same camp with her when the war broke out?" asked Harry.

"I was working as a house servant for a wealthy farm family upcountry in the Transvaal when it happened. I was only 16 and the family spirited me out of the country to save me from what they feared the British would do." She looked up at Mister Hogan. "I think you can remove your hands, young man. I'm not going anywhere." Hogan looked at me and I nodded. He lifted his hands but stayed in place behind her.

"It's interesting that Annake never mentioned you, at least as far as Mr Perry remembers," I said.

"Annake and my father both believed I would be better protected if no mention was ever made of me. I never met Mr Perry until I made his acquaintance on board, so I'm not certain of how he saw a resemblance of me with my mother."

"There was a tintype photo on the mantlepiece that he remembered seeing," I said. "Your mother was in it."

Mrs Morgan nodded. "Ah, that. Yes, I remember when it was made. I was sick that day so I wasn't in it. Funny, isn't it, how the slightest thing can come back to trip you up."

"If Mr Perry hadn't remembered seeing that photograph, you would have left the ship as Mrs Morgan," said Harry.

She gave him a slight smile. "But I really am Mrs Morgan. What I told Nurse Chandler about my late husband being a doctor and me a nurse is absolutely true. Aleid is my real first name, and Adelaide is the Anglicized version of it." She glanced over at Mister Harvey. "Shall I hold the purse now and let you answer the knock at the door?"

Harvey glared at her but retained his grip on the purse as he let Mister Armstrong and Doctor Harper in. Harper glanced down at the purse. "Another syringe of curare tucked away," said Harvey. He indicated Mrs Morgan. "And there's your killer." He handed the purse to Harper, who in turn handed it off to Mister Armstrong.

"Don't open it," he said to Armstrong. "You don't want to risk being stuck."

"Not to worry, Doctor." Armstrong closed a paw over it. "Safe as a babe in arms."

Harper nodded, then turned to me. "You're certain of her?"

"Yes. She was trying to dig out the fakes in the bathroom door when we got here. That, and the dose of what we think is curare in her purse."

"And as a way of clinching it, she's also Annake's younger sister," added Harry.

Harper was momentarily taken aback. "Really? How did you find that out?"

"A tintype photo that she wasn't in," I said. Harper gave me a curious look. I shrugged. "I'll tell you later."

"Well, Mrs Morgan?" asked Harper.

"I'd prefer that you call me by my Dutch name. Aleid. I haven't heard it in so many years, you know."

"Aleid," said Harper. "I doubt you'll hear it much where you're going, either."

"Probably not."

"Well, then." I sat on the couch opposite her. "I'll get right to the point. You killed Mr Isaac?"

"Yes. And do you know why?"

"I think, from what we heard from Mr Perry about Isaac killing your sister, we can all see your motive," I said.

"It took me all these years to find him. And that I should finally find him and his ex-partner both on the same ship at the same time was luck I never dreamed of."

"Then why is Mr Perry still alive?" I asked.

"Because of what he said when he was under the influence of the scopolamine you gave him this morning. I realized he had tried to save my sister, probably had loved her." She looked at me. "You're a nurse, you've seen him. He probably doesn't have that much longer to live, anyway."

"Neither did Mr Isaac," I said.

"No, but whatever time he had left was far too long."

I held up a hand. "Aleid, can we start at the beginning, please? How did you come to be aboard the *Victoria* with Mr Isaac and Mr Perry?"

She settled back in her chair, raising a hand to warn off Mister Hogan as he reached for her. "It's a bit of a story, but I guess we're not going anywhere. I left South Africa for good after the second war started. The family I was working for moved to the Netherlands, and then finally to Great Britain. When I turned 21 in 1907, they handed me an envelope containing the sworn testimony of the British commander of the concentration camp where my sister met her end, implicating Nathaniel Isaac in her murder. The envelope also contained Annake's wedding band."

"The one that you placed on the chain with Isaac's," said Harry.

She nodded. "Yes. I wanted him to wear it to his grave so he'd never forget her."

"He wasn't buried in it," I said. "Jewish religion forbids it. His nephew Joel has both rings."

"Does he?" She nodded. "I guess that's fitting, then. When I received the ring I was already in nursing school. There was nothing I could do until I graduated, but by then the trail for Nathaniel Isaac, at least in London and Europe, had grown cold. I finished school, gained my diploma, and went to work for the Charing Cross Hospital where I met the man who would be my husband, an American doing an exchange residency. The excitement of life took over and pushed other thoughts out of my mind, at least for a while."

"But you never forgot, did you?" I asked.

She shook her head. "Would you have forgotten such a thing if it was your sister? No, it was always there in the back of my mind. It came to the fore again in 1910 when I received a letter and press clipping from a friend in New York. The newspaper account detailed the automobile crash that tragically took the lives of a young couple, but whose baby boy survived. The child was adopted by the mother's brother, a city diamond merchant named

Nathaniel Isaac. I could scarcely believe it; but being an orphan myself with no family but my adopted farm family, I couldn't bring myself to go to New York and confront Nathaniel and throw the boy's life into disarray. Much as it upset me, I knew I'd have to wait until he came of age and no longer needed his uncle. So I waited – and then the War broke out and that stopped everything. After the Armistice, my husband and I moved to Massachusetts, where he was from. I became a citizen, and we worked together. After he passed away I came into a rather sizeable fortune which survived last year's crash."

"You were fortunate," I said. "The crash happened while we were at sea." *

"I can only imagine what a circus that must have been," she said. "Anyway, since we never had children, I was left to my own devices. I located Nathaniel's place of business, a dirty little hole if ever there was one. I watched, and I waited. It was a pleasure, in a way, to see Joel grow up. I knew that had Nathaniel not murdered my sister and doomed her children that she would likely have been Joel's stepmother and her children his stepbrother and sister."

"I'm sorry," I said.

Aleid's face was grim. "It just made me more determined than ever to avenge my sister on that monster. I knew I'd likely go to prison or worse, so before dealing with Nathaniel, I decided to make one last trip back to London to see old friends. It was while I was browsing through the sailing schedules and passenger lists in the newspapers that I saw Nathaniel's name and believe me my heart jumped a bit when I also saw Mr Perry's name on the same list, both for the *Queen Victoria*." She gave me an earnest look.

---

*　　See Book One: *Shadow of the Queen*

"I knew I'd never get an opportunity like that again. I booked passage too and went to work. As you know, the sailing passenger lists are generally published two weeks out, which meant that the *Queen Victoria* was in New York at that time readying to return to Southampton. Nathaniel and Perry would be on the following sailing from New York. I had had plenty of time over the years to think of how I would deal with Nathaniel Isaac and was ready with an immediate plan that would only take a slight modification to be carried out on a ship. My husband and I had made the acquaintance of a friendly bootlegger to keep us supplied for all the entertaining we did, and I placed a call to him for some assistance. He was only too happy to go aboard the *Victoria* while it was still here in New York and make two key molds for me, one of a master, the other of a standard room key. While that was being done I caught passage back to New York on the *Berengaria*, arriving in New York at about the same time the Victoria was arriving in Southampton. My bootlegger had taken the molds to a little shop in New York's Bush Terminal area over between 36th and 37th streets and they had produced two keys which he handed over to me."

"I understand the master key," I said. "But what good is a regular door key?"

Aleid smiled. "By itself, not much good unless you know the door it's used on," she said. "In fact, I didn't care about anything but the bottom post of the key. The machinist needed that so he could pattern a tube to slip over it through the keyhole."

Harry looked at me with an air of victory, then back at Aleid. "A magnetic tube," he said.

"Yes. It snugged very tightly over the post of the key visible in the keyhole and could thereby from the outside turn the key already inside the door. When the *Victoria* returned to New York from Southampton, I went aboard and tried it out with the master key. It worked like a charm. I just opened the door enough to hold the room key in place with my right hand while I pushed the tube on from the outside with my left hand. After locking the door I just pulled the tube off."

"And where is that tube now?" asked Harry.

She shrugged. "At the bottom of the Atlantic. Shall I continue with my story?"

"Please," I said.

"I went back to my bootlegger friend after he had delivered me the keys and tube and asked him to supply me with some excellent counterfeit gems, a good couple of handfuls. While he gathered those, I went to a local hospital and borrowed three syringes full of curare."

"Three?"

"One for Nathaniel, one for Mr Perry, and one as a spare. After I boarded the ship on Saturday I took two of the fakes my bootlegger had gotten for me – which looked very real, you'll have to admit, I can't tell the difference – and bribed the young officer at the Purser's office to let me get Nathaniel's box out."

"I'm sure you'll be happy to know that he eventually questioned the veracity of those diamonds," said Harry.

"And he's been cashiered for his efforts," I added.

"Pity," she said, with no remorse. "Once I had Nathaniel's jewels, I went directly to his room, used the master and let myself in. He was sleeping soundly but he awakened nicely when I stuck the needle in him. The curare took effect quickly and I helped him to the chair in the sitting room." She looked at me. "By the way, how did you know about the injection?"

"A bit of the needle broke off when you jabbed him. Sloppy work for a nurse."

"I was motivated."

"Well, I very nearly pricked my finger on it, sticking up as it was through his pyjama collar." I said. "But once I knew what to look for I found the same mark on Van Effen."

"Ah. And I thought I'd been so careful." She steepled her fingers. "With Nathaniel immobilized, I slowly recounted his crimes to him, and with each crime I put more of the fake diamonds in his mouth, finally ending with a single real one as an offering for my sister. Once he was dead I left the room and turned the key in the manner I mentioned before."

"Why?" asked Harry. "Why go to the trouble of locking the door from the inside?"

"Why?" said Aleid. "I wanted the world to know that Nathaniel Isaac took his own life. That his conscience finally caught up with him and that he locked himself in his room and killed himself in the most hideous way possible."

"So you took all of his diamonds," I said.

"Yes. Why shouldn't I? Small recompense for what he did to my sister and her children, don't you think? And before I ever came on board I had thought of the perfect place to hide them, in that bathroom door. I brought along a small valise carrying the fakes intended for Isaac, as well as a hand drill and material to fill over the top of the hole."

"So you're Mr Silverman," said Harper.

"That's right." She smiled. "There were several empty cabins on this corridor and I booked this one in addition to my own. Business, I guess, is not what it was before the crash." Mister Harvey frowned but said nothing, and she continued. "I left Isaac's cabin with the diamonds I had gotten from his box at the vault."

"What about Van Effen?" I asked.

"Van Effen." She shook her head. "I have to admit I had not counted on a large bodyguard in my calculations."

"The reason for the bodyguard is that Joel is in trouble with the gangster, Dutch Schultz," I said. "It seems he took out a loan at exorbitant interest to modernize his uncle's shop. And the loan is very much due."

"Poor boy. He was never going to get any help from his uncle, was he?"

"Let's get back to Van Effen," I said.

Aleid nodded. "I had just locked Isaac's door and was going to this cabin when Mr Van Effen appeared out of nowhere and asked what I was doing and what was in the valise I was carrying." She shook her head. "He was just in the wrong place at the wrong time. I knew he could turn me in, so I cut a deal with him. I'd give him half of the diamonds I'd taken from Nathaniel in return for his cooperation. I used the master to let us inside this cabin, then Van Effen used the hand drill in my valise to put a hole in the top of the door. When he finished I climbed up on the chair and deposited the jewels from Nathaniel's safe box, and stuck one of Nathaniel's business cards in with them, in case someone other than me recovered them. It was my hope they'd be returned to Nathaniel's estate and go to Joel if they didn't come to me. Van Effen plugged the hole with putty I'd brought along, then we left. I threw the valise with the drill, putty and empty box overboard."

"When did you plan to retrieve the diamonds?" Harry asked.

Aleid gave a wry laugh. "Oh, I was never going to retrieve them myself. I had arranged for my bootlegger to get them the next time the *Victoria* arrived and visitors were swarming over the ship."

"When did things go wrong with Van Effen?" I asked.

"He decided he was going to renege on our agreement. He came to me a day ago and told me he'd discovered that all of Nathaniel's diamonds we'd hidden in the bathroom door were fakes – as if I'd believe him and he could scoop the entire lot. We had a brief argument, but I knew then that I'd have to deal with him."

"And how did you do that, beyond the obvious solution of killing him?" said Harper.

"I noticed he had been spending a great deal of time in that pretty young lady's company. I still had a counterfeit left from taking care of Nathaniel, so I gave it to her with instructions to lure him back to his cabin for a shared bath. I let myself in with my master beforehand and ran the water, then hid in the bath closet and waited for him." She gave a grim smile. "When he let himself in he was certainly in a hurry, it seemed. He kicked off his shoes and dropped his shoulder holster and gun on the bed then came into the bathroom. It was easy to stick him with the syringe, then I let his own body weight carry him into the full tub."

"Well thought out, it seems," I said. "Did you know that Mr Isaac's store was robbed a few days ago? The manager was found dead."

She shook her head. "No. I didn't hear about that. I'm sorry for Joel. And on top of that bad loan you just talked about." She thought for a moment. "All you haave to do is give him his uncle's diamonds. They're right over there in the door."

"No, they're not," said Harry. "Van Effen was right. The items inside the door are fakes. Every one of them."

"How would you know?"

"Because I checked them."

"They came out of Nathaniel's safe box."

"And they're fakes." Harry crossed his arms.

"Who checks in a box of fake diamonds?" said Aleid.

"A question we've been asking ourselves," I said.

Aleid looked irritated with herself. "Well, hell," she said, then sighed. "All of that for nothing." She looked up at Hogan. "I'm standing up now, young man. Please don't manhandle me again." Hogan looked at me and I nodded. Aleid got to her feet, then reached for the back of the chair. "Leg cramps. If this keeps up I'm going to need a cane."

"I'm sure Mister Hogan and I can get you to – to where, Nurse?" said Mister Armstrong.

"Her cabin is right across the hall, 32-A. Lock her up inside and post Mister Hogan outside the door." I glanced over at the table and the items from her purse. "I imagine the two keys over there that Mr Harvey dumped out of her purse are her master and the key to her own room."

"Right. I'll check them." Flanked by Mister Armstrong and Mister Hogan, Adeleide hobbled out of the room, then turned back to us.

"I am happy for Joel and his engagement. Don't look surprised, the entire ship knows. It was all the talk. I'll tell him myself when I can."

"I think Joel would be just as happy not hearing from you," I said.

"Do you think so?"

"Yes."

Aleid nodded thoughtfully. "At least he's free of Isaac," she said. "We're all free of him." She smiled at me "Please give Mr. Clayton my regrets. He's such a nice man."

I gave her a hard stare. "Goodbye, Mrs Morgan." She limped out between her guards.

"Well," said Mister Harvey. "That's that."

"Not quite," said Harry. "Mrs Morgan brought fake jewels on board to use on Mr Isaac. Meanwhile, for reasons best known to himself, Mr Isaac checked fake jewels into the ship's vault. So the question remains, where are Isaac's real diamonds?"

Inspiration, which had been pretty much sleeping on the job the past few days, finally kicked into gear in my head. "I think I know," I said. "And they've been there all the time. Mister Harvey, could you please go retrieve Joel and Mr Perry from the salon and bring them to Mr Isaac's cabin? I've still got your master key to let us in. We'll be waiting."

Ten minutes later we were all assembled with the exception of a snoring Mr Perry, who had to be placed into his bed in his cabin by Mister Harvey and Doctor Harper. After we filled Joel in on all that had occurred, I leaned up against the desk in the sitting room. "So. Mrs Morgan – Adelaide – Aleid, whatever you want to call her, brought her own fakes on board to use on your uncle, Joel. And I now believe your uncle, distrustful, brought on board fakes to check into the ship's vault. Which leaves us with the question, where did he put the real ones? Because there was no chance he was spending this kind of money and taking this trip to show up in Antwerp with nothing to sell or trade."

Joel looked puzzled. "They weren't anywhere in his belongings. You were there when we went through the baggage.'

"And there was only the one box taken from the vault, so he didn't check in another box," said Harvey.

Harper nodded. "And we searched this room the morning we found him. There was nothing here."

"I beg to differ, Doctor. There was something there. And it has been there all along. We just didn't see it."

"What are you talking about, Maeve?" asked Harry.

"Aleid didn't see it, either. But she just gave it away." I looked at Joel. "She had been sitting so long that when she got up she had what the Americans call a charley-horse."

"So?" said Joel.

"When you've got a cramp in your calf or have injured your leg, what do you want to use?"

"A cane," said Harry. He looked over into the corner where Nathaniel's cane was still leaning against the wall, untouched. "A cane," he repeated.

"Joel, you told me that your uncle didn't trust anyone. I suppose that after the stock market crash back in October, he became even less trusting. I've heard of some people burying their valuables in the backyard. Hard to do in New York City, I imagine. Money in a mattress? Not altogether comfortable and it's a fire hazard." I walked over and picked up the cane.

"This is a big, heavy cane for a small man to constantly lug about." I took a grip on the cane with my left hand beneath the knob and grinned. "And yet Isaac was never without it." I gripped the knob even tighter, then gave it a sharp counter-clockwise twist and smiled at Joel. "Hold out your hands."

"Like this?" He held them out before him, palms up, right little finger touching left little finger.

"Perfect," I said. I unscrewed the knob and set it on the table, then tilted the cane forward into his outstretched hands. A cascade of paper-wrapped tiny items descended from its hollow interior, overflowing his hands. Joel's jaw dropped.

"Good Lord," said Harper.

Harvey pushed his cap back on his head. "Bloody hell."

Harry plucked one from Joel's palms, unwrapped it and fitted his loupe to his eye. After a moment he nodded and put it back in the wrapper.

"Congratulations, Joel," he said. "If the rest of these pan out, you own a nice fortune in diamonds."

# XIV

You remember reading those fairy tales where it all worked out in the end and the Princess and the Prince got married and lived happily ever after? I'm talking about stuff like *Cinderella* (the French version is the best known), *Snow White* (German), *Sleeping Beauty* (again, the French), and the like. After all sorts of trials and tribulations, the beautiful and handsome couple win through to the end and are assured of domestic bliss and wealth for the rest of their lives. (Unless eaten by an ogre or put under a spell by an evil witch or turned into a rutabaga or something; do some in-depth reading of the source material and you'll know why the most famous fairy tale collectors were named Grimm for a reason.)

Thankfully, such was not the case with our happy couple. Alice, dressed now in her best shore leave clothing, stood next to Joel in the hospital. Mister Harvey had procured a bottle of champagne and flutes. "To your health," said Doctor Harper.

I handed Alice a handkerchief. "I know you're about to cry." She nodded, her eyes wet with tears. "Oh, honey," I said, taking her in my arms. "I'm so happy for you."

"Thanks, Mother."

I pinched her ear. "Not that happy." I looked at Joel. "Take good care of her."

"I will."

"And I promise we'll be back aboard," said Alice. "We'll be doing a lot of traveling as we build up Joel's business."

Mister Harvey shook Joel's hand. "Don't expect the Stoddard Lines to comp you a private dining room and dinner again, though. Best of luck, young man."

"Thank you, Mister Harvey." Joel turned to Alice. "We need to go, Alice. We're expected by Mr Perry and Mr Winston at the Promenade Lounge before we disembark with them."

Alice nodded, then looked at me. "What about Mr Van Effen?" asked Alice. "It won't be another burial at sea, will it?"

"No," said Doctor Harper. "Nurse Chandler said that Mr Van Effen told her he served in the French Foreign Legion. I met some Legionnaires during the War and they vigorously protect their own. Since Mr Van Effen had no family that we know of, as a Legionnaire he qualifies for burial in France; probably the Foreign Legion cemetery at Puyloubier in southern France."

"I think he would like that," said Joel. Harper nodded.

"His body will make a stop at the Institut Médico-Légal in Paris first, for an autopsy to confirm the presence of curare. Those findings will go to London for the criminal investigation."

"What about Mrs Morgan?" asked Joel.

"She's an American citizen who committed crimes aboard a British vessel. The Yanks and Scotland Yard will have to figure that one out," I said. "Now go, before you're late for Mr Winston and Mr Perry."

"Come with us," said Alice. "I'm not ready to say goodbye to you yet."

"Go," said Harper, looking at me. "I'm sure Mister Harvey and I can find a good use for the rest of this bottle."

"Thanks, Boss."

"Like you ever ask my permission, anyway." He turned to fill Mister Harvey's glass.

The lifts were slow and full this morning as passengers prepared to leave the ship. It took us nearly ten minutes to reach the Promenade Deck. Alice prattled on about splitting time between New York and London while Joel and I listened with indulgence and an occasional smile and roll of the eyes toward each other at Alice's flights of fancy.

Despite the relatively early hour of eight the Observation Lounge was at near capacity when we pushed inside and it took us a few minutes to locate Harry and Mr Perry seated at a table near one of the walls. Both men rose to greet us.

"This reminds me of last Saturday night," said Harry. "Seems like a million years ago."

"It does, doesn't it?" I looked around. "And all of these people have no idea."

"Harry told me everything that happened last night," said Mr Perry. "Hard to believe, but there it is." He took a sip of his omnipresent drink. "Carrying his diamonds in his cane. So typical of Nathaniel. Trusted no one but himself."

"Joel," said Harry, "My offer to take you on still stands."

"Thank you." Joel looked at Alice. "We've talked, though, and as generous as your offer of employment is, I want to try and make it on my own." He held Alice's hand. "We want to try and make it on our own."

"Are you sure?"

Joel nodded. "Yes, more than sure. And thank you for your offer of donations to help me start, but with Nathan's diamonds, I won't need them."

"What about your debt to Schultz?" asked Perry. "I'm still happy to take that on for you. Like I said, this is my last trip. I'm retiring."

"No, but thank you. I made the mess, I'll clean it up. I've got the means to do it now."

"To you, then." Perry raised his glass "You've more character than your uncle ever had."

"Maeve, how far is Antwerp from Cherbourg?" asked Joel.

"280, 290 miles or so. The train should get you there in about eight hours."

Harry glanced at his watch. "It leaves at ten."

"That gives you two hours to kill before you board," I said. "The four of you be safe. The docks have pickpockets and worse."

"Telegram for Joel Singer," a bellhop's strident voice could be heard above the crowd. "Telegram for Joel Singer."

"What now?" Joel stood and waved his arm. The boy came over, delivered the missive, was tipped by Alice, and left. Joel tore the message open, then put a hand on the back of his chair to steady himself.

"What is it?" I asked.

"The store," he said. "Listen to this. It's from the New York police. 'Mr Joel Singer aboard *RMS Queen Victoria* stop. Gems found in raid on Dutch Schultz establishment, stop. Believed stolen from you, stop. Held as evidence, stop. Inventory list and description required to release after court use, stop.'" Joel sagged against his chair as Alice hugged him.

"Well, then," said Harry. "Looks like you really are set to go into business for yourself."

"Good for you, Joel." Perry drained his glass and chuckled. "Paying Dutch off with gems he stole from you in the first place. I'm sure there's some sort of cosmic interplay at work there, but it will take me a few more drinks to figure it out. I will see you all at the train station. Nurse Chandler, a pleasure meeting you."

"The same, Mr Perry. Please see a doctor about that malaria reoccurrence."

"I will, thank you, Nurse."

"We'll be going too," said Joel. "Thank you for everything, Nurse Chandler."

"Oh, Maeve." Alice wrapped her arms around me. "You've always been the best. See you at the wedding." She smiled and walked away, arm in arm with Joel. I waved goodbye, then glanced over at the bar.

"Coo, look there. He didn't even make it out of the lounge. Miss Thomas has latched on to Mr Perry. She never quits."

Harry smiled. "I'd like to be a fly on the wall when she tries to sell that counterfeit jewel she thinks is real."

"That will be fun, won't it?"

"Maeve," a voice called from behind me. I turned and saw Mister Casey. "How did all of that work out for you last night?"

"Just fine, Mister Casey. Just fine."

He looked at Mr Winston. "Sorry, didn't mean to interrupt. Will you give me the story later?" I glanced at Harry. He shrugged. "Perfect," said Casey. He tipped his battered fedora to me, gave Harry a nod and departed. I sighed.

"Well, I need to get back to the hospital and do some real work. It's been quite the week. Thanks for shepherding Joel in Antwerp."

"My pleasure. Before you go, hold out your hand." I did as he asked and he dropped a small sparkling diamond into my left palm. "I think someone lost this. As Miss Thomas would say, finders-keepers."

I gasped. "Harry, I can't – " He closed my fingers over it.

"Never say no to a diamond. Besides, I think you earned it." He stood and shook my hand. "I'll keep an eye on Joel while we're in Antwerp, and we'll all meet again on the return trip to New York – which I trust will be less active than this one."

"I'll do my best," I said with a smile.


Nurse Chandler, Doctor Harper,
Mister Harvey and the *Queen Victoria*
will return in *Queen of the Sky.*

Read on for a preview of the next book
in the *Voyages of the Queen* series – *Queen of the Sky*.

# Queen of the Sky

by Scott Finley

# Prologue

I'm sure you read all about the Greek gods and goddesses and such when you were in school; my older brother and I certainly had to do our share. He was better than I at keeping them straight, though; I tended to cross-pollinate them with the Roman gods who, I'm reliably informed, usurped them from the Greeks with some minor changes, so it didn't make much of a difference as far as I was concerned.

While the all-powerful gods like Zeus (Jupiter to the Romans), Hera (Juno), Poseidon (Neptune) and others ruled humanity with an iron fist, some humans thumbed their noses and got on with life anyway, and, being naturally of a recalcitrant turn of mind, it was to these non-conforming people I gravitated. Two of my favorites were Daedalus and his not-too-bright son, Icarus. For those needing a refresher on their story, while imprisoned on the island of Crete (where he had designed and built the labyrinth that held the Minotaur), Pop Daedalus came up with the brainstorm of making wings from bird feathers and binding them together with wax, the idea being to fly to freedom. Long story short, the wings worked, but human nature did not. Despite warnings from

Dad, Icarus flew too close to the sun, melting the wax and causing him to plunge to his death.

Of course, that was a long time back. Nowadays, air travel is marginally safer (not that I'm doing it) but it still can't compete with going by sea. While it took Lindbergh 30 hours to cover 3,600 miles when he crossed the Atlantic solo just three years ago in 1927, it took 111 hours for the German rigid airship *Graf Zeppelin* to cross in 1928 because it flies slower carrying 24 passengers plus 36 crew.

My ship, the *Queen Victoria*, carries 2,100 passengers and 700 crew and while it crosses the Atlantic in about the same length of time as the flying *Graf*, the *Victoria* is much more luxurious and much less expensive. For instance, I'm told the *Graf* has two washrooms and two toilets for 24 passengers. Another thing is room to roam: the First-Class dining salon on the *Queen Victoria* could easily hold the entire passenger and operations area of the *Graf* and still have room to serve breakfast.

Of course, there are other reasons to go by sea and not by air in the big rigid zeppelins. The British *R38* crashed in 1921 killing 41, the United States' *Roma* cashed it in with 34 dead in 1922, followed by the French *Dixmude* exploding and killing all 52 on board in 1923. Two years later the United States' *USS Shenandoah* crashed with 14 dead.

Not to be outdone my countrymen are trying it again with the new *R100* and *R101*, but results to date seem sketchy to me.

While pictures of airships show them to be beautiful, even ethereal craft, and while they do make the Atlantic crossing faster than most ships, in my opinion the number one reason to stick to the tried-and-true safe sea lanes (*Titanic* issues aside) is because the zeppelins and other airships achieve their lighter-than-air status from being inflated with explosive and highly flammable hydrogen gas. (Except the Americans, who use helium.) I remember during the War seeing a German zeppelin burn and crash near our town back in 1916 when I was fifteen years old. When the wreckage cooled the next day, I watched townspeople removing the crew bodies for burial and almost all had burned to death, save for a few who had jumped from a great height to escape the hungry all-consuming flames.

Get me into an airship?

Not bloody likely.

# *Monday, May 19, 1930*

I

'm certain that wherever you are, wherever you grew up, you had traditions.

They come in all shapes and sizes and range from familial to international. For my older brother and myself, a familial tradition was always something simple, like being allowed to scrape and lick the bowls Mum used to make cake batter. (I suspect that was probably one of yours, too.) Another was that our father always placed the star at the top of our Christmas tree, proclaiming 'let the season begin' as he did. That went on for years and years. A national example, of course, would be the British predilection for afternoon tea and biscuits, or going to the local pub where everyone knew you and vice-versa. (Not something my brother and I were allowed to participate in during our formative years, try as we might.)

Then there are the traditions on an international scale. Despite the fact that we just finished fighting the War twelve years ago, the globe does harbor some traditions that are rooted in antiquity and in which every nation participates. One of these is a distress call at sea. By custom, the ship closest to the one needing aid is obligated to turn from their set course and come to the rescue. The most famous of these is the ship *Carpathia* coming to the rescue of the *Titanic*. Unfortunately, the *Carpathia* was over 50 miles away when they got the signal, and despite full speed arrived an hour and a half after the *Titanic* had gone under. They rescued the survivors in lifeboats, then made for New York.

The reason I'm telling you all of this is to explain why, one day out from Southampton and bound for New York, the *Queen Victoria* had begun a turn that put the Continent parallel to our left, or port side, while increased engine revolutions beyond our normal cruising speed added extra vibration to the ship. Doctor Bratton looked at me. "Do you feel that, Maeve?" he asked.

Situated as the ship's hospital was on C Deck, amidships and just above the waterline, it would have been impossible not to feel anything. I nodded. "And we're turning, too."

Our ship's surgeon frowned. "A sudden course deviation is never a good thing." He looked around at our trim facility. "And I had hoped for a quiet trip."

The telephone rang and I answered. "Hospital, Nurse Chandler." I listened for a few moments. "All right. On my way." I rang off. Bratton looked at me.

"What's going on?"

"That was Doctor Harper from the bridge. Seems we're answering a distress signal."

"From?"

"He didn't say. Some sort of medical emergency."

Bratton nodded. "Could be anything. I'll go prep the surgery. Did he give you any notice of when we'd rendezvous?"

"None, I'm afraid. I'll ring back with more information." I gave Doctor Bratton a smile. "Sorry to see your quiet trip spoilt."

He shrugged. "That's the way of it. Though I don't know why it couldn't have happened while we still had Alice."

Alice had been our other nurse and had nominally reported to me. She'd left the ship a couple of months earlier to marry a passenger and her position wasn't going to be replaced.* "She's happy and getting married next month. We'll just have to deal with whatever this is on our own. Stiff upper lip, Doctor."

"Yes," said Bratton, though he sounded more resigned than enthusiastic.

Normally I opted to take the stairs when going topside, but this situation seemed to call for some expediency. The lift man let me off on the Sun Deck and I took the stairs to the Sports Deck and bridge enclosure at the forward end. Principle Medical Officer Doctor Harper was standing in conference with Mister Cameron, our chief Marconi radio operator, and Captain Webster. Harper turned as I came in.

"Nurse Chandler. We have a situation."

"Yes, sir. I guessed as much."

"Medical emergency, Nurse," said the Captain. "From what Doctor Harper tells me, could be life and death."

"What is it?"

Mister Cameron shrugged. "The signal was a bit garbled, Nurse, and the sender has a heavy German accent. What we gathered in the radio room is it sounded like acute appendicitis."

I nodded. "If it's not removed, it could burst." I looked up at Harper from my five-foot stature. "That means peritonitis."

The Captain rubbed his salt and pepper beard. "Fortunately for the patient, we were less than a half hour distant from their position when we got their call. Much closer now; Chief Engineer Duncan has done a good job of ramping up our speed." The Captain gazed out through the large heavy plate glass windows on the bridge. "The weather's holding and visibility is good, but bad weather is coming, I'm told. Hopefully we'll stay ahead of it."

---

*    See book two, *Queen of Diamonds*

"Mister Cameron's men have been able to maintain radio contact and pass my instructions to keep the man as comfortable as possible until we arrive," said Harper.

"They don't have a big Marconi set like ours," said Cameron. "I think they're using several small six-valve receivers from medium to very low frequency. They do have a radio direction finder so they can lock us, as long as they hold their position." Mister Cameron looked at the Captain. "And as far as the weather goes, sir, they are very insistent that if bad weather or a squall line forms, they will leave immediately."

"You aren't serious?" I said to Mister Cameron. "Waiting on help from the *Queen Victoria* and they'll leave if it starts raining?"

"They are not a very sea-worthy vessel," said the Captain.

"What are they, sir?" I asked. "Some leaky old two-masted sailing schooner?" I looked at Harper. "If that's the case we'll capsize them getting close enough to run a bosun's chair and evacuate their man to our hospital. Or are you planning to put one of our lifeboats in the water and pay a house call?"

"Paying a house call with a lifeboat would be too dangerous, both for us and the other ship. And I can guarantee you that we won't capsize them," said Harper. "The bosun's chair is completely out, we will have to board and attend to him."

"I am not following you, Doctor." I crossed my arms and looked at the three men. "You're telling me this vessel is not sea-worthy, but if we draw close we won't capsize them, we can't take a lifeboat over to them because it's too dangerous and in any case we won't be able to use our bosun's chair to move from ship to ship." My frustration was mounting. "Just how do you expect us to get aboard and treat this man?"

Bells rang as First Officer Carter pulled the engine telegraphs back to signal the *Victoria* be brought to a gliding stop by the engine rooms. "She's coming in view now, Captain," he said. "We should come to a stop reasonably close to her."

The Captain was peering intently through the bridge front windows as well, his hands clasped behind his back. "To answer your question, Nurse Chandler, I expect you'll have to use a ladder."

Though still some distance from our slowing ship, another large ship could be seen on the clear horizon, and as we closed with her more horizon opened up beneath her until a discernible gap could be seen between her and the Atlantic Ocean. It suddenly dawned on me that this ship was not in the water, it was over the water, and I gasped at a sight made familiar to me in countless newspaper and magazine pictures, but not one I had ever glimpsed in person.

The German airship *Graf Zeppelin* floated serenely in the clouding sky, awaiting our arrival.

Dear Reader –

You reached this page, so I'm guessing you survived your journey on the *Queen Victoria*! I hope you'll come along on book three, *Queen of the Sky*, featuring Lady Grace Marguerite Lethbridge Hay-Drummond-Hay, more usually called Lady Grace Drummond-Hay. This intrepid woman was a ground-breaking journalist for the Hearst family of newspapers, and in August of 1929 became the first woman to travel around the globe by air aboard the German *Graf Zeppelin*. *Queen of the Sky* finds Maeve and Principal Medical Officer Dr. Harper responding to a medical emergency aboard the *Graf Zeppelin*, then made unwilling travelers as the airship heads aloft due to incoming bad weather. When a passenger is found dead the next morning, Maeve and Lady Drummond-Hay are soon dueling with a killer who will stop at nothing to achieve their goal.

If you enjoyed this book, thank you! Please consider recommending it to a friend (or more!). Your word-of-mouth in person and on social media is not only a terrific compliment but also the best advertising in the world.

Speaking of social media, please visit the *Queen* website at www.voyagesofthequeen.com for all sorts of surprises. Doing a costume party for 1929 and the '30's? Find out what fashionable men and women were wearing, head to toe. Need a vintage cocktail recipe? We have them! How about some period artists to ask Alexa to play? There's a list! If you're hungry, come to the Captain's Table for luxury liner recipes. Preview the published *Queen* books on Amazon and get a look at upcoming titles in the series. Go to the Radio Room and sign up for the *Queen's* own blog, or just drop a line, either on the site or here: scott@voyagesofthequeen.com.

You can also learn about the men and women who crewed the great ships and the tasks they performed, as well as get a deeper understanding of the *RMS Queen*

*Victoria*, what she carried, when she was built, how large she was and what her decks looked like. Find out more about the Golden Age of the trans-Atlantic liner, and there's a hand-curated list of websites with even more information.

Again, thank you for booking passage on the *Queen Victoria*. Who knows, I may see you on your next voyage (I'll be hiding behind the tall potted palms in the First-Class salon).

*Bon voyage!*
Scott Finley

# Reader's Group Guide

# Queen of Diamonds

## By Scott Finley

Questions and history to augment your club's reading of *Queen of Diamonds*.

1) It's love at first sight for Alice and Joel. Is this possible? If so, has it happened to you or anyone you know?

2) Maeve would support her best friend Alice up to and including telling little fibs for her, though it makes her uneasy. Do you have a friend who would do the same?

3) Harry Winston is a worldwide name in diamonds. Have you ever shopped a store or made a purchase?

4) "Diamonds are a girl's best friend," goes the song. What's your preference and why? Diamonds, emeralds rubies, etc.

5) Nathaniel Isaac is buried at sea. Would you attend such a service for a stranger if you were a passenger?

6) Maeve recounts the time she was made aware of the identity of Father Christmas. What is your memory and what happened?

7) Maeve takes an instant dislike to Caroline. Has that ever happened to you? Why?

8) Maeve and Doctor Harper have a pretty good grasp of Shakespeare, at least enough to apply to situations they find themselves in. Who or what is your cultural go-to for quotes and/or direction?

9) Perry wants to help Joel as much as he's able. Is he doing it out of love and memory for Annake, or does he realize his time is short and it's time to set some wrongs right?

10) Maeve believes Miss Thomas is a gold-digger. Do you think she's looking for someone, or just looking for temporary fun?

11) The mobster Dutch Schultz is never seen or heard, yet he casts a shadow over the action. Have you ever felt like you were under the thumb of something you couldn't control, but which could exercise control over you?

12) Mr Perry has a sudden flash of memory regarding Mrs Morgan. Does this sudden memory flash ever happen to you? If so, what memory pops up unbidden?

There are many references to period products, people, ships, places and more within the story. For anyone born in 1901, this knowledge would have been as familiar to them as Ryan Reynolds or Brad Pitt is to you. Here's a quick dictionary.

# People

THEDA BARA - Silent movie actress and early sex symbol. 1885-1955.

WARNER BAXTER - Movie actor best known for portrayal of the Cisco Kid in 1928's *In Old Arizona* for which he won Best Actor at the 2nd Academy Awards. 1889-1951.

CLARA BOW - Movie actress who successfully transitioned from silent to sound films. 1905-1965.

CHARLES CHAPLIN - Comic actor/filmmaker with a 75-year career. 1889-1977.

THOMAS EDISON - Prolific inventor of the light bulb, phonograph, motion picture camera and more. 1847-1931.

DOUGLAS FAIRBANKS - Movie actor and co-founder of United Artists pictures and founding member of the Motion Picture Academy; hosted first Academy Awards in 1929. 1883-1939.

F. SCOTT FITZGERALD - Jazz-age author of *The Great Gatsby*. 1896-1940.

SIGMUND FREUD - Father of modern psychoanalysis. 1856-1939.

GRETA GARBO - Actress from silent to sound films. Three Academy Award nominations. 1905—1990.

H. RIDER HAGGARD - Popular author of adventure stories. Most famous work is *King Solomon's Mines*. 1856-1925.

HER AND HIS MAJESTIES - Queen Victoria, 1837-1901; Edward VII, 1841-1910.

BOB HOPE - American comedian of radio, film and TV. Hosted Academy Awards 19 times, famous for his tours entertaining US military around the world. His radio career begins in 1933, so at the time of this book Maeve really would not know what became of him. 1903-2003.

HENRY HUDSON - Early explorer of Canada. Hudson's Bay is named for him. 1565-1611?

WASHINGTON IRVING - Author best known for short stories "Rip Van Winkle" and "The Legend of Sleepy Hollow." 1783-1859.

ARTHUR LAWEN - German surgeon who pioneered use of curare as anesthetic in 1912. 1876-1958.

KEN MAYNARD - Western movie star of the era and first singing cowboy. 1895-1973.

TOM MIX - Top-grossing movie cowboy appearing in 291 films, most of which were silent. 1880-1940.

POLA NEGRI - Polish-born actress popular in silent films. 1897-1987.

MABEL NORMAND - Silent film actress. Appeared in 12 films with Charlie Chaplin. 1893-1930.

EMMELINE PANKHURST - British suffragette instrumental in winning women right to vote in UK (to a degree) in 1918. 1858-1928.

SIR WALTER RALEIGH - English adventurer in reign of Elizabeth I. 1552-1618.

CECIL RHODES - Powerful British politician and diamond mining baron in South Africa. 1853-1902.

ROSENCRANTZ AND GUILDENSTERN - Characters in *Hamlet* tasked with escorting Hamlet to England while carrying a letter for the King of England to have Hamlet killed. Apparently unaware of the letter's contents, the pair meet their end when Hamlet opens and rewrites the letter designating them for execution instead.

DUTCH SCHULTZ - New York based mobster who was so unstable his fellow gangsters eventually had him killed. 1901-1935.

SILVER RING BOOKIE - British term for horse racing bookmakers offering lowest and cheapest odds at the track.

TUPINIQUIM INDIANS - An indigenous people of Brazil.

WALTER WINCHELL - Popular and powerful American gossip columnist. 1897-1972.

HARRY WINSTON - Arguably the most famous jeweler in history. Founded Harry Winston Inc. in New York in 1932, and also owned the Hope diamond, later donated by him to the Smithsonian Institute. 1896-1978.

# Yiddish

GOLEM - An animated being usually made of clay. Think Frankenstein's monster made of mud.

KHAZERAY - Trash, garbage.

MESHUGGENEH - A crazy person.

SHIKSA (plural, SHIKSAS) - A term for a Gentile woman or girl, usually used in a disparaging manner.

SHIVA - The seven-day mourning period after someone dies.

SHLOK - Junk, inferior items.

# Books, newspapers, magazines, films

*ANNA CHRISTIE* - Greta Garbo's first sound film. Released February, 1930.

*THE BRITISH MEDICAL JOURNAL* - Peer-reviewed publication, active since 1840.

*BRITISH PHARMACEUTICAL CODEX* - Supplemental reference work for pharmacists.

CISCO KID - Popular western character created by American writer O. Henry in 1907.

*THE DISPENSATORY OF THE UNITED STATES OF AMERICA* - Reference work for pharmacists and physicians.

*INFERNO* - Part one of three of the *Divine Comedy* written by Dante Alighieri in the early 14th century. The *Inferno* takes readers on a trip through the nine circles of Hell.

*KING SOLOMON'S MINES* - Adventure novel written by H. Rider Haggard in 1885. Still in print and has been adapted to radio, tv, film and comic books.

*THE LANCET* - British peer-reviewed medical journal, active since 1823.

*MABEL'S STRANGE PREDICAMENT* - 17-minute-long silent film featuring Mabel Normand and Charlie Chaplin. Released in February of 1914, it was Chaplin's third film and his first in his iconic "tramp" costume.

MICKEY MOUSE - Mickey made his sound film debut in the 1928 cartoon *Steamboat Willie*.

*MY HOME* - *My Home* was a monthly British magazine aimed at women. The cover art and articles Maeve references are from the February, 1930 issue.

*THE MYSTERY OF THE YELLOW ROOM* - Detective novel by French author Gaston Leroux. The novel is one of the first 'locked room' mysteries, published in 1907 and is still in print.

*NEW YORK DAILY MIRROR* - Popular tabloid newspaper. Active 1924-1963.

# Drugs

CURARE - An alkaloid poison and paralyzing agent.

LUMINAL - Trade name for phenobarbital, a sedative and anti-epileptic drug.

PANCURONIUM BROMIDE - Muscle relaxing drug.

SCOPALOMINE - Used to treat motion sickness and post-operative nausea.

SUCCINYLCHOLINE - Drug causing short term paralysis.

# Places

ANTWERPSCHE DIAMANTKRING - Established in Antwerp, Belgium in 1928. First global organization handling rough diamond trade exclusively. .

DIAMANT CLUB VAN ANTWERPEN - Representing the diamond trade since 1885.

INSTITUT MÉDICO-LÉGAL - Paris mortuary and forensic institute for autopsies on crime victims and others.

KIMBERLEY MINE - Diamond mine in Kimberley, South Africa. Operational 1871-1914.

# Objects

*BERANGIA* - British-flagged passenger liner that began life as the *SS Imperator*, a German liner. She remained in port in Hamburg, Germany during the War, was briefly taken and used by the US Navy to bring troops home from France, and then was renamed and transferred to the British Cunard Line as a war reparation for Cunard's loss of the *RMS Lusitania*, sunk by a German submarine in May of 1915. Under three nation's flags she was in service from 1913 – 1939.

*BRITANNIC* - British-flagged passenger liner. Sister ship to *Titanic*. In service as a hospital ship 1915-1916. Struck German mine and sank in 1916 with 30 deaths.

CUSTOMS SHEDS - Long, open air sheds that debarking passengers had to pass through to have customs officers check their baggage and other items.

DREADNOUGHT - Heavy battleships of the early 20th century. The sole survivor of the class is the *USS Texas*, launched in 1912, served in both world wars, and is now a museum ship in her namesake state.

GLADSTONE BAG - A type of small suitcase constructed on a rigid frame that parts into two equal sides when opened. Named after four-time UK Prime Minister William Gladstone.

LENK BLOW TORCH - Alcohol-fueled miniature blow torch used by jewelers and hobbyists in the 20's and 30's.

THE NARROWS - A tidal strait between Staten Island and Brooklyn, it's the primary waterway connecting the Hudson River with the Atlantic Ocean.

PALL MALL - A part of London that's home to many upscale social clubs.

PALL MALL - Cigarettes popular in South Africa.

SANDY HOOK - A natural barrier protecting Lower New York Bay from the waters of the Atlantic Ocean.

Specialized pilots have been guiding merchant ships over and around the Sandy Hook formation for over 300 years.

TELEGRAPH - Not a message, in this case it's the control on a ship's bridge used to signal speed commands down to the engine rooms.

WALTHAM - The American firm Waltham made pocket watches from 1852-1957.

WIRELESS - British term for radio.

# Groups

BOERS - Descendants of Dutch settlers who colonized South Africa.

FRENCH FOREIGN LEGION - Much romanticized French army unit allowing membership from foreign nationals since 1831. Current strength approximately 9,000 men.

FRENCH LINE - Compagnie Générale Transatlantique, also known as the French Line. French shipping company famous for its luxury liners. The company's descendant is now the world's third largest container shipping firm.

GIRL GUIDES - Offshoot of Boy Scouts. Founded in UK in 1910. Known as Girl Scouts in US.

LORD BADEN-POWELL'S BOY SCOUTS - Founded in UK by Lt. General Robert Baden-Powell in 1908. American Boy Scouts founded in 1910.

# Events

MARITZ REBELLION - Failed Boer insurrection in 1914 in South Africa.

SECOND BOER WAR - Conflict between the British Empire and the Boer Republics of the Orange Free State and South African Republic. 1899-1902.

THE WAR - Up until the Second World War, the First World War was known simply as The War. 1914-1918.

# Slang

BEE'S KNEES - Something that's really great or fabulous. From about 1922.

CAT'S PAJAMAS - Something that is coveted and sought after. Note that the UK spelling is 'pyjamas' while the Americans use 'pajamas'.

DIAMANTAIRE - French for a master diamond cutter or producer.

JACK ROBINSON - "Faster than you can say Jack Robinson." Phrase dating back to at least the mid-1700's.

THICKO - Slow witted, stupid, an idiot.

TORPEDO - Slang originating in the 1920's for a gun for hire or hired assassin.

# About the Author

Scott Finley's fascination with the golden age of luxury liners began with Walter Lord's minute-by-minute account of the *Titanic* sinking, *A Night to Remember* and continued through a career as a multiple award winning and Emmy nominated news producer.

His hobbies include electric trains and restoring radios from the 1930's and 1940's.

He lives in Dallas, Texas.